The Thirteenth Torment

PAM CHAMBERS

Copyright © 2013 Pam Chambers

First Printing, 2013

ISBN-978-0-9926295-0-2

Published by Pam Chambers

www.pamchambers.co.uk.com
Cover design and layout by: Justin Dutton
www.justindutton.com

***

ACKNOWLEDGMENTS

For my daughter Carleigh and sons Clark and Jordan

'Hope, dream, believe that anything possible.'

With special thanks to Justin Dutton, for his expertise,
for his help and support and for putting the dream
in my hands.

THE THIRTEENTH TORMENT

From 'A preparation for confession'

Thirteenth Torment: Bearing grudges

Have you nurtured evil thoughts against anyone?

Have you returned evil for evil?

Have you remembered wrongs anyone
did to you in the past?

Have you bore any grudges instead of
understanding, loving, and forgiving?

Have you kept in mind when anyone made
offences towards you?

Have you imagined ways you could have
revenge on anyone?

CHAPTER ONE

The boy was in shock. The air stank of burning flesh. He would smell it for weeks, even when he was asleep. It was the stuff of nightmares. It smelt like fried grease. Like blackened pork crackling. It was sticking to him, on his hair and skin. It stung his eyes and scalded his lips. The boy pressed himself against the large window and watched in fascinated horror as the man's face burnt away on one side. The eye was exposed above his scorched cheek. It was completely white, like a charcoaled fish eye. His hair was gone and his head was just an ugly mass of burnt skin, except for a patch at the top of his neck - this was bright pink and cracking open.

The man was lying against the opposite wall of the shed from where the boy stood looking in. The boy wanted to run, but could not drag himself away. He knew that the man had been on fire first, and then the flames had caught the brick and wood structure. It was a big shed but it was burning fast.

He stood there for six or seven seconds, that's all it was, when he saw the burning man start to move. The fingers of one grotesque and smouldering hand reached out towards him, one at a time, as if reaching for him, then snapped back into a claw. The boy started to scream.

Detective Inspector Kate Landers pushed open the double doors leading to the children's ward and walked in without seeing a soul. The nurse's station was deserted. A phone rang incessantly, unanswered. She was there to see Darren Martin, a four-year old boy who'd been admitted after a vicious beating from his father. She'd known Darren since he was born, and she didn't want to admit it, but she had a soft spot for the child. She didn't know what room he was in and there was no one around to ask. The silent vibration of her mobile phone against her thigh made her hesitate. She fished it out to check the message screen.

'SHF CALL BARMY'.

Her colleague, the laconic DS Colin Morris, was a man of few words. 'SHF' translated to 'Shit hits fan,' 'Barmy' was 'Louise Barnes' the woman who, for a brief spell, had been the Acting Detective Inspector on the Child Protection Unit until the 'powers that be' realised 'bullish and confrontational' weren't the best personality traits for child protection work and gave Kate the job. Kate pinched her bottom lip and frowned. Barmy had moved to the CID department where she'd quickly alienated just about everyone except her DCI, and he was too focused on himself to realise what a witch she was. Kate couldn't think of what Barmy might want her for, but whatever was behind Colin's message, it was obviously not good news.

'Oh, bloody hell.' Kate swore under her breath. She'd only left thirty minutes ago. What the hell had happened now?

A Nursing Sister suddenly appeared from a side ward, spotted Kate and smiled in recognition. 'Hey Kate. Come to see Darren? He's in the end room. We've almost had to tie him to his cot. In spite of his injuries, the little monkey won't be still for five minutes.' Her grin lit up tired eyes.

Kate smiled, 'I've known him to climb out of a second floor window and escape down a drain pipe, you've got no chance if you think a cot will cage him. How is he?'

'Three ribs fractured.' The Sister pushed stray strands of blond hair behind her ear and caught them in a large plastic clip. 'The bruises cover most of the right side of his body. He's also physically and emotionally draining, and I alternate between wanting to cuddle him and wanting to strangle him. Have you caught the bastard?'

'We will, trust me, we will.' Kate's eyes met the other woman's in silent understanding. Then she nodded her thanks and headed down the hall.

She heard him before she got there. Darren's profound deafness meant his attempts to communicate audibly came out as low, guttural noises and he sounded upset. Kate almost ran the last couple of steps to his room. Although he was only four years old, Darren was incredibly small for his age. He was wearing a pair of loose blue underpants and Kate winced as she saw the purple bruising that started just under his chin and ended at his right thigh. Darren's father wasn't a big man, no, but he was violent and on the run. He'd only been out of prison a couple of days when he'd beaten the living daylights out of his small son. God only knew why. Every uniform and CID officer in the division was looking to put him straight back inside... but they had to find him first.

Kate just managed to drop her bag in time to catch Darren as he leapt at her. His thin brown arms wrapped around her neck and his bare legs curled around her waist as he clung to her. She knew from experience that he would have his thumb in his mouth as he leant into her shoulder. His short, blond hair smelt of soap for once. Normally, he only smelt of dirt. The young Auxiliary Nurse he had escaped from looked hot and fed up. Her plastic apron was torn at one shoulder and there were large sweat patches under her arms. The stroppy look on her face was very unattractive.

Kate decided she didn't like her. 'Why is Darren upset?' she asked, bluntly.

'It's not my fault.' Stroppy face shrugged, 'I don't know what he wants. He won't wear his pyjamas and he keeps trying to escape.'

Darren's tears had turned to wrenching, silent sobs. Kate tried not to hug him too hard in case she hurt him. 'Darren doesn't understand pyjamas. In the summer he sleeps in his underpants, in the winter he sleeps in his clothes. Not all children come from homes where there are duvets, pyjamas and slippers. And he's scared – he doesn't understand what's going on.' Kate wondered why she was bothering to explain.

'I don't know sign language and I need to get him dressed.' Stroppy face snapped.

Kate had had enough of her. She reached up and tickled Darren behind his ear, making him giggle. 'I suppose playing with children isn't something you know how to do either.' she said, dismissively.

The Nursing Sister stuck her head around the door, 'Do me a favour, Kate,' she smiled brightly, 'when you find his father, kick him in the nuts for me.'

It was certainly tempting, Kate thought. Darren could cause

mayhem; he climbed out of windows, set grass alight, and stole other people's pets. But then he would turn his head questioningly to one side, fix you with a stare and say 'Wurghh?' He was one of those kids that just got to you.

Whatever was going on back at the station, Barmy was going to have to wait five minutes.

***

The boy could smell vomit. His puke was on his shoes. He looked down at his Nike trainers. Vile lumps of sick were splashed down his trousers and over his feet, but he didn't care. The smell of burnt human flesh was so strong he could taste it. It was in his mouth, coating his teeth.

A man was shouting, screaming over the roar of the fire. Wood was splintering, cracking and falling. And then someone, maybe the man who was shouting, grabbed his arm and pulled, spinning him around and away from the smoke and flames. The boy wanted to run. Every sense he still had was telling him to run, but his eyes were streaming and he couldn't see properly. How was he supposed to run when he couldn't see?

He was half lifted off his feet and shoved so hard he stumbled and fell forwards. He flailed his arms out, trying to find something solid, but his hands grabbed at thin air. He was falling and he couldn't see the ground. Suddenly there was a massive 'whoosh', like a screaming rocket on Guy Fawkes night.

'DOWN!' the man yelled. 'Get down boy!'

His face hit the ground. It was brutally hard after the hot weather. He tried to roll sideways but his legs were trapped. He struggled desperately, but had only managed to get one arm over his head when the explosion happened. Louder than anything he'd ever heard. The blast filled his chest and took all the breath away from him in a hot, searing rush. Heavy waves of heat scorched the back of his neck. His ears felt as though they were going to blow out from the side of his head. Then it was gone. The boy buried his hand as deeply as he could into the grass, pulled clumps of it between his fingers and held on.

***

CHAPTER TWO

Kate parked behind the fire tender, grabbed her bag and slid her legs out of the door of her old BMW. She paused for a brief second feeling the familiar cocktail of emotions, anticipation and excitement in equal measure. It was the feeling of something big about to unfold, something juicy kicking off. An unexpected event had taken place in this tucked away little cul—de—sac, something that would change lives. She took a good look around at the inevitable rubberneckers who had started to gather on the opposite pavement.

Watch the watchers.

You never knew who might be on the fringe of an incident. It was a habit she had been taught by a wise training sergeant during her early days on the job, and it was a good habit to have. Watch the watchers.

Two young girls on shiny bikes came along the path at full speed and skidded to a halt. 'What happened? Is it a fire? What are the police doing here? Is someone dead?' They were breathless with excitement. A clutch of women gathered on the opposite corner ignored them, too busy with nods and glances and half whispered opinions to pay them any attention. Further down the street a teenager with a baseball cap pulled down over his eyes spun a skateboard between his hands, feigning boredom. An old man leant heavily on a gate and rolled his tobacco in a cigarette paper, licking the edge with a practiced flick of his tongue as he surveyed the scene with sharp, bright eyes.

The uniformed policeman on door duty gave Kate's bum the once over as she passed him and entered the bungalow. He was seriously taking the mickey. Nearer forty than thirty, Kate described herself as 'long legs, no boobs,' athletic rather than voluptuous. *Moron.* She'd dealt with idiots like him her entire career, but she couldn't be bothered to pull him on it, not today. She stepped into the narrow hallway and took a quick look around. It smelt of beeswax. A small wooden table at the far end was covered in ornamental china frogs. A wall plate announced it was a present from Herne Bay. Old people stuck in their ways, Kate had been in a hundred houses just like it.

'Morning my dear.' A familiar face appeared from the kitchen on her right, 'Tea?'

Sergeant Lenny Owen, a community beat officer, already had a mug in his hand. 'Mrs Pink is getting the kettle on for the boys and opening a tin of biscuits.'

Kate smiled but shook her head. 'Quick update, Lenny?'

'A bit nasty really', Lenny was keeping his voice down. 'George Pink, aged sixty-four, is deceased. An explosion destroyed his shed, with him in it. Fire service put out the flames and found his body under the debris, *very nasty.* He looks like badly burnt meatloaf by all accounts. The wife knows - she thinks it was an accident. You can't see the shed from the house; it's behind a massive hedge at the end of the garden. Apparently, the first Mrs Pink knew about it was when the explosion went off. She dropped her tea cup.' He rolled his eyes. 'The lad's in there.' Lenny tilted his head towards a closed door that Kate assumed led to the living room.

'Is he hurt?' she asked.

'Bit singed around the ears, nothing serious. One of the fire officers is with him. The lad's not a hospital case, but he's not talking to us. He's not said a word to anyone since we got here. I thought it best to give him a bit of space and quiet until you arrived. Mrs Pink says she's never seen him before; she has no idea who he is or what he was doing in her garden. The next-door neighbour grabbed the boy away from the fire. A uniform is talking to the bloke now, but it seems he heard screaming, ran round through the back gate and found the boy by the shed, watching it burn.' Lenny shrugged.

'What? And no-one knows who the boy is?' Kate had already heard this from Barmy during her brief telephone conversation, but it seemed too bizarre. Before Lenny could elaborate further a bulky fire officer filled the kitchen doorway behind him. Kate recognised him; she knew most of the local fire crews.

'Morning Kate, nice day for it.' he said cheerfully.

'It always is, Kevin.' Kate nodded. Kevin Baxter was a square, solid looking man with a shaved head and a permanent cheerful expression. He'd taken his helmet and boots off and had rolled the bottoms of his trousers up to protect Mrs Pink's carpets.

He drew her and Lenny Owen away from the kitchen door, glanced back to make sure Mrs Pink was out of sight and lowered his voice. 'You might want to call the team in. Someone didn't like this bloke, Pink, very much.'

Here we go. Kate felt the skin behind her ears start to tingle. She knew, without doubt, that whatever was coming next was going to give her a whole heap of trouble.

'Shed door was padlocked on the outside, someone locked him inside.'

Kate stared at him. 'The fire was started deliberately?'

'That would be my guess. Forensics will be able to tell us how. Whatever happened, someone made pretty sure the bloke couldn't escape. The shed was solid; more like a garage, a brick base and timber walls. The body has burnt unevenly, but the ferocity of the fire would suggest an accelerant was used, maybe petrol.'

Kate snapped into action. 'Lenny, take Mrs Pink and get her to a neighbours or something. Stay with her until we get a Family Liaison Officer to take over. This is a crime scene, let's get it secured. I'll get the circus started,' Kate glanced towards the lounge door, 'and then I'll take the boy.'

Kevin gave her a very direct look, but if he had any thoughts about the boy he was keeping them to himself. 'Our forensics guys are on their way. Everything's doused down so we're backing off, we'll leave it to them.'

'Great, thanks.' Kate pulled her mobile out, punched speed dial and started giving rapid instructions.

When she walked into the living room five minutes later she wasn't surprised to find she knew exactly who the boy was.

⁂

Kate took one look at Dean Towle and knew she had to get him out of there fast. Vomit was splashed down the front of his cargo trousers and trainers. His long face was shocked into sickly paleness. Thin, in the way young boys are when they've just had a growth spurt, his bony shoulders shook violently under a silver-insulating blanket as he wiped his sleeve across his face. He didn't lift his head as the door opened. He was terrified, his mind somewhere other than in the room.

Kate nodded at the fireman who was squatting on the carpet putting bits of first aid equipment back into a bag. 'It's ok, I've got him.' She crossed the room in four strides, knelt down in front of the silent boy and put a firm hand on his arm. She could feel him holding himself rigid, trying to hang on against the trembling that wouldn't stop. The smell was truly awful, smoke and vomit and worse.

'Dean?' She tried to get down low enough to look up into his eyes. 'Dean... come on mate, you're coming with me.'

Dean's head lifted just slightly. He recognised her voice. Then, suddenly his whole body jerked and his breath caught in his throat. Kate stood up and pressed his shoulder for encouragement. 'Come on, stand up, I'm going to take you out of here.'

Dean stood. Kate was relieved he was responding, but he kept his eyes on the floor as she led him across the room. As they crossed the hall the front door opened and Mr Neanderthal policeman stuck his head in. Kate indicated he should keep the door open for them.

'CID's on their way, Ma'am. They want you to hang on.'

Dean froze.

Kate gave the constable the benefit of her look - the one she reserved for useless idiots - and he backed out of her way. She pushed Dean gently towards the door, 'Tell Barmy its Dean Towle and I've got him.' She said in a stage whisper to Lenny over the top of the boy's head.

She almost had to lift him into the front of her car because Dean's legs weren't quite cooperating. As she pulled the seatbelt around him, he retched horribly and brought up a thin dribble of yellow bile.

'It's ok Dean, you're going to be ok.' She pushed his hair back from his face and handed him a tissue.

His head slumped on his chest. 'It smells. The smell's on me... it's on me.' His hands shook, tears were not far away. Dean jammed his hands between his knees and rocked forward.

Once she'd climbed into the driver's seat the smell in the

confined space made Kate feel sick. She turned the BMW in a wide circle out of the cul-de-sac, opened the sunroof and sucked in the blast of warm air.

'Dean,' she grinned and glanced sideways at him. 'You stink, and you're making my car stink.' She laughed. She had to jostle him out of the blackness he was sinking into. She had to haul him back from the dark place his mind was trying to hide. A huge dollop of taking the mickey was the best move.

'But the good news is', she said conversationally, 'it will wash off you. I'm just going to have to buy another motor.' She shrugged as though this was no big deal, but she'd got his attention. *Come on Dean, hold on kid.* 'I'm thinking of getting one of those Smart cars, you know, the little funky coloured ones? I quite fancy a pink one, what do you reckon? Think it will suit me?'

Kate seemed to be seriously considering the matter. Out of the corner of her eye she saw Dean sit up straighter. God, the smell inside the heat of the car was vile, thick and clinging. She was beginning to get the mother of all headaches. She turned the air conditioning up full blast.

'You're off your head.' Dean wrapped his arms around his chest. He was holding himself together, just. 'They're for wankers, they're bollocks they are.'

Kate laughed. 'Right, so you've not quite made your mind up yet?'

Dean wiped his face on his sleeve again and shrugged, 'Can I open the window? I don't feel good.' He pushed the button and his window slid down.

Kate was worried he was going to be sick again, 'I'm really bad with gadgets... not like you.' She grabbed her hands free kit and held it in front of him. 'I hope you know how that thing works, it's brand new and I'm useless with it. I don't want to get arrested for talking on my mobile. Can you ring your foster mum? If you want to talk to her, go ahead, if not, I'll talk. We need her to meet us. We're going to get you checked over in case you've frazzled your brain,' She turned and grinned at him, 'or something more important.'

'Give it here then, let's have a look.' He wrapped his fingers around the phone.

At the age of fifteen Eddie was a couple of inches short of six feet, but he still managed to make himself invisible. He'd been doing it all his life. But no one was paying any attention to him right now. The squat little bungalow near the end of the cul-de-sac was sucking up all the attention and this was making him so scared his stomach hurt.

He spun his skateboard on its tail between his hands and made a wish. The front door of the bungalow opened and a woman came out. She was half pushing, half supporting Dean Towle towards an old dark blue BMW. Eddie watched as she helped Dean into the front of the car. Why was Dean wrapped in something that looked like silver foil? Why was she treating him like a disabled kid? Was he hurt? Eddie pulled the peak of his cap further down over his eyes and made another wish, and then he stood up, and in a single movement dropped the skateboard in front of him and placed his right foot on the front of it. Pushing off with his left he made a slow graceful arc towards the BMW. He was too late, the woman climbed into the driver's seat and pulled away from the kerb. As the car passed him Eddie got a good look at Dean. The kid looked worse than shit. Eddie's heart started pounding so badly he thought it was going to bust out of his chest. He couldn't figure out what the hell had happened. Something had gone very badly wrong.

Kate knew Dean's foster mum well. Joan was standing by the side of her car, anxiously twisting the handle of a plastic bag around her fingers, when Kate pulled into the surgery car park. Dean looked up and Kate grinned at him,

'Joan looks worried to death, quick, smile... otherwise she's likely to come over here and kiss you or something.'

The best Dean could do was nod. He made no effort to move as Kate threw open her door and climbed out.

'It's ok, he's ok, just talk to him for a minute, I'll be back in a sec.' Kate smiled reassuringly at Joan.

Joan held up the carrier bag she was gripping. 'Clean clothes.'

'Great, thanks, he needs them.' Kate ran inside and made arrangements with the Receptionist to take Dean straight through to the surgery. Back at the car she squatted down by the open passenger door and gave Dean a hard look. 'Can you walk, or do I have to give you a piggyback?' She winked at Joan who was hovering, still looking worried.

'Walk.'

'Good, cos' you look bloody heavy. Come on then.'

It was almost over when Dean started to unravel again. He was behind the curtain in the examination room putting on his clean clothes. The doctor was explaining to Joan about the burn cream for the singe marks on his neck and ears. Kate told Dean to kick his dirty clothes out so she could get them. She was bagging them up in large plastic evidence bags when he pushed back the curtain looking for his clean shoes. He stared at Kate writing his name on evidence labels. For a tiny moment he didn't move, he looked lost and confused, but then he started to yell.

'I didn't... what are you doing? I didn't do it!' He looked wildly around at Joan. 'You think... don't... I didn't.' He was crying hysterically.

Joan reached for him but he shook her arm away.

'I didn't, I fucking didn't, let me go!' He pushed Joan away and spun towards the door. His hand smacked into the doorframe as he groped blindly for the handle.

Kate dropped the bags on the floor and grabbed him. She gripped his elbows and pulled him around to face her. 'Look at me Dean. *Look at me.* I don't, I promise you, I don't think you did it.' Kate fixed her eyes on his. 'Give me your hands. Come on, turn your hands over and let me see them.'

Dean stopped struggling. He stood still, looking at her warily, blinking back tears. He had no idea what she was on about but he slowly lifted his hands and turned them over. Kate lifted his hands to her face, her eyes focused on his face. She sniffed deeply, smelling his palms. 'If you'd started that fire your hands would smell of petrol, all I can smell is dirt. I've got your clothes, so I know you don't have gloves. It's ok Dean, it's ok.' She let go of his hands and he crumpled.

'He was... he was burning. He was already burning. I didn't do it.' Dean's voice was a hoarse whisper. He swayed sideways and as Joan reached for him again he fell into her, almost knocking her over. She pulled him towards her, wrapping her arm tightly around his shoulders, trying to steady him, to calm him. His head was pressed against Joan but Kate could hear him gulping, pushing down the sobs. They waited quietly until he'd stopped snivelling, but he was embarrassed, still hiding his head.

'Are you wiping snot on Joan's t-shirt?' Kate asked him, conversationally. She winked at Joan.

'Are you?' Joan played along, pretending to be shocked. Without turning around Dean nodded and Kate could see a small smile creeping up the side of his face.

'Urgh, gross!' Joan pulled away from him, giving him a chance to stand on his own, back in control.

He grinned sheepishly at her. Joan pretended to wipe snot off her top, pulling a face.

'Boys are gross,' Kate commented, 'It's their job.' She gave a huge sigh as though that's just the way things were and flicked her hair behind her ears. 'That's why I had a daughter. Girls don't wipe their noses on you.' She looked at Dean, 'Can we go now? I'm gagging for a coffee and Joan needs a clean top.' She gave him a gentle push towards the door.

As soon as they got home Dean was sent upstairs for a hot bath with the promise of hot chocolate with squirty cream if he could manage to get clean before he came down.

'George Pink?' Kate leant against Joan's kitchen counter, crossed one ankle over the other and sipped black coffee from a mug that bore the legend 'Landscape Gardeners do it in Wellies.'

'No idea.' Joan spread her hands out in front of her, a gesture of bewilderment. 'I thought Dean was out with some mates. I don't know who the man is... or was.' She grimaced, embarrassed, 'Why was Dean in his garden?' She raised her hands again and shrugged. She had no idea.

'We'll take him to Hope House tomorrow.' Kate told her. 'Interview him there. Can you or Philip come? We'll have a social worker with us as well, someone from the children's team. Just keep a close eye on him until then.'

'Kate...' Joan looked at her, shocked, and then she started to get cross. 'Dean didn't burn that poor man. You said you believed him. I don't know what's happened or how Dean got involved. But burn someone? Bloody hell Kate.'

'Joan, I've got to talk to him because he was at the scene, and no one knows why. And I meant you should keep a close eye on him because he's had a nasty shock. There's stuff I've got to do, but as far as I'm concerned he's a witness and he's been through hell today.'

'Sorry, I'm sorry.' Joan lifted one hand to her chest. 'It's just when I saw the state he was in.'

'It's fine.' Kate reassured her, 'Look, I know you won't try and question him but if he starts blabbing on about anything important give me a shout.'

Kate yelled up the stairs to Dean as she left, 'It's no good just sitting there. The dirt won't magically float off your body - use a flannel. I'll see you tomorrow.'

***

CHAPTER THREE

The blazing row Kate walked into when she got back to the station was like the fire that had engulfed George Pink; short lived, fierce and destructive.

Making her way up the stairs to the third floor incident suite a CID officer told her DCI Neil Stacey had been assigned as Senior Investigating Officer, or SIO. Kate was dismayed. Stacey was thought to be a bit of a 'star' in the eyes of senior management. He'd had a couple of cases that had put him in the spotlight, and he was always happy to take the full credit for anything that went well - whether he was actually responsible or not. The uniformed guys at the station thought Stacey fancied himself. He was a pretty boy who never got his nice white shirt dirty. Kate thought they had a point. He also had a reputation for throwing his weight about and had an unpredictable temper. Kate's relationship with him had only bordered on the 'so so', until he'd made a clumsy and embarrassing pass at her. Now it was a bit cool.

Stacey looked up expectantly when she walked into the controlled mayhem of the incident room, but his eagerness soon turned to annoyance.

'So you didn't actually manage to ask him anything?' Stacey's tone suggested this was ineptitude on her part. 'The boy was standing at the scene of a crime, watching a man die and you didn't ask him what he was doing there? Didn't you think it might be a valuable question?'

'He's had a bad fright, Sir.' Kate deliberately didn't bite back at him. 'The most important thing was to get Dean seen by a doctor. He's not badly hurt but he's tired and upset. If he's fit enough, I'll interview him tomorrow in the proper manner, with an appropriate adult and a member of the Children's Services team present. Right now he needs a good sleep.'

Stacey leant back against a desk and folded his arms, his face grim. 'The boy is on your CPU files, Kate. Our only witness just happens to be one of your child protection cases, I take it you know something about him?'

Kate ignored the sarcasm. Stacey was a fast track copper with a degree in something clever and a couple of years in the city behind him. Kate thought he was bright, but his ego got in the way of him being any practical use. Or maybe he was still pissed at her for side stepping his advances when they'd met up at a 'successful end to a shitty job' drink up. He needed careful handling, but she wasn't sure she had the patience... or could be bothered. She'd follow up with Dean and do his interview, but she didn't believe for a second that the boy was in any way responsible for Pink's death. As soon as she found out how he'd ended up being in 'the wrong place at the wrong time' Kate intended to leave Stacey with his investigation and get back to her CPU work. She resisted the urge to sigh and patiently gave him a brief summary of how she knew Dean.

'Dean Towle is thirteen years old and he's been in foster care for two years. There hasn't been a father in his life as far as we know. His mother was an undiagnosed manic-depressive. No one realised how badly she was neglecting Dean until a couple of PCs found him in the car park behind Sainsburys. Two older boys had made him strip and put on some old clothes from a recycling bin. Then they hit him with a stick while they set fire to his school uniform. Dean hadn't had a proper meal or a wash in goodness knows how long, but he hadn't said a word to anyone about what was going on at home.'

'But the boy is known to us.' Stacey insisted. He wasn't interested in the boy's poor upbringing.

'He has a file with my office, yes.' Kate answered carefully; she didn't want Stacey running off with the idea that they had a suspect, 'But only because he was taken into protective custody. Dean Towle has learning difficulties. He missed a lot of school before he was placed in care, he's in the special needs group and he finds it difficult to fit in. He's been picked up a couple of times playing truant, and there was a shop lifting incident which didn't go anywhere...'

'Recently?' Stacey interrupted.

Kate tried to keep her face blank; keep the emotion out of it. 'Back in March. He took a cheap pink candle, only worth two quid. He was crying his eyes out when PC Littleman turned up. It was Mother's Day and he wanted to give Joan a present. The shop wasn't interested in pressing charges. Littleman used his discretion.'

'Joan's his mother?'

'No. His mother won't have anything to do with him, Joan's his foster mum.' Kate watched Stacey's face, but he wasn't moved. *Heartless Bastard.*

'Well I suggest you get your diary squared away for the time being, you're being assigned to the investigation team, temporarily.'

It was the last thing Kate was expecting, or wanted. 'George Pink's death is not a child protection issue, Sir.' She raked both hands through her hair in frustration. 'No child has been hurt, or is in danger. Dean was frightened. He'll probably have bad dreams for a few days, but he'll be ok after a bit of TLC. I simply can't leave my work to help on this. You've got a team of Detectives...'

'It wasn't a suggestion Kate.' Stacey cut her off. 'It's been cleared by Detective Superintendent Knowling. Although this is clearly a CID matter, he thinks your local knowledge might be useful. We're waiting for an analyst to arrive from divisional HQ, so you can help out for the time being. Colin Morris can cover for you, and help can be sought from Hockley CPU if he gets overloaded, but it might not be for too long - depends on what the story is with this Towle kid.'

'Overloaded?' Kate's anger focused her into diamond shattering sharpness. 'My Sergeant has enough of his own cases to work on without picking up more. Plus, my most experienced detective, Andrea Webster, is off sick - so we're short manned. What about Darren Martin? I'm doing his interview tomorrow. His father, Todd Martin, just beat him black and blue then did a runner. I'm sure you heard about it. The bloody Parole Board should never have released him early. The uniforms are running a book on who'll get the cuffs on Todd first, but no one from CID is near the top of the list so you should have plenty of manpower.'

Kate knew she'd overstepped the line.

Stacey didn't want to hear it. 'The Superintendent has put a lot of faith in you, Kate. Some people think you've focused far too much on child protection work to the detriment of other CID experience. Whatever Dean Towle says when you eventually get round to interviewing him may well lead to other inquiries that you can assist with. This is a murder investigation. Colin Morris will be supported, but if some of the CPU cases get put back slightly; well it can't be helped, that's the nature of the beast.'

Kate stared at him in astonishment. 'Sorry Sir, I thought the first principle of The Children's Act was 'The welfare of the child is paramount'. I didn't read the bit that says unless there's a bit of excitement going off elsewhere, in which case, they can get put back a bit'.

'You're being emotional.' Stacey's voice was rigid with anger. 'I've just told you Morris will get help if necessary. A man has been burnt to death in his own garden for God's sake.' His eyes narrowed, 'I suggest you go away and calm down.'

Kate stood her ground for a second longer than she should have before turning on her heel.

'Never mind,' Colin Morris grinned with mock sympathy when she gave him the bad news, 'you're not that indispensable, Gov. You've only scored a seven so far in the 'Strictly Come DI' contest. You've obviously practiced really hard, but your foot work still needs attention.' He was 'Strictly Come Dancing's' biggest fan. Yesterday, after she'd got a coffee shop owner to admit indecently assaulting a fourteen-year-old Saturday girl, Kate had walked back into the office to find Colin holding up a white card with a perfect score of ten written on it in huge bold numbers.

'I can do Darren Martin's interview for you at least,' he offered, 'and you can go and help on the murder - maybe you'll be some help there.' Colin looked sorrowfully at her as though didn't really hold out much hope for her success.

In spite of herself, Kate laughed, her anger evaporating, 'Is that fresh coffee?' He filled a cup and held it out to her. 'What about Dean Towle, any ideas?'

Kate perched on the edge of her desk and kicked her shoes off. 'Stacey would like him to be a suspect - but Dean didn't do this.'

'Is he alright?'

'He could have been far worse. Apparently he was just standing there, watching it. Pink was on fire, which must have been a horrific sight, the shed was going up in flames and he just stood there. It's so bloody odd. I mean, Dean's a bit slow, but what was he doing?' She pulled a face.

'What about this bloke next door? Could he have started the fire?' Colin leant so far back on his chair he was defying gravity.

'God knows. No doubt one of our crack team of CID detectives has interviewed him, but I don't think they're considering him as a homicidal pyromaniac. He seems to have only turned up in time to rescue Dean. Lucky for Dean - when the shed exploded he could have gone with it.' Kate paused and stared down at her cup, deep in thought.

'What?' Colin recognised the sign.

'It's always the same kids.' Kate met his eyes and sighed deeply, 'We'd have been surprised if we'd found a kid at the scene that we'd never heard of, but when it's one of our frequent customers?' She leant her head back and massaged her slim neck with her fingers.

Colin thought about this for a moment then sniffed loudly. 'That new perfume you're trying out isn't working for you. Bloody hell, what is it? Eau de le burnt puke?' He pulled a face, 'Oh, and don't forget you've got a new sidekick starting tomorrow.'

Kate sagged, 'Shit, another career climber. No doubt he's ticking off the CPU as a stepping-stone on his path to glory. Not a sausage of experience and I'm supposed to teach him. Steve... somebody?' His surname escaped her. She'd been so pissed off when she was told she was getting a secondment, someone with no CPU experience, she hadn't paid any attention to who he was. Detective Superintendent Knowling had refused to listen as she'd tried to wheedle him out of giving her the placement, eventually dismissing her with a 'put up and shut up,' comment that sent her packing from his office.

Colin nodded, lazily swinging his foot as he reclined at an impossible angle, 'Astman, Steve Astman. He's done Fraud and Drugs and he's supposed to be something special on the Rugby squad.'

'Great,' Kate's voice was thick with sarcasm. 'We don't rugby tackle many people in child protection work, but if that changes he'll come in really handy. Actually...' she looked at Colin thoughtfully, 'If he's that good... I wonder if he could drop kick Stacey for me?'

***

CHAPTER FOUR

Running, for Kate, achieved several things. It gave her body a work out, it gave her a chance to untangle the problems that clogged her brain, and she kidded herself that if she ran hard enough she could sweat off some of the filth and depravity that she dealt with every day. After four years on the Child Protection Unit there was no depth of human depravity that shocked her, but there were far too many days when she felt as though the filth had stuck like a vile black tar to her skin.

Exercise also blew off the aggression. She knew she'd lost her temper with Stacey and the row had left her feeling uneasy. As soon as she got home she threw her running kit on and headed out to the bridle paths that crisscrossed the woods and fields around her house. Some of her colleagues ribbed her about living so far out of town; a forty-five minute drive without traffic, but she needed this. She needed to be able to close the door and shut herself away from the wretchedness, the hopelessness and the cruelty that filled her working day. She needed peace and fresh air.

Her normal circuit took her five miles around Tockers Wood and back - with a steep climb at the halfway point. As she started up the incline sweat trickled down the side of her face and a wet patch spread across her chest. She put her head down and took smaller steps. The inside of her knees started burning as she pushed on. To take her mind off her knees she wondered what it was like to burn to death. It was one of those gruesome questions that came up in games played by bored police officers. What was worse – burning to death or drowning? Kate knew she'd much rather drown than burn. Burning someone alive was unbelievably cruel. But someone had hated George Pink with a vengeance –

hated him enough to throw petrol over him and light it. What must it have been like for Pink as the flames took hold and his escape was cut off? Who would do such a thing, and why?

Kate started to play a mental game of 'ask the right question,' while she climbed. Ask the right question and you've got a much better chance of getting the right answer. It was a good habit; and not just for interviewing sex offenders. Her thigh muscles started complaining, but she focused on the case, ignoring the pain. In spite of what she'd said to Stacey she was in this thing. A man had burnt to death in bizarre circumstances and a vulnerable child had been found at the scene. It was an interesting enough case without the added mystery of Dean Towle. How had he ended up witnessing the horror of Pink's death? She needed answers.

One: How did Dean know Pink? Even when the boy was crying that he didn't do it, he'd never once said the man's name. Kate knew this was significant. If Dean knew Pink's name then why couldn't he say it?

Two: Dean had got into the garden, presumably through the back gate, without meeting Pink's wife. Why was he there?

Three: Why wasn't there any family, other than Mrs Pink, at the house after the incident? There were no 'nearest and dearest' gathered. It was normally the first thing that happened after some tragic event or drama; people came out of the woodwork. Even Sergeant Lenny Owen would have happily given up 'widow watching' if there'd been a family member to take over. But there'd been no one. That was bloody odd - but so was everything else about it.

Kate made the crest of the hill and stood hands on hips, breathing deeply. The countryside opened up below her bathed in the last lazy glow of sunlight. It had been one of Duncan's favourite spots. He'd always made it to the top ahead of her and waited, cheering her on as she pushed herself up the climb.

'Keep going babe, come on you can do it, get your arse up here!'

She no longer woke every day with the terrible pain of missing her husband and best friend lying beside her. Too many years had passed and the hurt, once so overwhelming and so constant that she felt she was wearing it like a skin, had faded. But she always felt close to him when she looked at this view. Duncan had been as fit as a Butcher's dog, as her dad would have said, but it hadn't made a bit of difference in the end. They say only the good die young. Kate hated the word 'widow'. She refused to use it. It made her too sad. She knew her friends wondered why she hadn't remarried; or at least settled into a permanent relationship with someone new. It wasn't as though she'd made a conscious decision to remain single, she'd had a couple of chances; she hadn't given up on men entirely, but the bar had been set pretty high. She'd raised their daughter, Angel, on her own and they were doing ok. Kate smiled as she pushed her damp fringe back from her face and wiped her hands on her shorts. Her daughter had been christened 'Angelica' but from the first moment she'd opened her eyes she'd only ever been referred to as Angel. At the age of eighteen she was a gifted player on her college volleyball team. She had her Daddy's eyes and had inherited his talent for sport along with his absurd laugh.

Kate shut her eyes, took a deep breath and gave herself a mental shake. *Come on girl, standing here being soppy isn't going to get your butt in shape.* She took another deep breath, spun around and tore back down the hill at a gallop.

Eddie knew it was hopeless. Everything had gone tits up. He knew he was too late - but he went to the meeting place anyway. Their plans had been made so carefully. He wasn't good at writing things down so he'd memorised it: *Meet at the corner of Drakes Avenue. It's close enough to skate to, but tucked out of the way. Bring what you need, but don't let anyone know you're leaving.*

He'd totally followed the instructions. All he had with him was a small rucksack with a clean t-shirt and some socks and pants. Tucked inside one of the socks was a fake fur collar from an old coat. He couldn't leave it behind – it had belonged to his mum and was his only reminder of her. He'd been carrying it around since he was three years old. His one clear memory of her was being dragged through an outdoor market just before Christmas. It was very cold. His nose and eyes were running but he didn't want to wipe them on his blue mittens. The ground was wet, and there were legs and heavy bags dangling from tired arms all around him. The stalls were lit up with coloured lights; stallholders yelling out, their breath visible in the cold dark air.

'Come on ladies, two for a pound, that'll make your old man happy.'

Boxes filled with rolls of cheap wrapping paper, toy figures and plastic cars, the smell of cabbage and hot dogs everywhere, plastic cups trodden into the black, sodden path. He'd been excited because he was going to get a Christmas present from Santa, but scared because it was dark, his mum was hurrying and his legs hurt.

He'd begun to cry. His mum lifted him onto her hip and told him to shush. She'd wiped his nose, roughly, with a tissue, and he'd buried his face into the fluffy collar of her coat. It smelt of shampoo and cigarettes. He'd wanted to be hugged, he'd wanted to be comforted, but she'd dumped him back down on the ground and pulled him on.

Not long after that she was gone. He'd had to live with strangers; aunties and uncles, other children whose parents didn't want them. Of course, some of the children made up stories; their dads were soldiers fighting secret wars and would come back for them when they'd won. Their mums were just waiting to get a brand new house so they could live together. The secret wars never ended, the new house didn't happen. If anyone moved it were just to another aunty and uncle. He'd found out that there were no choices in foster care. You didn't get to choose what to wear, you didn't get to choose where you went, you didn't get to choose who touched you, or how.

There were rules - rules that you had to obey or things would go from bad to really fucked up. You had to be available, you had to play nice, but if you followed the rules you got stuff. You got to go back to your bed instead of having to sleep in the shed, you got to be warm, and sometimes, if you played really nicely, you got money.

But suddenly, and without warning, his life had changed. He'd been promised an escape, a way out, totally unbelievable, but it had really happened, something he'd never even dreamed of. But now everything had gone wrong. First Dean being at the fire and now this, and it was his fault. He was too late.

Sweat plastered his hair to his head under his navy NYC baseball cap and the back of his t-shirt was sticking to him. Everything was his fault. If only he'd been able to get away in time. He'd had to wait until no one would see him leave and now he was too late. If only, if only – fucking if only, it was the story of his life.

He'd ridden so hard the wheels on his skateboard were

knackered, but he didn't give a shit. At last someone wanted him, someone who cared about him, but he was too late, he'd missed his chance, his only chance.

His life had been full of disappointments but this was the worst. He couldn't bear it. He was alone - he'd always been alone, but now he had nowhere to go. Tears came so hard he choked, unable to catch his breath. He smeared the tears into the sweat until his whole face was wet and his lips tasted of salt. He picked up his skateboard and started to walk. He didn't know where to go and it would be dark soon. He was afraid of the dark. Suddenly, the sound of a powerful car coming up behind him made his heart stop. A car door opened and slammed shut again. Someone was running towards him.

'Eddie! Wait. WAIT!

His heart lurched so suddenly he tripped and almost fell. It wasn't too late. She'd waited for him. She was here!

***

CHAPTER FIVE

Kate was at her desk by seven in the morning. She made fresh coffee when DS Colin Morris arrived and they made a futile effort to try and juggle the caseload. The atmosphere in the station was vibrating, gearing up, running on snippets of information, speculation and total bullshit. Kate had only been in the building for four minutes when one of the uniforms told her a gang of kids had killed George Pink.

Colin had also arrived early and he was leaning back in his chair, his eyes half closed. He looked thin and exhausted. Kate was worried about him. She knew he hadn't slept properly for two weeks, not since he'd found Callum. The bruised and broken tiny two-year-old boy who'd clung to his finger with such pathetic hope that it had done something to Colin's spirit. After years of dealing with abused kids Callum had got to Colin. The child had pierced his protective shell and left him a troubled man.

When Colin had related the story to Kate, the point he couldn't get past was 'this baby had the biggest, saddest blue eyes I've ever had the horror of looking into.' He'd choked up as he'd tried to explain it. Callum was still on the critical list in hospital and Colin had been to see him three times. Her Sergeant was a soft touch, but Kate was the only one who knew.

'Go on then, bugger off and leave me all alone.' Colin opened his eyes and grinned at her. 'Don't worry, Gov, I've got everything covered.'

Kate wasn't so sure, but she didn't have a choice. 'We could get lucky - it could be all over by tonight.'

Colin smirked, 'Yeah, right. And you could marry George Clooney and have lots of fat babies.'

'Actually, that's far more likely.' Kate nodded solemnly. 'The man's been practically stalking me for months, begging me to have his babies.'

Colin threw his head back and roared with laughter. He was

still laughing when there was a knock on the door; so quiet they almost missed it. He stopped laughing and stared at her. She stared back until they both grinned.

'Enter!' Kate yelled, and swivelled her chair around to face the door. *Bloody hell, he's a big bloke.* She had to tilt her head back and look up as Detective Constable Steve Astman walked in. *He's going to frighten the kids.* He was six feet something of solid bulk; square shoulders with a broad chest wrapped in an expensive shirt. Kate stood, shook hands and did the introductions.

Colin offered him coffee. 'Be warned, it's espresso strength. Governor won't drink it any other way, and it's her coffee machine so we don't get a choice.'

'Fine', Steve grinned at him, 'I'm happy if it's hot and wet.'

'What happened to your nose?' Kate was peering at his face. Steve's nose was twisted sideways with the bulbous tip flattened and spread out. His complexion was smooth under very short tidy blond hair, but his broken nose gave his blue eyes an squinty look.

'Rugby.' Steve grinned and rubbed it with his index finger. He seemed proud of the fact. He took his coffee cup and looked for somewhere to sit. There was a spare chair at the end desk, but he lowered his immense frame onto the edge of the coffee machine table. Kate sensed disaster.

'It's great to be joining you, Gov.' He grinned at Kate.

'Drugs and Fraud not stimulating enough for you?' Colin asked.

'To be honest, I was boring my friggin' tits off on the Fraud Squad, I'm looking forward to something a bit more challenging, something a bit more interesting than your normal CID crap.'

Kate was not impressed. She gathered up her bag and nodded to Colin. 'Good luck with Darren's interview. Tell him I said 'hello' and I'll see him very soon.' She walked out of the room.

As the door closed behind her Colin looked sideways at Steve. 'Aren't you supposed to be sticking with her?'

'Where's she going?' Steve shifted his weight on the table.

'Well she's been assigned to the murder inquiry so I'm guessing it's something to do with that.' Colin shrugged and tipped his chair upright again.

Steve checked to see if he was serious, decided he was and dumped his coffee cup down. 'Shit!' He was out of the door a moment later. He had three flights of stairs to negotiate but he was confident he wasn't going to lose her. He passed a couple of uniforms on their way to the incident room. They turned as he took three steps at a time.

'After her mate!' One of them yelled. 'That's the spirit. Don't let her get away!' There was a shout of sarcastic laughter behind him. 'No wonder our rugby squad is crap. Is that the best you can do?'

Steve ignored them, plenty of time to catch up with the piss takers later. He careered around a corner and out of the rear station doors. Scanning the car park he saw Kate gingerly backing an old blue BMW out of a bay. She was staring in her rear view mirror, chewing her lip in concentration.

God woman, you could get a bus through there. Steve watched her inch forward. As she eventually managed to line up with the exit he casually sauntered over, opened the passenger door and climbed in. Kate didn't acknowledge him so he put his sunglasses on, leant back and waited. They turned left towards town and Steve's heart rate rocketed as Kate took both hands off the wheel and her eyes off the road to reach for her sunglasses and plug in her hands free kit.

'I don't appreciate bad language in my office.' she told him, her eyes back on the road.

Steve half turned in his seat to look at her, not sure if she was being serious.

'We sometimes have children, parents, social workers or even teachers in the office. I don't want anyone making a mistake in front of the wrong people, so we don't use crude language in the CPU suite. Clear?'

'Clear, Gov.' Steve felt like a three year old.

Kate turned towards him, let her sunglasses slip down her nose and gave him a big smile. 'Thank you.' She turned her attention back to the road just in time to narrowly miss a transit van parked half on the kerb. Steve's foot involuntarily shot out towards an imaginary brake. It was all he could do not to grab the wheel.

'Can I ask where we're going?' He wondered how long he'd survive her driving.

'You've fallen on your feet Detective Steve Astman.'

'Sorry?'

'DCI Stacey has requested my assistance on the investigation into the sudden and violent demise of George Pink. You're assigned to me, so you just got yourself on the murder. Dean Towle is our only witness. He's thirteen years old. We're going to talk to him, or at least I am, with a social worker and his foster dad present. You can record it.'

'What's Dean's connection to the murder victim? George... ?'

'Pink, George Pink.' Kate helped him out. 'Absolutely no idea.' She swung the car left off the main road. 'I'll ask him, shall I?' She was being sarcastic.

God, I've been here five minutes and she's pissed off with me already. Steve wondered what he'd let himself in for.

'I know one thing,' Kate's voice softened. 'Dean Towle didn't kill Pink. I don't know what the hell happened, or why he was found at the scene, but the boy needs help. This could have serious repercussions for him.'

'What are we going to do?' Steve asked.

Kate turned towards him again. 'We're child protection. We're going to protect him.'

The children's interview suite was part of a large building known, bizarrely, as Hope House. It belonged to the County Social Services and was used by the Families and Children's division for a number of purposes, most of which were hopeless. Supervised access visits took place in the rather worn, but comfy lounge areas and walled garden. Children's therapy groups met around the enormous kitchen table, and extremely 'challenging' children were brought here by child psychologists and expert 'play' teachers to give their parents a break.

Kate thought a lot of children with challenging behaviour were the product of extremely dysfunctional parenting, but she kept that view to herself. She introduced Steve to the staff and then showed him the recording room where he would watch the interview on a monitor and film it. 'Just watch out for significant points during the interview and make a note so that we can find them quickly.' Kate left him to it.

He was practicing camera angles when the door opened and Mivvie Levin, the social worker partnering Kate, held out a plate of milk chocolate digestive biscuits. 'I always lick the chocolate off first.' She teased.

Steve helped himself to two. 'Sounds good to me.'

'I knew you wouldn't disappoint me.' Mivvie gave him a wink before disappearing again.

Steve knew a flirt when it batted its eyelashes at him. Mivvie was a bit skinny, with hardly any tits, but Steve thought there was something bloody attractive about her. She was forthright and sassy and she'd come on to him as soon as they were introduced. He'd caught a disapproving look from Kate, but what the hell?

On the monitor he saw Kate, Mivvie, Dean and Dean's foster dad, Philip, spread out around the interview room. Dean sat next to Philip on the settee, his eyes fixed to the floor as Kate made the introductions for the benefit of the tape.

Five minutes later Steve was engrossed in the interview. Kate was good, in fact she was very good. She'd got a reluctant Dean talking and the boy was visibly relaxing. He seemed to have forgotten about the camera and the others in the room, all his attention was on Kate. She'd got him to talk about his life, his school, about how he loved playing football at The Marville Community Sports Centre where he'd met Pink - who did odd jobs in the grounds. Another five minutes and Steve realised he hadn't made a single note. Shit! He grabbed his pen.

'Draw the route for me.' Kate said.

Dean had slid onto the floor and was leaning on one of the coffee tables. He had a black marker pen in his hand, drawing a map. He looked up at Kate, checking that she was following. Kate was taking it slowly, not rushing him. She was treating him as a grown up; asking straightforward questions, taking him seriously. It was working.

'Did Mr Pink tell you what time he wanted you to come to his house?' She asked.

'Twelve. I was supposed to go at twelve.'

Kate hesitated, there was something wrong. 'What time did you get to Mr Pink's house?'

Dean looked up, puzzled. 'Twelve, I told you already.'

Kate nodded. 'How did you know what time it was?'

'On the clock in our kitchen. It said half past eleven when I left and I had to walk.'

Kate knew he was wrong, but she let it go. 'Did anyone go

with you?'

Dean shook his head. 'Nope, I was on me own. I was going to go with the dog, but I couldn't find him so I went anyway. I just walked by myself. It's just round the corner from the MCSC where I play football.'

'Tell me about anyone you met, or saw on the way,' Kate said.

'Didn't meet no one.' Dean shrugged.

Kate pointed at the card where the drawing of the road led to a path. Kate knew the path cut between the row of houses in the cul-de-sac and doglegged right, leading behind George Pink's house and the houses adjoining his. It gave access to the back gardens. 'What about when you got here?'

Dean rubbed the corner of his eye with his thumb, thinking. He was replaying the journey in his mind. 'No one, I don't think. I don't remember if anyone was walking on the road. There weren't no-one on the path.'

'How did you know how to get into the garden?'

Dean shrugged again. 'He told us, when he said about coming round, to come in that way.' He looked back at his map and started filling in some details. He wrote 'my house' very slowly and carefully over a small square in one corner of the card. Philip looked across to Kate and smiled. It was as if Dean was establishing his safe place.

Kate looked intently at the boy. 'How many times have you been to George Pink's garden?'

Dean didn't look up. He hesitated while he put more details on his drawing. 'Yesterday were the first time. He never asked me before. Fucking wish he'd never asked me.' He was getting emotional; breathing faster, the pencil scribbled furiously.

Kate was pretty sure he was lying. 'Ok, who...' she stopped as Philip leant forward.

'Dean, you're on tape mate, don't say 'fucking'. Philip was grinning, making the comment light hearted.

In the monitor room Steve burst out laughing. The kid gets to watch a bloke burn to death, but he isn't allowed to say 'fucking' when he talks about it. On the monitor he saw Mivvie smile.

Kate didn't react. She put a new piece of card in front of Dean. She'd slowed him down, given him a break. 'Draw the garden for me.' She smiled encouragement.

Dean went to work. The first thing he drew was the burning shed, smack in the middle. Flames shot across the paper from one corner wall. Then he started filling in details around it; the gate in the fence, a path leading to a greenhouse, a large hedge.

'Explain what happened when you got into the garden.' Kate said.

'I smelt the smoke.' Dean hesitated again and stuck the end of the pen back in his mouth. 'And I could hear the fire.'

'Then what did you do?' Kate prompted.

'I could see the flames. It were the shed, the wall were burning at this end.' He pointed at the drawing. His voice was beginning to rasp slightly. 'I could see the smoke coming out at this corner at the back. The door at the front were closed, so I walked round the side.'

'Then what happened?'

'I looked through here, at the window, and saw him burning.' Dean pointed slowly at the drawing, then jerked his hand away and sat bolt upright, perfectly still, his eyes focused on the picture.

'Why did you look inside, Dean?' Kate spoke softly, completely focused on the boy.

Dean shrugged. 'I just did.'

'What could you see?'

'He was lying down, not properly, more fallen over like. All his top half was black and burning. There was smoke on the back of him, on the back of his neck. There was something sticking out underneath him that was on fire and his arm were sticking out.' Dean's voice cracked, 'He'd fell into the wall and the wall were burning too.' Dean's eyes met Kate's and she saw how scared he was. He was holding himself rigid, trying to keep himself together.

'Then what happened, Dean?' Kate's eyes never left his face. She kept him focused on her.

'He waved. He waved his hand at me.' Dean jammed his fists into his eyes and started to cry.

'He got the time wrong.' Kate was holding the informal de-brief in the kitchen of Hope House after Philip and Dean had left. 'He thought the clock in his kitchen said half past eleven, but it must have been half past ten. I didn't say anything because I didn't want to embarrass him, but he was an hour early.'

'Dean's not good with numbers. He can't tell time very well and if he's in a hurry he's more likely to get it wrong.' Mivvie said. 'Because it's the school holidays he hasn't got a structure to his day, so he gets mixed up.'

Steve looked puzzled.

'When he's got a structure he tells time by what's happening. He knows it's eight o'clock when Joan gets him up for school. He knows he gets out of school at three-thirty. He knows his dinner is at six, so he works out the time by events.' Mivvie explained it to him.

Steve shook his head. 'No, I understand that. What I was thinking... does it make any difference?'

'If he'd got there at twelve, like he was supposed to, he would have missed it all. Pink would have already been dead.' Kate flicked her hair back off her neck. She felt damp and sticky. It was so hot, eighty odd degrees during the kids school holidays. A bloody miracle – no doubt it wouldn't last.

'But is that significant?' Steve asked.

'Timing is always significant. And I think there's a whole load of stuff he's not saying.' Kate gathered up the cards that Dean had drawn on. They were already marked up as exhibits.

'Are you thinking of talking to him again?' Mivvie looked reluctant. 'He's had a traumatic experience. He was frightened stupid. Surely, he'd have told us anything important?'

Kate shook her head. 'I think he's worried about something. He was too guarded. He's not clever enough to get away with lying, but I think he's leaving stuff out, something important that he doesn't want us, or maybe Philip, to know about. Let's give him a chance to think about it - but I want to do a follow up interview.'

Mivvie shrugged, she wasn't convinced. 'What else do you think there is? Why would he be hiding something? Dean's a bit slow and he gets confused, but he understands how serious this is. I think he'd tell us everything he knows just to make sure he wasn't in trouble; so we didn't think he had anything to do with the fire.'

'He didn't tell Philip or Joan where he was going. He said Pink offered to pay him to help in the garden, but he never mentioned it to them. And I'm concerned that he hasn't once said Pink's name.' Kate said.

'He's thirteen. I didn't tell my parents lots of stuff when I was thirteen. Maybe he didn't want them to know he was getting some money. Maybe he was afraid they'd stop him going.' Steve suggested.

Kate didn't agree. 'Dean's not your average thirteen year old boy. He looks younger than he is. He's in the 'special needs' class at school and he's in foster care. He's not street smart or full of himself. He watched the horror of a man burn to death. But why did he watch? Why didn't he run; run to the house, scream for help, run away? Something? He just stood there.'

'He got mesmerised.' Mivvie said. 'It happens. Its car crash mentality... you know? You don't want to look but you can't help yourself.'

'I always look. Something to do with my job I think.' Steve was being flippant.

Kate ignored him. She was thinking. It wasn't right. There was *something,* something more, something Dean wasn't saying. She was going to have to report back to Stacey that her interview with Dean was 'on-going' and he wasn't going to like it.

She was about to top up her coffee when her mobile went off. As she listened to the message she saw Mivvie give Steve a flirtatious look and Steve smirk back. They were both beginning to seriously wind her up. She snapped her phone shut. 'Sorry to break up the party but we've got work to do. We need to speak to some kids on the Backridge estate.

Mivvie pulled a face. 'Lucky you, just as well you've got a bodyguard. The Backridge residents aren't very friendly towards the police.' She looked at Steve, 'The Backridge Crew are just a bunch of delinquent yobs who think they're hard, but to a certain extent they're kept in check by the really hard core older residents who've been around for ages. You're a stranger to the area... they won't like the look of you.'

Steve narrowed his eyes, but before he could speak Kate cut him off.

'Don't worry, they love me. I catch child abusers and even the most hardened criminal hates child abusers. You'll be perfectly safe as long as you're with me.' She swung her bag over her shoulder and was out of the door before he could think of a reply.

***

CHAPTER SIX

The whole estate was a dump. A warren of narrow streets lined with wrecked and broken down cars. Rubbish spilled out of black plastic bags and mixed with the debris of a section of humanity that was past caring.

Kate parked in front of one of the only well kept houses in the street. 'Aunty Sharon's place.' She nodded towards the blue front door. 'We'll walk from here. If anyone messes with the car she'll skin them alive.' She grabbed the keys and hopped out.

'Why are we looking for these kids, Gov?' Steve fell into step beside her.

'We're not looking,' she told him. 'Justin Coleman is four years old and he's got a broken arm. I know exactly where he is. Apparently he and his older brother, Terry, know a new song... a song about George Pink.'

'Sorry Gov?' Steve had no idea what she was talking about. 'These kids are singing a song about the murder victim? How's that?'

Kate looked over the top of her sunglasses at him. 'Let's ask them.'

She turned onto a path leading between the backs of two rows of identical terraced houses, pushed open a gate and Steve followed her into a small square garden. An enormous trampoline filled the centre space. A skinny blond woman in a pair of pink micro shorts and a bikini top was lying flat out in the centre of it, sunbathing.

'Hey Kate.' She sat up and eyed Steve suspiciously. 'Who's your mate?'

'Hi Jules.' Kate made the introductions. 'Aunty Sharon called me. Something about the kids singing a little jitty she thought I should hear. Can I talk to Justin and Terry?'

Jules nodded. 'Aunty Sharon were here earlier, she took Justin for a walk. He's doing my head in. Keeps wanting the paddling pool out 'cos it's so friggin' hot. But he gets his plaster wet. I knew she was going to call you. He's dead then, is he... this bloke, Pink?'

Kate nodded, but before she had a chance to say anything a small boy in a pair of red surfer shorts shot out of the back kitchen door. He was holding an orange ice-lolly, which was melting and dripping down his right arm. His left arm was encased from wrist to elbow in a dirty plaster.

'Oi! I told you no lollies.' Jules shouted at the boy.

'I had it already. Look.' The boy held his hand up. He was right, most of it was gone and the rest was melting quickly.

'Kate! Kate! Come on the trampoline. Come on! You have to take your shoes off.' He started jumping about excitedly.

Kate grinned at him and shook her head, 'I'd love to, but I think my friend Steve would really like to have a go first. He's very good at jumping. He loves trampolines.'

'Thanks, Gov.' Steve knew he'd been stitched up.

Justin craned his neck to look up at Steve, his eyes wide with interest.

'What happened to your arm?' Steve asked him.

'I was jumping like this.' The little boy started leaping in the air, 'And Terry pushed me after Mum had told him to get off and leave me alone and I fell off the trampoline really hard and it broke all on this bit all in here.' Justin was gushing, not pausing for breath. He waved the lolly over his plastered arm.

Steve looked a bit stunned.

Kate shook her head in amusement. 'That was daft, wasn't it? But it's nearly better now, isn't it? Can I talk to you about something really important, Justin?' Kate tried to get his attention back.

'Tell Kate the song, Justin, sing that song again.' Jules told him.

Justin licked his lolly. He didn't want to sing the song.

'Can you sing it? Can you sing it for me? I'd really like to hear it. So would Steve... wouldn't you, Steve?' Kate nodded at him enthusiastically. Steve nodded back.

'Tell you what Justin.' Steve bent down and started undoing his laces, 'How about you sing the song and we'll have a go on the trampoline?'

Justin's face broke into a huge grin. He started to sing loudly.

'Pink the Perv had a BBQ.

He had it in his shed

He roasted his balls and his hair caught fire

And now the Tosser's dead.'

Kate stared at him in astonishment. 'Where did you learn that?' Goosebumps pricked the back of her neck. Justin obviously didn't understand what he was singing. Pink the Perv? What the hell was that about?

'Bev's house.' Justin started pulling himself up on the trampoline. 'Mum, get off. I'm jumping with Steve.'

Steve put his hands up to help Jules down but she ignored him and did a forward flip over the side, landing squarely on both feet. He climbed up behind Justin, giving Kate a questioning look over his shoulder, but Kate didn't respond. Her mind was racing with questions as she watched them.

'Did Bev teach you the song?' She stood at the side of the trampoline and stretched her arms out, ready to catch Justin or push him back on if he got too close to the edge.

'Nope. The boy told me it. The Zebedee boy. Bev laughed when we sung the song, she said it were really funny and served him right.' Justin was shouting out words breathlessly between jumps.

'Served who right?' Kate wasn't sure if he meant the Zebedee boy or Pink.

Justin shrugged, 'Don't know. Look at me Kate. I can go this high.' He bounced as hard as he could.

'What else did Bev say?'

Justin grinned cheekily and looked at his mum as though he knew something he shouldn't.

'Go on, Justin, what else? What else did she say?' Jules nodded at him encouragingly.

'Pink burnt his sausage and no-one would eat it now.' Justin stuck his index finger in his mouth suggestively.

Jules exploded. 'I'm going to friggin' kill 'em. What are they teaching him that filth for?'

But Kate was thinking about something else. 'What were they doing at Bev's house?' She asked Jules.

'Terry took him over there late yesterday afternoon.' Jules told her. 'Terry said there were older boys there. They were planning to have a party with Bev last night. Some idiots obviously thought it were funny to teach Justin that filth. I made Terry come home and bring Justin wiv him. It aint right, Bev having kids round, all drinking and smoking, with her little baby there and everything. Oi... stay in the middle.' She shouted at Justin, 'I never knew the bloke was really dead until Aunty Sharon told me this morning, poor Bastard. Who was he?'

But Kate wasn't listening. They had to leave... right now. She jerked her head at Steve who got the message and lifted a reluctant Justin off the trampoline.

As soon as they were out of the back gate Kate started running.

***

CHAPTER SEVEN

'Get it open now!' Kate gave the order and stepped back from Bev's front door. She'd hammered on it loudly enough to wake the dead, with no response. 'There's a five week old baby in there somewhere. GET IT OPEN.'

Steve smashed the lock off with his third kick.

Two uniformed policemen had turned up within a couple of minutes of Kate's call for support. Steve was first in through the ruined door and they crowded in behind him. PC Greg Thomas disappeared up the stairs while PC Jaz Gulzer headed for the back room. The air was thick with the stench of dank stale booze, fags, and worse.

There was a shout from the back room and Kate heard Greg thundering down the stairs again.

'Ma'am, in here!' Jaz was yelling, 'We need an ambulance!'

Jaz was on his knees besides the prone body of Bev. She was on her back on the sofa. Her head was tilted back at an awkward angle, her dirty blond hair stuck to the back of her head, rigid, like the plastic head of a cheap doll. A small woman, no more than five feet tall, Bev was thin in the way that some women were when they smoked rather than ate. A new mother, twenty-three years of age, she should have been vibrant, and blooming, with breasts full of milk and a stomach still rounded after childbirth. Instead she was a stinking, empty husk.

Bev had vomited violently. The smell was overpowering. Kate felt bile rising up in her own throat and swallowed it back down. She forced herself to take shallow breaths. *Don't breathe it in girl, keep breathing, but don't breathe it in.*

Jaz pulled rubber gloves from his pocket and tried to find a pulse. Kate knew it was a waste of time, so did he, but he tried anyway.

It can't have been that long, Kate thought, she must have died today, this morning, or late last night. *Shit.* It was what she'd been afraid of, from the moment Jules had mentioned Bev having a party with kids drinking. Beverley was an alcoholic who'd only been allowed to keep her baby with her because there was supposed to be a team of supporters ensuring she didn't go off the rails. *So much for that.*

Jaz shook his head. 'She's gone... and not just now, she's been dead a while, stupid girl, she's choked on her own vomit.' He stood up and took a step back, careful not to tread in the mess on the carpet.

'Where's the baby? Where's Crystal?' Kate looked at Greg, but he shook his head.

'Nothing upstairs, Ma'am.'

'She's here.' Steve's voice was surprisingly quiet. They'd all been looking at Bev. Kate hadn't realised that Steve had gone behind the sofa. He stood up suddenly, filling the room, looked around quickly, came to a decision and pulled his tie and shirt off.

'I need some help here'. He disappeared again as he knelt down.

Kate stepped quickly around the sofa and saw what he was looking at. Greg crowded up behind her, a hanky held over his mouth to block out the smell. Jaz unhooked his radio from his belt but waited at the other side of the room. He didn't want to look. He could handle most things, but not dead babies.

'Jaz, call in... she's alive. How many minutes away is the ambulance? I need to know *now*.' Kate said urgently.

Baby Crystal, five weeks old and barely alive lay on a grubby cot blanket on the floor. A blue t-shirt soaked through with urine and worse covered her little body, over what was left of her nappy. She'd been left for so long that her nappy, saturated with faeces and urine, had disintegrated. Her tiny bare legs were still and lifeless, red raw from the burn of urine and chaffing where she'd struggled and screamed, but no one had come.

Kate knelt down and touched one finger to the baby's neck. Crystal wasn't moving, but there was the faintest whimper as Kate touched her. Kate could feel her own throat constricting. She wanted to grab the baby up, pull it close to her chest and comfort it, but she knew she'd hurt the child more than she was hurting already. *Please God, where's the ambulance?*

Steve bent forward close alongside her. His sheer bulk made Crystal look even more tiny and vulnerable.

'Guys see if you can find something in the kitchen that will hold water; tepid water, and a clean towel, tea towel... anything clean.' Kate leant over the child, she was afraid to touch her, but she had to.

Steve laid his shirt on a dry piece of carpet next to the baby as Kate tenderly lifted the blue t-shirt, and as gently as she could, lifted it over the baby's head, and off. The whole of Crystal's tummy, chest and under her arms was red raw. Kate slowly pulled rotten pieces of the nappy away from the baby's body, until the child was naked. Crystal's lips trembled, as she was touched. The whimpering grew louder. Kate thought this was a good sign. She put her finger to the baby's cheek and stroked it. The child was hot and feverish. Kate leant forward and blew gently on her face - a gentle breath of cool air on the fevered skin. Crystal opened her eyes. She looked directly at Kate and held her gaze, and then she started to cry. Kate smiled.

'It's alright baby,' she said, 'it's alright now.'

She placed her hands under the tiny body and lifted slowly and gently, until Crystal was clear of the floor. Trying desperately not to add to her agony, Kate placed her down on Steve's shirt. Crystal cried out as she was lifted, but seemed soothed by the stroking and blowing.

Greg came back with a saucepan of water and two pink ladies t-shirts. He handed them to Steve. 'That's the only thing I can find. The water's just slightly warm, not hot.'

'Ambulance is entering the estate.' Jaz said, from the hallway, his voice croaked. 'I'll go out the front and wait for it.' He disappeared.

Kate looked up at Steve as he placed the saucepan by the side of her. The look on his face was one of controlled anger, and something else she couldn't make out; pity maybe? He dipped one of the t-shirts into the water, and went to hand it to her, but she shook her head.

'No, just let the water run over her legs and tummy, we need to wash some of this urine and mess off her.'

He nodded, twisted the t-shirt and the warm water ran down over the baby's legs. It soaked into his shirt underneath her and Crystal took off crying again. Kate stroked and blew and shushed her, and closed her eyes in relief as she heard sirens approaching.

***

CHAPTER EIGHT

J ohn Bishop's office space was only separated from the open
plan office inhabited by the 'plebs and dregs' as he liked to refer
to them, by a large glass panel. The Social Services management
had adopted an 'open door' policy - which meant that he had to
suffer the annoyance of being visible and 'on hand' to the other
members of staff whenever he was at his desk. The up side,
however, was that he got to look at his new Administration
Assistant's tits whenever he wanted to, and Michelle's tits were
worth the look. The fact that he couldn't use the word 'Secretary'
anymore was just another bloody indication of how local
Government, the County Council and the world in general had
gone to hell on a donkey. Political correctness ruined everyone's
fun, not just his.

He shifted his weight onto his left buttock, spreading his legs a
bit wider to accommodate the semi hard-on he was nursing. There
were eight people currently sitting in the office on the other side of
his glass partition, they could all see him quite clearly - but they had
no idea that he had an erection, which made him want to laugh.
The fact that he was aroused had nothing to do with Michelle's
boobs pressing against the front of her red cardigan - like two fat
puppies trying to escape from under a blanket. Most days she wore
low cut tops, showing off a cleavage you could park your bike in,
and she had more than enough buttons undone today to give a
man whiplash. Bishop picked up the handset from the new office
phone contraption that he'd never really got the hang of. He
stretched his legs out under his desk and leant back, pretending to
talk to someone. At the same time he slid his other hand down his
thigh and let his fingers slip into his groin, pushing into the

material of his trousers as he gently stroked himself. *That felt good.* But it wasn't Michelle that was making him squirm in his seat, no, what he was thinking about was something Michelle would never be able to offer. Not in a million years.

He started flipping through the pages of his computerised diary. How the hell had Michelle booked him in for so much crap? He had to find time to get away and see the boy. Something had happened; Pink was dead and there was rumour and speculation all over the place. He needed to find out if there was anything going on that he should worry about. He didn't want to worry, everything had been going so well, but he wasn't about to take a chance. He was Mr No Risk Man. But looking for information was a good enough reason to get some one on one time with the boy. Bishop felt the familiar hot rush and pressed his thighs together to control himself. It had been too long, it would be good to see the boy again.

Baby Crystal was on her way to the local hospital, and Steve's shirt had gone with her. The ambulance had left, and a lot more people had arrived. A traffic officer, the only bloke on duty who was bigger than Steve, had turned up with a spare white shirt. The uniform boys were mostly outside the house. The smell inside was too bad, and there was nothing to be done anyway - Bev was dead. The Coroner's car was parked behind the traffic car. The ambulance crew had said Crystal would be ok; just dehydration and severe nappy rash... oh, and she was minus a mother, but a bloody poor one, as the general opinion seemed to be, so that might be a bonus.

The obligatory gawpers and gapers had turned out in force. Several women with kids hanging around their legs and babies in arms were on the pavement outside the next-door neighbour's gate.

'I did me best, helping her out and all, but that baby should have been taken off her. I said it didn't I? She weren't fit to have a dog, never mind a baby.' A woman with purple mottled arms and enormous bosoms was holding forth, expressing her views loudly to the women gathered around her. Several of her listeners nodded in agreement,

'Bloody useless Social Services.' The woman continued,

encouraged, 'And none of these could give a shit, too bloody late turning up now... not you Kate.' She called across the path, 'You're alright, shame about your mates.'

Kate gave the woman a brief nod in recognition, but she wasn't in the mood to chat. She looked around and surveyed what was fast becoming a small, yet serious incident scene. This was her second sudden death in two days, and it was the first one, Pink's death, that had brought her here. She suddenly felt one of those weird moments; as though something had got away from her, shifted her reality into something unexpected. This wasn't supposed to be part of her job description, adult deaths, but there had been a child at both scenes, and children were her job.

Steve was standing off to one side, waiting. He hadn't had much to do for the last twenty minutes, so he was watching his DI giving her report to the young uniform Sergeant who was trying to cover up his anxiety by looking earnest. Kate's sunglasses were perched on the top of her hair, pushing her long red fringe back from her face. Steve could see freckles on lightly tanned skin. Her voice was low, he could only make out a few words - she was saying something about a case conference and a sister.

Greg Thomas plodded over and lit a cigarette, 'How long have you been with the CPU?' he asked.

Steve studied his watch before looking up, his eyes focused somewhere over Greg's head while he calculated. 'Four hours and eighteen minutes.'

'Good start then.' Greg blew smoke straight up into the air. 'One dead woman, a half dead baby, and you've lost your shirt.'

Steve just shrugged, 'Straight into the scrum, no point in pissing about.' The banter was part and parcel of any event - he wasn't bothered. He was still looking past Greg, watching Kate, but he knew Greg was grinning at him.

'If you're assigned to our lovely DI Kate Landers you'll have fun.' Greg smirked.

Steve waited for him to elaborate, but he turned and started to walk over to the two traffic boys. They'd turned up, had a look, found there was nothing for them to do and had decided to hang about until something more interesting showed up.

'Anyway,' Greg threw the comment over his shoulder as he left. 'You want to stop pissing about; you're supposed to be on the murder enquiry.'

'That's why we were here.' Steve said under his breath.

Kate eventually stepped away from the Duty Sergeant and in doing so stepped away from the event.

'Let's go.' She turned and started back towards her car. 'I've spoken to the Social Services Children's Department and they're gearing up for the fall out.' She told him as soon as they were out of earshot. Her glasses slid down the length of her nose, shiny in the heat, but she didn't have a hand free to push them back up. Steve wasn't sure if the look on her face was one of exasperation or she was just pissed off.

Opposite her parked car were two teenage boys Steve had clocked earlier. They were leaning against an ancient Renault 5, cultivating a look of 'bored witless'.

Kate knew both of them - B.Zed and Noel. 'I think we're being watched by a couple of Bev's party guests.' she said. 'The one on the right is Zebedee boy.' As they drew level she nodded across, acknowledging their presence without blowing their 'cool'. Kate's guess was right on the mark - B.Zed wanted a word.

'Hey Kate, who toasted Pink the Perv?' He leant back and stuck his hands deep into his front pockets. His jeans, only just belted above his crotch, slid further down.

Kate stopped walking. B.Zed was watching her, but she pretended to look puzzled, 'Pink the Perv? I don't know who you mean.'

B.Zed grinned, 'Like I said, Pink the Perv. Reckon he's barbequed, fried in his shed, who done that then?' He rocked backwards and forwards on his toes. Was he drunk, stoned? It was never too early for B.Zed. Noel seemed to have found something really interesting on his foot that was taking all his attention.

'I don't know.' Kate said. 'You tell me.'

Before B.Zed could answer Steve had crossed the road and was standing in front of the boys. His sheer size barricaded them against the vehicle, deliberately hedging them in. He casually looked past them and down the road, over Noel's left shoulder. 'Who told you about George Pink then?'

B.Zed shrugged and grinned at Steve sarcastically. He didn't know who this bloke was, but he knew he was filth, and he recognised a pissing contest when it stepped in front of him.

'Anyway, I weren't talking to you mate, I was talking to her.' He tilted his head in Kate's direction.

Kate sighed. B.Zed was a player in a lot of stuff; some of it a nuisance, some of it bad, and occasionally stuff that was downright evil. He wasn't going to be easily intimidated.

Steve nodded, as though to say; 'fair enough', and leant in closer. 'No-one told you... but you heard it right? Where? Were you at Bev's house last night? Do you know George Pink?' He looked from one boy to the other and back again. Noel kept studying his shoes.

'He's mute is he?' Steve nodded towards Noel.

B.Zed looked out from under the peak of his grey baseball cap and smiled chummily, 'No, he just don't like talking to fucking pigs, that's all.'

Steve nodded, his expression didn't change, but Kate saw his jaw harden and watched him take his weight on his back foot. *Oh shit*, she thought, *he's going to head butt him.*

'DC Astman, could I have a word?' Kate yanked open the front passenger door on her car, left it open, and strode around to the driver's side. Sitting with both hands on the steering wheel and staring straight ahead, she waited for Steve to join her. As he climbed in she sensed his hostility and ignored it.

'B.Zed and Noel.' She told him. 'Noel is on an ASBO. B.Zed has just been released from a Young Offenders Institution. Don't bother putting your seat belt on, you're getting out again in a second.' For a full minute she just sat watching the boys over her left shoulder.

Steve was confused. 'What are you...?' He didn't finish the question.

Kate suddenly revved the engine and jammed the gear lever into reverse. She backed up fast, swinging the car in a tight curve back towards where the boys were still standing. Steve fell against the door and braced his right hand against the dashboard to hold on, then realised he looked a twat and let go. Kate braked hard. The car rocked as its rear end stopped six feet short of Noels toes. Kate snatched her keys out of the ignition. 'When I give you B.Zed's mobile, hang on to it and stay with Noel. Watch him - he's pretty to look at but he's an evil git. Ready?' She raised her eyebrows at him.

Steve smiled and reached for his door handle. 'Where's B.Zed's phone?' He asked.

'It will be in his hand any second now.'

Kate pushed open her door with one hand and pushed buttons on her mobile with the other. As they climbed out Steve saw B.Zed look at the monitor on his mobile, a look of puzzlement on his face. Neither boy had moved. Noel was looking at them as though he'd die of boredom any second. Kate stepped in close to B.Zed, placed her foot directly over his right training shoe and leant into him, tilting him off balance. B.Zed opened his mouth and started to drop his hand, but Kate wrapped her fingers around his wrist, twisted his hand up and, before he knew it was happening, she was holding his phone. She casually passed it behind her back to Steve who stuck it in the front pocket of his trousers, placing himself between B.Zed and Noel.

'What the fuck?' B.Zed's eyes started jumping in his head.

'Walk with me B.Zed.' Kate turned her back on him and started to stroll away.

B.Zed's eyes went from her to Steve and back again. He licked his lips nervously. 'Give me the fucking phone back, man.'

Steve ignored him and kept his eyes on Noel. The boy was looking at his shoe again, a small smile on his face.

'You'll get it back, walk with me.' Kate called over her shoulder.

B.Zed gave Steve a filthy look then turned and jogged after her. He was wired, restless and jittery, either on the way up or the way down from a drug-induced mood, Kate wasn't sure which.

'Talk to me B.Zed before my Detective Constable gets bored and starts searching your contacts list, tell me about Pink the Perv.'

'He's toast Babe - he's gone. Someone lit the perv up. Whoosh, barbequed.' B.Zed bounced on the balls of his feet as he walked.

'Why's he called Pink the Perv?'

'Cos he's a fucking pervert.' B.Zed grinned.

'Help me here,' Kate said, calmly. 'Why is he a pervert?'

B.Zed bounced in front of her, his eyes skitting left and right as though he couldn't quite focus. His small goatee beard made him look like a demented Leprechaun. 'Likes to do young boys. He pays them to perv about with him.'

'How do you know that?' Kate stopped walking. She fixed her

eyes on his face, trying to get his attention.

B.Zed rocked backwards on his heels, still grinning. 'Everyone knows it.'

'How?' she insisted. 'How do they know? Who told you?'

B.Zed looked over her shoulder back at Steve. He wouldn't meet her eyes. 'Same people as told you. The lost boys no one gave a shit about, a couple of tossers. Perv was fiddling with them, but the filth didn't believe them. But he got more boys. Street kids that'll do stuff for money. He pays them for kinky stuff, fucking pervert.' B.Zed rocked back on his heels. He was laughing at her.

Kate's mind was racing. She'd just opened a huge can of worms. 'Give me details. What boys? Where? When?' She tried to get him to make eye contact but his constant motion made it impossible. 'B.Zed!' She said furiously, and moved closer to him, invading his space. She had to make him calm down and focus - she needed answers. 'Who are the lost boys? Where does this happen?'

B.Zed stood still for a second, hunched his shoulders and made a huge effort to focus. 'Round the back of his house, in the garden. Anyone meeting him goes in the back way.' He burst out laughing, doubled over and pointed at her with an unsteady finger. 'Goes in the back way! Fucking shirt lifter – that's funny that is.' He hooted, yelling with exaggerated laughter.

Kate had had enough. Turning around she called out to Steve, 'DC Astman, find my contact number on that phone and delete it. Oh, and while you're at it, there might be some other numbers of interest.'

Steve nodded and pulled B.Zed's mobile from his pocket, keeping his eyes on Noel.

B.Zed's eyes darted to his phone; a look of panic crossed his face and he started blabbing. 'Ask Andy Frazier; ask him where he got his new trainers, and Martin... what's his name? Josh Martin. He's Pink's little boyfriend. That little shithead won't tell you fuck all, but he knows.'

Kate nodded at him encouragingly. Nothing on her face showed the alarm bells that were starting to ring in her head. She recognised both names. Andy Frazier was a delinquent fifteen year old who was 'known to the police' for all sorts of yobbish behaviour. Josh Martin was the eldest son of the Martin family –

brother to Darren Martin, the little four-year-old boy she'd been visiting in hospital when all this kicked off. *It's always the same kids.*

B.Zed started chewing his bottom lip, his eyes locked on his phone, which Steve was studying intently. 'There's more. Maybe The Toad knows. That Andy Frazier is right up for it, and Pink the perv pays. And that little prick Martin will do anything for cash.

Kate looked at him blankly, but her mind was racing. *Was George Pink into young boys - young boys like Dean Towle?* She turned, sauntered back to her car and got in without a backwards glance.

Steve pressed a couple of buttons on B.Zed's phone then casually threw it back to him. He climbed into the passenger seat and grinned at her. 'That was interesting, Gov.'

Kate didn't respond. Her mind was busy working over what she'd just heard. *The lost boys had told the police? Who were the lost boys? What the hell was that about? Did half the town know something she didn't know? She'd never heard of Pink before yesterday.*

Steve was silent for a moment, and then he turned in his seat to look at her. 'How come you've got B.Zed's mobile phone number?' He asked.

'I bought him the phone.' Kate said.

***

CHAPTER NINE

'It could be chinese whispers.' There was doubt in Kate's voice. Perched on the side of a spare desk in the incident room, she folded her arms and stared at a point over Steve's left shoulder, thinking it through.

'You don't think it's true, Gov?' Steve asked.

Kate looked up sharply at the touch of sarcasm in his tone. He'd obviously already made his mind up, his shoulders twitched impatiently as he waited for her to answer. She was still thinking, pulling on her bottom lip with her thumb and finger when Colin Morris came in and wordlessly handed over a cup of espresso. Kate gulped at it quickly and asked him what he thought; knowing he'd play Devil's advocate.

'It could have happened like this,' Colin spoke slowly, 'someone hears that George Pink pays young boys to help him in his garden and someone calls him a pervert. No evidence or anything, just a throw away comment by someone who likes to think that any man who entertains young kids in any way must have a sexual deviance, the sort that calls every scout leader or swimming coach a pervert. Next thing you know, 'Pink's a pervert' is being branded about as though it's a fact.'

Kate wasn't so sure, 'Dean Towle went to Pink's place for money. Dean's vulnerable; he's an easy target. What if he knew he was expected to do something other than work in the garden for the cash? What's he not telling us? It's worrying that he hasn't once used Pink's name - he's never said it.' She drained her coffee. Standing next to Steve she heard his stomach rumble and tried to think when she'd last eaten anything. She came to a decision, Stacey wasn't around and the analyst who would examine every facet of Pink's life still hadn't arrived. She needed information.

'Steve, find out if Pink has ever come to our attention for anything, ever. Has anyone checked the Sex Offenders Register?'

She turned to a young female officer, Natasha Blackley, who was making a spirited effort to handle several ringing telephones and listen in on the conversation at the same time. 'Who's the Family Liaison officer looking after Pink's wife? I want to see a copy of Anne Pink's statement.' Before the girl could answer Kate looked across at the computer wizard, Detective Constable Rogers, known to all and sundry as 'Ginger', who'd been borrowed for the incident room. 'Ginger, do an internet search. Google Pink, check Facebook, You Tube, all the usual places.'

Ginger looked uncertain.

'What?' Kate glared at him.

'Sorry Ma'am, from what I've been told, the victim didn't seem the sort to be on the cutting edge of technology or running his social life on line.' He shrugged.

'I agree, but do it anyway. Don't assume anything.'

'Julie's the Family Liaison Officer, Ma'am.' Natasha called out. 'She's at the neighbour's place where Mrs Pink's staying until we can let her back in her house.' She flipped through a stack of papers on her desk. The neighbour is Cynthia Alma - she's a widow. Julie's been there all day taking a statement. Apparently it's taking forever because Anne Pink is a bit of a 'Poppet'.

Kate gave her a sideways look.

'You know, the sort that talks non-stop, makes tea constantly, but is difficult to tie down to details. Julie's taking it slowly.'

'Right,' Kate nodded, 'Get Julie on the phone. Why is Anne Pink at the neighbour's? Where are the family?'

The girl turned and pulled a desk phone towards her. Kate issued instructions until everyone, except Colin, had a job. Colin wasn't involved in the investigation, he was just lingering.

'They'll die if you don't feed them, even the big ones.' Colin said in his slow, laconic voice.

Kate peered sideways at him, 'Sorry?'

'You haven't eaten, have you?' He looked at her accusingly. 'Detective Constable Astman is not covered in a layer of fat. He's not like a bear. That's a layer of muscle sticking out all over his body. If you don't feed him he'll fall over – and you'll be in trouble with Knowling.'

Kate snorted, 'Looking at your skinny arse I'd say you were the last person to be lecturing anyone.'

'What are you going to do?' Colin ignored the jibe.

'Well, I'm not taking him home to my house for dinner if that's what you think.'

'No, what are you going to do about Pink?'

'I'm going to call the search team working at Pink's house and tell them what to look out for - keepsakes, computer stuff, hidey holes, you know the score... then I'm going to set up a meeting with the guy who runs the football club at the centre where Dean plays - find out everything I can about Pink's relationship with these boys. And at some point I'll give Stacey a heads up.'

'And Josh Martin? Andy Frazier? The kids B.Zed told you about?' Colin looked worried.

'They'll have to be spoken to, but you know what they're like. Dean Towle might open up, but if Josh Martin or Andy Frazier visited Pink for money there's no reason on earth why they should tell us about it...'

'Excuse me, Ma'am'. Natasha called out. 'Julie says no family. Mrs Pink had a sister, lived up north somewhere, but died two years ago. And George Pink was an only child. They never had kids, so there's no-one close. Cynthia Alma is Anne Pink's best friend, they go to the WI together. Julie hasn't got into too much detail on George Pink's background or social life yet. Mrs Pink has just taken a sleeping tablet so she's going to carry on with the statement tomorrow. Was there anything else?'

Before Kate could answer, Ginger jumped up and pulled a sheet of paper from the nearest printer. 'George Pink was given a community award for 'Good Citizenship' by the Mayor of Hockley three years ago. Something to do with his volunteer work at a kids club.'

Hockley? Kate looked back at Natasha - she was still hanging on the phone. 'How long have the Pink's lived here, in Marville?' There was a creeping suspicion just building up in the back of her mind.

Natasha asked the question into the receiver, and then looked up, 'Two years. Moved here from Hockley when George Pink retired. They've been at the bungalow in Clare Walk the whole time.'

'That's fine.' Kate told her. She ran her hands through her hair and turned back towards Colin. 'B.Zed called them *The Lost Boys*. He said they'd told us about Pink but we didn't believe them. Who are the lost boys? No one told us... not here at Marville. But the Pink's have only been here two years.' Kate stopped suddenly and stared at Colin. She knew he was thinking the same thing.

'B.Zed spent time in a Young Offenders Institute in Hockley.' Kate narrowed her eyes and turned towards the computer wizard, 'Ginger, get me the sheet on B.Zed. When was he sentenced, and when was he in Hockley YOI?'

Steve was walking towards her. 'You need to see this, Gov.' He was holding a page he'd torn from a notebook. Kate saw the look on his face and the tiny hairs on the back of her arms stood on end. She made no move to take the paper from him. She knew, before he said anything, she knew.

'Pink was arrested in Hockley nearly three years ago.'

Kate stared hard at him. 'Arrested for what?'

'Inciting sexual activity with a child.'

***

CHAPTER TEN

DI 'Barmy' Barnes knew she was breathing heavily but she couldn't help herself. They were waiting for the post mortem to start on George Pink and she was excited. Pink had been burnt to death! She knew the body was in a right mess - he'd had petrol thrown over his head before being set alight. It was the best sort of post mortem, much better than some dreary old 'Sudden Death' where some old fart had inconveniently waited to get to work before he dropped dead on the toilet... no, this was a proper post mortem.

Barmy took a deep breath, stuck her finger in a tub of Vicks, scooped out a generous blob and rubbed it around the outside of her nostrils. Her eyes started to water as she wiped her nose on the back of her hand. Her companion, DC Edwards, didn't bother with the Vicks and she peered at him in disgust as she pulled on her mask. She didn't think there was anything clever about being a knob. Edwards was already in her bad books. He was dishevelled, stunk of cigarettes and looked massively hung over. His complexion matched the coverall he'd pulled on over his suit. When she'd refused to let him smoke in the car he'd had a sulk and then stopped at a petrol station to get two cans of Red Bull, nearly making them late. Oh well, nothing like a good post mortem to sober someone up. Barmy grinned to herself.

The Pathologist, Eric Brewton, acknowledged their presence with the briefest nod of his head and went to work. He didn't believe in idle chitchat in his domain. He liked discipline and respect around the deceased. Any police officer that tried black humour in one of his post mortems would be firmly shown the door.

As the body of George Pink was exposed, Edwards took a long step back from the table. His hand shot up over his mouth and nose.

If he faints, I'm going to fucking kill him. Barmy decided.

Eric Brewton ignored them. It wasn't that he didn't like police officers; he didn't like anyone very much. He found the living generally a lot less interesting than the dead. He started his preliminary examination of the body, pulling a powerful overhead light towards him and dictating aloud as he began.

Whatever George Pink had been in life was long gone. The spirit had departed. Barmy didn't believe in Heaven, but she damn well believed in an afterlife. She knew there was an eternal torment waiting for child abusers. Standing calmly, she let her anger with Edwards seep away as she studied the charred remains on the slab. Pink's torso had burnt unevenly and one side showed far greater damage than the other. The facial features were gone, only a charcoaled mess remained. The upper body was barely recognisable as the human it once was. Pink's right arm was angled upwards, bent at an awkward angle. The limb had contracted; it stuck out rigidly as though thumbing a lift. Barmy smiled: A deathly Hitch Hiker, destination Hell.

As he worked his way down the torso Eric Brewton paused, bent low towards the charred remains and poked about in Pink's groin with his gloved finger. Behind her Barmy heard Edwards make a small gagging sound. Brewton waved the forensic photographer over. Barmy leant forward, trying to get a closer look.

'Now that's interesting,' Brewton said, to the room in general. He reached across to a tray of instruments and picked up a small measuring tool. 'Whoever did this, really didn't like him.'

DC Edwards made it to the car park before he threw up.

Eddie Lead was doing tricks on his skateboard. It was late enough for it to be dark outside but four ornate lamps, positioned high up on the back wall of the house, threw light onto the large garden. He was focused on landing the tricks, one after another as fast as he could. He was distracting himself, trying not to think about how scared he was. *Pink is dead, Pink is dead, Pink is dead.* He chanted it like a mantra, whispering the words over and over. *Pink is dead.* He wanted to be glad Pink was dead, but his stomach was churning. He knew if he stopped jumping and twisting with the skateboard he'd start shaking, or worse – he'd throw up. Everything had changed. In one day his whole life had been turned upside down.

He didn't want to be scared anymore but he didn't know how to make it stop. He raced back down the patio as fast as he could, crouching low on the board as he hurled himself off the top of a steep set of concrete steps, his skateboard turning over in the air beneath him as he jumped. He landed neatly with both feet on the board, bending low to keep his speed up, before flipping the board up with his foot, catching it easily in his hand and running back up to the patio taking the steps two at a time. He tucked his head down and pumped his arms, racing to the top to start over again. He didn't know what the time was – he didn't have a watch, but he knew it was past midnight. At some point he would have to go in the house and go to bed, but not yet. He wasn't ready for that yet.

In the split second it took for him to raise his eyes from the ground and look up he realised there was a dark figure standing just inside the glass patio doors watching him. Silhouetted by the light from behind, their features were invisible and Eddie jumped with shock. He heard himself shout out in fear and his arms flew up, protecting his face and head.

The patio doors were thrust open and she rushed to him; wrapping her arms around his waist, pulling him towards her. 'I'm sorry, I'm so sorry.' She was pressed against his chest, her head tilted back so that her eyes could search his face. 'It's ok, everything's ok, it's only me. You're safe; no one can hurt you now. It's just me.'

Eddie dropped the skateboard and clung to her.

Kate was exhausted. As soon as she got home all she wanted to do was climb into bed, but she was too wound up to sleep. Instead she ran a bath that was so hot she had to lower her body down slowly into the water an inch at a time. Her skin prickled and reddened as the heat spread up her legs and back. The glass of Merlot sitting within reach was her second, but there was no-one counting. It had been a long day. Her mind was running riot with questions about the case and her shoulders were knotted with tension. She leant back until the water lapped her breasts and she closed her eyes.

Pink had been arrested but nothing had come of it. The news had stunned the team. It wasn't chinese whispers. It appeared that what B.Zed had told her was true - his intelligence sources on this case were better than hers. A bloody punk kid, who'd spent time in a Young Offender's Institute, was way ahead of her. What was it he'd said? '*Every fucker knows it?*' Well almost everyone. She had a list of names: Josh Martin, Andrew Frazier and The Toad. Apparently, even Bev knew about Pink. She'd been celebrating, laughing about Pink's death before she died. Even little Justin was singing songs about it. They all knew.

Someone had told the police about Pink - two young boys had, and no one believed them. Pink's life went on as before, uninterrupted. If he was a paedophile then he was a successful one. He'd been challenged once and walked away, untarnished.

Questions rattled around in her head. What did she believe? Was George Pink a paedophile or were the allegations against him malicious? Was he a victim rather than a sinister predator? She mulled over what she knew: Pink was sixty-four years old when he died, so he must have taken early retirement. Retired from what? What had he done for work? She didn't know. They were still waiting for a full victim profile to be established. Two boys, who'd been in foster care at the time, had made accusations against him, accused him of inciting them into sexual activity, but the Crown Prosecution Service didn't take it on. They decided that the case wasn't going anywhere and it was dropped. Pink was never charged and he'd moved to Marville shortly afterwards. Why? What was the reason for the move?

Pink had been a volunteer at a kids club. He'd been recognised by the Mayor for his community service. Was his community spirited endeavours also his alibi? Lots of paedophiles hid their offences under a blanket of 'good deeds', helping out where there were vulnerable children and trusting adults.

He'd died violently.

Kate sunk lower down into the bath, stretching her long legs out until she had to lift her feet out and prop them up on the taps. She took a sip of wine and balanced the glass precariously on the edge of the bath. Why didn't anyone believe the two boys? Why had their allegations been so easily dismissed? Was Pink so plausible, so respectable? Or was it because his accusers were less plausible? Why would two teenage boys go through the embarrassment and drama of making the accusation if it wasn't true? As the hot, scented steam cocooned her, Kate closed her eyes. It was such a familiar story: Middle aged men, on the surface respectable members of the community, but with dark secrets hiding behind closed doors. Did George Pink keep dark secrets behind his shed door? Kate was disturbed, but she knew she didn't have enough evidence - yet, to make a decision.

She'd worked on a case with Colin only a few months ago. A fifty-two year old man had befriended young boys he found playing truant from school whilst out walking his dog. He knew the areas around the local park where they hung out. He'd cosy up to them by offering them cigarettes or food. Then he'd invite them home, give them money, buy them gifts and groom them until they took part in sex games with him. Colin had nicknamed him 'Fagin' because of the way he'd gathered wayward boys into his den. He'd encouraged them to smoke drugs; drink alcohol and generally do whatever they liked while he lusted after them. Then when a boy got too old for his tastes; he'd dump him and look for a new one – and he'd been doing it for twenty-six years before Kate caught him and put him away for twelve years.

Was George Pink a paedophile? Local gossip seemed convinced that he was. But if the accusations were nothing more than sordid rumours then most of her colleagues had already jumped on the bandwagon and decided Pink was a child abuser, which troubled Kate. She didn't know what the truth was... not yet.

***

CHAPTER ELEVEN

As DCI Stacey stuck photos from the crime scene to the white board at the front of the incident room there was a collective sharp intake of breath. It was only eight o'clock in the morning. Some of the team hadn't had their breakfast yet. They had all seen dead bodies before, but this was nasty. Pink's head had burnt fiercely on one side, but the side where he'd been pressed against the ground was blistered and swollen, like a large boil waiting to burst. Bizarrely, a full-length view showed his left shoe was virtually undamaged. The black laces on his brogues still neatly tied.

Stacey waited for the full impact to take effect. 'This is what the fire service found once the fire was extinguished. George Pink was doused in accelerant, probably petrol, mostly over his head and shoulders, and torched.'

'No chance of suicide then, Sir?' One of the less bright uniform boys was foolish enough to open his mouth and speak before his brain was in gear. Several of his older and wiser colleagues snorted. *Prick.*

Stacey ignored him. 'So far we don't know what was used; a lighter, matches or what, or whether or not the petrol came from the shed or the perpetrator brought it with them. What we do know is that the attack was deliberate with the intent of inflicting intense pain and suffering to Pink before he died.'

Kate was looking at the piece of paper Stacey was holding in his left hand. She knew what was on it, she'd given it to him.

But Stacey was drawing it out, playing to his audience. 'The results from the post mortem show that Pink was still alive when the fire started, and that he was stabbed in the genitals with a long, stiletto type blade, probably just before he was set alight.' He paused for effect. Several male members of the team winced loudly.

'This would have left him pretty helpless in fighting off his attacker...'

'Slashed and burned.' DC Evans quipped, and loud comments started to buzz around the room. Evans looked smug.

Stacey's face was thunderous as he waited for them to settle down. Kate sighed, willing him to get on with it. He glanced once at the piece of paper in his hand and started to write on the board. Kate felt the room re-focus. Officers were straining and shifting position so that they could read it.

ADAM DYER
TONY CONTELLI

Several heads turned, experienced eyes met hers. Are we up and running? Has it suddenly grown legs? They were beginning to feel it; the pulse was quickening, growing stronger, adrenalin started fizzing. Something was going to shunt the investigation forward, give them something to run with.

Stacey turned around and faced the room. 'DI Landers?'

Kate nodded and made her way to the front. Stacey moved aside. She turned and quietened the room with a look. 'Adam Dyer and Tony Contelli made accusations against Pink nearly three years ago in Hockley. Both boys were in foster care with Hockley Social Services. Both were fourteen years old. Pink was arrested on suspicion of inciting sexual activity with a child. He was interviewed but never charged. We won't know the full story until we've spoken to the CPU team at Hockley who dealt with it.' Kate paused and looked around the room. They wanted something to go on; something to chase, but she couldn't give it to them. She turned and added to the information already on the board.

'Other boys whose names have been linked to Pink since he moved here two years ago, Josh Martin - he's fourteen; Andy Frazier is slightly older. The Toad has also been mentioned - but he's seventeen...'

'He looks younger, Ma'am.' A CID bloke interrupted.

'Yes, yes he does.' Kate agreed. 'But what's the link between these boys?'

'Other than the fact that they're all a shit load of bother?' DC

Edwards chimed in. There was a murmur of agreement around the room.

'But not Dean Towle.' Kate told them briskly, bringing the focus back to her, 'Dean is only thirteen and he's not in the same league. Josh Martin and The Toad live on the same estate, they would obviously know each other, but I doubt that they're mates.'

'Has The Toad got any mates?' Someone asked.

Kate grinned, 'Good point. He doesn't exactly invite warm, fuzzy relationships.'

'What about the thing with these two boys in Hockley, Dyer and Contelli? Is it right B.Zed knew about it; knew Pink was a pervert, messing about with kids? How was that?' Edwards chipped in again.

Kate winced. She knew the team had all heard the 'Pink the Perv' label, but she didn't like the fact that Edwards, and no doubt others, were jumping on that band wagon. It would cloud the investigation if they accepted, without proof, that the murdered man was a child abuser. She looked to Stacey to see if he was going to object to Edward's comments, but he remained silent, which in Kate's book was as good as an endorsement.

'We don't know yet where the gossip about Pink came from.' Kate gave Edwards a hard look, which he seemed not to notice. 'First we're talking to Hockley... get the information on their case, and more importantly, why it was dropped.' Kate looked around for a member of the search team. 'What have we got from the house?'

'Not much. No computer, and no journals or keepsakes that we've been able to find. We're back there today, but so far all we've got is a large amount of cash.' He flipped open a notebook, 'Found in a tin under the sink in the bathroom, five hundred quid in twenties and tenners.' He closed the book. 'The forensic team from the fire service are still working on the shed. It doesn't look as though there's much to recover from there, but you never know. We're waiting on their full report.'

Kate nodded and turned to Julie, the Family Liaison Officer. 'Ask Mrs Pink about the money. It's not unusual for elderly people to keep cash in the house.'

Julie nodded. 'I should have her full statement finished today.'

Stacey stepped forward. 'The analyst won't be here until at least tomorrow – some cock up or other, but it doesn't matter, she'll have to catch up when she gets here. I want bank details. Where did Pink's income come from? Where did the cash come from? What's their expenditure, you know the score. What about a will? Was there an insurance policy?'

Julie stuck her hand up and the DCI nodded at her. 'He was with the Local Authority, Sir, a Facilities Officer, but he took early retirement. Mrs Pink said he was a bit delicate - apparently he got upset easily. He was on tablets from his doctor to help him sleep... '

Stacey cut her off and nodded towards Edwards. 'Follow up on his job before he retired. Get the full story from the employers.'

Kate saw Julie bow her head looking embarrassed, as though she'd said something stupid. Her eyes were cast down, fixed on her notebook. Kate made a mental note to follow up with her afterwards; find out what it was she was going to say.

Stacey was in full flow, 'Dean Towle arrived in Pink's garden just after Pink had been attacked. He didn't see anyone on this path leading to the back gate. Could someone have gained access to the back of any of the other houses in that row? Are the gates kept locked? Behind the path is just this piece of scrubland, but the size of the bushes would make it almost impossible for someone to get over and escape that way. The search team will be moving into that area today.

'We haven't got anything from the garden yet.' A SOCO spoke up. 'We're still looking, but so far we've got sod all, no footprints, nothing. Not surprising with the recent heat wave, the ground is rock hard.'

'Step up the house to house enquiries.' Stacey ordered. 'Anyone who lives in the vicinity, or was there at the time needs to be spoken to. Someone must have seen the attacker leave.'

'It's a big garden,' Kate said, 'Maybe they were still there when Dean turned up. There are plenty of places to hide.'

Every head in the room turned towards her, but she was looking at the power board, deep in thought. Dean Towle had walked in moments after the murderer had set Pink alight and locked him in the shed. Was it possible the attacker had hidden in the garden and slipped away in the chaos after the explosion? The neighbour had grabbed Dean and hauled him up to the house. Mrs Pink took the boy into the lounge. Did the neighbour go back into the garden? Did he try to fight the fire, or look for George Pink?

'Who spoke to the neighbour? The bloke who made the triple nine call?' Kate took a step forward again, addressing the room.

A look of annoyance passed over Stacey's face. He knew where she was going with the question and he didn't like the competency of his staff being questioned. 'He didn't go back to the garden. He stayed with the boy. Apparently he was afraid the boy was hurt, or would do a runner. He didn't want to leave him alone with Pink's wife. They were all in the house when the first response got there.'

Raised eyebrows sent signals around the room and a buzz of conversation broke out. It was possible someone could have been hiding and slipped away before the first response got there. Someone could have been watching the whole time; watching as the shed became an inferno, inhaling the acrid smoke and the crisp smell of burning human flesh.

The sun was bouncing off the silver bonnet of the car as Kate and Steve left for Hockley. If Kate had known what type of car it was she might have been impressed, but she didn't have a clue. Not that she cared much. Her daughter, Angel, knew more about cars then she did. In fact, her mother knew more about cars... and her mother couldn't drive.

Steve rolled the cuffs back on his shirt and put his sunglasses on. Kate saw him glance at his reflection in the visor mirror and she almost laughed. *Who does he think we are? Bloody Miami Vice?*

'Do you know the CPU team at Hockley?' He asked her.

Kate nodded. 'We all go on the same courses, help each other out; try and learn from each other. Hockley deals with fewer Crown Court cases than we do, but they've got a really good team of people.'

'Less cases?' Steve was confused. 'I would have thought they had more. The town's not that much smaller than Marville but they've got some real dodgy areas.'

'There's no rhyme or reason for it. It's just the way it is. Maybe Marville is a bigger den of iniquity and there are more paedophiles on our patch. Not a nice thought is it?' Kate crossed her ankles and tucked her feet sideways as she turned in her seat. 'We get more cases into Crown Court than Hockley. And there are more and more cases reported every year, to both teams. None of us will ever be out of a job.' She smiled wryly at him.

'The thing you said in the briefing, Gov, about a link between the boys we've heard about. What sort of homes do they come from?'

'Josh Martin lives with his mum. His father, Todd Martin, was released from prison four days ago. He went on a bender to celebrate and then gave his four-year-old son, Darren, a beating. Todd was fighting with his wife and I think Darren got in the way. Darren ended up in hospital and Todd did a runner. Andy Frazier lives with his father. The Toad lives wherever he chooses on any given day.'

'Sorry?'

'The Toad's a law unto himself, a Maverick. He's super intelligent, but...' Kate paused, *but what?* The Toad was also a bit scary. She could never put her finger on it but there was something a bit sinister about him. Sometimes he was around and she saw him every day, then he'd disappear and she wouldn't see him for weeks. He didn't seem to have a job and Kate had no idea where he went or what he did. Other kids gave him a wide berth.

Steve was just starting to say something when Kate's mobile went off. She smiled at him, half apologetically, before answering.

'Not such an outstanding citizen then, your man Pink.' It was a local journalist Kate knew well.

'Sorry?' she stalled. *What the hell did he know about Pink?*

Steve looked across at her questioningly and she rolled her eyes at him.

'Pink the Perv, is that right? The paper wants to run it Kate, before everyone else gets it. But there's the wife to consider. It might sound better if you could give me something decent to wrap it up in.'

'I'm not sure I follow you.' Kate wondered how much, exactly, he knew. 'I'm aware that there are several lines of inquiry being followed into the death of George Pink. But you would need to call the communications officer, or maybe wait for a press conference.'

'Bullshit... sorry Kate, but you would only give me that 'several lines of inquiry' crap if you couldn't tell me anything real. We've got it that Pink was up to some nasty little hanky panky, messing about with young boys, I just want to get the story straight.'

'Bullshit.' It was Kate's turn to sound incredulous. 'I will not confirm any speculation concerning the case you're referring to, and you know better than to ask. I can't help you.' Kate started to smile, and knew that the caller would hear it in her voice, which she intended.

It was always a difficult relationship. Both sides needed each other, and this journalist had helped her out in the past. But with child abuse cases things were fairly straightforward - the law took a very serious view of irresponsible reporting.

'Right, you win,' The caller sighed, dramatically, 'but it's going to break at some point, I can feel it in my water. It's going to be one of those 'the poor wife suspected nothing whilst her husband secretly twiddled with young boys. I bet you're the one that has to tell her and all.' The caller seemed delighted by this idea. 'Look, buy me a drink sometime; I'll be nice, I promise.'

'No you won't. You'll try and get me drunk and make me tell you things.' Kate laughed and hung up. Then she swore. 'Bugger, the papers know the 'local hero stories' about Pink might have been a bit premature. I don't know where they're getting their information. For a moment there I thought he was going to ask about Tony Contelli and Adam Dyer. Bloody press.' She used her mobile to call the police communications officer.

'He's even less impressed.' Kate said as she hung up.

Steve's thoughts were elsewhere. 'So Gov, you can't be trusted when you're drinking, is that right?' He looked sideways at her, something of a smirk on his face.

Kate let her sunglasses slide down her nose until she was peering over the top of them. 'You'll never know, will you? Now shut up and drive, I need a coffee.'

DS Colin Morris tapped on a desk to get everyone's attention, 'Steve Astman just drove the lovely Kate Landers out in his car.'

'Bollocks.' DC Evans swore loudly.

Everyone in the incident room turned towards Ginger. He lifted up a scruffy piece of white card. It had names and times written in various scrawls down the left hand side.

'I do believe I've won, again.' Colin reached for the board, 'Astman has, remarkably, survived Kate's driving for eleven hours before, rather tactfully it must be said, taking over in the interests of saving his own sanity and skin.'

'Hold up, hold up. What time, *exactly*, did they drive off?' Ginger asked, holding onto the board.

'Eight-thirty,' Colin was confident.

'Well tough shit, that's eleven *and a half hours* of duty with her. You are a big fat loser, Superintendent Knowling wins the pot.'

The sweepstake was run every time Kate worked with someone new. Her lack of driving skill was as legendary as her skill as a child abuse investigator.

'Give Astman credit for surviving so long in the face of terrible danger'.

All heads turned as Detective Superintendent Knowling entered the room. He looked disapproving when a smattering of applause broke out.

Colin accepted defeat graciously. 'We're wondering why the wife didn't mention Pink's arrest in Hockley, Sir.'

'Maybe she didn't know.' Knowling said. 'It's not unusual for a spouse to be kept in the dark, and remember, it got dropped.' It was clear he believed the wisdom of that decision might be re-examined.

'Maybe she just forgot.' Ginger addressed the room in a singsong voice.

Knowling just shrugged. 'It wasn't that long ago. I'd put money on her not knowing... Pink didn't tell her.'

'I'll take that bet.' Someone called out cheerfully. 'I think she definitely knew what he was up to.'

'I'll have a fiver on it with you, Sir.' Natasha called out from behind her computer monitor. 'Bloody men never tell you anything important.'

Knowling chose to ignore the jibe at his sex and the fact that most of the officers in his station would bet on anything. He squinted at the power board and then turned, smiling, and left the room.

'Jammy bugger. Don't know why he's grinning like an idiot, it's only fifty quid.' Ginger said.

'And you know he'll put it behind the bar at the next drink up.' Colin replied. He knew exactly why his Superintendent was grinning and it had nothing to do with money.

***

CHAPTER TWELVE

Steve had been part of the area CID unit at Hockley and knew DS Maggie Fratta and DC Boz Orudo even though he hadn't worked directly with them before.

If Maggie looked exactly as you'd imagine a child protection officer to look, Boz Orudo looked like an American football player. His parents were from Jamaica, and Boz had black shiny skin, no neck and arms the size of Steve's legs. He had a smile so white it could make your head hurt looking at it. Kids looked up to him as though he was the Terminator.

'Did you think Adam and Tony were telling the truth?' Kate asked the question, but she was pretty certain she already knew the answer.

Nearly three years ago Tony Contelli and Adam Dyer had both been fourteen years old and living in foster care. They were best mates. They went to the same Sports Club where George Pink acted as a volunteer driver. Together they had accused Pink of trying to incite them into sexual activity in his garden shed.

Maggie and Boz looked at each other, knowing they were in agreement.

'It was right.' Boz said, 'It sounded right, it felt right, and although Tony and Adam were your worst case scenario for reliable witnesses, we were prepared to take it on.'

'What about him? What about Pink?' Steve leant forward, resting his elbows on his knees, 'What were your feelings about him?'

Boz hesitated before replying. He spoke slowly and thoughtful as Maggie, who was folded into a corner chair with her hands wrapped round a cup of tea, nodded her head vigorously.

'Oh, he was perfect, solid gold. No question about it, George Pink was a paedophile.'

'So why didn't it go anywhere?' Steve was perplexed.

Maggie explained it for him. 'Both boys were in local care and both had been in trouble. Nothing major, you know, just a bit of vandalism, criminal damage, truancy... practically the same shit that most of these kids get into. Anyone who dealt with them knew they treated lying as a hobby – would swear black was white just for the fun of it, so we knew we had problems with it from the start. The story was that they'd both been offered money by Pink to help him in his garden, but they didn't go there together... no, Pink was too cautious for that. He got them there separately, first Adam, then Tony.

'Tony was small for his age, but gorgeous in a 'pretty boy' way. He had that 'Mediterranean look', all olive skin and dark eyes. Pink tried it on with him, but Tony wasn't playing. He started fighting; punching, kicking, biting, what have you. Pink probably would have backed off as soon as the boy started; he wasn't the aggressive sort, but now he was the one getting attacked. He gave Tony a couple of hard slaps that put him on the floor and gave him a bloody nose.' Maggie pulled a pack of Silk Cut from her bag, scooted her chair back towards the open window behind her and lit up. 'Tony told Adam what happened, and how he got hurt and Adam says Pink tried the same thing with him. They decided to tell a teacher that they got on well with at school, a Roland O'Dowd, a seriously good guy, and it came to us.'

At this point, Boz picked up the story, giving Maggie a chance to smoke. Kate watched the unlikely couple thinking what a good team they made.

'The Crown Prosecution Service didn't want it.' Boz said, and there was genuine regret in his voice. 'Both boys were 'in the system', whereas George Pink, to all intents and purposes, was an upstanding member of the community. Oh, he was arrested without any bother. He played the 'bewildered, wrongly accused,' role to the hilt. Never got angry, never really looked worried, but it was obvious it was an act. He'd been waiting for the day when it happened... practicing what he was going to say, expecting it. So out came some bullshit about trying to help the boys; how he'd felt sorry for them. How they'd preyed on his generous nature and then tried to blackmail him. The Crown Prosecution Service thought the chances of getting a conviction in court were pretty much shit - and it was dropped.'

Maggie stood up and ground out her cigarette in a small metal ashtray on the window ledge.

'When you say 'sexual activity with a child' what are we talking about here?' Kate wanted to know what George Pink was after with these boys.

'Showed them pornography; masturbated in front of them, wanted them to do the same - normal stuff.' Boz shrugged.

'Are you still in touch with the boys?' Kate asked.

A puzzled look passed between Maggie and Boz and Kate waited for, what she knew, was bad news.

'We thought you knew.' Maggie pulled another cigarette out, lit up and took a deep drag.

'Tony's dead, he hung himself in a Young Offenders Institute. Adam is in prison.' Boz said it for her.

'I knew Tony pretty well.' Maggie dragged her hair back from her face with her free hand, 'I dealt with him many times before his death. I wasn't surprised when he committed suicide. He was delicate and painfully shy; he couldn't keep up with the other boys, he wasn't in the same league.'

Kate understood exactly how her colleague felt and she knew Maggie's regret was genuine. For every success, for every bastard locked up, for every child taken out of danger, there were these 'went nowhere, ended in tragedy' cases that were quietly laid aside.

'Tony Contelli hung himself whilst on remand in the YOI.' Boz filled in the details. 'The story about him and George Pink had got out. Other boys spread the word that Tony was gay; a 'ponce' a 'rent boy'. The stigma of the case never left him, it clung to him like a toxic smell; dogging him wherever he went. Pink was restored to the community, without charge, without blame; free to carry on his 'good works' and before long Tony started making a nuisance of himelf. He became withdrawn and was prone to violent moods, then two months after his fifteenth birthday he hung himself.'

'What about Adam?' Kate looked at Maggie.

'Adam progressed from petty crime to the big boys league, but at least he's still alive. He's doing four years for robbery. A bloody stupid escapade trying to do over a jewellers, but he'd pushed the self-destruct button one too many times. The shop owner and a customer took him on and he fell through a glass display cabinet... not pretty.'

Steve winced, sucking air through his teeth. 'How bad?' He asked.

'He nearly bled to death at the scene.' Maggie told him. 'So, sorry, but we can't help you with a suspect for your burning man.' She grinned, ruefully. 'Being dead or in prison are pretty good alibis.'

There were no avenging relatives to follow up. No one turned vigilante to get justice for Adam or Tony. As Maggie pointed out, no one gave a shit at the time, so it wasn't likely they'd bother now.

Kate left with a copy of the file and a sense of uneasy disquiet. The thought of Tony Contelli, shamed, disbelieved, branded... and alone, taking his own life, weighed heavily. The whole professional protection service had failed Tony Contelli; failed in the worst possible way. And there was no coming back from that. It was too late.

He didn't want her to go. He didn't want to let her go. But like most things in his life, Eddie knew he probably didn't have a choice. She was facing away from him with her back against his naked chest, his arms circled around her, pulling her close. He swayed gently from side to side, holding her against him, pulling her into his groin, dancing with her. Maybe she'd stay a bit longer.

'I'll be back as soon as I can.' She pulled away and turned to face him. 'Please don't. Please don't look like that.'

'I'll be lonely. Please don't leave.' He quietly pleaded with her, dipping his head so that his eyes were level with hers, his face almost touching her.

Her eyes started to fill with tears. *Shit, she was going to cry.* That's not what he wanted. He wanted to go back to bed and lie down naked with her.

A tear ran down the side of her nose. She wiped it with a finger then reached up and ran her wet finger across his lips. Eddie trembled. He'd never felt anything as intimate as a woman wiping her tears on his face.

'Please don't be lonely.' She whispered. 'I won't be able to bear it if I think you're sad, not even just a little bit. You're making me cry already. I have to go, you know I do - but I won't be long, I promise.' She pulled one of his hands from behind her back, lifted it to her face and sucked gently on the tips of his fingers. Eddie's eyes locked on hers as he took a deep breath and tried to keep himself under control.

'Well, can I go and find Dean? I just want to see if he's ok.' He stepped back, letting her go.

She looked up; her eyes gave him that 'I'm going to tell you something really simple' look that he'd come to know. 'You know you can't.' she said slowly, 'Dean will be fine. Nothing is your fault baby, nothing. Do you understand?'

Eddie didn't, he didn't understand anything. He didn't understand how she'd chosen him; he didn't understand why she wanted him. All he knew was his whole life had changed and he never wanted to go back, but she didn't know how scared he was. He wasn't good at talking, but he tried again. 'Something must have gone wrong, something bad. I just need to know that he's ok, that it's ok.'

'I promise it's alright, trust me.' She begged him.

Eddie nodded, his long fringe covered his eyes; he had no idea what trust meant.

She pulled his face towards her, and pulled him into a kiss, sucking at his lip. Then she pulled away from him and a moment later she was gone.

He found the directory in the lounge, mixed up with a bunch of magazines in a rack. She hadn't said anything about not phoning Dean. Maybe Dean hadn't told anyone anything yet, maybe he could, like, warn him. He ran his finger slowly down the 'T's. He read them all out loud, softly, sounding them out, stumbling over the letters. There were four entries for TOWLE, but he didn't recognise any of the addresses. Then he realised his mistake. Dean didn't live with his parents. He lived with foster parents.

He didn't know what their name was.

***

71

CHAPTER THIRTEEN

Dean wasn't home. Kate made the coffee while Joan tried to clear enough room on the kitchen table for them to sit down.

'He's gone with Phil to get that football shirt he wanted. We thought it might cheer him up, take his mind off things a bit.' Joan gave up on tidying the table, 'Do you want to sit outside?' She slid open the patio door and led the way to a garden table set under a green umbrella.

'How is he?' Kate took the corner seat in the sun.

For a moment Joan looked away, staring at a point somewhere in the distance, 'It's hard to explain. He's... jittery. Whereas he'd normally be begging to be on the PlayStation or something, he's just traipsing around.' She paused and looked up, 'He seems to want to be near us. If the phone rings he looks terrified; chewing his fingers and waiting to see who it is.'

'Who does he think is going to ring?'

Joan shrugged and shook her head, she didn't know.

'Has anyone called for him, or been round to see him?' Steve asked. He was trying to get comfortable in a metal chair that was too small for his bulk.

'No, no one. I rang the doctor again this morning because he's not sleeping. I found him standing in the kitchen at two o'clock this morning. He had the fridge door open, but he was just standing there as though he didn't know what he wanted. Then I realised he was crying; really sobbing. I got to him and he just collapsed; crumpled into a heap on the floor. I don't know how to help him.' Joan looked devastated.

'Has he said anything?' Kate asked.

'Nothing about that man, George Pink, or what happened, not a word. And I haven't mentioned it.' Joan leant forward and met Kate's eyes. 'But he's holding something in and whatever it is... it's not good.'

Kate nodded. She wished she didn't have to tell Joan what they knew about Pink, it was only going to cause more upset. 'Has Dean had more money than normal recently? Unexplained cash; presents maybe, something he's had difficulty explaining?'

Joan looked puzzled, 'There was a football bag, a couple of weeks ago. The football coach at the Marville Community Sports Centre gave it to him. It's quite an expensive one, but Dean said everyone on the team got one because they'd got some sponsorship or something. Why?'

Kate raised her eyebrows. 'Really?'

A look of confusion passed across Joan's face. 'Well, that's what he said... maybe not. Oh, shit. You mean that man might have given him stuff?'

Kate placed her hand on the woman's arm. 'There's a strong possibility that George Pink was inviting boys to his shed for something more indecent than gardening. We think he may have bought their participation and silence with presents or money. Right now I don't want Dean to think we don't trust him, but he may have been to Pink's before. What's the name of his coach, the one at the MCSC?'

'Lion, they call him Lion, something to do with the fact that his surname is Hart and he's got a sword.' The reality of what Kate was telling her started to take hold, 'Oh, bloody hell Kate, are you serious?' Joan was distraught.

Steve gave Kate a sideways look, which she ignored. She didn't have time to get into it right now. 'Do you have a number for the coach? Can you call and ask him?'

Joan nodded. She got up and headed back into the kitchen. Kate leant back and lifted her face to the sun, closing her eyes. It was on days like this that she wished she still smoked. Another life, another time... fags, booze and reckless fun, God, she felt old sometimes. She smiled to herself. Right, and yet here she was; a single parent with an eighteen-year-old daughter, a proper job, as her father would call it, and a new sidekick the size of a tank. She wondered if Steve was sorry he was assigned to her; not that she really gave a monkey's, but he'd certainly had a baptism by fire. Kate knew Dean had lied about the sports bag, she knew before Joan came back with the news.

'Lion didn't buy the bag. Dean just turned up with it one day and was showing it off to him. He told Lion he'd got given it, but he didn't say who gave it to him.'

Kate nodded but didn't comment. She waited for Joan to settle herself back into a garden chair. She could see lines of anguish on Joan's face and she felt sorry for her.

'Why would Dean do that? Does this mean that Pink gave Dean the bag and Dean was...?' Joan couldn't say the words. She stared bleakly at Steve, 'What could he want badly enough for that?' For a moment she looked completely lost, and then her eyes flew to Kate's face. 'Oh shit, Kate. He wanted the shirt; the football shirt, he was desperate for it, we've heard nothing else for the last couple of weeks. Apparently everyone had the new shirt and his life wasn't worth living because he still had the old version. He wanted that shirt so badly - and now he's getting it.'

Kate leant forward, fixing her eyes on Joan's. 'You've got a great relationship with Dean, look at what happened last night when he was upset. You're brilliant with him - you really are, and I'm going to need your help.'

Joan nodded, 'What can I do?'

'Go and get the bag.'

The sports bag was sitting on the kitchen table when the front door burst open and Dean came running in, wildly excited, brandishing his new football shirt. He saw the bag, saw Kate leaning against the counter by the sink sipping a coffee with Steve perched next to her on a stool, and he ground to a halt. Rooted to the spot halfway between the door and the table, his eyes went from the bag to Kate and back to Joan.

Kate waited. Joan fixed a smile on her face.

Philip walked in behind Dean. 'Hi Kate, how's it going?' He was going to say something else, but either the look on Kate's face or the tension in the room stopped him. He put his car keys carefully down on the kitchen counter. 'I'll be in the garden. Shout if you need me.'

Joan nodded gratefully. Steve followed him out and slid the

door shut behind them.

'Why's my bag on the table?' Dean made a valiant attempt to brazen it out. He was struggling to keep a nonchalant tone; a questioning look on his face. It lasted all of three seconds before his big act fell apart. His hands came up and he buried his face in his new football shirt. Joan flew to him. She tried to wrap him in her arms, but he pushed her away, shouting at her.

'Did you look in it? Did you? It's mine! You had no right. No right!' His face flushed red as he yelled. Crossing the room he grabbed at the bag pulling it off the table.

'It's private. You had no right to look in it, it's mine.' He was hysterical. He turned away from them and started to unzip one of the side pockets. But before he'd got it open Kate stood up, took two steps around the table and placed her hand over his wrist, holding it firmly.

'Dean, stop a minute, stop!' She crouched down until she was eye level with the boy, her voice insistent, leaving him no options. Dean hesitated and stared back at her, breathing hard.

'Dean, I've never lied to you have I?' She waited, her eyes searching his. Dean's face was full of resentment and she didn't blame him; he was caught and he knew it. She had to bring this round so that he'd talk to her. 'Have I?' she demanded.

There was a slight shake of his head.

'No one has looked in the bag, ok? I promise you. It's your bag; no one has looked in it, not me, not Joan, no one.' She took her hand away from his wrist and Dean looked down at the pocket he'd been trying to open. His eyelashes were wet with un-spilt tears.

'It's mine. He gave it to me and it's mine.' His voice cracked, the dam broke and the tears fell.

Kate cupped her hand around the back of his neck and pulled him in until he was leaning against her. 'It's ok mate, it's ok.' She ruffled his short hair with her fingers. She knew more than anything else what a shit situation this was for him. He'd lied, and he'd been caught out in the lie. He'd been keeping a secret; a horrible secret and he was hurting. But it could all come out now.

For several minutes she held onto him while he cried and Joan watched in silent agony from across the room. Then he started to get a grip. He sniffed loudly, turned his face and wiped his nose on the short sleeve of his t-shirt.

Kate laughed, 'Thank God! For a moment there I thought you were going to get snot all over your new football shirt. That would have been a disaster.'

'And I would have killed him.' Joan laughed too, grateful for the break in the tension.

Kate bent down, pulled Dean round by the shoulders, 'I'm on your side, mate. You know that, don't you? We're here to take care of you, although to be honest you're a bit of a flipping nightmare.' She grimaced comically at him.

Dean couldn't help himself, he grinned back.

'I mean, it's not like you're making it easy on us is it?' She shook his shoulder, teasing him.

'I like making it tough for you.' Dean was playing along, pulling himself together.

'And you're very good at it.' Kate nodded, 'Now let's make some really big milkshakes and you can tell me what's in the pocket of that bag, ok?'

'Will you help me find him?' Dean looked up at her, his face wet, his eyes full of childish hope.

Kate stopped smiling and crouched down again to look him in the eye. 'Find who, Dean. Who do you want me to find?'

'Brian. I can't find him. He aint in my school and he don't come to the Community Centre. I don't know where else to look. I *have* to tell him, but I can't find him.'

Kate had absolutely no idea what Dean was talking about, but years of experience told her it was important. She glanced across at Joan who was at the sink rinsing out the milkshake maker. Joan gave her a look that said, 'don't look at me - I haven't got the foggiest idea either.' Kate turned her focus back to Dean. 'I don't think I know a Brian. Who is he? And why have you got to find him?'

Dean's eyes never left her face. He was giving it up, the big problem, all the worry, and the fear. He'd had enough; he couldn't do it by himself anymore. He wanted to give it over to an adult, someone that could take it and fix everything. He was going to trust Kate to make it right. 'He gave me money. It's in my bag, look.' He finally unzipped the pocket of the sports bag, reached in and pulled out a small canvas wallet. Slowly, and with great care, as though he wasn't used to having a wallet with such treasure in, he pulled back the Velcro strap and pulled out some ten-pound notes. 'I kept it. It was nearly enough; nearly enough for the shirt.'

There was thirty quid in his hand.

Kate looked at the pathetic little stack of notes and wanted to scream. *Thirty quid! Thirty bloody quid! What had it cost Dean to get it?* 'Do you mean George Pink?' She said, calmly.

Dean nodded. 'He give me money 'cos of Brian. He wanted to be with me 'cos he was missing Brian and I reminded him of him. And I did... I did,' He faltered and took a deep breath, 'I did stuff 'cos he give me the money and he was sad.'

Kate had a good idea what Pink had asked him to do. She squeezed his arm. 'It's ok Dean, everything's going to be ok now.'

'Can you find him? I have to tell him.'

'Why? I don't understand. What do you want to tell Brian?' Kate was confused by the desperation she heard in Dean's voice.

'I have to tell him about him, about him... being dead, he'll need to know. Brian's special, he were his best boy. I think he really loved him because he... he cried about him.' Dean gulped and started chewing his lip. 'Brian won't know. He needs to know, you have to find him. *Please.*'

Kate gripped his shoulder. 'I'll find him.' She made the promise. 'You don't have to worry anymore; it's going to be ok. I'll find Brian.'

———※———

At his home, a couple of hours drive away from Marville police station, Raymond Greggs hung up on a telephone call and stood stock still, waiting for the pain in his chest to subside. Although he was only in his thirties, Raymond looked older, but his features were so unremarkable that he wouldn't stand out in a crowd of two. Raymond didn't want to stand out – ever. He'd spent a whole lifetime trying not to be noticed too much. His wife, Cheryl, was forever telling him to stand up straight - he invariably looked down to avoid the embarrassment of making eye contact with people.

Now he fixed his gaze on a small vase that Cheryl had made during a brief fling with pottery classes. He focused all his attention on the object, trying to get his breathing under control. Thank God she was at work already. She'd think he was having a heart attack. Many years of putting distance, time and space, between himself and his past and none of it had mattered. One telephone call was all it took, one bloody busybody who couldn't wait to throw it all back at him. All the feelings, the hurt and the confusion shook loose inside him, everything he'd tried to bury since he was a child. *Focus! Look at the vase; breathe slowly, in, out, in, out.*

'I thought you might not have heard, seeing as how you've been away from the area for so long,' the telephone conversation had started innocently enough. 'George Pink was found burnt to death in his garden shed yesterday morning. The police are treating it as suspicious. Apparently a young boy was found in the garden when it happened.'

A young boy.

'Weren't you close to the Pinks at one time? Poor bugger. What a way to go. His wife was home at the time, didn't know a thing about it until the shed exploded. It's really weird about this young lad that was there.' The caller was revelling in having some juicy, upsetting gossip to share. 'I only know about the boy because he was seen being ushered away from the house by Kate Landers. She's the child abuse police person, you know, one of those specially trained sorts that just deals with abused kids. A neighbour recognised her and said who she was. I wonder what that was about then?'

Raymond's brain threw the words around his head in a disjointed panic. *Young boy, child abuse police person, wife... focus, breathe, don't fall down.*

He replaced the handset without speaking. To his surprise his legs supported him over to the sofa. Falling heavily back against the cushions he closed his eyes. George Pink burnt to death in his shed. It was the best news he'd ever heard. Raymond clenched both his hands into tight fists and pressed them into his eyes. The best news he'd ever had. It made him cry.

***

CHAPTER FOURTEEN

'He'd been there before.' Kate was in the incident room giving DCI Stacey an update. 'Dean had heard stuff about Pink; smutty comments about other boys who'd been there. But he's a bit of an outsider, a bit naive, not one of the lads. He's mentioned a couple of names; a couple of them match what B.Zed told us. And there's another boy, a Brian, but I don't know any more about him yet. I'll talk to Dean again, but I don't want to push him too hard.'

'So why did he agree to go to Pink's? If he knew something was up, something sinister going on, why would he still go?' Stacey didn't understand the allure that cash had on a vulnerable boy.

'Like I said, he's a bit naive. He's not in the same league as Josh Martin or Andy Frazier, and Pink offered him ten quid, that's a fortune to someone like Dean. Pink would know that.'

'What happened when he was there?'

'Cuddling is all he's been willing to say so far. He's talked about Pink stroking his face, holding him and crying, apparently because he missed this boy, Brian. Again, I'm not pushing him because I want him to consent to a full medical examination. But it gives added weight to Tony Contelli and Adam Dyer's accusations. Pink was into young boys.'

Stacey wasn't happy. He stood in front of the incident board and looked at the list of names that they'd been given so far, starting with Josh Martin. The crime scene photos of Pink had been removed and replaced with a photo supplied by his wife of him when he was alive. It was now thought to be more respectful to have a photo of the victim, as they'd been in life, to remind the team that they'd been a person, someone with a life, before they became a mutilated body.

'If that's true, and Pink was abusing other boys then there's a distinct possibility that someone wanted to stop him; one of the boys, or an Avenging Angel, an older brother maybe.' Stacey stood back and surveyed his list. He'd made his mind up. 'You've discounted Adam Dyer and Tony Contelli so we need to get onto these others.'

Kate thought she understood where he was going with this, and she hated the idea.

Stacey turned towards her smiling, but the skin around his eyes was taut, almost translucent, giving it a bluish tinge. The smile was only on his mouth. 'Talk to all of these boys, interview all of them, plus any others whose names crop up.'

'You want me to interview these kids with the view that they might be suspects?' Kate wanted him to confirm what he was asking her to do.

Stacey's face clouded. 'Yes Kate, or find out if someone is acting on their behalf. And don't look like that... someone very deliberately made sure George Pink died; someone who was there only moments before Dean turned up. Maybe someone knew Dean was on his way, but didn't know he'd get the time wrong and turn up an hour early. If that's true, then it's someone Dean knows.'

'CPU doesn't stand for Child *Persecution* Unit.' Kate was furious enough to be rude.

Steve looked away, embarrassed. He didn't want to be part of the row.

Stacey stepped closer to Kate, his face set. 'Let's take this in the office.'

'That's ok, Sir,' Kate's voice hung on the 'Sir' she would say what she had to. 'George Pink is dead. Nothing will change that, but there are kids who will continue to be abused and it's my job to try and change that. I'm not prepared to ruin my relationship with all of them - not when it's taken me years to build up some trust.'

Stacey opened his mouth to speak, but Kate wasn't finished. 'If Pink was a paedophile, he didn't suddenly wake up one morning last week and discover the fact. It would have been his life. We should be digging into his background more, his history. Where's the analyst? This may not be about our local kids at all. It's more likely to be about his past, ancient history even. Pink may have been at it for years, God knows how far back his offending started. He's only been on our territory for two years and he's spent time grooming the boys he's picked - recruiting and enticing them into his shed. Dean said there were photos of other boys there - shame we didn't manage to salvage any because I'd have a better idea of where to look for victims.'

Stacey opened his mouth again to reply but Kate needed to get away from him before she got herself into serious trouble. She turned, picked her bag up from the floor and swung it over her shoulder.

Steve noticed her hand was shaking, but he was the only one who saw it. He stayed where he was and let her go.

As Kate entered her office the desk phone was ringing but she ignored it. She had a pretty good idea who was calling and she needed to be calmer before speaking to them. She checked her appearance in a small mirror on the wall of the cloakroom. Her flat, shiny hair looked a bit ruffled, but not as though she'd been dragged through a hedge. She pulled out a pack of scented wet wipes, lifted her t-shirt up over her boobs, slipped her arms out and, without taking it off completely, wiped under her armpits and across her chest. It was a temporary job, but she was going to get much dirtier soon. She fished a pale pink lip-gloss out of her handbag and glossed in the outline of her mouth. Her mother had taught her never to face anything without lipstick in place.

She crossed the hallway and, without knocking, stuck her head around Superintendent Knowling's door. 'Looking for me?' She put on a bright smile.

Knowling put down the telephone receiver he'd been holding to his ear and scowled, 'How the bloody hell would you know? You never answer your bloody phone.' He nodded towards the chair in front of his desk. Kate stepped in and sat down. Her boss studied her face for a long moment, 'I want you to apologise to DCI Stacey.'

Kate waited, knowing there was more.

'He's absolutely right. If Pink has a history of sexual activity with boys it makes perfect sense, in fact we'd be negligent if we didn't follow it up as a motive for his murder. I've told him you'll apologise and I expect you to do it.' He sighed heavily as Kate gave him a blank look. 'You don't have to do it today. Wait until you feel you can apologise properly.'

Kate relaxed. He'd just given her a get out clause.

Knowling's face was weathered and lined, with intense blue eyes under thin, pale eyebrows. He was older than Kate but he kept himself in shape, his shoulders bulged under his tailored suit. Kate didn't want to apologise, but she didn't want to let Knowling down either. At least she didn't have to do it straight away. 'Yes Sir.' She tried to sound as though she was contrite.

Knowling didn't buy it for a second. He leant back in his chair and looked at her suspiciously, 'Lost Astman?'

'Apparently he needs food.' She gave a little shrug as though this was something of a mystery to her.

Knowling glanced at his watch and raised his eyebrows. 'You're being uncharacteristically soft on the guy. He hasn't got time to eat, get him back and do something useful.'

'I'm taking him to the Martin's place,' Kate tried to look the picture of innocence, 'Josh Martin has got his name on DCI Stacey's board.'

Knowling pressed his lips together and nodded solemnly, but his eyes were smiling. 'I trust you've warned Astman?'

Kate didn't answer. She stared at the diary that was open on his desk, trying to read upside down. His handwriting was awful.

'I'll take your refusal to answer as a 'no' then.' He shook his head at her and changed the subject. 'Do Dean Towle and Josh Martin know each other?'

'They're at the same school, but I wouldn't say they're friends. I'm not sure Josh Martin has any friends. He's not a friendly person.'

'He's his father's son in every way. God help us, one Todd Martin is bad enough, and we can't even bloody well find that one.'

'Oh, we will. Todd Martin isn't clever enough to outrun us for long. After what he did to Darren every uniform and plain clothes officer in the division is after him - it's only a matter of time.'

Knowling nodded, but he was looking at her appearance and he didn't miss much. He took in the slightly flushed cheeks, her tousled hair and the state of her outfit. He liked looking at her; liked the fact that she wasn't one of those 'girlie' women, always checking their lipstick. He swallowed, trying to divert his thoughts.

'You're a bit creased,' he said.

Kate's blue eyes flashed with humour, 'That's ok, I'm going to get *really* filthy very soon.' She had him and she knew it. She knew he was thinking about something, and it sure as hell wasn't the creases in her outfit.

'Go away Kate,' he said, roughly, 'and consider your apology, I'd rather Stacey didn't have any further reason to complain to me about you, but no doubt I'm pissing in the wind.'

'Yes Sir.' Kate said, solemnly. She swung out of her seat and left.

Knowling sat rock still for a small moment, deep in thought. Then he shook his head and tried to put Kate Landers out of his mind.

***

CHAPTER FIFTEEN

'I wouldn't house a dog here.' Kate pulled the BMW hard over to the left to avoid several crater-sized holes in the unmade road. She waved cheerfully at two men lounging in the doorway of the first apartment building on their right and Steve was thrown forward as the car hit a ridge.

Red-bricked two storey buildings lined each side of the track. A narrow strip of ground, which might have been lawn once, but was now just burnt scrubland, separated the buildings. Kate pulled onto the ground in a space between the third and fourth block and tooted the horn twice before opening her door and sliding her legs out.

There was an explosion of yelling and screaming as a gang of kids of all shapes, colours, ages and sizes appeared out of nowhere and ran towards them. Everyone clamoured for Kate's attention at once, pulling her in six different directions.

'Hey!' Kate's shout was almost lost in the din. 'Whoa up.' She raised both her hands in the air in mock surrender. A slim, scruffy adolescent girl stood in front of her. The girl was struggling to hold a fat grubby looking baby; her arms wrapped under its bum as it clung to her neck. Kate took the baby from her and swung it easily onto her left hip in one quick movement. There was a brief skirmish over who was going to hold Kate's spare hand as she jiggled the baby up and down, making it laugh and dribble. It grabbed a handful of Kate's t-shirt; its small chubby fist was black with dirt.

'Who's that man?' One of the kids pointed at Steve. He was standing by the car watching Kate organise her gang.

'Is he a policeman?' A boy wanted to know.

'Is he your boyfriend?' A small dumpy girl asked.

Kate burst out laughing but the others took up the theme.

'Kate's got a boyfriend, Kate's got a boyfriend.' The chorus was deafening. 'She loves him, she wants to kiss him.' The chorus got louder, 'She wants to marry him!' The baby laughed and kicked its legs, delightedly.

'He is not my boyfriend.' Kate shouted over the din. She started leading the way towards the nearest building but their progress was slow. 'Don't worry,' she called across to Steve, 'I'll protect you.'

Steve cocked an eyebrow at her, 'Cheers Gov.'

Kate was surprised to see him holding hands with a dishevelled, timid little boy. She hadn't thought him to be the holding hands type. The boy seemed to have taken a shine to the giant, his big eyes looking up in wonder, his little legs scrambling to keep up with Steve's long gait. As the noisy procession headed towards the corner of the apartment block a small boy erupted from the doorway, his brown plastic sandals slapping loudly on the ground as he charged towards Kate.

'Burgh, burgh!' He yelled, his arms outstretched towards her.

Kate lifted the baby off her hip and dumped it unceremoniously on a startled Steve. She dropped her bag on the ground behind her, crouched down and opened her arms. The rocket boy leapt at her, wrapping his arms tightly around her neck, his legs gripping her waist. He held his small brown face a few inches from Kate's nose for a second or two and studied her eyes. Kate held him protectively against her as she stood up. The boy snuggled into her chest and rested his head on her shoulder; twisting her hair around his fingers he stuck his thumb in his mouth contentedly.

'This is Darren Martin, he's a special friend. He's deaf.' Kate told Steve.

Steve frowned. He had the baby in a sort of one-armed bear hug and he was afraid he was going to drop it. 'What, totally?'

'Yes, he was born deaf. He thinks he said 'Kate' but it comes out as 'Burgh'. He's very clever at sign language though.'

'Kate, Kate, Todd give Darren a kicking. He were in 'ospital and everything.' The plump girl was excited, thinking she was first to tell Kate the news.

'I know,' Kate said gently, 'but he's going to be ok now. Aren't you?' She shifted around, trying to get Darren to look at her. He lifted his face to hers. He put his right hand to the side of his nose and then moved it forward slightly.

Sad

With his other hand Darren lifted his t-shirt up to his neck and Kate winced. A mass of ugly bruises snaked from his hip to his neck. He'd had a kicking all right. It looked worse than when she'd seen him at the hospital, the bruises had come out, angry and vivid.

'Bloody hell,' Steve was shocked, 'his father did that?'

Kate nodded, 'Todd Martin. He's number one on our 'Most Wanted List' at the moment, there's a book running for whoever gets him first.'

'Mister, her nappy's dirty.' The baby's sister told Steve, cheerfully, 'She's going to get pooh on your best shirt.'

'It's not my best shirt,' Steve shook his head, but he lifted the baby away from him and handed it back.

Kate led the little parade through the open door of the first apartment on the left and into an open plan living/dining room. The kitchen was off the dining area, only separated by a flimsy looking partition wall. A battle was on for the most prominent smell; fags, chip fat, or mould. The fags were winning... just.

'Tea is it, Kate?' A woman's voice yelled out.

'Yes please Pat,' Kate yelled back, 'make it two, I've brought a colleague.'

A short skinny woman wearing a black vest with no bra underneath and sprayed on pale blue jeans appeared from the kitchen section. She eyed Steve with interest, nodded once, apparently satisfied, and disappeared again.

Kate rolled her eyes at the kids who'd plonked themselves on and around the settee. She was swinging around one way and then the other, making Darren giggle behind his thumb.

'Put the bugger down.' Patricia yelled, 'He'll get your nice clothes messed up.'

'Doesn't matter a bit.' Kate kept swinging.

Steve looked down at the small boy hanging off his arm. 'What's your name?' He asked.

Before the child could answer, the chubby girl on the settee yelled 'Brum'.

'Is that right?' Steve nodded at the boy, 'Is your name Brum?'
The child shook his head slowly.

'No?' Steve looked at the other kids but no one offered any
help. 'What is it then?' He tried to crouch down so the child didn't
have to strain his neck quite so much to look at his face.

'Abrum', the boy said, solemnly, eyes like saucers.

Kate decided to rescue Steve. 'Abraham, his name's Abraham.'
She nodded at the child, encouragingly.

'Abrum', he agreed, his face cracked into a huge grin.

'Told you.' The chubby girl said.

Once she'd had a couple of sips of tea Kate looked pointedly at
Patricia, who was sitting at the dining table with Darren plonked on
her lap. She was smoking in short quick puffs, blowing the smoke
around the side of her son's head. 'I need Josh'. Kate told her.

Patricia's expression didn't change. She knew exactly why the
two officers were in her apartment, and she knew why Kate wanted
her oldest son. She tipped Darren on the floor, stood up slowly
and ground her cigarette out in a red tin ashtray. 'Right you lot,
fuck off home.' She waved her hand at the kids. 'Josie, go get your
brother, take Mickey with you. Tell Josh if he aint here in five
minutes he'll be sorry.'

All the kids stood up. Abraham looked crest fallen, but there
wasn't a word of dissent from any of them.

'Mickey's bums dirty.' Josie told her mum.

'Right, leave her here then. Go get your brother.'

'I'm getting him! I can!' Abraham shouted and ran towards the
door. All the kids except Darren shot off after him.

Patricia lit another cigarette. She looked across at Steve, 'I don't
suppose you could help us out with me shoplifting charge?'

Five minutes later the door banged and Josh walked in alone
and sulking. He was small for his age, his skinny frame hidden
under a pair of cheap dirty tracksuit bottoms. Kate noticed he was
wearing a pair of brand new, expensive looking Nike trainers.
Either he'd stolen them, or his dad had. The boy slouched in the
centre of the room and stared at Steve rudely; almost as a
challenge, but Steve had enough experience with young louts to see
past the bravado. Josh was nervous as hell.

Darren put his arms up to Kate, so she picked him up.

Patricia blew a stream of smoke up towards the ceiling. 'Kate needs to talk to you. No lies now, you hear?'

Kate immediately knew it was hopeless; they were wasting their time. She wished Colin were doing this, he was much better with teenage boys then she was. She always felt she was better with little kids. She could normally manage ok with adolescent girls, but when it came to the male variety Colin was the expert at getting them to talk.

'Josh, I need to ask you about George Pink and this is very important, I think you might be able to help me.' She swung sideways, shifting Darren onto her left hip, so she could face Josh straight on.

The boy said nothing.

'Did you know George Pink?' she asked.

Josh sneered slightly, and shrugged his shoulder. 'Nope.'

Kate tried again. 'George Pink died, Josh. He died by burning to death in his shed. If you know anything about him at all, I need to know.' She waited, looking at Josh intently, trying to convey a sense of trust and sincerity. She doubted it was working. Josh was closed down; he wasn't going to talk to her.

'I don't know nothing. I saw him with those tossers outside the centre. He was always trying to get them to his house to do stuff for him, but I never talked to him. He was just an old fart.' Josh looked down at his shoes.

'Did you go to his house, Josh?' Kate kept going, 'Ever? Or do you know anyone else that did?'

'Nope.' Josh lied.

'The others that George Pink talked to at the centre, who are they?'

'I dunno. That Andy Frazier sometimes and some others; don't remember.' He sniffed loudly.

Kate jiggled Darren on her hip and watched Josh closely, knowing he had nothing to gain by talking to her. Had he been one of Pink's victims? It was entirely possible - Josh always needed money. His home life was dreadful, his father would be back in prison as soon as they found him and his mother was the last word in inadequacy. All in all, he was pretty screwed up.

'Those are pretty cool trainers,' Steve nodded towards Josh's feet, 'where did you get them?'

Josh looked up with a start, but seemed unable to answer.

'His dad got 'em.' Patricia said quickly. She stared at Steve in a direct challenge.

'Right.' Steve nodded slowly. *That's how it was then.*

Patricia didn't bother to get up as they started to show themselves out. Josh shuffled over to the settee and sat down heavily. Kate got to the doorway and turned back towards him, 'Where's your dad?' she asked, casually.

'On a lorry to Ireland.' He replied, but he couldn't look at her and Kate let it go.

'Think about it; think about what's happened, and then talk to me. You don't need to be in the middle of this mess, Josh. You know where I am.'

'Yup, at the cop shop, and I aint got nothing to say.' Josh turned the volume up on the television.

Darren was waving at Steve, slowly and shyly with a grubby hand, his huge eyes looking up under sleepy lashes.

'Thanks for the tea, Patricia.' Steve called back over his shoulder. He hadn't touched it.

Kate remembered to ask Patricia about the alarm system. There were two panic buttons, one in the kitchen and one in the main bedroom. Patricia promised she'd use them if Todd ever came back. Kate didn't believe her. She nodded towards Josh. 'Get someone to call me.'

Patricia nodded absently and lit another fag.

***

CHAPTER SIXTEEN

Walking back to the car Kate sucked in fresh air greedily. She knew she smelt bad. Clicking the remote to unlock the BMW she glanced across at Steve and decided to be human. 'Come on. I'll find you a decent cup of tea, as you obviously didn't like the one Patricia made you.'

Steve knew she was expecting him to ask where they were going, so he didn't. They climbed into the car and he braced himself as Kate pulled out gingerly onto the track. 'Is Mickey short for Michelle?' He leant forward; watching the front of the car, sure she would hit something.

'Nope,' Kate said, cheerfully, 'Just Mickey. When Patricia was pregnant she was depressed and couldn't think of a name, so she let the kids choose. They chose Mickey, because it was their dog's name.'

'So they've got a dog and a baby girl called Mickey?' Steve thought that was stupid.

'No, just the baby, the dog got run over. Mickey was named in his memory.' Kate was laughing.

Steve was amazed how different she seemed when she laughed - not the Iron Lady at all. 'Right, sorry I asked.' He turned his attention to the road and realised they were heading back towards the Backridge Estate.

'Have you and Mivvie worked together much? She seemed ok, has she been on the team long?' He was talking to fill the silence in the car.

Kate turned in her seat and gave him a look full of distain. 'Mivvie transferred here from somewhere in the Midlands. I don't have a problem working with her, she calls a spade a spade, sometimes to her disadvantage; she can be a bit blunt, and she's not always as politically correct as her bosses might want, but the kids like her.'

Steve squirmed, knowing he'd said the wrong thing.

'As I'm sure you don't give a Monkey's about any of that, and are only really interested in her *availability*,' Kate's tone would strip paint. 'She's been favourably divorced, as she would put it. She is therefore, not only available, but is ideal if you're the toy boy type.' Kate turned, dipped her head and her glasses slid down again.

He didn't want to read the look on her face. He was happy to change the subject when she pulled over a few moments later and parked the car in the same place they'd stopped before. 'Remind me again who lives here?'

'Aunty Sharon.' Kate said, before she climbed out and went to get something out of the car boot.

He wondered if she trusted him to knock the door by himself, but it opened before he got there. He stared in surprise at the woman standing in the doorway. She was barefooted; wearing rolled up denim dungarees, the bib top stretched over a tiny gold bikini top. Her hair tumbled in a mane of gold and reds around her bare shoulders.

Bloody hell, I wish all my Aunties looked like you. He thought. His second thought was that Aunty Sharon knew exactly what he was thinking. The look she gave him back was disturbingly confident and sexy.

She grinned and called over his shoulder. 'Coffee's on Kate. What else do you need?'

'To borrow your bathroom for five minutes.' Kate walked up the path carrying a small nylon gym bag. 'Can I leave Steve with you? He's just joined us on attachment.'

'Oh, I'm sure I'll be able to look after him for a few minutes. How much trouble can he be?'

Steve gave her the benefit of his sexy eyed grin and stepped into the hall. 'If I'm *very* lucky you might just find out.' He spoke softly, but he knew she'd heard him.

The interior of the house was cool and fresh and smelt of lilies. It was a sharp contrast to what was outside. Kate disappeared upstairs as Steve was led to a stylish glass conservatory overlooking the garden. Through the glass he could see a tiny square lawn almost entirely taken up with an expensive looking garden swing under a green and beige awning. Two Garden Gnomes stood guarding each end of the swing. One Gnome held a small England flag, the other, inexplicably, held both hands over his eyes.

'Grab a seat.' Aunty Sharon gave him a grin and disappeared back to the kitchen.

Steve plonked himself down into a large wicker armchair, suddenly conscious of the fact that he was dirty. He was afraid he could smell himself. The visit to the Martin's had left an unpleasant aroma clinging to him. There was the sound of cups and a fridge door being opened and closed a couple of times and Steve looked around while he waited. There were photos of Aunty Sharon with a couple of pretty blond headed little girls. There were no photos of a man. Steve wondered what that meant.

'How are you getting on?' Aunty Sharon yelled.

'Crap,' he yelled back, 'I haven't got a clue what's going on, I'm just following the Governor and doing what I'm told.'

Aunty Sharon stuck her head around the kitchen door and squinted at him. The dungaree strap had fallen down her arm; a tiny triangle of gold material was just about covering her left boob. Steve swallowed and tried to look at her eyes. She was laughing at him. 'Right.' She said, and disappeared again.

To Steve's dismay Kate returned dressed in a fresh pair of dark denim jeans, and a clean white t-shirt. She looked fresh and shiny and full of energy. He groaned inwardly, so that was what was in the bag. There was a lovely lemony scent coming from her as she kicked off her shoes and curled her legs under her on the cane sofa. Aunty Sharon brought in a tray with a pot of coffee and matching espresso cups. Steve felt like a troll at a beauty contest.

'George Pink.' Kate looked at Aunty Sharon.

'Pink the Perv, I've heard about it. He was working as a handyman or gardener at the Community Centre. Rumour is he had some of the boys from the centre to help him out in his garden. Have you got any names?'

'Andy Frazier and Josh Martin, and The Toad might know something. We've seen Josh Martin...'

'How's little Darren doing?'

Kate smiled, 'Bruised, but he's still a little monkey, and it hasn't slowed him up any.'

'I'm going to kidnap him. I'm just going to bundle him into the back of my car and bring him home so I can take care of him. How that bastard could beat up that small boy and the poor little poppet can't even hear!' Aunty Sharon shook her head in disgust, 'I bet you got nothing from his brother. Josh is a miniature Todd. He won't tell you anything even if it hurts him not to.'

'I've got nothing.' Kate agreed. 'No one's made a complaint. George Pink has gone about his business, apparently enticing young boys to his shed without fear of discovery. But that's not unusual. Teenage boys are unlikely to complain, especially if they're getting paid in some way. But then Pink gets himself dead in a rather nasty way and my DCI thinks one of these kids did it.'

Aunty Sharon rolled her eyes mockingly.

'*I know.* I didn't say it was a good theory. You know these boys - they can all be trouble, but murderers?'

Steve wasn't so sure, 'But if one of these boys, even one we don't know about yet, is linked to the murder, it makes sense that Pink's actions; his behaviour with these boys led to his death.'

'Yes,' Kate said, 'But not by one of these boys. There's different things going on here, and we only know about one of them - the boys visiting Pink's house.' She leant back and blew her fringe out of her eyes.

Steve had seen her do the same thing several times. It was obviously a habit, like some people played with their glasses or their rings. He looked to see if either woman was wearing a wedding ring - they weren't.

'Yup,' Aunty Sharon agreed, 'I haven't seen Andy Frazier for a while; I'll see if I can find out what he's been up to. The Toad is another story.' She picked up the coffeepot and topped up Kate's cup.

'What's up with The Toad?' Steve's coffee was still too hot for him to drink. He wondered if his Governor had an asbestos lined mouth. 'I take it he's got another name?'

'Not one that's been used in the last five years.' Kate said, 'But he's William Hogarth Todsworth. And he's *super* intelligent, although he doesn't let on. I'm pretty sure that in a proper test his IQ would be off the scale. He's a complete maverick in every sense of the word. He has a whole bunch of urban legends attached to him, some bizarre and others downright scary. There's an element of truth to some of it.'

'I like him. There's something of the Johnny Depp about him.' Aunty Sharon flicked her hair back, suggestively.

Kate snorted. 'Seriously? You'll be telling me he's sexy in a minute, God, you're a disgrace!'

Aunty Sharon grinned, 'I'm just saying there's something magnetic about him.'

'What are the other things?' Steve had had enough of The Toad. 'What are the other things you said are going on apart from the boys visiting Pink's shed?'

Before Kate could answer she had to put her cup down to retrieve her mobile that was vibrating in the bag at her feet. She flipped it open, looked at the screen and stood up. 'We need to go.'

Steve didn't want to leave, 'What's up?'

'Dean Towle has been beaten up.'

***

CHAPTER SEVENTEEN

J ohn Bishop raised the beer bottle to his lips and realised his hand was trembling. It wasn't a good sign. Maybe his blood pressure was up again; it was more than bloody likely with all this nonsense going on. He looked at the half smoked Benson and Hedges cigarette dangling from the fingers on his other hand and wondered if he could give up the fags. It wasn't a serious thought, he'd smoked since he was fourteen years old, and it usually calmed him, but not now, not today. He was angry and he was getting increasingly agitated, he'd need a horse tranquiliser to calm him down if he carried on like this.

'Why the hell didn't you tell me? Why did I have to come over here to find out? You should have let me know as soon as you realised Eddie was gone; you should have rung me, not waited for me to turn up. If I hadn't come looking for him I still wouldn't know.' Bishop looked across at the shapeless woman who had heaved her large bulk into a cheap white plastic garden chair next to him. They were sitting in the back garden of her house because she had some stupid rule about not smoking indoors. She said it set off her asthma. Bishop didn't give a toss about her asthma. The boy was gone, had been for a couple of days, and this stupid lump of a woman hadn't bothered to say anything. He needed to calm himself down and think about what this might mean, but he couldn't, he was too angry and he didn't seem to be getting through to her.

'He goes sometimes; you *know* he does. He takes himself off, but he comes back. Its not like he's got somewhere to go, is it?' She scrunched up her dark eyes against the sun and looked at him.

She looked hot and bothered. Maybe it was the wretched heat

that was making her uncomfortable, or maybe she was miffed that she was getting yelled at. Bishop didn't care. Her long greying brown hair was scraped back into a ponytail, keeping it off her neck and face, but he could still see sweat dribbling down onto her chest. She lifted the hem of her voluminous black t-shirt and wafted it, fanning herself. Bishop caught a glimpse of fat white belly and he winced.

'What did he take?' Bishop distracted himself by taking a deep drag on his cigarette. He felt the nicotine hit and blew smoke out through his nose. 'Has he got any money?'

The woman shrugged. 'I dunno, do I? Not much, his room looks the same, he couldn't have taken that much wiv him, 'cept his skateboard. That thing's stuck to him, he don't leave it anywhere. And talking about money – I aint been paid properly this month, I'm short. Its hardly bloody worth it for what the Social pays now. I'm not doing this anymore – Eddie's my last, I've lost some of my benefits taking him in, and those aren't what they used to be neither. Bloody Government want us to starve.' She was beginning to ramble.

Bishop ground his cigarette out in a chipped flowerpot and took another swig from the bottle. It tasted vile; cheap rubbish, but at least it was cold. He'd had enough of her winging. 'You'll have to take that up with the office. But you can't tell them Eddie's not here. Do you understand? You'll have the bloody police knocking the door; there'll be all sorts of questions asked, and one of them will be why a foster care kid wasn't reported missing by his bloody foster carer until she realised she was short on her money. You don't think they'll pay you when he's not even here? Do you? Don't be bloody stupid. You get money to look after him; feed him and stuff. You don't even know where the fuck he is.'

The woman bristled. 'I told you, he's gone off before – he always comes back. He's a sad little thing, never says a word, and he don't even have any friends. Where's he going to go? I bet he's sleeping rough somewhere. Boys do that. They like to sleep outside and stuff, especially when it's hot. He'll be back when he's hungry enough or he starts to miss his bed.'

Bishop wasn't so sure. The woman hadn't seen Eddie since the day Pink died, but she wasn't even sure if he'd been home the day before that. She obviously didn't pay much attention to him. He came and went as he wanted. Her lack of scruples was exactly why he'd placed Eddie in her care in the first place. Now it had come back to bite him, but what could he do? He considered his options and realised he didn't have much choice. He would have to hope she was right – that Eddie was sleeping out somewhere and would be back soon. He couldn't report the boy missing; too many complications, and not just with his department at Social Services, no, there were other people that might be anxious about the boy's disappearance, and he didn't want that either. Shit! Where was the kid? Eddie was a frightened rabbit, no gumption to him at all, never had been. He did what he was told and kept his mouth shut. He never talked to anyone – about anything. In fact he barely spoke. Surely he hadn't gone off and done something stupid? Not on his own?

Bishop drained the last dregs from his bottle and pulled himself out of the chair. He needed to find him.

'You're going to frighten the horses.' Kate told a sorry looking Dean, 'I hope you've got a good story for that mess on your face. Maybe a little girl was about to get run over by a speeding car - you saved her life but fell on your face.'

Dean smiled painfully; at least Kate had got a response. When they'd arrived Joan had pulled them aside, so that Dean couldn't hear her, and told them he wasn't responding to anything, not even hot chocolate with squirty cream.

'Let's have a look then. Is plastic surgery required? Will we have to fly you to Hollywood to see a top surgeon? We don't want anyone cheap, you might end up looking like Michael Jackson.'

'Um, he's dead.' Steve said.

'I meant before he died.' Kate put her hand under Dean's chin and lifted his face up. He winced. 'Ooh, that looks pretty nasty but I think you'll live.' A chunk of skin had been taken off his cheek and another out of his chin, but Kate was relieved to see it wasn't anything more serious.

Philip came into the kitchen and looked sheepishly at the group. 'This is my fault and I'm in the dog house,' He looked to Steve for sympathy, 'I let Dean go to the centre to show off his new shirt.'

Dean was still wearing the shirt and there was a nasty

bloodstain on the collar. 'Are you hurt anywhere else?' Kate asked.

Dean shook his head, but Kate didn't believe him. Joan had patched his face up with some basic first aid, but she was worried in case he had other injuries she couldn't see. 'So you're ok? You're sure?'

Dean nodded.

'Do you want to tell me how it happened?'

He shook his head. He was trying to tough it out, scared of being a grass.

Kate decided to leave it for now and give him a bit of space. They'd made him feel uncomfortable, all standing around looking at him. 'Steve's pretty good at rugby,' She told him, 'or at least that's what he tells us. He's probably pants at football though. Why don't you go outside and see if you can teach him? But try and stay on your feet ok?'

Dean jumped up and ran outside, desperate to escape.

Steve looked at Kate questioningly.

'See if he'll talk to you, there's too much attention on him in here. Go gently, just have a chat, but I want to know who did this and why.'

Steve nodded and stepped out to the garden where Dean was already putting a small goal net up against the far wall.

'I'm sorry.' Philip was apologetic, 'He really wanted to go and I gave in. I thought it might do him good to do something normal; take his mind off things. I should have stayed with him.'

'If he'd known he was going to get a hiding he wouldn't have gone, so he wasn't expecting trouble. The question is who did it, and why won't he say?'

Philip shrugged, 'I think he's scared. Maybe he thinks they'll come after him again.'

'So how did he get home?' Kate asked.

'Some boy called my mobile,' Joan looked bewildered and upset, 'I don't know who it was. He said 'you need to come and get Dean from the centre; he's had a bit of bother, he's hurt.' Then he hung up. When I got there Dean was sitting on the kerb on his own and he's refused to say what happened.'

'Do you know the other kids who would have been at the centre today?' Kate thought there must be a witness. She had to get someone to talk to her.

'Oh God, Kate. There's dozens of them and the same ones don't always turn up every week. You need to speak to Lion; he'll tell you who was there today.'

'Can you give me the number?'

Joan nodded and went to find it.

Outside a rather frenzied kick about was in full swing. Kate watched as Steve ran towards the goal. The ball bounced in front of him, he stretched for it but Dean nipped in off his right and took it away from him. Two touches and the ball hit the back of the net. At first Kate thought Steve was letting Dean win, but as she watched she realised the boy was running circles around him. She smiled.

Joan came back and handed her a piece of paper.

Kate got her mobile out and started punching numbers. Outside, Steve bent over and leant his hands on his knees. He was puffing and Dean laughed at him.

Kate's call went to voicemail. She left a message that she hoped conveyed how important it was for Lion to call her but didn't put the fear of God into him.

Fifteen minutes later Steve opened the door and stuck his head in. 'You wouldn't happen to have a rugby ball somewhere, would you? I'm getting killed out here.'

Philip laughed at him, 'Welcome to my world.'

'No answer from the coach.' Kate told him. 'I've left a message. Apart from getting killed, how are you getting on?'

'I need to get a rugby ball.' Steve wiped both his hands over his face; he was sweating. Through the glass door Kate could see Dean bouncing the ball continuously off one foot.

'What for, so that you can show off?' Kate gave him a sideways look.

'No, I said I'd show him some moves. He's pretty keen but they don't play rugby at his school and he'd like to have a go. He's starting to talk but he's embarrassed. I just want to hang out with him for a while until he feels comfortable talking a bit more.'

'What has he said?' Kate was losing patience.

'I don't know who attacked him yet, but some kid filmed the whole thing on a mobile phone.'

'Oh, for Christ's sake!' Joan exploded. 'What the bloody hell is the matter with these kids?'

Kate got her purse out of her bag and looked at her watch; they had time. 'How much is a rugby ball?' She looked at Steve. 'Take the car, take Dean with you and go get one. Find out who's got that mobile.'

***

CHAPTER EIGHTEEN

By the time Kate got back to the Station she was tired and frustrated. Stacey was waiting for her report but the information she had wasn't going to help the investigation into Pink's death.

'We're going to pick up Andy Frazier tomorrow.' She told him, 'He cornered Dean at the MCSC earlier today and assaulted him. Dean's not badly hurt, and he's reluctant to talk about it, but his face looks a bit of a mess. Another boy, Bisby Alouni filmed it on Andy's mobile phone, so we'll pick him up too.'

'How old is this Andy Frazier?' Stacey asked.

'Fourteen going on twenty-seven. He lives with his father but he's not exactly under parental control.'

'And he's known to us.' Stacey seemed rather pleased about this.

Kate realised why he sounded hopeful and she paused. She didn't want the DCI to home in on Andy Frazier quite so readily. 'He was cautioned last month for being in possession of a knife. There was some trouble after the local school prom. A couple of uniforms went out to it and Frazier got stopped and searched.'

'You've seen the report from the autopsy?' Stacey asked.

Kate knew where he was going with this but didn't know how to head him off. 'Yes Sir.'

'So you know that George Pink was stabbed in the genitals before being set alight. Andy Frazier's name has already been linked to Pink and he's known to carry a knife. A bit of a bloody coincidence, don't you think?' Stacey underlined Andy Frazier's name in red on the power board.

'Sir, the vast majority of boys in Frazier's circle carry knives.

101

That's exactly why they get stopped and searched so frequently. Frazier wasn't charged with assault, there was no evidence that he was even involved in the fracas outside the school. And we don't know what, if anything, his involvement with Pink was. Andy Frazier's a nasty little coward, he likes to play the role of a thug, but he never tries anything on his own - he's always got back up.'

'There could well be more than one person responsible for Pink's death.' Stacey wasn't distracted. 'Maybe Dean Towle got a hiding because of something he knows, or something he saw. Maybe it was a warning.' Stacey liked this idea. 'Maybe that's what it was for; to make sure he kept his mouth shut.'

'Dean didn't see Andy Frazier or Bisby Alouni or anyone else near Pink's house. If he had he would have said so.' Kate was getting cross.

'Really? What makes you so sure?' Stacey said with exaggerated patience.

'Because when I picked Dean up at the scene he was terrified - he thought I believed he'd killed Pink. If he'd seen anyone there he would have told me.'

Stacey wasn't convinced, 'But he lied to you about the number of times he'd been to Pink's house, so what makes you think he's reliable? Was Pink involved in sexual activity with this Frazier kid? Maybe the man hurt him; or maybe Frazier decided he'd had enough, wouldn't play anymore and there was a fight. Frazier's a yob, he's perfectly capable of throwing petrol over someone and making sure they couldn't escape to get help.'

Kate couldn't drag up a plausible argument, 'I'll pick Frazier up early tomorrow morning. I'll take a couple of uniforms with me to search his house.' She could feel a tension headache just starting behind her eyes. She needed a bath and a glass of wine. It had been a bloody long day. 'I haven't heard from the search team at Pink's house. Do you know if they've come up with anything new?' She changed tack.

'Nothing significant; it's looking more and more likely that anything relating to Pink's offending was in the shed and was lost in the fire. Maybe he didn't trust his wife not to pry.'

'I don't believe that,' Kate was too tired to be anything but blunt, 'There should be something; some memento or keepsake, something he kept close to hand. It might be well hidden - but it'll be there. I need to see what they're turning up; it might not be easily recognisable. They're not just looking for kiddie porn.'

'Oh good, maybe you can tell them to stop looking for that then.' Stacey drawled, sarcastically.

Kate started getting an impression of herself as a hamster, constantly running on a wheel, never getting anywhere. Arguing with Stacey and trying to get him to understand paedophile behaviour, was getting old. She decided to fulfil her promise to Knowling.

'I'm sorry, Sir. I apologise, excuse me.'

Stacey opened his mouth to speak but she brushed past him and walked away. Sticking her head around her office door she wasn't surprised to see Colin was still at work. He raised tired eyes and grinned at her, waiting.

'Why don't you and Sarah come to dinner tomorrow?' She was worried about him, an evening off would do them all good.

'Oh God,' Colin pulled a face, 'you're not going to cook are you?'

Kate grinned. 'Well someone will, probably Mr Marks and Sparks. Can you come?'

'Well I was going to spend the evening getting run ragged by my two sons before collapsing in front of the telly, but I can give that a miss for one evening. Will there be surprise dessert?'

'Absolutely,' Kate nodded solemnly. 'And the surprise is...'

'There's no dessert!' Colin chimed in. It was an old joke. 'We'll bring a bottle.'

'Which reminds me - there's a glass of Merlot beckoning me as I speak.' Kate winked at him and left him to it. As she passed Knowling's office she paused, leant towards it and listened. She couldn't hear anything. *Was he in there? Should she knock?* She wanted to see him, for no other reason than to be with him for a few minutes. For some reason she couldn't fathom, she wanted to be close to him for a minute or two. Glancing over her shoulder she saw Colin standing in the doorway of her office watching her. He had a 'caught you' grin all over his face and she heard him 'tutting' loudly at her. Stupidly she felt herself blush. *Bugger!* Mustering what dignity she could she walked down the stairs.

Eddie didn't want to talk about it. He'd never talked about it to anyone before and he didn't want to start now. It was a horror locked deep inside him. He'd buried it; pushed it down, found a way of shutting it off. What had happened to him since he'd lost his mum wasn't the sort of thing you told people. He would rather slash his own wrists and bleed his way out of his misery then start this conversation.

A lifetime of being messed about, of having no control over anything, of being scared and hurt all the time and now he wanted it gone, he didn't want to think about it ever again. He was going to be with her, he was going to stay with her. This was his new life, his chance. He had feelings he'd never had before, the feeling of being held by someone who cared about him, the feeling of being special to someone, being wanted. He didn't know how long it would last, he couldn't think too far ahead. She was older than him, but she wanted him. No one had ever wanted him before.

He wanted to bury himself deep inside her, blocking out everything except the heat of her grip around him. He wanted to shut his eyes and put his hands on her. He loved watching her face when he was doing it to her, loved the way she whispered his name. But she wouldn't do it now, not now. She was waiting for him to say something.

Eddie lay back against his pillows and flung one arm up over his head, but he couldn't stay like that. For reasons he didn't understand the thought of telling the story made him curl up on his side, like a baby. He rolled against her and she turned to face him until she was almost nose-to-nose with him, but he couldn't look at her. He closed his eyes, took two very deep breaths, in out, in out, knowing how much the words would hurt, and began.

Kate stood in the shower for twenty minutes just letting the hot water wash over her. Leaving her hair wet she pulled on a pair of frayed cotton shorts and headed out to the garden. Eight o'clock in the evening and there was still enough sun to get her legs out. She knew she'd pay for it later. She'd have prematurely wrinkled skin and end up looking like the present day Bridget Bardot. Kate smiled ruefully to herself. She might even end up wearing ugly hats and spend all her time rescuing skinny cats. She leant back in the lounger and had almost dozed off when her mobile chirped on the table beside her. She picked it up and the metal casing felt hot where she'd left it in the sun. She smiled when she heard his voice.

'Hello dear.'

'Hello Dad, I was just thinking about rescuing cats and wearing ugly hats, but I think I nodded off. How are you?'

'You sound more like your mother every time I speak to you.' He was laughing.

Kate smiled. Her father was the rock in every storm, the voice of calm in every episode of her often-crazy existence. He also cared in a kind, tender way for her mother, whose senility was slowly and painfully pulling her down to a place where nothing made sense. Kate had hardly known her dad when she was growing up. His job as a Geologist working for a scientific research organisation had kept him away from home for long periods of time. When she was in Junior School she'd told classmates he was a spy and was away on secret missions. It was her way of explaining why he never came to sports days or school concerts. And then suddenly, when she was in college, he'd decided to make up for lost time; gave up his job, only taking occasional high paying consultancy work, and gradually they'd got to know each other.

'Your mother sends her love. I told her I was calling and she said to tell you she can baby-sit.' Kate's father never made a big deal of his wife's illness.

Kate smiled sadly, 'Bless her. She forgets Angel's eighteen, not eight.'

Whenever her daughter visited her parents in Dorset her mother would be surprised that she was so grown up. Then Angel would leave and she'd forget again.

'I want to come down Dad. Angel's on tour with her college volley ball team and then she'll be home long enough for me to do her washing before driving down to you. I'll join her as soon as I can.'

'You've got a lot on, love.' Kate's dad always said he didn't so much read between the lines as 'listen between the words'.

'I've been pulled into a murder enquiry, Dad.' Kate closed her eyes briefly, and took a long sip from her wine glass.

'With Colin?' Her dad had met her colleague and liked him immensely.

'I wish,' Kate smirked, 'I've got a new sidekick, Steve Astman, CID career climber.'

'He's lucky to be with you.'

She laughed out loud, 'Could you please tell him that?'

By the time she'd hung up Kate realised she was starving. Drinking red wine was nice, but it wasn't exactly nourishing. She couldn't remember when she'd last had a proper meal. She was heading back inside when her phone went again. She didn't recognise the caller's number.

'Kate Landers.'

'Hi Kate. Kevin Baxter, hope I'm not disturbing you.' It was the senior fire officer that she'd met in Pink's house the day he died. 'I'm sorry to call you at home, but you said you wanted to know if we found anything significant in the shed at that sudden death in Clare Walk.'

Kate's scalp prickled. Walking into the kitchen with the phone clamped to her ear, she picked up the bottle of wine, topped up her glass and took a bigger slurp than she meant to. 'Kevin! No, its fine... of course, what have you got?'

'Is that alcohol you're knocking back?' He was laughing at her.

'Oh God, sorry.' Kate was mortified. 'Merlot; my second glass I'm afraid, but I deserve it. It's been one of those days.'

'Wish I could join you. Maybe another time?'

'You're on. What did you find?'

'Two metal tins. They survived pretty well, probably because they were a long way from the seat of the fire. They're similar; a bit like old-fashioned toffee tins, not that you're old enough to remember those. We also found a couple of large bits from a wooden chair that survived. A bit of an odd looking thing. We've put our reports in to your colleagues.'

'Right,' Kate was desperate for him to get on with it. 'Was there anything in the tins?'

'One's got money in it. Ten pound notes wrapped inside a sort of canvas money pouch; four hundred and twenty quid.'

Kate was taken back. They'd already found cash in the house, why did Pink need to keep more in the shed?

'Lots of old people keep money in a teapot or under the bed - they don't trust banks; like to have cash handy.' Kevin was telling her something she already knew.

'What about the other one?' She tried to sip her wine quietly.

'A mouth organ. Looks pretty old, but it's a decent one, it's inside its own case, which was inside an old velvet pouch, but it's in good nick. It's got initials engraved on the top.'

Kate's glass stopped half way to her mouth.

'Now, about that drink?' He was playing with her.

Kate groaned. 'Come on! I'll buy you a bloody drink, I promise. What are the initials?'

'MBB. Nicely engraved; a professional job, like. Mean anything to you?'

Kate closed her eyes and thought about it. *Nothing; it meant nothing to her.* She didn't know who MBB was. But she knew damn well she'd have to find out. She'd found the keepsake.

***

CHAPTER NINETEEN

'That's not good.' Kate snapped her phone shut and threw it into her bag on the floor at her feet. 'Aunty Sharon says Andy's not been around since yesterday, and she's pretty certain he knows we're coming for him. The chances are he's not in there.' She blew her fringe out of her eyes and checked over her shoulder.

She and Steve were sitting in the car waiting for two uniform officers to turn up - Jaz and Greg. After being with her at Bev's house when they'd found baby Crystal, they'd both shown an interest in what she was doing, so she'd got them assigned to help with the search of Andy's house.

'She's sure?' Like Kate, Steve was dressed casually in jeans and trainers.

'Aunty Sharon is always sure.' Kate was getting restless, fed up with waiting. She peered over her shoulder again and fiddled with her watch. It was five minutes past seven in the morning and the day was threatening to be another scorcher. She was already hot, she could feel her bra sticking to her. She pulled the front of her t-shirt open and blew down her front - it didn't help much.

Steve leant forward and draped his long arms over the steering wheel. 'Can I ask you something? How does she know so much about these kids, about what they're up to? She seems to be your 'go to' for a lot of information.'

'She makes it her business to.'

'Right,' Steve was going to say something else, but hesitated.

'What? You think informants only come in the guise of skinny little runts hanging around the drug scene; the ones who swap sides as soon as the benefits or perils change?' Kate stared at him, waiting.

Steve kept his face turned to the front of Andy's house, his eyes watchful, 'No, it just seems a bit odd that's all, the way Aunty Sharon knows what's going on. They talk to her, at least some of the kids do, and she tells us anything interesting.'

'Good, huh?' Kate grinned.

'Gov,' Steve turned towards her, his face blank, 'She's not really your Aunty is she?'

Kate gave him the benefit of her withering look. 'Give me the cigarettes.' She held her hand out.

Steve reached into the glove compartment and fished out a packet of ten Benson and Hedges. 'Remind me again why I'm buying you fags? You don't smoke.'

Kate ignored him. 'Here we go, backup's arrived, about bloody time.' She was out of the car before he'd even got his door open.

Thumping loudly on the front door for several minutes eventually brought a dishevelled looking Mr Frazier to open up, but he wasn't very welcoming.

'Oh for Christ's sake! Why can't you lot fook off? Go on, fook off, get off my step.' He peered at Kate, saw Steve and the uniformed officers standing behind her and started cursing.

'Morning Mr Frazier,' Kate greeted him, cheerfully, 'that's not very nice is it? And here I was hoping you'd already have the kettle on for the boys.' She waved the search warrant at him and he swore even louder, but he stepped aside to let them in. Kate led him into the kitchen as the team spread out around the house, she knew he wasn't going to be any trouble. He was all noise and bluster.

'He aint here and he's got the phone with him; he always has it with him, sleeps with the fooking thing on his pillow.' Frazier leant back against a sink overflowing with dirty dishes and crossed his arms defiantly.

'When did you last see him?' Kate kept up the cheerful tone. She knew Frazier well; he wasn't exactly the sharpest knife in the drawer.

'Dunno. Yesterday, they day before maybe, he comes and goes as he likes. Why, what's he done?'

'He left a boy looking as though his face had been rubbed against a cheese grater. Bisby Alouni was with him and I believe they took the trouble of filming the assault on Andy's mobile.'

'Well, I dunno anything about that. The other boy must have done sommat, or maybe he started it.' Frazier pushed greasy grey hair back from his face and wiped his nose on the back of his hand.

'Except he didn't,' Kate put him straight, 'and the boy who was hurt is younger and smaller than your son. Two against one isn't very nice is it? A bit cowardly if you ask me.'

'Then he's lying.' Frazier started worrying at a dirty fingernail with his teeth. He was defending his son, but he was as nervous as hell about something.

Kate watched him thoughtfully. What was bugging him? She'd dealt with him before and normally he didn't give a shit about Andy being in trouble. Was there something hidden in the house?

'Gov?' Almost on cue, Steve called from upstairs.

Kate raised her eyes at Frazier and smiled, 'Let's go and see what he's found shall we?'

Andy Frazier's bedroom was a tip. An explosion of clothing, possessions and tangled bed sheets covered the floor and the very strong aroma of body odour assaulted Kate's nose as she walked in. Steve was crouched by the wardrobe, he was holding a new shoebox in his hand. 'Nice gear these, the price tag is still on the box.' He held it out to her.

Kate looked at the logo and the picture on the side. Nike Shox hi-top trainers, size ten. The sticker said they cost eighty-three quid. The box was empty. She looked at Frazier who was standing in the doorway, still biting his nails.

'He got 'em off a mate for twenty quid.' He told her.

'Right,' Kate nodded at Steve, 'Andy must be wearing them. Keep hold of the box, what else have you got?'

'Just this so far.' Steve pointed at a crumpled magazine that was on the mattress, 'It was under the bed.'

Kate realised she was looking at the cover of a gay porn magazine.

'That aint his.' Frazier was looking over her shoulder shaking his head.

Kate turned towards him, a questioning look on her face.

'It fooking aint, I'm telling you! He's got a girlfriend, I've seen her here with him, and he's no fooking poof.' Frazier swore.

It was the first Kate had heard about any girlfriend. 'Bring it.'

She nodded to Steve and then turned to make her way back downstairs; taking Frazier with her and leading him back to the kitchen. She needed him to give up the sulky, protective attitude and talk to her. She picked up the kettle, filled it with water from the tap, looked around for some tea bags and then opened the fridge and kept her fingers crossed that the milk was fresh. She sniffed the open carton before she tipped it into the mugs, she didn't care that Frazier was watching her. She pulled the Benson and Hedges packet out of the back pocket of her jeans and held it out to him. Frazier grinned, helped himself to a fag, opened a cupboard and plonked half a bag of sugar down in front of her.

'Does Andy have a mate he stays with when he's not here? What about this girlfriend?' Kate was just chatting, making the tea and chatting, chummy like.

'Fook knows where he goes, he don't say, he never does.'

'What's the girlfriend's name - is she local?'

'Dunno.' Frazier slurped his tea noisily, 'Gina sommat, Gooden or Grodden maybe. I only seen her a couple of times.'

'Gina,' Kate nodded encouragingly, as though this was really helpful. 'What does she look like?'

'Skinny little thing. Taller than you maybe, but tiny, like a doll.' He shrugged, 'She don't say much, bloody moody if you ask me. I didn't pay much attention to her.'

'How long has Andy been seeing her?'

Frazier looked at her as though she'd just asked him the stupidest question in the world. 'Fook knows. She's stopped here, so you can forget about him looking at that poof's magazine.'

Kate thought about the girl stopping over, she thought she knew what he meant by that. 'So this Gina is how old?' She asked.

Frazier opened his mouth to speak but stopped and Kate saw it dawn on him about where she was going with the question. He was allowing a girl to stay in the house with his fourteen year old son. 'Sixteen.'

Kate knew damn well he was lying. 'Does your son visit Gina at her house?'

Frazier wiped his nose on the back of his hand again, 'Must do, she turns up with him sometime so he must go and get her. Have you got another fag there?'

Kate tipped one out for him to take and lit it for him. 'Do you know where Gina lives?'

'Nope.'

Kate stared at him, a look of utter disbelieve on her face. 'Think about it a bit more.'

'I don't, I swear.' Frazier blew smoke out of his nose, 'She aint far though. I remember Andy asked her how long it took her to get here once and she said it was ten minutes. She walks here, so it can't be far.'

'Where did he meet her?' Kate took a step back and sideways out of the path of Frazier's cigarette smoke. Her clothes were going to reek again.

'School, they goes to the same school. She come here once in her school uniform. Mind you her bloody skirt just about covered her arse - more like a fooking belt. Her mother wants her head seeing to, letting her daughter out like that. Surprised the bloody school don't do sommat, these young girls, they're all bloody like it nowadays.'

'Where does Andy get money?' Kate changed tack.

'He helps out at the market sometimes, you know, in the square on Saturdays. The bloke, the guy with the fruit stall, pays cash.'

'Would Andy go to Bisby's house?'

'You're fooking joking, Bisby aint even allowed in his house half the time. I don't like the idiot, he's a bad influence.'

Kate looked at him in astonishment. He either didn't know his own son, or chose not to. 'Does Andy have any other mates that he hangs out with?'

Frazier squinted at her, his right eye closed as he blew cigarette smoke out of the corner of his mouth. 'Have you tried Todd Martin's kid, Josh?'

She was about to say something when Jaz, who was outside the back door, stuck his head in. 'You'd better have a look at this, Gov.'

A small brick shed was attached to the back of the kitchen. There wasn't room for more than one person inside, so Kate stood in the doorway adjusting her eyes to the gloom. Jaz pointed into the corner. Partially hidden behind a pile of junk was a brand new Jerry can. He lifted it out carefully with a gloved hand and gave it a slight shake, then unscrewed the cap and sniffed.

'Petrol, Gov. There's a drop left in the bottom, but not much.'

Shit! Stacey was going to love this. Had the DCI been on the right track all along?

'That's mine.' Frazier was crowded up behind her.

Kate turned, frowning. 'You haven't got a car.'

Frazier looked from her to Jaz and back, he was thinking furiously. 'It's for me lawnmower.'

'Where's the lawnmower?' Jaz asked, quick as a flash.

Frazier searched for an answer. 'It broke down. Andy said something about having a mate that might be able to do something with it.'

Kate fixed him with a hard look; she'd had enough of being chummy. She turned to Jaz. 'Bag it.'

As they walked away from the house Kate rang the Incident Room and got hold of Ginger. He was acting as analyst on the case as the one they'd been expecting had become unavailable. She was sending Jaz and Greg back with the items they'd picked up. The forensics team could match the composition of the petrol with any residue from the accelerant used in Pink's shed. She told him to let Stacey know they were still looking for Frazier and to get the word out in case he was spotted. When she'd hung up she saw Steve looking at her quizzically.

'What?' She demanded.

'You didn't seem surprised when we found that gay mag.'

'It's not unusual for paedophiles to use porn when they're grooming young boys.' She told him, 'It's a conspiracy thing, being naughty but grown up together, a secret. It's a way of sexualising their time together.'

'So you think Pink gave it to him?' Steve clicked the remote and climbed into the driver's seat.

'Where did you get porn from when you were fourteen?' Kate asked as she slid in next to him.

Steve was shocked, she'd completely thrown him. 'Well, um, I think my older brother had some stashed away in his room, of course I never actually looked at it.'

Kate tilted her head and smirked at him. *'Of course you didn't.* Andy Frazier is a kid. To start with Newsagents are not supposed to sell porn to kids, and secondly, as a kid would you try and buy gay porn over the counter? We can trace it later if we need to, but yes, I think it's possible that Pink gave it to him.'

'What's next Gov?' The subject was making Steve uncomfortable. He started the car and fiddled with the air vent as he pulled away from the kerb.

Kate looked at her watch, 'Let's get Joan to make us a coffee. We can see how Dean's getting on and Joan might know who this Gina girl is - or where she lives.'

Steve looked over his shoulder and pulled the car into a tight U-turn, throwing Kate against the door.

Joan looked a bit dishevelled when she answered the door. Kate thought she probably hadn't been up long, but she ushered them into the kitchen and put the kettle on.

'Dean's not up yet, he's still not sleeping too well.' Joan heaped coffee into three cups and leant back against the counter, 'He talks about you, though.' She smiled at Steve. 'He's asked me several times if you were going to come back to play rugby with him again. You'll cheer him up no end.'

'Oh great,' Kate rolled her eyes, 'I do all the flipping work and he gets all the attention because he can throw a misshaped ball around, thanks.'

Joan laughed, 'It's a boy thing I'm afraid. You and I just don't measure up. And however hard he tries; Philip is really crap at football – or any kind of game that involves physical exercise, so Steve has become something of a hero in Dean's eyes. I'll give him a shout.'

'Let me.' Steve got up and went to the foot of the stairs. 'Oi!' He yelled, 'Dean! Get your skinny little butt down here. The days' half over and Kate's going to make me go and do important police stuff in a minute.' He banged on the wooden banister.

Kate was grudgingly impressed. Steve had made a connection with Dean through their shared love of sport. There was a thump and a scuffling sound from the floor above. Sixty seconds later Dean charged down the stairs with the rugby ball under his arm. Joan sent him straight back up again to wash his face and brush his teeth. When he came back down Steve promised to have a kick about as soon as he'd drunk his coffee.

Joan put a bowl of cereal in front of the boy. 'Here, eat some of this while you're waiting.' She told him.

Kate studied Dean's face. The ugly graze down his cheek and

chin looked swollen and bruised, like a friction burn. Some of the scab had come off and the wound was weeping. 'Does your face get stuck on the pillow when you're asleep?' She asked.

Dean grinned and nodded, his mouth full of cornflakes.

'Hurts like hell when you have to peel it off in the morning, doesn't it?' Steve laughed, 'If you think that's bad, I once had a friction burn all down one bum cheek - it was this big.' He held up his hands, eight inches apart to show them. 'I mean, that's an impressive wound you've got there... but mine was gross. And at least people can see your face so you get some sympathy. It wasn't like I could go around all day showing people my bum.'

'Thank you for sharing that lovely story with us.' Kate pretended to be cross.

Dean laughed out loud, spitting cornflakes.

'Don't laugh at him, it only makes him worse.' Kate shook her head and waited for Dean to calm down before she changed the subject. 'Does a girl called Gina, Gina Godden or Grodden go to your school?'

As soon as she said the name Dean's head swivelled round and he looked at her, eyes wide. He swallowed, nodding, 'Gina Godden.'

'Do you know where she lives?'

He nodded again, his eyes never leaving her face.

Kate saw the start of a blush creeping up his neck towards his cheek. *Now what the hell was that about?* She glanced at Joan.

'Gina's only a couple of streets away, in Grant Road. I took her home once but I'm not sure what number she is, I think its four doors down on the left from this end.' Joan was trying to be helpful.

Kate was confused, 'Took her home?'

'We played computer games. She's good at the fighting ones but I'm much better than her at the racing ones, I beat her every time on the racing ones.' Dean was babbling.

Kate was intrigued. Andy's father had said that Gina Godden was Andy's girlfriend. Why would she be spending time with Dean playing computer games? Was Dean blushing because he had a crush on her?

'Gina's mum, Arlene, was on the school Activities Committee with me. She brought Gina round a few weeks back when we were planning the end of year school prom.' Joan tried to mop up the mess Dean had made. 'Dean was on his computer game and Gina ended up having a go. I invited her to stay for tea and took her home afterwards. I think she might be a bit sweet on our Dean.' Joan rolled her eyes, nodding at Dean as he tried to shrink to nothing from embarrassment. His neck was crimson.

'Do you know if Gina is friendly with Andy Frazier?' Kate asked.

'Hates his guts.' Dean's face shut down into a scowl, but for the briefest of moments Kate thought she saw a flicker of shock, or was it panic on his face? He avoided more questions by dragging Steve out into the garden.

Joan topped up Kate's coffee. 'Can I ask why you're looking for Gina?'

'Andy Frazier's dad thought she was his girlfriend.'

'Oh.' Joan looked troubled.

'What does 'Oh' mean?'

'It seems a bit odd, that's all. She called here on her own last week, or maybe it was the week before? Anyway, she's... well, you'll see what she's like when you meet her - you'll wonder why she'd want to come here. And to be honest I'm not that keen on her.'

'Really?' Kate waited,

'Oh Dean dotes on her, well he would do, but I don't know, this sounds a bit stupid but I think she's a bit cruel. She has a cruel streak hidden under a pretty face.'

Kate really wanted to meet Gina Godden.

The girl had the stature and build of a model. She was tall, stick thin, and had an elfin face under an ultra fashionable short haircut. When Gina Godden opened the door she was wearing tiny white hot pants with a soft blue t-shirt that hung loosely off one shoulder.

Her mother was a similar build but had bronze curls falling around her shoulders. The house was ex-council, but nicely done up and nothing like the home Andy Frazier came from. Mrs Godden looked confused and worried as Kate made the introductions and walked straight through the hall into the kitchen. She wanted to keep this casual; informal and the best place to do that was the kitchen.

'It's just a general enquiry really; maybe you can help us. We're looking for a boy called Andy Frazier - he goes to Gina's school. We were told they might know each other?' Kate was playing it out gently. She was pretty sure that Mrs Godden wouldn't approve of any kind of relationship between her daughter and Andy Frazier; let alone sleepovers at his place.

Mrs Godden looked at her daughter and for a second Gina took on the appearance of a rabbit caught in headlights. Kate knew she was right - Mrs Godden had no idea who Andy Frazier was and Gina didn't want her to know.

'I don't know him, I only see him at school sometimes.' Gina shrugged.

'I'm sorry,' Mrs Godden looked back at Kate, 'I think someone's mistaken. I don't know where you got your information from or what this is about, I've never heard of him.' She looked back at Gina. 'Is he in any of your classes?'

Gina shook her head vigorously, 'He's older than me. I told you, I don't know him.' She sucked on her lips nervously.

Kate could almost see the girl's heart pumping against her chest with nerves. 'Have you seen him since school broke up, maybe in town or somewhere?' She gave the girl a chance to cooperate.

Another vigorous shake of the head, 'No.' Gina wasn't looking at Kate, she was looking somewhere over Kate's shoulder towards Steve. It was an obvious lie. Kate saw Gina tilt her head and give Steve the benefit of her big cow eyes. *Bloody hell, she's trying to flirt with him.*

'What year are you in?' Kate was getting a really bad feeling about this.

Gina lowered her eyes, 'I'm going up to year ten.'

'Really? Do you have Drama classes with Mrs Ranu?' Kate was thinking furiously, trying to work out the class structure. She was pretty sure that if Gina was in year ten she was only thirteen, although she could be mistaken as a lot older.

Gina nodded, hope growing in her eyes, desperate to get away from the awkward questions.

'Well, when you get back to school, tell Mrs Ranu you met me and ask her about the man with the painted gloves.' Kate rolled her eyes mischievously. She was using distraction techniques; getting away from the subject of Gina's knowledge of Andy Frazier - she could come back to that later if she needed to. There was no way Gina was going to talk about him in front of her mother, not now. 'Sorry to have bothered you.' Kate smiled at Mrs Godden.

'I hope you find him.' Mrs Godden was relieved they were going.

'Bye Gina, and thanks again.' Kate nodded at the girl and gave her a look; a look that let Gina know that she knew, but she was on her side. 'Can I give you my card, just in case you're out and about and you spot him, or you need to call me?'

Gina took the card and showed them out.

Steve waited until they got in the car to give Kate his opinion. 'Frazier didn't dream her up, the girl's lying.'

Kate nodded, 'Because her mother doesn't know. You saw the house; the way they are, do you think Mrs Godden would encourage any sort of relationship between her daughter and Andy Frazier?'

'Fuck no! And if she were my daughter I'd lock her up until she's thirty. God, she's stunning – in a jail bait kind of way, but what's she doing hanging out with Dean Towle? That's bloody strange.'

Kate stuck her sunglasses on her head and gave him a long sideways look. 'And she's only thirteen.'

'Shit!' Steve couldn't get over it. He thought about it for a moment longer and shook his head in disbelief, 'Shit! No wonder Dean's got a thing for her. If a girl like that had played any sort of games with me when I was his age I'd have thought I'd died and gone to Heaven.'

'You mean you didn't have girls clamouring all over you when you were thirteen?' Kate was teasing him.

Steve swallowed hard and to Kate's amusement, started to look a bit self-conscious.

'Fat chance. Girls were a complete mystery to me until I was eighteen. Most of them still are.'

Kate swivelled in her seat, leant back against her door and looked at him, intrigued. 'So no big moments at the school disco?'

'I sort of missed the disco era. Wasn't that the seventies?' Steve kept his eyes on the road.

'Smart arse. The school dance, prom night, whatever it was that you were doing - same thing.'

Steve pulled a face. 'If you gave me a rugby ball I knew exactly what I was doing, but dancing? I looked like some sad cretin at that age. It was all about rugby for me, but the girls at my school only seemed to fancy the boys on the football squad.'

'So no snogging in the bike sheds then?' Kate was still laughing.

'I think it's called *making out* now, Gov.'

Kate threw him a sarcastic look and turned back to face the windscreen.

'So what about you?' Steve asked.

'What about me?'

'Any big moments *snogging* in the bike sheds?'

'I invented it.' Kate flicked her fringe out of her eyes, 'I was a trail blazer when it came to bike shed snogging, but we weren't talking about me.' She turned and grinned, teasing him again.

Steve frowned. He wondered why she was in such a funny mood today. 'If we'd met at school and been about the same age, I wouldn't have spoken to you – not in a million years,' he said, seriously.

'Why not?'

'You'd have frightened the living daylights out of me.'

***

CHAPTER TWENTY

J ohn Bishop checked his watch as he walked into the apartment
block. He didn't have long; he'd had to fake an emergency
family visit to get away from the office, and he needed to get
back in time for a case conference. He was starting to get rattled,
not seriously, not yet, but enough to make him need some
assurances. He pressed his hand over his nose and mouth to block
out the stench in the passageway. How the hell did these people
live like this? The smell was grossing him out, making him feel
nauseous. Animals had cleaner habits than this lot.

He banged on the apartment door and was glad he didn't have
to worry about Todd Martin being at home. The bloke was still on
the run - although Bishop had heard he hadn't gone far and was
still in the neighbourhood somewhere. He probably had to stay
close to home to get access to money and it would take a brave
person to turn him in. Bishop had dealt with Todd before, he was
an evil bastard, a big bloke with a nasty temper, and anyone who
had any sense gave him a wide berth.

Josie Martin opened the door just wide enough to eye him with
suspicion. She was struggling to keep a squirming baby on her hip
and made no move to let him in.

Bishop tried a smile. 'Hi, do you remember me? My name's
John, from the Social?'

Josie didn't return the smile. She hoisted the baby higher onto
her hip and cradled it under its bum with her free arm. The baby
stuck its finger in its mouth and stared at Bishop, eyes big with
curiosity.

'My mum's not in.' Josie leant forward, starting to shut the
door with her shoulder.

Bishop stuck his hand out and stopped her before she could

close it in his face. 'Just a second! I'm actually looking for Josh – just need a word with him about something. I don't need to see your mum.'

'I'm not allowed to let anyone in.' Josie said, and leant against the door much harder.

Bishop pushed back again. He wasn't about to be seen off. He was used to kids doing exactly what he told them, didn't she realise who he was?

'I'm not just anyone. Your mum knows me. I'm from Social Services – we've met before, remember?'

'No,' Josie's stare was hostile. 'We've got an alarm, right? And if I press the button the police will come right away. They'll be here in two minutes, right? Go away 'cos I'll push the button.' Josie put her shoulder against the door again and Bishop let go.

The door slammed in his face.

Bishop took a step back and stared at the door. Bloody kid slammed it on him! He kicked the door hard, anger and frustration getting the better of him, and then took a step back, hoping like hell he hadn't frightened her into pressing the alarm. He fumbled in his pocket for his fag packet, pulled one out and lit up. The kid deserved a good hiding. Serve her right if he took the lot of them into care. He dragged smoke down into his lungs and frowned. Had she pushed the panic button? Was she going to? He'd heard the police had installed alarms after Todd attacked his wife and kid. The last thing he needed was the police turning up, asking questions. He exhaled, blowing smoke up towards the ceiling as he thought about what to do. He realised he didn't even know if Josh was in there. The mother not being at home was a bonus though; saved him a lie by means of explanation for his visit, but no bloody use if he couldn't get inside.

He decided the girl was bluffing. She knew who he was; she wasn't about to summon the police. He'd just have to be a bit more persuasive. Without putting his cigarette out he stepped forward and used his right fist to knock sharply on the door three times, then he leant forward and listened. There was no sound from inside, no footsteps, no baby noises, and no telly even. He knocked again. 'Hello. Can I talk to you again for a second? You don't have to let me in, I just need to know where Josh is. Can you come to the door again please?'

Suddenly he heard sirens approaching, fast. They must already be on the estate. He hurried outside and saw the first Patrol car just screeching to a halt fifty feet away. As he walked towards it the doors were thrown open and two uniformed police officers jumped out.

'Sorry lads, sorry, false alarm!' He spread his hands out in front of him and tried to keep the smile on his face. 'Misunderstanding. I'm John Bishop, Team Leader on the foster care section of Social Services. I'm here for a welfare visit. There's nothing to worry about. I've got identification – and that's my car behind you. Josie just got a bit mixed up that's all... and her mother's not in.'

A loud scream made them all turn towards the adjacent apartment block. Patricia Martin was running towards them at full pelt, her eyes wild, and her hair streaming behind her, closely followed by another woman dressed in a matching outfit of sprayed on jeans and tank top.

'What the hell's happened? What's happened?' Patricia didn't stop or wait for an answer. She nearly knocked Bishop over as she barged past him and into the building. He could hear her yelling for Josie as she disappeared.

By the time he'd given his details and a grovelling explanation to one of the officers - which he seemed to accept, and the other officer had checked Josie's version of the 'emergency', a small group of onlookers had gathered and Bishop was seething. So much for being discreet, it was a frigging circus! He nearly bit his tongue when he apologised to Patricia for causing alarm, and was told that Josh was out fishing with his mates and not expected back until much later. He knew it was a lie. Josie watched him, a smug look all over her face, when he had no option but to leave them alone. As he climbed back into his car he spotted the message light flashing on his mobile and realised he'd missed a couple of calls, both from his office. Probably wondering where the hell he was, he thought as he retrieved the last message.

Your Case Conference has been cancelled today and will be re-scheduled for next week. A Detective Chief Inspector Stacey is trying to reach you – can you give him a call please? He said you have the number, but just in case it's...

Bishop deleted the message, sat back in his seat and chewed on his bottom lip. Perfect. He had time to look for the boy. And DCI Stacey could go to hell.

It was thirty minutes later, as he turned the corner at the back of the deserted market place that his luck changed. He spotted Josh Martin on the right hand side of the narrow alleyway. The boy was slouched over with his back against the wall, smoking a fag - and he was alone. If he hadn't taken a short cut he would never have seen him. Bishop took a quick look around; there was no one nearby. As he pulled over the boy looked up quickly, recognised him and almost took off, but Bishop had had enough pissing about for one day. The boy had left it too late and Bishop was out of the car and had him by the arm before he could run. Without saying a word he yanked open the passenger door and bundled the boy into the car.

Josh sat back in his seat, scowling and sullen, his eyes following Bishop as he strode around the front of the vehicle and climbed into the driver's seat.

Bishop pushed his seat back as far as it would go and turned the whole bulk of his torso to face the boy. 'Where's Eddie Lead?' He demanded.

'How the fuck would I know?' Josh said, his voice angry.

Bishop punched him in the face.

By late morning Kate was jumping out of her skin with frustration. She hadn't found Andy Frazier, Bisby Alouni or the mobile phone. Everywhere they'd been they'd come up empty handed. Kate didn't know where else to look and she really didn't want to report back to Stacey that they'd got nothing. She leant against the car, tilted her face to the sun and called the Incident Room to get an update. Ginger answered. His voice sounded distant, distracted. She guessed she'd interrupted him from a long spell at his computer.

'Search team has given an interim report but there doesn't seem to be a lot to get excited about. The fingertip search has finished with the path at the back of Pink's house but they didn't get much. They're also working in all the neighbouring gardens along that row but it looks a bit bleak - the ground all around the scene is rock hard from the glorious weather we've been enjoying.'

Kate heard the note of sarcasm. None of the team had been enjoying the hot weather, they were too busy, and Ginger was cooped up in the incident room at a desk all day.

'There was one item from the garden, a pair of sunglasses, found just outside what's left of the shed. Mrs Pink has been asked, but they're not hers or the victim's. Some stuff has been picked up from the path at the back - empty fag packet, cigarette butts, and a few bits of paper, general trash. But it's a public path, so they're not too hopeful. Everything's gone to forensics.'

'What sort of sunglasses?'

'Sorry?' Ginger sounded a bit blank.

'I said what sort of sunglasses? What make, what do they look like?' Kate was frowning into her phone. There was a pause and she heard papers being shuffled and a chair scraping against the tiled floor. She pinched her bottom lip between her thumb and index finger as she waited.

'Brown tortoise shell - large frames, cheap stuff. Someone's been tasked with identifying them, but the DCI wants you to check with Dean Towle first.'

'I'm pretty sure the answer is no, but give me five minutes and I'll call you back.' Kate cut the connection, pulled up her contacts list and redialled.

Joan picked up after the second ring. 'I was just about to call you, but I wasn't sure if I should. I don't want to sound wet but I'm a bit stuck, not really sure what to do.' She was babbling.

'Ok,' Kate said cautiously, 'what's the problem?'

'Gina rang here about an hour after you left. She wants Dean to meet her in Scrub Park.'

Kate frowned. She'd thought from their earlier conversation that Gina only came over to Joan's house to play computer games, but she hadn't explored the matter very much because she was only interested in Gina as a means to finding Andy Frazier. 'Has he been out to meet her before?' She asked.

'Well I've only just found out, but yes, he has. When I hesitated about letting him go he told me he'd met her there before.'

Kate heard the disbelief in Joan's voice and she couldn't blame her. Playing computer games was one thing - but for her to want to meet Dean outside? 'Does he want to go?' Kate still wasn't sure what the problem was.

'He's desperate to go, but he's nervous and I'm not happy. What if he's getting set up?'

'In what way, what do you mean?'

'Well it just seems odd. What if she's up to something, shall I let him go?'

Kate thought about it. There might be something in the fact that Gina called Dean after she and Steve had paid her a visit, but she couldn't see what harm could come from him meeting her. In any case, Steve could always ask him about it later. Maybe he'd open up a bit more to him.

'It doesn't make sense Kate, you saw her didn't you? What do you think?'

'I honestly don't know,' Kate was truthful, 'I understand what you're saying, but I can't see how he would come to any harm. We haven't found Andy Frazier, but I think he's running from us and he's not stupid enough to go after Dean again.'

There was silence as Joan struggled to make a decision, then she turned and yelled, 'Dean! If you still want to go, get your shoes on.' Kate heard Dean making loud whooping noises in the background.

Kate asked about the sunglasses. Joan confirmed what she already knew: Dean didn't own any sunglasses.

'But I have got another bit of news. After getting all stroppy and digging his heels in when you asked him about consenting to a medical, he's sort of come round.'

'Really? So he's said he'll do it?'

'He said he doesn't want to – keeps insisting he's alright and Pink didn't hurt him, but he asked me if Steve would go with him if he said yes, or if you had to go. I told him Steve would take him. I hope that's ok. It is isn't it?' Joan was anxious.

'Of course Steve can take him.' Kate was relieved. She told Joan to call her anytime she needed to talk and hung up.

'What?' Steve was intrigued.

'It would appear that dreams do come true. Dean is meeting Gina in the park, and not for the first time.' She spread her hands out in a 'beats me' gesture. 'And he's consenting to a medical as long as you go with him.'

Kate called Ginger back and gave him the update, and then she pulled her mind back to the problem of finding Andy Frazier and making sense of his connection with the case. What tied Dean Towle, Andy Frazier, Bisby Alouni and Josh Martin together? Had they all been victims of George Pink? She couldn't think how The

Toad could fit into the picture; he was the odd one out in every way.

Dean Towle had been groomed by Pink and had been given money and a new sports bag. Pink had been killed on a day when Dean was visiting him. Dean believed Andy and Josh had also visited Pink before, but he hadn't mentioned Bisby Alouni - and Josh and Andy both had expensive new trainers. Bisby Alouni was also the odd one out in that he came from a better home background than the others. Maybe he was just Andy's henchman.

Bugger! Kate suddenly realised what else linked the boys. She should have thought about it earlier, when Steve asked about their home conditions. She pulled her mobile phone from the back pocket of her jeans again and speed dialled.

Steve waited, watching her with interest. She was suddenly animated, her fingers flicking impatiently as she waited for the call to be picked up.

'Mivvie, are you in the office? Great, I need a favour. Josh Martin was taken into care briefly earlier this year. I think it was for a couple of weeks at Easter, and then Patricia got him back. Has Andy Frazier ever been in foster care, or Bisby Alouni? Can you find out and call me back? Cheers.' She snapped the phone shut.

'Patricia had a bit of a melt down last year - well, more than normal.' She turned to Steve, her sunglasses slid down her sunburnt nose as she explained. 'Josh pushed her buttons once too often. She'd had a drink and she punched him in the face; gave him a black eye and a cut on his cheek where her ring had caught him.'

Steve was impressed. 'Shame she couldn't find a bit more of that when Todd was around.'

Kate grinned. 'Anyway, the school rang us and Josh spent a couple of weeks with foster carers until things had calmed down and Patricia got help from everyone under the sun. I'm sure Andy Frazier was in a similar situation recently but I don't know about Bisby... and all these boys go to the Community Centre. Come on.' She turned and grabbed the car door handle.

Steve clicked the remote and opened it for her. 'Where are we going?'

'To talk to Lion.'

***

CHAPTER TWENTY ONE

The Lion wasn't what Kate was expecting at all, but then she wasn't really sure what she'd been expecting. In contrast to Steve's solid bulk of muscle he was slim and athletic looking in baggy shorts and a t-shirt. He couldn't match Steve for height, but he wasn't far short. Kate noticed a few flecks of grey in the close cropped dark hair and judged him to be in his late thirties or early forties. She made the introductions.

'Do you mind if we sit outside?' She led the way over to the grassy area and a picnic table with wooden benches at the back of the sports hall.

He brushed the seat off politely for her and asked if she would prefer the shade of an umbrella. Kate saw Steve give her a sarcastic sideways look. 'You're called the Lion? Something about a sword - anything I should be concerned about?' She smiled at him, ignoring Steve.

He threw his head back and laughed, 'Fencing, I fence. It's not a sword it's a foil, and my name's Richard Hart. Some kids kicked off the 'Richard the Lion Heart' tag and it stuck, but it was a bit of a mouthful so it got shortened over time to 'Lion'. Call me Rick.'

'Are you any good?' Steve gave Rick a direct look.

'National Team a couple of years back.' Rick held the look.

'I'm impressed.' Kate saw the two men sizing each other up, but she didn't have time for macho bullshit. 'Right then, Andy Frazier and Bisby Alouni.'

'Yes, I'm sorry about what happened to Dean - Joan called me. How is he? I take it it's not too serious?' Rick's face creased with concern.

Kate shook her head, 'A badly grazed face where it was shoved

127

into the pavement, but it could have been worse. Can I ask you some questions? Were Andy Frazier and Bisby Alouni in the Club that afternoon? Did something kick off earlier?'

'No, Andy definitely wasn't playing. Not that day. He comes and goes, and I see him hanging about quite often, but he doesn't use the Club regularly. Bisby Alouni was here. He was playing football with Dean, but there wasn't anything... at least nothing that I saw, or was aware of. Dean seemed ok, if a bit quiet. Philip had dropped him off and I spoke to him before he left. I mean; I knew what had happened to Dean at Pink's house so I was surprised to see him. Philip said he wanted to play and it would do him good; take his mind off things, so I just let him get on with it. I didn't want to draw attention to him, or make him feel awkward and he was chuffed to bits with his new shirt.'

Kate smiled, 'He really was. Does Andy or Bisby hang around with anyone else in particular?'

Rick leant back, stretching upwards and clasping both hands behind his head. Kate's eyes were drawn to his smooth flat stomach as his t-shirt rose up. She quickly lifted her eyes and looked back at his face.

Rick shook his head. 'Bisby Alouni is cocky and makes out he's a bit of a 'hood', but its all front. He hangs off Andy's shirttails and Andy uses him; treats him like a lackey when it suits him. Andy's only got mates because he's occasionally got money and he likes to show off.'

Kate nodded, 'What do you know about George Pink?'

Rick looked down at the table, his face troubled. 'He was working here before I started helping out with the coaching. He was a part time handyman cum Gardener. I always took him to be a bit of an old woman.' He lifted his face and his eyes met Kate's, 'I don't mean to be unkind now that the bloke's dead, but he was a job's worth; always making a bit of a drama over things. I tried not to get too involved with him to be honest.'

'Did you see him spending time with any of the boys in particular?' Kate was trying to decide how much to tell him.

'In what way?' He looked from Kate to Steve and back again. 'Oh, shit. Don't tell me he was one of those? Shit! Is that right, was he? Shit!'

Kate suddenly felt sorry for him. Normal heterosexual adult

men don't understand how another grown man could be interested sexually in young boys. It was abhorrent to them. And the boys in question were young boys that Rick knew; boys he worked with, trying to keep them off the streets and out of trouble.

'I'm sorry, but I can only tell you that we're following a line of enquiry that suggests he may have had reasons for working here other than his love of gardening.'

Rick looked as though he'd been punched in the stomach. All the air went out of him and he slumped forward onto his elbows, pushing his hands through his short hair. 'Oh for fuck's sake!' He suddenly exploded. 'Sorry Kate, but that's awful. Shit! Dean... that's where Dean got the bag wasn't it? The one he told Joan I'd given him? Was Pink doing something with Dean?'

Kate looked at him glumly, and gave him a moment to calm down. 'We don't know the extent of what was happening; whether there was any serious sexual activity between Pink and Dean or anyone else for that matter. But we have information that suggests Pink may have been grooming boys that he was attracted to. If you can tell us anything... '

'Dean's good. He's really good. Did you know that?' Rick interrupted, 'He's a really talented footballer. I'm trying to get him into somewhere where he'll get proper coaching. If he keeps developing the way he is he'll be good enough for a trial with a club. He's quick; runs like a demon, an awesome little player. I hope this won't knock him back.' Rick was obviously fond of Dean.

'He ran circles around me.' Steve grinned ruefully.

'Is he going to be ok?' Rick looked at Kate.

'We hope so. He's getting the proper help. Look, what I've just told you – it's confidential, but what can you tell us about George Pink? There might be something that didn't seem important at the time, but might have seemed a bit odd, anything?'

Rick thought about it, 'He was always here on the afternoons that the boys play football, so when we were outside inevitably he'd be working around us. Did you meet him, before?'

Kate and Steve both shook their heads. 'Well, he was a typical old Bodger. He'd wait for me to come in so that he could make a fuss about something. I used to dread having to talk to him to be honest. He didn't work for me but he acted as though I was his boss, almost bowing and scraping, doffing his cap like. He fawned over the female members of staff too, opening doors, carrying stuff from their cars. We all took the mickey out of him because of his trousers. It became a standing joke.'

Kate's ears pricked up, 'What was wrong with his trousers?'

'They were ridiculous, he had... hang about.' He jumped up and disappeared back inside the centre, returning two minutes later with a ten by six inch print in his hand. He handed it to Kate. Steve shoved up along the bench so that he could look at it with her.

'The under fourteen team had got their new sponsored shirts and Pink managed to get himself in the photo.' Rick pointed.

A group of grinning boys were lined up in two rows, a typical team pose, with Rick standing at one end and George Pink standing just slightly apart from the group on the other end. Kate spotted Dean Towle in the middle of the back row, and a couple of other boys she knew. Pink was wearing a checked shirt, red tie, and a pair of very shapeless baggy blue trousers held up with a belt and tucked into the tops of black wellies. She had only seen pictures of him after he'd been killed so she studied him closely. He had a smooth round face under a tuft of grey hair that was too long over his ears. He stood ram rod straight, his left hand rested on the shoulder of boy nearest to him, his right hand was in his pocket.

'How long ago was this?' Steve asked.

'Not that long ago, Easter time maybe, I can always check if you need the exact date.' Rick looked from Steve to Kate. 'You could have got three of him in those trousers they were so baggy. He wore the same pair every time I saw him.'

Kate nodded, solemnly. She knew exactly why Pink was so fond of his trousers. 'There's a reason for those.' she said, 'Look what he's doing with his hands.' She passed the photo over for Rick to look at it again.

He studied the photo then looked up at her, puzzled, 'I don't get it.'

'He's probably aroused,' Kate said, quietly. 'It's easier in baggy trousers. And he's got physical contact with the boy next to him.'

Rick closed his eyes, screwed up his face and threw the photo onto the table. 'That's sick! And we were laughing at him, telling him to tell his wife his proper waist size next time she shopped for him. That's Tommy Bowden next to him. He was only here for a couple of months before his family moved away.

Steve got his notebook out and started scribbling. Kate asked if she could hold on to the photo for a while. Rick nodded and handed it over to Steve.

'Did he ever do work inside when you were here? Was he ever in the changing rooms with the boys?' Kate asked.

'Yes, of course he was. He was just always around. As I said, I tried not to get too involved with him.' Rick's head suddenly jerked up and he met Kate's look. 'He would have been CRB checked to work here, everyone is. Isn't that supposed to throw up anyone who's on the sex offender's register?'

'Only if they've been caught and the evidence against them allows it.' Kate didn't mention the previous arrest and the fact that it had gone nowhere.

'So no bloody use if you're a clever bastard.' Rick was devastated. 'What else can I tell you?'

'We can't find Andy Frazier or Bisby Alouni. Do you have any idea where they might be?'

Rick was looking over her shoulder. 'Well don't look now, but Bisby Alouni is over there, behind you. He's got Josh Martin with him.'

Kate and Steve spun around. Josh and Bisby saw them and stopped dead. For a heartbeat and a half everyone froze and then Bisby took off running with Josh right behind him. Steve got his legs tangled up getting off the picnic bench - giving Kate a head start.

'Stop, Bisby, wait!' She shouted. She had no idea why Josh Martin was running, but the two boys were fleeing as fast as they could. She got to the path leading from the car park just as they veered left and started towards some industrial units. Josh was trailing slightly but was running flat out. Kate could hear Steve pounding up behind her. 'Go left!' she pointed and shouted over her shoulder, 'Block them off!'

From her right she was surprised to see Rick racing like a sprinter around the other side of the squat single storey buildings. They were closing in on three sides.

Suddenly both boys disappeared from view and Kate realised there was a gap between the units. Shit! She had no idea where it led, or if they could escape out the other side. She pushed herself forward, breathing hard but steady. As she got closer she could see that a narrow concrete passage cut through the brick built units. The sunlight didn't penetrate the cut through and as she raced into the opening she was plunged into darkness, but she didn't slow up. She'd wasted half the bloody day already; she was damned if she was going to lose them now. A dozen yards further and she exited back into bright daylight. It was so sudden that for a moment she was blinded and she had to pull up to get her bearings. She was in a large concreted yard. Several loading docks for forklifts opened against the units on her left, double high roller doors were on her right. She stood still for a moment, catching her breath. There was no sign of them.

'Kate!' Rick vaulted over a fence off to her right. He was gesturing frantically, one hand pointing high and to his right towards a row of large waste storage dumpsters at the back of the yard.

Kate ran. Where the hell was Steve? She saw Rick circling around the back of the dumpsters, crossing the ground fast. There was enough space between each dumpster to fit through so Kate went for the centre of the row. She glanced to her right and saw Rick gesturing again. He was pointing up – pointing at something over the containers. Had he seen them climb up? She found a metal access ladder on the side of the dumpster nearest to her and grabbed a rung. She was half way up when she heard it; a loud scraping noise, something sliding. She scrambled up, reached the last rung and stuck her head over the top just in time to see Bisby disappear from view on the other side, ten feet away from her. Swearing under her breath she scrambled backwards and jumped the last four feet to the ground, racing back the way she had come.

Bisby was crossing the yard trying to double back but there was no sign of Josh. Before Bisby reached the entrance to the cut through Steve exploded out of it, cutting him off. Obviously there was no way through on the other side of the buildings and he'd had to turn back to follow them. Kate found Rick alongside her - they had the boy trapped. Bisby skidded to a halt, almost falling but just managing to stay upright. Steve and Rick both shouted at him at the same time and Kate put her arms out, like a goalie, hedging him in from behind.

Bisby twisted right, catching Steve unawares. He ran flat out towards the building and leapt into the air, landing heavily on a low brick power-housing unit. He reached out with both hands, grabbed onto the network of piping above him and pulled himself up, climbing.

Kate realised the danger and shouted. 'Bisby! Don't be stupid! Stay still!'

He kept going, scrambling up until he ran out of pipe just short of the roof. Stretching up he got one hand, then the other up onto the flat roof and hauled himself over.

'Steve, go back the other side, see if there's a way down.' Kate's heart was thumping as she flicked her phone open and called for backup. Shading her eyes, she walked the short length of the building, scanning the roof, Rick in step beside her.

Where the hell was he?

Suddenly a loud crack rang out. Bisby screamed and there was the awful sound of glass breaking. Kate's heart jumped into her throat and she yelled, 'BISBY!'

Silence.

'He's fallen! Steve!'

Steve was already running back towards her.

'How do we get in?' She turned to Rick.

He shook his head, 'It's locked up.'

'Window!' Kate dashed towards the building, her phone in one hand calling for an ambulance as she ran.

Steve got there before her. The window was a couple of feet off the ground and covered with a thin wire mesh - it didn't look that solid. Steve looked up. There was a metal pipe running along the top. Grabbing it with both hands he pulled himself up, balanced one foot against the building and kicked at the mesh with the other. Rick followed his lead, jumping up onto the other side. Both men threw all their weight into kicking at the mesh as hard as they could.

'Where is he? Where is he? Is he dead?' Josh appeared at Kate's side, shouting, almost hysterical.

Kate grabbed his shoulder and pulled him around to face her. There was a large red swelling on one side of his mouth, but she didn't have time to ask him about it. 'We're going to find him, ok? It's ok, go over there and sit down.' She pointed at the grass verge at the side of the yard.

Josh didn't move; he looked terrified.

'Go over there and sit down.' Kate made him look at her. 'Stay there, do you hear me? Do not move until I come and get you. We'll find him.' She gave his shoulder a shake and he did what he was told. She turned back just as the window gave in.

Rick took his t-shirt off, wrapped it around his hand and pushed out the larger bits of glass that remained. Steve went in first, turning to give Rick a hand through. Kate ran over to join them.

'BISBY!' She shouted into the gloom. 'Can you hear me? BISBY!'

Silence.

***

CHAPTER TWENTY TWO

The boy was face down and motionless; arms splayed out either side of his head. Steve got to him first. He bent down to check the boy's breathing and Bisby stirred as Steve touched him. Kate took a deep breath in and blew it out again.

He's alive.

She looked up and saw the broken skylight high above them.

'Stay still mate, ok? Don't try and move. Can you talk to me?' Steve leant over the boy, his hand gently pressing down on his shoulder.

Bisby groaned. He opened his eyes and tried to push himself up on his hands.

Kate saw his legs move as he struggled to get to sit up. Thank God! At least he's not paralysed. She dropped to her knees by his side. 'Stay still Bisby. You're going to be ok; everything's going to be ok. Just keep still while Steve checks you over, if you've hurt your back you might make it worse. Can you tell us what hurts?' She spoke calmly, reassuring him, they had to keep him quiet until help arrived. She turned to Rick; he was standing to one side looking as worried as anyone could. 'See if you can find me a blanket, anything like that.' She told him.

He nodded, grateful to have a job.

Bisby coughed, screwed up his face and winced with the effort, 'Me knee, me knee,' he struggled to roll onto his side, breathing heavily, 'I've done something to me knee, and my bum hurts.' He pointed back towards his left leg, 'I want to get up - I can get up.'

'He must have landed on his backside and bounced,' Steve looked at Kate, relief all over his face. 'It's a good job you've got some padding back there.' He told Bisby.

Where's my phone?' Bisby was reaching behind him.

'Sorry.' Kate wasn't sure she'd heard him right. 'Don't worry, we'll call your mum, just hang on and keep still for a moment.'

'My phone, it's in my side pocket. If it aint broken take a photo. I've got a six megapixel camera.'

Kate couldn't believe it. He'd just fallen through a roof, was lucky to be alive and all he could think of was getting a photo of it to show to his mates.

'What do you think you're going to do with it? Put it on Facebook or YouTube? Make yourself famous?' She was teasing him, keeping him alert and occupied. There was still the danger he could slip into shock.

Steve shook his head at her, 'I can't find anything broken. He says nothing on his back or neck hurts. Apart from that bump on his head, a bruised bum and what looks like a sprained knee he seems to have got off bloody lightly.'

Bisby looked up at Kate and grinned. 'I flew, man, I flew!'

Kate burst out laughing.

None of their efforts to keep him lying down did any good. By the time the paramedics and a couple of uniformed police turned up he was sitting up wrapped in the large padded coat Rick had found in a cupboard. Steve followed the ambulance to the hospital, while Kate phoned Bisby's mum and arranged for a car to pick her up and take her to meet them. When the ambulance left she sent Josh home in a police car with the promise to talk to him later and she found herself alone with Rick. He was still bare-chested, having thrown his t-shirt in a bin.

Standing in the yard in the sunshine he looked down at Kate's jeans. She was covered in grease and dirt from climbing on the dumpsters and she'd touched her face and some of it had rubbed off her hands onto her cheek.

'Why don't you walk back with me?' His eyes creased up at the corners as he grinned at her, 'You can get cleaned up and I can find another t-shirt to cover my modesty.'

'Have you got a kettle?' Kate kept her face serious.

'Yes.'

'Coffee?'

Rick narrowed his eyes, perplexed. 'Yes.'

'Thank God.' Kate gave an exaggerated sigh, flashed him a quick smile and took off at a fast walk.

He jogged after her. 'I've actually got an espresso machine and a choice of Turkish, Arabic or Columbian blends. It's in my office; I'm a bit of a snob when it comes to coffee.'

Kate stopped suddenly and spun to face him.

'I might just have to marry you.' She told him.

Most of the grease came off her face. There was nothing she could do about her clothes so she didn't bother trying, and the glorious smell of Columbian coffee brewing was driving her crazy. Rick's office was opposite the main sports hall. She helped herself to the coffee and sipping at it gratefully, plonked herself down in a small battered armchair in the corner.

'I thought you police types only drank tea.' Rick said.

'You thought wrong.'

'What's going to happen next?' He looked intently at her.

'Bisby will be spoken to about the assault on Dean when he's given the all clear from the hospital. I'll find Andy and arrest him and I'll try and figure out what all this is about.'

'What about Josh?'

'He ran because Bisby did. He's not very bright. I'll talk to him later when he's had a chance to calm down.'

'Don't you want to hit someone?'

'Sorry?'

'Child abuse; people like George Pink. Don't you want to hit someone? I just think it would make me feel like that, like thumping someone.'

Kate shook her head. 'No, it doesn't. And I couldn't do my job if it did. We have a motto in my office; 'Victim safe, villain confesses', that's the aim. If I can go home at night knowing that a child who was in danger is now safe, then I'm happy. If I can lock up the villain by getting a confession and prevent the victim from having to give evidence in court, then I'm very happy. That's it.'

She got up and helped herself to some more coffee, aware that he was studying her.

'That all sounds very professional, but I'm sure it's not as simple as that.'

'I try not to overcomplicate it,' She told him, 'by the time I get involved I'm dealing with history. What's happened has happened, and although child abuse is not like any other sort of criminal behaviour, I am a criminal investigator. My job is to investigate – not to get wrapped up in the psychology of why abusers do what they do. And there's an army of professionals lined up to help the victim. If I got emotionally wound up, involved with the victims or their families, I couldn't do my job. With the number of cases that we deal with any sort of emotional entanglement would be a short ride to a nervous breakdown. The only way to remain sane and to have any impact is to 'DIP', detect, investigate, prosecute – and move on.'

Rick watched her as she made this speech, impressed, but still unconvinced at how she could do what she did and not have some emotional fall out. 'What about George Pink?' He asked, 'Did someone take the law into their own hands do you think? Someone who knew what he was doing?'

Kate turned to face him. She realised she liked him; his charm, the way he'd jumped into action with no hesitation, his intelligent questions. 'What was Pink doing? We don't really know...' Kate didn't finish the sentence; her mobile phone ringing distracted her. Excusing herself she stepped out into the hallway.

'Josh Martin was in foster care for a month with the Matheson family last April. Andy Frazier was in foster care with the Murphy's for three weeks in May.' It was Mivvie Levin, calling back with the information Kate needed.

'Bisby Alouni?'

'No, not on our books, I don't know anything about him.'

'Well he's just fallen through a roof and is on his way to hospital with a bruised bum and a sprained knee...'

'What? What the hell happened? Is he something to do with George Pink?' Mivvie interrupted.

'It's a long story. Can you come to the Martin's with me, Steve's at the hospital?' Kate suddenly realised she didn't have any transport, but Mivvie didn't mind picking her up. She stepped back into Rick's office as soon as she'd hung up and apologised for the interruption.

'Desperately important detective stuff?' He was teasing her.

Kate gave him her sarcastic look, 'I only do desperately important detective stuff. I've got a badge and everything.'

'Well I'd like to help.' He was serious again. 'If there's anything I can do.'

'Thanks.' Kate narrowed her eyes at him. 'If you find Andy Frazier for me I'll definitely marry you.'

Patricia Martin was chain smoking and edgy. Something had changed. Kate and Mivvie exchanged looks as they made their way down the hall and into the sitting room. The baby was busy entertaining herself on the floor with an old rubber flip flop so Mivvie scooped her up and perched on the settee with her on her knee.

'He's got the shakes. He thought his mate, Bisby were dead.' Patricia told them. 'Josh don't want to talk to you, but he ain't pissing me about any more.' She disappeared behind the kitchen partition.

Darren suddenly erupted into the room - he was signing to Kate, shouting 'Wurghh, wurghh,' in his funny little voice, desperate to tell her something

Kate couldn't keep up. She recognised 'Dad' and 'see' or 'look', but that was it. She put both her hands out and lowered them slowly towards the floor. Slow down,

Josie walked in behind her little brother and spun him round to look at her. She watched him for twenty seconds and then shrugged, nonchalantly. 'He says he's seen his dad.'

Kate shot Patricia a look, but the woman didn't flinch. 'He's making it up,' she said, casually. 'He thinks he sees him all the time, I think he dreams it.'

Kate wasn't going to let it go at that. 'Where, when? Ask him Josie. Where and when did he see his dad?'

Before Josie could respond, Patricia cut in, 'He aint seen him. No-one has.'

But Darren was nodding his head, pleading with Kate for understanding.

'Where, when?' Josie signed. Darren looked down at his feet as though the answer was on the floor. Everyone waited. When Darren looked up he locked his eyes on Kate and his little hands flew, signing frantically. Josie used the same sign back at him, 'The Castle?'

He nodded excitedly, 'Wurgh!'

'See, told you he was making it up.' Patricia said. Josie was shaking her head at Darren in disbelief. Darren looked as though he was going to cry.

Kate picked him up and swung him round, making him squeal. 'You're a good boy.' She told him, although she knew he couldn't hear her. She tickled him, making him squirm and giggle. His long blond hair smelt dirty and his shorts were hand me downs, but for a moment at least, he was happy.

Josh walked in carrying a can of cheap fizzy drink. He popped the ring pull, slurped noisily and belched. Kate winced, she couldn't help it - Josh was obnoxious.

'I aint told 'em.' Patricia said to him, 'But you will, or I'll clobber your head again.'

Josh's face took on a look of sulky defiance.

'What do you need to tell me?' Kate knew Patricia meant it.

'I went to Pink the Perv's place, he give me a tenner. I was supposed to do garden stuff, but when I saw the shed I legged it.'

Kate stared at him. What did he mean about the shed? 'Start at the beginning, when did this happen?'

Josh couldn't meet her eyes. 'Easter maybe, I was off school and I weren't suspended, so it must have been Easter holiday.'

Easter - that was April. Josh was in foster care last April. Kate glanced across at Mivvie - she nodded. 'Was it when you were staying with the Matheson's?'

Josh thought about it. 'I suppose, Yeh, that's right, I walked there from that prison house where I was supposed to be staying.' He threw a disgusted look in Mivvie's direction. 'Stupid waste of time that was. Bloody social don't know nothing.'

Mivvie looked at him blankly, refusing to bite.

Kate ignored the sarcasm and nodded, encouraging him to go on.

'That's it,' Josh shrugged again and sniffed loudly, 'Pink said he'd give me a tenner - so I went back to his place with him.'

'Was anyone else with you when he asked you?'

'No.' Josh didn't even try to think about it.

Kate moved on. 'Explain to me what happened when you got there.'

'He took me to the shed, like I told you. It were filthy; sex stuff. I told him I weren't doing nothing for him, like, and he could

140

give me the money he'd promised or I'd get the policeon him.'
That was better.

'What did you see in the shed, Josh?' She tried to maintain eye contact, but his eyes slid away.

'Pictures of some boys in their pants. Magazine stuff, like. He had loads of it. And there was lights; like Christmas lights, around the ceiling, and a stupid poncy chair he wanted me to sit on.' 'What was wrong with the chair?'

'It were a big wooden thing, like a rocking chair thing, but for two people. Stupid gay thing.'

Kate didn't react. She was watching Josh closely, was he telling the truth this time? Why was the chair so important? 'Describe it to me.'

'I can't.' Josh shrugged.'

But Kate wasn't letting it go at that, 'Try.'

'It had big curly ends and the bit where you sit was a funny shape - not flat.' He made a scooping motion with one hand and then wiped his nose on the sleeve of his hoody.

'Get some bog roll!' Patricia shouted at him,

Josh shuffled off down the hall and Kate shifted her weight. She was getting cramp in her knees sitting on the beanbag with Darren. Mickey had gone to sleep on Mivvie's lap. When Josh came back Mivvie patted the space next to her on the settee, 'Plonk yourself down here.'

'The chair, was it something he'd made?' Kate tried to get him talking again.

He thought about it for a moment. 'Don't think so, looked like it came like that.'

Kate made a mental note. 'What was said Josh? What did he ask you to do?'

'He never had a chance to ask me to do nothing. I wouldn't sit on the chair with him and he got scared when I said about the cops.'

'What did he say?' Kate was pushing for details.

'Told me I was special. He said he'd always noticed me. He said I was like Brian, that he could look at me and remember about Brian, he kept blabbing on, like, wouldn't let up about it. He kept trying to put his arm around me; trying to cuddle me, like. Stupid tosser.'

'Do you know who Brian is?' Kate looked across at Patricia, but the woman was watching her son.

'Nope.' Josh belched again.

The baby woke up but Mivvie ignored her, all eyes were on Josh. Kate knew there was more.

'He cried. When I told him to fuck off he started bawling like a baby. He were looking at sommat in a tin when I legged it, holding it like it were precious or sommat, with big stupid tears running down his fat face. He never even wiped 'em, he just stood there crying.'

Mivvie pulled out a packet of Marlboro Lights, and offered one to Pat before lighting her own. Josh looked across hopefully, but the packet went back in Mivvie's pocket.

'What did the tin look like?'

'Just an old metal thing.' Josh shrugged.

'What was inside, what was he looking at?' Kate was thinking about the mouth organ they'd found in an old tin in the burnt out shed. If that was what Pink was crying over then it definitely a keepsake, something that reminded Pink of something or someone very special to him.

'Dunno, didn't look.' Josh was kicking his heel against something behind him, making an irritating thumping noise.

'How many times did you go to Pink's garden?'

'That were it.'

Kate was sure he was lying. 'Josh, it's very important that you tell the truth. What did George Pink ask you to do? Why were you there?'

Josh didn't blink, 'He wanted me to sit on the stupid chair with him, but I never.'

'Was there anything else he wanted you to do? Was there anything else that made you uncomfortable?' Kate pushed it.

Josh grinned and then touched his face where it was swollen at the side of his mouth as though it hurt him to smile. 'No. He gave me a tenner out of his money box and were still crying when I left.'

Patricia got up from the table and crossed to where her son was sitting. Before Josh realised what was coming she smacked him across the back of his head.

Josh yelped. 'What were that for?' he scooted sideway trying to get out of her reach.

'Lying to Kate before. Now, get out and don't come back till I calls you.'

Josh bolted for the door.

Kate needed to ask him something before he disappeared. 'Did you tell your dad about this? Did you tell Todd about George Pink?'

The boy paused in the doorway, 'Dunno, can't remember, maybe.' He was gone.

'More tea?' Patricia asked.

Kate and Mivvie looked at each other. They both shook heir heads.

'If you keep using physical violence against Josh you're going to get into serious trouble, and I know you don't want that.' Kate said, softly. 'How did he get that bruise on his face?'

Patricia shrugged, giving Kate a direct look, 'Ask him, he come home with it.' Kate knew the woman was telling the truth, Patricia wasn't afraid to admit to smacking Josh. But if she hadn't hit Josh in the face – what had happened to him?

***

CHAPTER TWENTY THREE

Mivvie's office was deserted. Kate asked where everyone was.

'Buggered off to lunch, but as you never eat you'd have no idea what that is.' Mivvie smirked. 'I've got lunch.' Kate held out her cup of coffee.

They were searching through the files looking for Brian, the boy Pink had told both Josh and Dean about. Kate was convinced that, whoever he was, Brian was *The Special One*. Pink was obsessed with him. She was an expert on fixated paedophile behaviour and she knew it was likely that Pink's behaviour was an attempt to recreate what he had with Brian. But she didn't know who Brian was and she needed to find him.

So far all they'd found was a Brian who'd been in care for four years, but he was only five years old and he was black. The boy wasn't Pink's target age or type - he wasn't anything like Josh. Josh was like Dean, blond and small for his age.

'I need a fag.' Mivvie pushed her chair back from her desk and headed to the back of the room. Kate went with her, glad of the chance to get up for a moment. They went out onto the fire escape and propped the door ajar with the fire extinguisher. It was against the rules, but Mivvie used the first floor landing at the top of the fire escape as her own personal balcony. She even had a folding deck chair against the wall and an ashtray perched on a railing.

Kate leant against the rail and tilted her face to the sun while Mivvie leant with her back to the rail, blowing cigarette smoke straight up in the air.

'Is it a coincidence, the foster care thing?' Mivvie asked. 'Dean is in care, and Andy and Josh have been in the past. Does it mean anything?'

'I don't know. It may just be that they're from disadvantaged backgrounds in one form or another. It makes them more vulnerable; better targets for someone to prey on. The link seems to be that Pink met them through the Community Centre. Maybe he studied the boys, singled out the ones that he thought he could groom; the ones he had a chance with.'

'Christ Kate, everyone knew about this except us. Even little Justin knew about Pink, although he didn't understand what he was singing. Don't you feel like we're getting the piss taken out of us?'

Kate thought about it. It was bloody frustrating that Pink had gone unreported, but not surprising. He'd coerced the boys, drawn them in with attention and bribery. He'd picked on boys who were at the age when they were struggling with developing sexuality, hormones raging and their bodies changing quickly.

Kate started to speak, but stopped suddenly as a hurried click clack of high heels sounded on the floor of the office behind them.

'Oh shit,' Mivvie hissed. She stubbed her cigarette out and they both peered cautiously around the door.

A short, chunky woman with huge boobs under a tight fitting t-shirt was crossing the room towards the Foster Care Team Leader's office, which was behind a glass partition at the far end of the large open plan area. Her stilettos clacked on the floor as she walked.

'Who's that?' Kate mouthed to Mivvie.

'Michelle. John Bishop's new tart... I mean secretary.' Mivvie whispered, grinning.

Kate was going to step back inside but she stopped when she saw Michelle go straight to Bishop's jacket on the back of his chair. The woman lifted out a mobile phone and after a quick glance over her shoulder, switched it on. The ring tone rang out loudly and Michelle tried to smother it with her hands. She looked around guiltily, as though the noise might have summoned someone. As soon as the music stopped she looked at the screen and started punching keys. Still holding the gadget in her left hand she opened the top drawer of Bishop's filing cabinet and started flicking through some papers.

'What's she doing?' Kate whispered to Mivvie, she was intrigued.

'Fuck knows.' Mivvie pushed open the door and walked into the office. 'Can I help you with something?'

Michelle nearly jumped out of her skin. Pushing the filing cabinet drawer closed with her hip she pressed her hand with the phone in it against her chest and grinned. 'Bloody hell! You made me jump.' She was over acting trying to cover up her embarrassment.

Mivvie wasn't laughing. 'What are you looking for?'

Kate stayed in the doorway; slightly embarrassed by the confrontation.

'God Mivvie, I'm so sick of him letching all over me. He's always pretending that he's doing confidential stuff, winding me up. I'm just checking what he's got planned. I need a break, and don't look at me like that, you've just had a crafty fag.'

Mivvie couldn't give a damn. 'I suggest you put the phone back.' She told her. 'And do something about your neckline so that Bishop doesn't have to peer at your cleavage all the time. In fact that would do us all a favour. You could always report him if you're that upset with his behaviour. We have a disciplinary procedure, you know?'

Michelle blushed, but before she could reply the door swung open and John Bishop walked in. Kate started to feel as though she was playing a bit part in an improbable soap opera.

Bishop looked delighted when he saw them, 'Ah, it must be my lucky day.' He rubbed his hands together. His shirt, two buttons open at the neck, had come loose from his trouser belt, which was pulled in tightly somewhere under his beer belly. He looked dishevelled and unsavoury. He was a soft, plump man with fat fingers and greying curly hair that was going thin on top. His tongue worked over his lips constantly as he spoke, giving Kate the creeps. 'Letch' was the right word - she almost started feeling sorry for Michelle.

'All my favourite ladies in one place, is there something going on I should know about?' He looked from Kate to Mivvie, his eyebrows bobbing at them as though they were all part of some jolly secret. Kate was uncomfortable; she didn't want to be involved in Mivvie's office politics. Over Bishop's shoulder she saw Michelle slip the phone back into his jacket pocket and slide away from his desk.

Mivvie's face was expressionless, 'We've already eaten.' She tucked her fags into her trouser pocket and headed for the door.

'Thanks anyway.' Kate smiled as she followed Mivvie out. She had no idea why she felt the need to be polite, the man made her skin crawl.

Eddie was nervous. He roamed around the house trying to find a distraction. He had an excellent antenna for detecting trouble. He couldn't explain it even to himself; it was like he felt small changes in stuff that was going on, or some weird thing that would ring his silent alarm. Right now his alarm bell was ringing persistently and he didn't know how to stop it. He was worried about Dean. He wasn't sure if the boy knew he was still in terrible danger – the worse sort. Eddie wanted Dean to be safe, he liked the kid, although Dean was a bit slow and had no idea how to take care of himself. But she'd said not to talk to Dean, and he couldn't go into town because someone might see him.

He went upstairs, pushed open the door of her bedroom and looked out of the window. There wasn't much to see, just a bunch of fields. She said no one ever called; she didn't have any friends, well that was fine, neither did he. He opened the wardrobe and ran his hand over a sheer silk blouse. He really wanted to open her underwear drawer and touch her knickers; the little bits of lace and silk she wore. But he'd save that for later - she wouldn't be home for ages yet.

There were a variety of boxes on a shelf over his head. He pulled them down and laid everything carefully on the bed. He picked the largest box first and pulled out several soft pouches full of jewellery then turned to a small leather case, unfastened the strap and looked inside. It was full of old cards. Lifting the first card out, he tried to slowly read the front, sounding out the letters: Deepest Sympathy. He didn't know what that meant. He opened it. You are in our prayers. He couldn't read the name at the bottom. Eddie put it face down on the bed besides him. He had to keep them in order so he could put them back the way they were. He didn't want her to know he'd been looking at her stuff. He picked up the next card, then the next. They were all cards about people being sorry 'cos someone had died. He suddenly felt unbearably sad. Who had died? It must have been someone she loved a lot.

Her mum? He knew what it was like to lose your mum.

The last card in the box was different - it was a plain brown card with no writing on the front. Eddie opened it, took out a newspaper cutting, faded with age and unfolded it.

'Boy, 12 dies saving sister in boating accident.'

There was a photograph and a whole load of writing in small black letters. He read the article slowly, not sure if he was getting all the words right as he struggled to understand what it said. The story was sad and he started to feel really bad reading it, but he couldn't stop, he'd never read about a child dying before. There was something about the funeral and how children from the boy's class at school were going to be there. He thought about the boy's body in a coffin and wondered what it must be like knowing that a kid you knew was lying dead in a box. He wondered if the box had been kept open for people to see the dead boy's face. How would you feel? Would you touch it – would you touch the face of a dead boy? He didn't think he could, not even if he'd liked the boy a lot. He didn't want to touch anything dead, not again, not after his mum. He wondered what the boy was wearing when they put him in the box. Would his mum have had to dress him before they laid him inside? That would be sad. How would she choose his clothes, knowing it was the last thing he'd ever wear? He thought about the boy's mum lifting the arms up on her dead son to put a t-shirt on him; holding his dead foot to put his sock on; touching his skin and his hair and knowing they would soon come and shut the lid on him. It made him want to cry.

There was a picture of the boy, the sort you have taken at school, just a head and shoulders shot, and Eddie stared at it for a long time. There was something familiar about the boy in the photo. He walked over to the window, held it in the light and looked closely at the boy's face. There was something about it, something he recognised, but it took him a while to see what it was. Then all of a sudden he knew.

He felt his skin go cold.

Steve finished a very late lunch alone in the station canteen. He was draining a cold coke when there was a shout from the doorway.

'Hey, Astman! Hear the child protection team just dropped a

kid through a roof. Not really the idea is it? Have you lost your Governor as well?'

Looking up, Steve recognised Greg Thomas as the piss taker, with a couple of uniform boys behind him.

'She didn't want to leave me, but a man needs to do what a man needs to do without the shackles of a woman'. Steve stood.

'Don't let Kate Landers hear you say things like that, she'll have your balls for earrings,' Greg told him, pleasantly.

Steve looked over his shoulder as he pushed through the swing exit doors, 'Her little ears would never carry the weight.' He shook his head and left them laughing. He was filing his report about Bisby when Barmy appeared in the doorway and shouted at him.

'Astman! DI Landers is looking for you... has been for ages, it would be helpful to let someone know where you are; ring her on her mobile - pronto.'

Several nearby heads looked up over their computer screens and a few sarcastic whistles rang out. Steve made a point of leaving the room before making the call.

Kate picked up before it hardly had a chance to ring. 'What happened with Bisby?' She demanded.

'Sprained knee and a bruised bum. The knee will be bloody painful for a while. He won't be running anywhere, he'll be at home so we can talk to him about the assault on Dean at any time. I'd give it a day or two. Oh and you might want to check out Facebook.'

'Don't tell me.' Kate could see where this was going.

'Oh yes. He was posting a report of his adventure from his mobile while he was still sitting in casualty. He's playing it up big time. You get a mention.'

'Great, fame at last.' Kate said sarcastically. 'I'm at the Social Services office with Mivvie, we're going over some records here.' She quickly filled him in on what Josh had told them. 'There's a boy somewhere who has been in a relationship with Pink, possibly a long-term relationship. I need you to get back over to Hockley. I've rung Maggie and she's going to wait for you. See if you can find any trace of this Brian that Pink talked about – that's all I have, just his first name. From what Dean and Josh have said, Pink was obsessed with him. He's likely to be another vulnerable kid. Get Maggie to run it past Social Services over there and see if you can come up with anyone. Mivvie and I are not getting very far.' Kate paused.

Steve waited. He could tell she was trying to remember something else that she wanted to tell him.

'He could have told Todd.' Kate eventually spoke, 'Josh Martin could have told his dad that Pink tried it on with him.'

Steve sat down on a window ledge in the corridor and thought about it. Todd Martin was released from prison, when, several days ago? Certainly before Pink was murdered. He got drunk for two days and then beat Darren up before disappearing. Did he also pay a visit to Pink's garden? 'And why couldn't I get through to you?' Kate asked.

Steve ignored the question. 'What about Adam Dyer?' He asked, 'we can't talk to Tony Contelli, but maybe Adam knew this Brian, especially if you think he was from Hockley. We could ask him.'

'It might be worthwhile,' she didn't sound convinced, 'but let's see what you can get from Hockley CPU and Social Services.'

'Well if we visit Bristol prison, I'm driving.' Steve hung up and grinned to himself. He'd probably just pissed her off again but it was worth it. He dug his car keys out of his pocket and headed back down the stairs.

***

CHAPTER TWENTY FOUR

There was the prickle of an idea forming in Kate's head but she couldn't quite grasp what it was. Steve had said something that had started it off but then she'd lost the thread; she'd been focusing on sending him off to Hockley. She thought back over what he'd said about Bisby. The boy really was lucky not to have been killed. She gave a silent prayer of thanks. What if he'd landed on his head? It didn't bear thinking about. But he'd survived to enjoy his moment of fame. That was it!

She rang the incident room and got put through to Ginger. 'What are you doing?' She asked, bluntly.

'Processing data for the Office Manager. We're waiting for some forensic test results to come in, Gov.' Ginger said.

'Well while you're waiting I need you to do some research for me. Get into Facebook and see if Gina Godden is on it; see what you can get, find out who her friends are, anything interesting about her.'

'Right. She may have restricted her information but leave it with me. It's not a common name, but just in case there's more than one match, what's she like?'

'Thirteen going on nineteen. Very pretty, very tall and slim with a short blond bob. She goes to Marville High School. Get onto it – I'll be back shortly.'

'Done.'

Kate could already hear him taping away on his keyboard.

By the time Kate got back to the nick she was exasperated and edgy. She felt as though she was chasing whispers in a fog. Snippets of information kept distracting her, but she had no real evidence, nothing solid to tell her what was going on. She stared at the information on the power board. There were hardly any updates; just the information about the money, the mouth organ and the sunglasses they were now trying to trace. She noticed someone had put Todd Martin's name next to his son, Josh.

Nothing added up. Nothing was breaking fast enough.

'Do we have any policemen out on patrol at all?' She addressed the room in general but the only response was a few pulled faces and knowing looks. 'So why the hell can't they find Todd Martin, or Andy Frazier? This isn't Jason Bourne we're looking for.' Kate sighed. Maybe Steve would come back with something from Hockley.

'I've put the coffee machine on in your office.' Natasha said, 'but I'm not sure how you like it.'

Kate could have hugged her. 'Very strong and very black, thank you,' She smiled, 'have you ever thought of applying for the CPU?' The young woman looked slightly embarrassed as she turned and hurried out the door.

'Ginger, talk to me about Facebook.'

'No Gina Godden, sorry Gov.' Ginger grimaced at her apologetically.

Kate was surprised and disappointed; she wanted to know more about Miss Godden. 'I thought the whole bloody world was on Facebook – what about a Marville School Group?'

Ginger nodded, 'I've checked, but I haven't got anything yet. She may be registered under another name, or we could get to her through a friend...'

Before he could elaborate Natasha reappeared through the door carrying her coffee. 'I'm helping Ginger work on Pink's finances, Ma'am, but I keep having to wait for people to get back to me. I do know Pink wasn't short of cash.'

Kate nodded, she liked Natasha; she was earnest and keen to get on with the job. She'd only been half joking when she'd suggested a trial on the CPU. She looked around at the incident room team; they were getting bored with computer work and were looking for diversions. The atmosphere was getting a bit rowdy.

'Hey, Ginger!' A computer techie called from across the room. 'Is it true Stacey's Facebook photo is of him in full riot gear, helmet, shield... everything?'

'Yeh, but you can tell it was taken in his bedroom.' Someone deadpanned.

The uproar died quickly as Stacey walked in looking agitated.

Kate diplomatically caught his attention and steered him to one side of the room. 'Todd Martin is a distraction,' she got straight to the point, 'Even if Josh told him about being propositioned by Pink, Todd didn't kill Pink. He might have got drunk one night and turned up on the doorstep shouting the odds and having a pop - but not this. Todd's too stupid and lazy to plan this, and it was planned. Whoever wanted Pink dead was determined in making sure he died nastily - it's personal.'

'Todd Martin is still outstanding,' Stacey narrowed his eyes, 'with his history and his son's connection to the case he needs to be found and questioned... even if he's not in the frame, which I'm not convinced about.'

'But if Pink is a paedophile, he's been one for years, probably his entire adult life.' Kate said. 'This is about his past. It's about someone who's been so badly hurt by him that they wanted to inflict torture on the man. It's about the man's history... not Dean Towle, or Josh Martin, or Andy Frazier. Remember, none of them, not one ever made a complaint about him. No one ever turned up and told us about Pink's shed. Why? Why didn't anyone tell us? Well, maybe because they were all aware of what had happened in Hockley. If B.Zed knew, then every other one of these kids knew too.'

There was something more that was bothering Kate; George Pink's death was brutally violent and cruel, but she hadn't found anyone so far that he'd physically hurt. 'Maybe we're all jumping to a fast conclusion here. We don't have any evidence that Pink sexually assaulted any of these boys. All we know at the moment is that he wanted to cuddle Dean Towle and kiss his face, and that he tried to get Josh Martin to sit on some sort of rocking chair with him.'

Stacey seemed taken aback, but she kept going, not allowing him a chance to speak. 'Even with Tony Contelli and Adam Dyer – if they were telling the truth – there's no evidence that he assaulted them.' Kate paused, checking to see if he was following. 'Pink picked on the vulnerable, the less acceptable, slightly damaged ones. He chose boys who needed things, even if it was just attention. And he gave them money.' She had Stacey's full attention. She was also aware that the clatter of typing on keyboards had muted - the team were listening in. It struck her that she sounded like she was preaching. She needed him to understand the psychology of paedophilia - but she didn't want to piss him off by telling him his job in front of his own team.

Stacey shook his head, 'Pink was known locally for being into young boys. Half the bloody town knew there was a pervert living in Clare Walk. He enticed young boys to his home on the pretence of helping him in the garden. And what about the medical on Dean Towle? As you've failed to get any of these boys to tell you what was really going on, what about the results from Dean's medical? Did Pink assault him?'

Kate heard the rebuke. He was convinced Pink was a fixated paedophile and he was blaming her for the lack of evidence to support his conviction. 'It's being arranged.'

'Well, as the only concrete information we have about the victim's past offending is the case involving Adam Dyer, he might want to talk about it again. Set up a prison visit.' Stacey cut her off dismissively.

'What about interviews with previous colleagues, people who knew him?' Kate tried not to let her frustration show, but failed badly, 'Pink was using his job at the Community Centre to make contact with kids. If he was a fixated paedophile the chances are he was using the same tactics in Hockley.'

'We're looking for someone local.' Stacey was adamant, 'If someone from Hockley wanted to kill Pink why wait until he'd moved? Why didn't they go after him while he was still there?' He gave her a dramatic sigh. Kate wanted to slap him.

'But the mouth organ is a keepsake, something from his past,' she insisted, 'it's important to identify who it belonged to.'

Early on in her CPU career she'd arrested a man who could relive every moment of his offences with a five-year old girl just by holding a Care Bear the child was fond of. Keepsakes were very important.

Stacey wasn't listening. 'We've got someone on it, but it's a bloody long shot and I'm not going to waste too many man hours on it.' He was getting defensive. 'To all intents and purposes Pink was a bit of a hoarder. A lot of these old people are; they don't like throwing stuff away. We can ask questions about it, but I'm not convinced we'll come up with any helpful answers.'

'It's a keepsake.' Kate was determined, 'something that was linked to a boy that was special. It would make sense that if this boy, Brian, was the special love of his life, that he kept something that reminded him of his time with him.'

'Still doesn't mean that this Brian had anything to do with his death. Half the bloody town seem to have thought he was a pervert – we're looking for a local vigilante.' Stacey argued.

Kate was beginning to feel like a hamster again. The argument was going nowhere. She leant back and folded her arms. Something had occurred to her, something she hadn't considered before. What was the connection between Dean, Josh and Andy Frazier from Pink's point of view? Was it something other than their vulnerability, their need for money? Was there some other link that attracted him to them? 'Is the FLO still with Pink's wife?' As Kate asked the question she saw something set in Stacey's eyes. He was digging his heels in because he thought he was being challenged. His ego was going to get in the way of him making any worthwhile decisions.

'Mrs Pink's taken a bad turn. She's under the Doctor, sedated. We're leaving her alone for now.' Stacey was being dismissive.

'Does she have any understanding yet of the suspicions about her husband?' Kate persisted.

'Absolutely not.' Stacey turned and walked away; the discussion was over.

Kate sidled up to Ginger's desk and gave him the benefit of a smile. 'Print me off a copy of the Anne Pink's statement please,'

Ginger grinned and opened up a database.

'Is there anything in the system that could match the MBB initials found on the mouth organ?' She put the question out to the room in general as she waited for the file to open.

'The Chief Constable's got an MBE.' Natasha called out from behind her monitor, and Kate laughed out loud, which only encouraged further comment,

'And a rather scary photo of him and Mrs Chief Constable outside Buckingham Palace. At least we were told it was her. It could have been anyone under that hat,'

'Shall I take that as a 'no' then?' Kate asked.

'A big fat no with knobs on, Ma'am.'

Kate wasn't a bit surprised.

John Bishop shifted his weight awkwardly. He lifted his left buttock off the car seat, making the leather squeak noisily. The new Jag was his treat to himself and he'd gone for the whole works, full leather trim, alloy wheels, upgraded sound system - all the electronic gizmos you could want. His two favourite things were the leather seats and the satnav system. He didn't really need the satnav – he didn't go off his patch very often, and he knew the local area like the back of his hand, but he liked to have it on and listen to the woman with the Swedish accent telling him what to do. There was no point in having money if you couldn't treat yourself, and just the smell of the leather when he opened the car door turned him on.

His other new toy was tucked away somewhere safe. He'd only used it a few times, no point in getting greedy, but it was the best purchase he'd ever made using the Council's money. It made him smile thinking about how he'd put that money to use. High quality DVDs, in strictly limited numbers, had enormous value to specialist collectors, and now he could turn them out in less time than it took him to have his dinner. Bishop settled his backside down comfortably into the seat and leant forward against the steering wheel. If he leant back the sweat running down his back made his shirt stick to the seat. He wiped his forehead on his shirtsleeve; he hated this weather, he spent every day in a state of damp discomfort. A bit of rain, that's what was needed, a bloody good downpour.

He tried to curb his impatience. He'd never been a patient man, no, he could act as though he had patience, when he had to, but it wasn't easy. He had a need to get on with things, to dominate everything – and right this minute his patience was running very short. He was fed up with waiting; fed up with having to chase around after bloody kids who were more of a frigging nuisance than they were worth most of the time. He knew he was in the right place; it was just a matter of sitting it out. Sooner or later the boy he was looking for would walk around that corner.

He'd had the flaming heebie-jeebies since the thing with Pink and, what with Eddie doing a bloody disappearing act; he needed to get things straight. He was pretty certain there was nothing to worry about, but no point in taking chances, not now, not when things were going so well. And anyway, he had a pretty good insurance policy – in fact it was a blindingly good insurance policy, the best. Bishop grinned to himself. He was in control, everything was fine and there was nothing to worry about.

He wondered what the boy would be wearing. Low slung jeans? Tight t-shirt?

Bishop shifted his weight again, reached down and slid his right hand inside the front of his trousers and down inside his underwear. He had to adjust things a bit, but he managed to give himself a little fondle. Baggy trousers - that was the trick. Sweet mother it had been too long, much too long. He needed a little sugar; a little play time... private time. This one was just for him. He leant across with his left hand and turned up the volume on the CD player. Music soared out of the speakers, filling the car and making him sigh deeply. 'L'Amore Sei tu', and the voice of the beautiful Katherine Jenkins – you couldn't beat her. Her version of 'I will always love you' was ten times better than that Witney Houston crap. A good strong pair of lungs on a hot Welsh chick would beat any American shit any day.

Bishop was so preoccupied that, at first, he didn't spot the boy. The kid was only twenty feet away by the time he'd got himself together. He composed himself; he needed to do this right, he wasn't wasting any more time farting about. He took two twenty-pound notes and a tenner from his wallet and laid them on the dashboard near the passenger door, and then he leant very gently on the horn, just enough to get the boy's attention.

Andy Frazier opened the car door and slid into the passenger seat, reaching for the money and slipping it into the front pocket of his jeans. He looked up at Bishop uncertainly.

Bishop ignored him. He threw the car into first gear and, without checking his mirror, pulled sharply away from the kerb. Andy was thrown back against his seat as Bishop turned left at the T-junction, away from town, and picked up speed.

'Where we going man?' Andy was struggling to get his seat belt fastened. He was fumbling with the catch but couldn't lock it in, so he gave up and leant his arm against the door, trying to act nonchalant.

Bishop didn't answer. His state of growing excitement didn't allow for chitchat. It was better than he'd hoped; the boy was wearing loose fitting dark denim jeans rolled up at the bottom, a pair of sporty flip-flops and a white V-necked t-shirt. As the car pulled off the B-road and onto the country lane he made no effort to slow down. Taking a left hand bend much too fast the car clipped the hedgerow.

Andy's passenger side window was filled with greenery and he shrank back as branches scraped against the glass, and then all four wheels bounced back onto the tarmac and the road straightened out. His head snapped round to face Bishop as he gripped the door handle and hung on. 'Shit! What's the matter with you?'

Bishop took his left hand off the wheel and, sticking his tongue out, licked his palm from its base to the tip of his fingers. Then he spat on his fingers; a glob of spit moistening the tips. He rubbed it in, spreading the wetness. He was holding his left hand in the air, like it was half way to a salute but couldn't quite manage to make it all the way up.

Andy shrank back as far as he could, jamming himself against the door. 'What the fuck man? Where the fuck are we going?' He was trying to bluff it out, but he was scared.

'I've missed you.' Bishop said, reasonably, still not lowering his hand. 'And I need you to help me with something.'

Andy knew it was no good. He'd got in the car... he'd got in the car.

***

CHAPTER TWENTY FIVE

Kate unlocked her office, walked in and threw her bag down on a chair. Sun was streaming in through the blinds but the room was empty and lonely. She sat facing the stack of casebooks she'd pulled out of the filing system. Six large metal cabinets crowded against the back wall stored the records of each child that came to the attention of the CPU. Every story reduced to black and white print on standardized forms. There was one aspect of the paper system that Kate loved: Smiley faces. They were the symbol of a confession. The wall calendar above Colin's desk had several yellow smiley faces doted about, some of which Colin had put great big exclamation marks next to. Those were the days when a suspect had confessed during the interview... good days. Every interview that resulted in a confession was a conviction in the bag. No trial, no need for the child to suffer the trauma of giving evidence. All that remained was the sentencing, and the greater the confession, the greater the sentence. Good days.

The folders laid out in front of her told the story of her life and work on the CPU; full of sadness and shame, loneliness and longing and the sort of depravity and perversion that nice, normal people would never imagine, not in their worst nightmares. She lifted the top folder and flipped the cover over. Pink's fantasy, what was it that pushed his buttons? Dean Towle, Andy Frazier, Josh Martin, Adam Dyer, Tony Contelli... these were the ones she knew about, but how many more were there?

What she did know, what she believed was they were all wrapped up with Pink's fantasy boy, Brian, the boy he'd obsessed over, cried over. The mouth organ was a keepsake, a tangible link to someone he cherished. Colin could have run a book on it, and she would have bet her month's pay that she was right. Finding the link between the boys she knew about might lead her to the one that remained a mystery, Brian, and help her find the key to Pink's murder. Kate pushed her chair far enough away from her desk so that she could stretch her legs out and put her feet up. It was quiet, and she needed quiet. She wanted to be calm, to think. She went through the folders one at a time, making notes.

She knew before she got to the last file. Pink liked young, pretty and vulnerable. The boys on her list all looked younger than they were and Kate knew this was important. The boys had similar colouring, and similar builds. It was their youthful, childish looks that linked them, even though they were all in their teens. She was looking for a particular type, a boy between twelve and fourteen years old - a boy who turned Pink's world.

Setting the folders aside she picked up the copy of Anne Pink's statement. It ran to about twenty-five pages, which was about right. If the Family Liaison Officer had done her job properly all of Pink's life would be in these pages, or what Anne Pink knew of it. But how well did his wife know him?

Half way through reading the utterly boring details of the Pink's daily existence, Kate felt as though she knew nothing about George Pink's true existence. There were no surprises in the neatly typed pages; just details of an elderly couple that, according to Anne Pink, never did anything more exciting then visit a garden centre. Anne Pink had a couple of elderly lady friends who called at the bungalow occasionally. They lived in the same street and they went to the local WI meetings together.

More interestingly to Kate she'd stated that George Pink never had visitors at the house. He didn't have any living relatives that his wife knew of, and they didn't socialise as a couple. To all intents and purposes Anne Pink led a very quiet, ordinary life for a woman who was five years older than her husband. She knew very little of what her husband did when he left the house, but she knew he 'was always doing marvellous things for the community, helping out with young people and he loves his garden.' Kate drained the last of her coffee and decided to call it a day. Maybe tomorrow something would start to make sense.

She was crossing the car park to her car when her mobile rang.

'Don't go.' Knowling's voice was low, conspiratorial,

'Sorry?' Kate smiled into her phone.

'Don't go. Hang on, just for half an hour or so. I could buy you a drink, a glass of wine somewhere.'

Kate closed her eyes, damn it - why now? 'Sorry, Can't. Colin and Sarah are coming over and I'm cooking dinner.'

'Bollocks,' He taunted her, 'you don't cook. You've got time to wait. I can't leave yet, not just yet, but I'd like to see you.'

It wasn't in his vocabulary to say 'please'. Kate knew that he was expecting her to fold because she always did. He never made arrangements in advance. He'd suddenly decide that he wanted to spend time with her and expect her to be available.

'Could you do tomorrow?' She asked, brightly, 'doesn't matter what time, I'm free all evening.' Kate realised she sounded like a sad loner.

'Not tonight then? Well ok, but don't know about tomorrow, depends what turns up here.'

Kate almost gave in. Bugger! She wanted to see him, more than she was prepared to admit, and there'd been so little opportunity lately, they'd hardly had any time together, but she stuck to her guns, hating herself.

'I want to touch you,' Knowling's voice was soft and caressing.

She closed her eyes and took a deep breath. She wanted to feel his hands on her. A moment's silence hung between them.

Kate closed her eyes again. 'I know.'

He hung up first.

Because he was deaf, four year old Darren Martin couldn't hear the bedroom door open behind him, but he knew instantly that his brother, Josh, was there.

Darren was sat cross-legged on Josh's metal-framed bed. He'd been playing with the money he'd found in Josh's secret hiding place. Now he knew he was in big trouble. The look of fury on Josh's face terrified him, but he had no chance of escape. He scooted backwards up the bed trying to shove the money under his bum. A couple of ten pound notes were lost in the gap between the bed and the wall as he pressed himself into the corner. Josh took a swipe at him and caught him by the leg, digging his fingers into Darren's skin as he yanked him out towards him.

Darren ducked and tried to wriggle under Josh's arm and out

of his grasp, but he was pinned down. He couldn't hear the bad words Josh was shouting but he felt them and he shrank away. Josh smacked him hard on the side of his head and then punched him, pummelling over and over into his skinny little body as he held him down.

'Urghh, urghh!' Darren wailed loudly. Josh was hitting him on his bad side; his injured side, he tried to bring his knees up to protect himself.

Josh hit him again, and Darren's head snapped back, bouncing hard off the metal bed frame behind him. For a second he lay perfectly still, and then slowly he lifted both his hands, wrapped them around the sides of his head and started to scream.

Josh scooped him up onto his lap and pulled him into his chest, 'Shush, shush! Shut up you little prick.' Josh didn't know if Patricia was home but if she heard Darren screaming he'd get hell. Josh held his brother's head to his chest with one hand and scooped up the bank notes with the other.

Darren kept crying; he was holding his head, his body shaking. 'Here,' Josh scrunched a ten pound note into the boy's hand, curling Darren's fist around it. 'Ice cream, I'll take you for ice cream.' Josh mimicked holding a cone and taking big licks at it. He pulled a dirty t-shirt off the floor and used it to wipe the tears and snot off Darren's face.

Darren almost stopped crying but he couldn't stop shaking.

Josh wondered if he could just take the money away from him again and dump him - forget all about ice cream. He looked down at the boy's head. There was a small trickle of blood running down towards his right ear. If he kept his promise about the ice cream Darren wouldn't tell.

Shit! He wouldn't have been bothered about it except the Money Cow was dead. It was a shame. Thirty quid for a bit of messing about was easy money and he needed the cash to get away. Ireland maybe, somewhere they wouldn't find him. Josh reached up and felt along his face with the palm of his hand. The swelling was going down, but his mouth hurt inside still, especially when he forgot to keep his teeth away from the inside of his cheek. He'd go to Ireland, his dad would take him - they could hide out together, like two bandits on the run.

Darren was staring up at him, holding out his hand, pointing towards the bank notes; hoping Josh would give him more money. And that's when Josh had an idea. He thought he knew how to get the extra cash he needed to get away – he'd ask the Perv's wife for it.

Awesome!

He'd take Darren with him; play up the 'little deaf brother' bit. He'd get the money for sure, no problem. Josh separated another fiver from the bundle of notes and tucked it into Darren's fist. Having a snotty nosed deaf kid for a brother could come in handy. Why hadn't he thought of it before?

Darren closed his fingers tightly around the money and smiled at his big brother as Josh helped him put his flip-flops on. He thought he had enough for a big ice cream with a chocolate in it and red sauce on top.

***

CHAPTER TWENTY SIX

Colin got drunk first, he always did. There was a gap between dinner and desert because Kate had forgotten to thaw out the frozen Pavlova, so they moved to the sitting room to put their feet up while they waited. Kate had known Colin and Sarah for a long time. In spite of her being his boss they were good friends and comfortable with each other. There was a golden rule that when they met socially they left the job behind. The rule, as always, got broken.

'So you don't think it's about any of these boys you've been told about, and CID aren't having any luck finding anything?' Sarah held her glass out for a refill.

'CID couldn't find a sock in a sock drawer.' Colin shook his head as though this grieved him greatly. Kate rolled her eyes.

'But this isn't the Bronx; people don't get stabbed and burned in Marville! That's *awful*, that is.' Sarah didn't drink very often; she was the far side of tipsy after three glasses.

'Awful.' Kate agreed, pleasantly.

'But he was a very bad person,' Sarah looked from her husband to her friend and back, 'In fact,' she sat up straighter, a rather serious look on her face, 'he was a total bastard.'

Kate gave her a sideways look. 'So that's ok then, is it?' Sarah was drunk and Kate knew she shouldn't make too much of anything she said, but she was beginning to get seriously miffed with the 'vigilante and local justice' tag that had stuck well and truly to George Pink's case.

Sarah looked contrite. 'You know what I mean. Of *course* it's not ok that he got killed like that. But he'd probably been messing about with boys for years. What about her? What about Mrs Pink? She'd have to be stupid not to have known. Why did she put up with it?'

'I'm not convinced she knew anything. She certainly had no idea who Dean Towle was, or what he was doing in the garden. Whatever Pink's motive was, his actions regarding the visitors to his garden were his business; something he didn't involve his wife in.' Kate said firmly.

'But he was doing it in the garden shed! How the bloody hell did he get away with it?' Sarah was not going to drop it.

'Which Anne Pink never went into - it was his domain. Her domain was the house; she never went in his shed. *And* she couldn't see the shed from the house. Pink could have had any number of visitors and she wouldn't know they were there, not unless they came up the garden to the house. She cleaned, polished, and cooked, the perfect little housewife.' Kate tried to end the discussion.

'I'm like that. I'm a bit of a Stepford wife.' Sarah decided, distracted at last.

Colin nearly choked on his wine; 'If I bought you an apron you'd strangle me with it.'

'You haven't got a shed.' Sarah punched him in the arm.

'Only because you won't let me have one.' Colin topped his wine up again, a hangdog expression on his face. 'I'd quite like a shed.'

Kate knew the conversation had gone way past the point of making any sense, but at least they'd got off the subject of George Pink.

'So, tell me about your new man... Steve?' Sarah turned to Kate and lowered her voice like a conspirator. 'What's he like? Any good? Or is it too early to tell?'

Kate threw back her head and laughed out loud. Sarah was far more interested in her new colleague than she was in the case. 'What do you expect me to say? He's only been here five minutes; I haven't had a chance to knock him into shape yet, but he'll learn.'

Sarah wasn't satisfied. 'But what's he like?'

'Big...' Kate started to speak but Sarah cut her off.

'Oooh, you've already discovered that and he's only been with you for five minutes!'

'I apologise for my wife's smuttiness.' Colin said, with false mortification. He leant sideways as he spoke, trying to prop his elbow on the table, but he misjudged it. His arm fell back onto his leg, he jerked as he tried to steady himself and then carried on as though nothing had happened. Kate was concerned. Colin was getting drunk very quickly; knocking the wine back as though it was his last chance. He had to be back at work in the morning, she thought she'd better try and slow things down. Put the kettle on and make coffee, maybe that would help.

It was midnight before Kate poured them into a taxi and waved them off. She stood for a moment looking down the country lane as the car's lights faded away. It was one of the things she loved about living in the middle of nowhere: there were no streetlights, nothing to pollute the darkness and interfere with the intensity of the myriad of stars above her. She took a deep breath in and let it out slowly. She would never live in town again. She'd tried it once – because of a man, but the town wasn't for her, and as it turned out, neither was the man. With Angel away at college she practically lived alone, but she cherished her independence. She smiled to herself in the darkness; it was probably that very quality in her that kept men at bay.

Her 'thing' with Knowling certainly wasn't going anywhere; it was hardly a relationship.

They'd wound up at a bar together on the first night of a child protection conference. They'd talked until the place closed and they were in danger of being thrown out. The conversation had started out being stilted and polite, both making small talk and pussyfooting around until a couple of glasses of wine and the feeling that Knowling was somehow *teasing* her, had made Kate far more open and reckless than she'd meant to be. He'd responded by giving her a far more honest insight into what made him tick and she'd suddenly realised that he excited her. She didn't want to leave him – they were jumping over each other's words, squabbling over a disagreement one second and laughing like kids the next.

When, to her amazement, he'd walked her back to her room and kissed her goodnight, the kiss had turned into more kissing until he had her pressed up against the wall and she was melting into him, her tongue exploring his mouth, recklessly ignoring the fact that she was snogging her boss in a hotel corridor like a pair of sixteen year olds. Since then they'd grabbed odd hours together, but it never went to the next stage. She hadn't even slept with him. They'd only ever 'made out' as Steve would have said. Knowling was desperately protective of his position - she'd kidded him that he was so 'police' that if you cut him in half he'd have a blue line all the way through him like a stick of rock. And he was obsessed with his privacy. It was all so bloody awkward, and at the end of the day he was still her boss.

As she undressed, Kate realised she wanted to hear his voice, if only to say 'goodnight'. She glanced at the bedside clock. Hell, it was seriously too late to call him. If she rang him now he'd panic, think something was wrong. It would be a mistake. *SHIT!* She'd told him she'd see him tomorrow. Angel was coming home tomorrow. How the hell had she forgotten? The man made her crazy! Now she'd have to cry off – damn it. Kate connected her mobile phone to the charger on her bedside table and opened her picture files. She had a video of Knowling that she'd taken without his knowledge. She'd caught him standing on the 'fag corner' at the back of the nick, earnestly in conversation with some poor CID moron, who was obviously trying his patience. She clicked open the video and watched it play through. The look on Knowling's face was so intense, so full of intelligence and conviction in what he was saying, his whole body leaning forward as he drove his point home, his blue eyes locked on the face of his annoyer – Kate loved it. Her mobile beeped and told her she'd missed a text message. She closed the video and opened the message.

The dunbars 2nite.

What the hell did that mean? Kate knew the Dunbar family. They lived in the Barracks not far from the Martins. Fred Dunbar was serious low life. What was going on at the Dunbar's tonight? Kate didn't have a clue. She'd read it twice before she realised who the message was from - *Aunty Sharon.* Kate smiled; if she hadn't had a couple of glasses of wine it would have made sense sooner. Now she knew exactly what it meant. She set her alarm for six.

***

CHAPTER TWENTY SEVEN

Kate was up half an hour before her alarm was due to go off; she needed to get started on the day. She scrolled through the 'calls received' list on her mobile; found what she wanted and pressed 'call'. As she waited for an answer she pulled a very old pair of shorts from a drawer and bent down to put them on. She was pulling an equally ancient t-shirt over her head when a rather gruff voice answered.

'Morning Gov.' Steve's voice was muffled; he sounded asleep and a bit bewildered.

'Can you pick me up at my house in an hour? Oh, and wear jeans, you'll get dirty.'

There was a pause, 'Sure Gov, Why?'

She'd hung up.

Steve realised he had no idea where she lived. He called back, but got no reply so he called Colin to find out. Colin sounded very hung over and wasn't very polite. Following the most basic of directions, Steve pulled up outside the cottage almost exactly an hour later. He didn't need to get out of the car; Kate was climbing into the front passenger seat before he had a proper chance to admire the setting.

'Thanks.' She chucked her bag onto the back seat. Steve nodded and threw the car into a tight circle. The tyres kicked up gravel as he spun out of the courtyard.

'Andy Frazier is at the Dunbar's flat.' Kate tucked her feet sideways so that her knees were pointed towards him.

Steve took in her slim legged black jeans and short white t-shirt. She had flat canvas pumps on her feet. The look was sporty and ready for action.

'Let's go and wake him up.' Kate grinned at him.

'Great, where do these Dunbar's live?'

'The Barracks - I'll tell you where to park when we get there.

He won't be any trouble, but no point in announcing our arrival too early.' Kate was enjoying herself.

Steve looked across at her, 'Didn't your mother tell you not to go out with wet hair, Gov?'

Kate turned her head and gave him a disdainful look over the top of her sunglasses.

'Don't worry,' he smiled, 'I never did anything my mother told me to either.' He pulled up at the crossroads and looked in both directions, then hesitated.

Kate realised he didn't know the way to the Barracks from her house. *Why the hell can't men ever ask for directions?* 'Turn left,' She told him, 'Bugger - I meant to bring a torch. Is there one in the car?'

Steve frowned, 'In the boot, but if there's any bother I'll probably manage without hitting anyone over the head with a torch.'

'We're not hitting *anyone*. The Dunbar's never feed the electricity meter; the flat is as dark as a cave most of the time. I think it suits them like that.'

'How many people are in the flat?' Steve asked.

'Take a guess. There could be three; there could be ten. Fred might have had a lady friend stay over. There are a couple of cheap vodka ladies locally who might have got lucky.' She was being sarcastic.

'He's not much of a catch then? And I take it there's no Mrs Dunbar?'

'There was once. But it wasn't a happy relationship. I think she decided to take up with Fred at some point and there wasn't a lot he could do to stop her.'

Steve squinted at her sideways, confused.

'Ava Dunbar wasn't just a large lady she was colossal.' Kate explained, 'I arrested her once for battering Fred. She hit him so hard he nearly lost an eye. She was a nasty piece of work *even though* she was disabled.'

'Disabled?' Steve wondered how weird this story was going to get.

'She only had one leg.'

'You're joking, right?'

Kate laughed again. She looked around the dashboard, found the control for the sunroof and opened it right back. A rush of hot wind blew her hair up around her face. She leant back over the seat again, grabbed her bag, lugged it over onto her lap and started searching for something while she told him the story.

'Would I joke? One-legged Ava was a handful, the uniforms hated arresting her – and she got arrested *a lot*. She was so big it was like trying to arrest a Zeppelin airship. She also had a nasty habit of lifting up her skirt and taking off her false leg. She threw it at an unfortunate new Probationer once. He ducked, but they were outside the Dunbar's apartment and of course as soon as she chucked her leg at him she fell over.'

Steve was picturing the scene in his head. Kate pulled a CD case from her bag, took the disc out and stuck it in the player on the dashboard. She started pushing buttons. Steve winced. He hated anyone messing with his car, but he took a deep breath and stayed silent.

'The uniforms had sent the kid in first.' Kate continued, 'Typical new boy wind up - before they went to give him a hand. Three of them were struggling to get her up, with her rolling about flashing her stump at them and swearing.' Kate was in full flow. 'Back up arrived by way of a second patrol car. Unfortunately, they were distracted by their mates trying to arrest Ava and they ran over her false leg.'

'Fuck!' Steve nearly choked. 'What happened?'

'Everyone blamed the Probationer and The Commissioner had to buy her a new leg. He was rather unhappy about it if I remember rightly.'

They hit the main road and she told him where to turn. 'So you didn't get any good leads on Brian over at Hockley then?' She changed the subject.

'No.' Steve swung the car left, 'Maggie is going to keep looking, but I'm pretty sure there's nothing to find.' He paused, 'How do you know where Andy is, Gov?'

Music blared out of the audio system that Steve had paid a small fortune for when he bought the car. The powerful voice of Bruce Springsteen surrounded them. Steve recognised the track: *Glory Days*. She had it on volume seven - it was *loud*. He looked across, but Kate had her sunglasses on and was leaning back against the seat, her hair wild streamers in the wind. She spoke without turning her head. 'This is good, it's 'let's go and arrest someone' music.'

She never did answer his question.

Kate knocked loudly enough to wake the dead but it was several minutes before the door opened. Fred Dunbar peered around the door at them, his eyes puffy and bloodshot. His shapeless grey cardigan was on inside out over his vest and he smelt bad.

'Morning Fred' Kate greeted him cheerfully. 'Can we come in? This is DC Astman.' She put one foot over the doorway.

Fred shrugged and moved back out of her way. 'Whatsa matter?' He turned and started down the hall. He didn't seem all that bothered.

Kate and Steve followed him in, leaving the front door open behind them to let some light and fresh air in. The flat was in a poorer state than the Martin's and the general odour was far worse. Steve could feel the soles of his shoes sticking to the floor. He didn't want to touch *anything*. He could barely see the end of the hall it was so dark. Kate stopped halfway between the two bedroom doors on her left.

'Is Andy Frazier here?'

Fred had shuffled into the gloom of the living room cum kitchen. 'Dunno.' He couldn't have been less interested. Kate saw him lift a cushion off the seat of a dilapidated armchair. He found a crumpled pack of ten fags, shook it, looked inside and found a single cigarette. He stuck it in his mouth and started searching again. He needed a light.

'Mind if I have a look?' Kate hadn't moved. Steve was right behind her. He had his torch in his right hand, but the front door had stayed open. Light from outside illuminated the squalor.

'Do what you like.' Fred was intent on finding a light for his first nicotine hit of the day.

'Kate stuck out her left hand and slowly pushed open the door on her left. It opened four or five inches and stuck fast. She pushed harder; nothing, something was wedged behind it. She glanced over her shoulder at Steve and indicated to him with a tilt of her head. 'Open the door.' She was whispering.

Steve stepped around her and pushed. The door moved another inch or two further; his weight forcing back whatever was behind it. He stuck his head into the open gap and looked down. Then he stuck his foot through the gap and started kicking at something. Suddenly the obstruction moved and the door opened wide enough for Steve to squeeze through. He couldn't get very far into the dark room. Two mattresses were jammed up against each other on the floor. Bundles of clothes and various items of junk were piled everywhere. At first it was difficult to make out any sign of human life amongst the mess. Then his eyes adjusted to the gloom and he saw three boys and a dog. The boys were all sleeping in their clothes.

'What the fuck?' There was a mumble, followed by a shouted, 'Fuck off!' Two of the boys didn't seem too happy about the rude awakening. The other boy didn't move. Neither did the dog.

'Which one's Frazier.' Steve asked.

Kate stuck her head around the door behind him and tried to make out what she was looking at. 'The good looking one.' She pointed at the boy nearest the wall. 'Morning Andy, fancy breakfast at the station?'

Just then the front door slammed shut and everything went black.

'Shit.' Steve swore. There was the sound of someone scrambling and something banged against the door. The dog yelped loudly.

'Torch!' Kate shouted. There was a crash from the kitchen. She started moving slowly back towards the front door to open it again. She felt along the wall, looking for a light switch. *Why the hell hadn't Steve got the torch on?* Then someone crashed into her in the dark, throwing her sideways, pain shot through her shoulder as she fell heavily against the wall. A boy rushed past her. She put her hand out to grab them, but only managed to get an inch of material between her fingers. The boy struggled so violently Kate was knocked off balance again. She was spun around and tripped over in the dark, falling onto one knee, her hands pressed into something damp and tacky on the floor, but she didn't have time to worry about it. The front door was flung open and as she turned towards the light she saw Andy Frazier making a run for it.

Shit! Here we go again. 'Andy!' Kate yelled. She was back on her feet, but Steve was ahead of her. He was out the door and running.

The chase was on.

Kate got to the doorway and saw Andy dodge around the back of the building opposite. Steve had some catching up to do but he was running flat out. A moment later Andy appeared around the far side and doubled back along the dirt road. The boy's arms were pumping and his head was stretched way out in front of his chest, like a hundred metre sprinter going for gold.

Bloody hell, Kate thought. *He was asleep a minute ago.* She ran as fast as she could across the other side of the building, heading him off. He saw her coming and swerved. He skidded to his right but the change of direction slowed him down, not much, but enough.

Steve gained fast. The boy dodged again, but he was running out of options. On one side of him was a building, Steve was close behind him and Kate was coming in fast from the side. He pumped his arms harder. He was running as fast as he could, trying to get ahead of them, out of reach, but Steve was still gaining on him. A couple of people shuffled out of their hallways to watch the fun.

'Go on boy!' Someone yelled encouragement. 'Run! Don't let 'em catch yer.' Kate heard the shrieking of kids behind her.

'The police are chasing Andy! The police are chasing Andy!'

More kids started tumbling out of the apartments. Some of them ran towards Kate, joining in the fun. 'Kate, Kate! Why's you chasing Andy?'

Kate didn't have time to stop and explain. She saw Andy look behind him. It was a mistake. Steve got a hand to his shoulder and spun him around. The boy nearly fell, but Steve kept him on his feet. Andy ducked one way and then the next. He tried to swerve out from under Steve's arm. Andy had played this game before, but Steve was a master at it. It would take someone a lot bigger and better than a kid like Andy Frazier to get away from him. Steve pinned the boy's arms behind him and held him still.

'Will you stop pissing about and calm down?' Kate pulled up in front of him.

Andy Frazier stopped struggling. He looked at the giant holding him by the arms, looked at Kate and shrugged, 'Made you run.' he said, smirking.

She resisted the urge to slap him around the back of his head.

***

CHAPTER TWENTY EIGHT

There was something terribly cruel about it. Dean hadn't stood a chance. Kate chewed her bottom lip as they played back the video on Andy's phone. She watched Dean suffer a couple of rough slaps around the head and a punch in the gut before Andy pushed him to the ground and used his foot to grind Dean's face into the concrete. Dean was sobbing with hurt and humiliation. He curled into a foetal position; his hands over his genitals, obviously afraid there was a kicking coming. Andy could be heard laughing and shouting in the background, calling Dean a loser.

Kate scowled in anger.

There was a close up of Dean's face; the skin scrapped off his cheek and chin, blood dripping onto the concrete, his eyes pleading but helpless. Then a different voice was heard over the sound of him crying and the screen went blank.

'Play it again.' Kate nodded to Steve. He pressed the touch screen and the film started at the beginning. They watched it again. This time Kate was listening out for it and she heard it more clearly. Just before the film finished a voice in the background said, *'Do you tarts want to play?'* The words were spoken casually; no aggression in the voice, just a simple question.

'Gov?' Steve looked at her expectantly.

'I'd put money on that being The Toad - the voice in the background. The Toad stopped the fight, now *that's* interesting.' Kate thought about it for a moment longer. 'That's who called Joan; it must have been The Toad. *Why?* What was he getting involved for?'

'Maybe he felt sorry for him?' Steve suggested, 'didn't like the odds; two against one.'

Kate pinched at her lip as she thought about it - she wasn't convinced. 'I've never thought of him as the sympathetic sort. Luckily for Dean, Andy and Bisby together aren't stupid enough to take The Toad on.'

'His reputation's that bad?' Steve raised his eyebrows.

'And then some.' Kate rocked back on her heels, nodding. 'Andy and Bisby would get out of his way very quickly.'

'But Dean never mentioned The Toad. Why tell us who hurt him, but not tell us who helped him?' Steve didn't get it.

'Maybe The Toad told him not to, that's the only reason I can think of. You have to understand the 'aura' around The Toad. Dean's probably terrified of him, but now he has reason to be grateful to him too. If The Toad told him to keep his mouth shut then Dean would do just that. Have we got the results yet from the M-Scan on the petrol in the Jerry can?' She changed the subject.

Steve shook his head. 'It might take a while.'

'Not good enough, I need Ginger to chase it.' Kate wasn't happy.

When they went downstairs they found Andy Frazier finishing up a plate of bacon, eggs and toast in the Custody Suite. He looked perfectly happy and at home by the time his father turned up, but Mr Frazier wasn't happy about anything.

'Your son has been arrested for the assault on Dean Towle at the Community Centre.' Kate started to explain.

'He's got bad feet.' Frazier interrupted, rudely. He looked at Kate as though she should have known this.

'Sorry?' Kate didn't remember asking about Andy's feet.

'His toenails don't grow right. They cut into his toes. His feet are a mess; he had an operation but they still aren't right.'

'Right.' Kate wondered what he wanted her to do about it. Did he think Andy's bad feet were a 'get out of jail free' card? It hadn't stopped the boy running.

'So he don't play football at the Community Centre.' Frazier spoke as though that put an end to the matter.

'Mr Frazier,' Kate spoke slowly, 'your son was at the Community Centre. He and another boy were responsible for an assault on Dean Towle. They filmed it on your son's mobile.'

'But he don't play football. What would he be doing there when he don't play football?'

Kate gave Steve a 'help me' look. He just grinned at her.

'Well his bad feet didn't stop him beating up another young boy. Do you understand? This is *very* serious.' Kate wondered if she was getting through to Frazier at all.

'Will you be long?' Frazier asked, 'I've had to park in the 'Pay and Display' car park. I've only got an hour on the ticket.'

'I don't know Mr Frazier. You might have to go back and put some more money in.' Kate was running out of patience.

'Well I don't know about all this nonsense at the Community Centre...' Frazier stopped and tutted to himself. 'I remember now. He'd just been to the foot Doctors. His feet always seem fine for a while after he's been to have them done. He was there Monday.' Frazier smiled, happy that he'd solved the puzzle.

Monday. Kate stopped wanting to strangle him for a second. 'What time on Monday did he go to the Doctor's?'

Frazier looked from Steve to Kate and back. He wiped his nose on the back of his hand while he was thinking. Eventually the answer came to him.

'He had to be there for half past nine, but the Doctor was running late. He's always running late.' He pulled some scraps of paper from his back pocket and started to unfold them, slowly going through each one. 'Here, I've got the card here somewhere; the appointment thingy, but I don't see how it matters.'

'How long was he there?'

'All morning, I told you, he had to wait ages. He never even got seen until after eleven, fooking waste of time the lot of them.'

Kate felt Steve shifting his weight from one foot to the other besides her and she glanced up at him. *Andy Frazier couldn't have been at Pink's on Monday morning.*

Kate wasn't surprised. She would have been surprised if Andy *had* been involved in Pink's death. The boy was a coward; shrewd and clever, but still a nasty little coward. He had no problem giving another boy a hiding, as long as he had help from one of his followers, but he was a cocky little nuisance who was going to get himself into serious trouble at some point.

'Which foot Doctor does he go to?' Steve wrote down the details.

The interview with Andy was as easy as pulling teeth.

'I don't like him, he's a tosser.' Andy shrugged.

'So you attacked Dean?' Kate was taking the lead. She put a photograph on the table face up. It was a close up of the mess on Dean's face. 'You slapped him about the head, pushed him to floor and stood on his face with your foot causing these injuries. Is that right?'

Andy looked up from the photograph, still grinning, 'Serves him right. Dean's a grass, him and that faggot Josh. They both want to learn to keep their mouths shut.'

Andy's father leant forward, looked at the photograph and started to say something but Steve raised his hand to stop him. Kate kept her eyes on Andy. 'What did Dean and Josh grass about?'

'Everyone knows Josh is a liar. He lied about me.'

'What did he lie about?'

'Pink the Perv. It was him that got money off Pink, same as Dean. They told you I got money off Pink for poof stuff, but it never happened. They're both lying little faggots.'

Kate narrowed her eyes at him. 'So you assaulted Dean Towle outside the Community Centre because you believe he'd lied to us about you and George Pink. Is that right?'

'That's what I said aint it?' Andy shrugged.

'What has The Toad got to do with this?'

There was a flicker of surprise in Andy's eyes; he obviously hadn't played the film back on his phone, he didn't know The Toad's voice was on it. He stared at Kate, unwilling to answer.

'That's who stepped in wasn't it? Stopped you doing any more damage to Dean?'

Andy tried a blank look, 'Don't know what you're talking about.'

Kate sat back in her chair and folded her arms. She saw Steve glance sideways at her out of the corner of her eye. He was getting some fast lessons in The Toad's ability to wrap a cloak of secrecy around him and have everyone else play along. Neither Dean nor Andy was even willing to admit The Toad had been at the scene. 'How did you know that Josh and Dean had been to Pink's house?' Kate asked.

Andy leant forward and smirked at her. 'Josh is a ponce. Pink the perv had a thing for him; he used to ask for him all the time.

We'd be having a fag round the back of the centre and he'd come shuffling over looking for Josh. Dean is just thick; he's simple like, a bit slow. He needed the money and he found out how he could get some.'

'Do you know what happened to George Pink?' Kate kept her eyes on his face.

'Every bugger knows. Burnt dead in his shed.'

Again, Mr Frazier looked as though he was going to speak, but a warning look from Steve stopped him.

'You attacked Dean because you thought he'd lied about you and George Pink. Did George Pink invite you to his house, Andy?' Kate asked, conversationally.

He looked at her warily; he wasn't sure how much she already knew. 'He invited me.'

'When did he first invite you?'

The boy looked at the ceiling, searching for an answer and Kate knew he was going to lie to her.

'Two weeks ago.'

'What exactly did he say?' Kate glanced sideways at Mr Frazier - she couldn't tell if any of this was news to him.

'He said he thought I looked strong.' Andy's voice was full of sarcasm. 'He said he'd pay good money if I helped him.'

'Helped him, how?'

'In his garden.'

Andy was slouched back in his chair, his right foot balanced on his left knee, nonchalantly, but Kate knew it was put on – his leg was trembling with nerves.

'When he asked you to help him in his garden, what did you think he meant by that?'

'He wanted help in his garden?' Andy said sarcastically, a look of exaggerated scorn on his face.

'And yet you've just said that Josh and Dean had been to his house for some sort of sexual activity with Pink.'

Andy thought about this, 'Maybe I didn't know about that until afterwards.'

Kate didn't believe him. 'When did he want you to go?'

Andy shrugged and didn't answer, but Kate waited, letting the silence play out. The boy folded first.

'That day - he told me to come that day. He said he were going

178

home and I could go with him.'

'And did you go with him?'

Andy nodded, his eyes fixed on his shoe.

'And what happened when you got there.'

'We never got there.' Andy's mouth opened in a huge yawn as though he was bored to tears by the whole thing.

'Why not? What happened?'

Andy didn't look up, 'He changed his mind. He said he wanted to take me shopping instead.'

Kate glanced across at Steve - he was looking at Andy's foot. 'Shopping?' She knew what was coming.

'Yup, shopping. He bought me these.' Andy lifted his right leg up and placed his foot on the edge of the table to show off the trainers. 'He were such an old poof. He picked 'em out and helped me try 'em on, fussing about like an old woman. He wanted me to have them.'

'So George Pink bought you an expensive pair of trainers, then what happened?'

Andy Frazier took his foot off the table and looked directly at her. 'I legged it.'

'Ran away?' Kate raised her eyebrows at him.

'When we were walking out I told him I remembered I was busy. I told him I'd help him another day, 'course I never.' Andy was pleased with himself.

'What did Pink do when you told him you weren't going with him?'

There was a flicker of uncertainty in the boy's eyes and Kate knew that whatever he said next would be bullshit.

'He said he'd see me later.'

'Wasn't he upset? I mean, he'd just spent all that money on you just for you to turn around and tell him you weren't going with him?'

Another shrug, 'I told you, he weren't bothered.'

Kate stared hard at the boy. He was lying, she was certain of it. She didn't believe for one moment that Pink hadn't reacted when Andy let down his side of the deal. By the time Andy had the shoes on his feet and they were walking out of the shop Pink would have been in a state of high excitement, anticipating getting the boy back to his shed. Andy walking off and leaving him high and dry would have got some reaction, maybe even a nasty one.

'Did he mention a boy called Brian?' Kate changed tack, watching closely for a reaction.

'Who?' Andy looked up.

'Brian. Did George Pink ever talk to you about a Brian?'

'He never talked to me about no-one.'

Ten minutes later Kate knew she'd got all she was going to get. Steve charged him with assault and released him into the care of his father

Sergeant Barry stuck his head around the door as they were getting the file together.

'Excuse me Ma'am, there's a phone call for you, it's important.'

If there was something about the tone of Sergeant Barry's voice that indicated the trouble that was about to unfold, Kate missed it. 'Can you finish this up?' She looked at Steve and he nodded.

'Who?' She asked the Sergeant as she followed him back to the Custody Suite

'Andrea, and she sounded upset. I wouldn't have called you out, but she insisted it was important.'

Kate lifted the receiver on Sergeant Barry's desk,

'Andrea?'

'Gov, I'm sorry to interrupt but its Colin – he needs help, he's crying.'

***

180

CHAPTER TWENTY NINE

He was afraid to breathe in deeply in case his chest broke, which was a stupid thought. You couldn't really break your chest, could you? Even if it hurt as badly as his did right this minute, it was only his heart that was breaking. He had no flesh on his backside, just skin and bone. He knew this because the cold floor was pressing against his bum, the cold seeping into the back of his thighs.

He gripped the edge of the wall-mounted radiator with his left hand. His right one was fully occupied pressed against the pain in his chest. He told himself he'd get up in a minute. He'd haul himself off the floor, wash his face and go back out. But every time he went to do it, the thought of actually opening the door of the bathroom to face what was out there pushed him back down.

The knees of his trousers were wet. Why was that? He didn't remember kneeling in anything. He'd slid down the wall behind him, and into the hunched over position he was in now, so where had the wetness come from? He tried to stretch his eyes wide open, tried to blink some sort of reality of his surroundings back into his head. But he knew his mind was a bit screwy. His brain refused to be tricked, and nothing clear came into focus.

Breathe you tosser, breathe, in and out, in and out. He wrapped his arms around his body and hugged himself. He'd get up in a minute... very soon. He was surprised when the door opened. He was confused when he heard Kate's voice and felt her drop down beside him and wrap her arms around him. He didn't resist being held, he was cold and her arms were warming him. Maybe he could let go now.

He pulled his head away from her shoulder and managed to pull his eyes round to her face. 'Callum died. The poor little bugger died.' He was happy because in spite of the pain he'd managed to say the words. But his chest hurt really badly. Now he knew why his trouser knees were wet because the same big, wet splotches were falling on Kate's chest. She was saying something; speaking to him, but he couldn't make out the words.

Colin closed his eyes, but the terrible image behind them was still there, all he could see was the brutally abused little boy holding out his thin arms, eyes pleading with him, saying the same word, over and over.

'Please'.

Andrea looked pale. Whether it was as a result of her recent illness, or as a result of finding her colleague having a nervous breakdown, Kate didn't have time to find out. 'It's ok, Sarah will be here in less than ten minutes, go and wait in the car park for her.' She said.

Kate squatted down and placed her hand on Colin's knee. He looked up with such an expression of anguish a lump caught in her throat. She felt the fragility of the situation and she was afraid. She was afraid for her friend. She didn't know what to say, so she told the truth.

'You're frightening the life out of me,' she tried to smile. 'I need you to be ok. You're the only thing that keeps me sane. If you go barmy I'll have two nutcases to contend with and I'm really not up to it.'

Colin's head started to nod and he almost managed to smile, but he gripped his coffee mug as though his life depended on it. Kate kept talking softly, cajoling him. She was focusing so completely on her friend that when her mobile went off she nearly jumped out of her skin. She reached out to grab it. *Thank God, Sarah's here.*

It was Knowling. 'Why is Andrea pacing in the car park?' He asked.

Was the man psychic? How did he find out about stuff so bloody fast? She was acutely aware that Colin could hear her. 'Colin's been taken ill. Andrea is waiting for Sarah to pick him up. He needs to get home as soon as possible.' There was a pause; Kate doubted her boss was buying it. He could read her better than she wanted him to.

'What do you need?' He asked.

Kate could have kissed him. 'I just need to get Colin out of here quietly, and on his way home as soon as possible.'

'I'll ring down and make sure there's a parking space available, even if it means Stacey moving his ugly great Ford out of the way. In fact that's a very good idea, he's probably parked nearest the door.'

Knowling paused and Kate waited. She didn't know what else she could say; didn't know what else she could tell him. Colin seemed totally oblivious of his surroundings again. His coffee was forgotten, the cup balanced on his lap. She needed to get back to him.

'Kate,' Knowling cut into her thoughts, 'Talk to me as soon as you can.'

'Thank you.' She hung up, but as she went to put the phone down it went off again. She was still expecting Andrea, so couldn't quite get her thoughts together quickly enough when a male voice said, 'There's a Raymond Greggs in reception to see you, Ma'am.' It was one of the staff at the front desk.

'What's it about?' Kat searched her brain for a reference to a 'Greggs' and came up empty.

'Apparently, he heard about you taking the boy out of George Pink's house the day of the fire and he's got information for you. He asked specifically for you.' The reception staff had a talent for sounding bored to death in the midst of a crisis.

'Ring the incident room - get one of the team to talk to him.' Kate's mobile bleeped in her ear, she had another call waiting. She pushed the button to accept it and cut the receptionist off.

'Sarah's here, the car's right at the door and Steve asked if you needed a hand. Do you want Sarah to come up?' It was Andrea.

'No...' Kate looked at Colin and thought he might, just might have a bit more colour in his face than he'd had five minutes ago. Maybe the coffee had helped. 'We're coming down.'

Kate had managed the two flights of stairs between her office and the ground floor in seconds on occasions, but the journey she made down with Colin took, what seemed like, hours. The fact that they made it without Colin falling down, or bursting into tears again was, Kate thought, nothing short of a bloody miracle. Colin pulled himself together long enough for Sarah to fold him into the car. She gave Kate a look that said 'I knew this was going to happen' and pulled away.

'Ring me.' Kate mimicked holding a mobile up to her ear as Sarah turned the car around to leave.

Colin lifted his head and looked at her out of the passenger window. He smiled, almost apologetically, and then they were gone.

The wet stickiness was still on the inside of Eddie's thighs and perspiration was dribbling down his back. It was the best feeling in the world. He'd just lie back for a minute; get his strength up and he'd be able to do it again. He closed his eyes. Just the thought of her sitting on top of him, leaning back against his thighs, he'd be hard again any second.

He felt her small hand stroking his chest and he breathed in deeply. She was naked alongside him. He felt her let out a long sigh. Her hand reached up and her fingers flicked gently through his hair, over and over. It felt good.

Eddie half opened his eyes. Something had changed and for the briefest moment he wasn't sure what. He was about to sit up when he saw her tiptoe slowly to the chest of drawers against the far wall. He must have fallen asleep because she was fully dressed. But why was she tiptoeing? He lay still; his eyes barely open, watching her through his lashes.

She slowly picked up his mobile phone; the one she'd bought for him, slid it into her back pocket and tiptoed out the door. Eddie didn't move.

Kate climbed up three flights of stairs and strode through the incident suite without acknowledging anyone. Her chest felt tight and she was breathing rapidly through her nose. It wasn't just the shock of seeing Colin fall apart so dramatically, it was the fact that she had seen it coming and she'd ignored it. She was blaming herself and she was furious. She'd let him down. Colin was a member of her team and she'd let him down. She hadn't kicked back hard enough when Stacey had attached her to the murder investigation. She should have insisted on some help for Colin, but she'd got wrapped up and she'd ignored the warning signs. She'd seen his weariness; seen how tired and strung out he was, and she'd done nothing to help him.

'Where's the DCI?' She snapped at Ginger more harshly than she'd intended to.

He looked up startled. 'He's gone out to the scene, they've found...'

'The search team on an extended tea break - if they've got any sense.' DC Edwards interrupted with a quip, which he obviously thought was funny. He stood at the vending machine waiting for a white plastic cup to fill with something masquerading as coffee. He turned and grinned at his audience.

Kate's head whipped round, words of reproach ready on her lips, but a couple of snorts and appreciative coughs erupted and she realised Edwards had support. She turned back to face the team. Heads lowered to keyboards and eyes were averted as she scanned the room. So that was how it was. Some of them had decided that the murder of a suspected paedophile didn't merit looking into too closely. They might as well find the person responsible for it; pat them on the back and go back to fighting *proper crime.*

'Is there anyone in this room that did not make an attestation on becoming a Constable?' Kate was angry. 'It's a long time ago, but I seem to remember it said something about discharging your duties with fairness and integrity and...'

'Look Gov,' Edwards interrupted, 'if there's a kid that was being abused by Pink – some kid that he hurt, someone who maybe tried to fight him off and things got out of hand...'

Before Kate could respond Natasha called out from across the room, her voice urgent. 'Ma'am, I've got a bloke on the phone. He says he was in Clare Walk just before the explosion. He says he saw two kids going up the path behind Pink's house just a few minutes before it all kicked off. I've got him on hold.'

Kate spun round. 'Transfer it.' She pointed firmly at the phone on Ginger's desk. The call forward light lit up and she snatched up the receiver. 'Hello, this is DI Kate Landers.' She was aware that the room around her had gone still. The team of officers were all waiting; watching her for a clue. The voice on the other end of the line was polite and well spoken. Kate guessed the man to be in his twenties or thirties. He certainly didn't sound like a crazy.

She listened to his story, asked where she could meet him and told him she'd be there in fifteen minutes. Hanging up, she turned and nodded to Natasha.

'Log it. And let the DCI know.'

'I don't know if you're aware, Gov.' Ginger was looking at her sheepishly. 'But the back of your t-shirt is covered in something black and nasty.'

Kate twisted her neck to look over her shoulder, but she couldn't see. She looked down; one knee of her jeans was covered in something disgustingly greasy. She'd got filthy scrambling about in the Dunbar's hallway in the dark. She glanced at her watch; she'd got time to change, she had a clean pair of jeans and a shirt in her office. 'Thanks Ginger.' She swung out the door.

Knowling caught her just as she was about to pull out of the car park in a CID car. He indicated for her to wait, so she wound her window down.

'You were supposed to come and talk to me.' He said.

'Well I can't right now.' Kate said, rudely. 'I'm working on a murder enquiry where half the bloody investigation team seem to think someone did us a favour, and my own Detective Sergeant has collapsed under the weight of what I dumped on him! It should never have come to this. God! Colin's looked like hell for weeks. Callum dying was just the final straw. Colin went to pieces when he heard. He was already under too much pressure before Stacey threw his weight about and I left him with even more work. I just ploughed on like I always do, hoping it would be ok. *You* did nothing about it either; we could have seen this coming a mile off!' She ran her hand through her hair in exasperation, staring at him. 'I hope you're going to charge that baby's parents with murder. Callum didn't have one day on this earth when he was safe or loved - *not one single day!* All he knew was neglect and abuse.' Kate's voice trembled; she was close to tears with worry and guilt. She loved working with Colin but she was pretty certain he wouldn't be able to return to the CPU any time soon.

Knowling took a step forward and laid a hand on her arm. 'I'll do whatever needs doing. And I don't just mean Callum's parents, I mean Colin.'

She searched his face; his eyes were full of concern. She swallowed back the tears and sniffed loudly. 'I know you will.

Thank you.'

'Is there anyone in particular I should be *speaking to* about their attitude... I mean on the Homicide Team?'

Kate swallowed and shook her head, 'Forget it. I'll deal with it.' She told him about the witness.

Knowling was standing at the side of the car, the sun was behind him and Kate had to squint as she looked up at him.

'Why are you going alone? Where's Astman?' He asked.

'He's finishing up the file on Andy Frazier and then he's going to have another talk to Bisby Alouni - see what he's got to say for himself.' She saw his eyes narrow at her. 'It's ok, I'm meeting the witness at Costas... I can park right outside. I'll just stop when the wheels hit the kerb.' She managed to grin at him.

'I'm not worried about the car, I'm concerned about you.' Knowling spoke softly. He leant towards her, squeezing her arm gently. Kate wanted to get out and hug him. She tried to distract herself by putting the car in gear. 'I'll be back as soon as I can.' She held his look for a moment and gave him a brief smile before pulling away. He didn't go back inside until she was out of sight.

***

CHAPTER THIRTY

The witness wasn't hard to spot; he'd described himself perfectly over the phone: Five feet ten, grey chinos with a white shirt carrying a blue Nike back pack, sitting at a table just inside the door of Costa coffee shop.

'Thanks for waiting Mr Jeffries.' Kate shook his hand.

'Call me Bruce. And you're welcome; you're the only person I've spoken to today that's not over sixty, needs a hand rail to get off the loo or wants to talk to me about their grandchildren or their last visit to the doctors. Is this ok?' He stood up and indicated the table, smiling broadly.

Kate smiled back. He seemed a cheerful sort. She supposed you needed to be if you spent most of your working day with the elderly trying to decide what sort of bathroom fitments they needed to aid their mobility.

'This is fine. Can I get you a coffee? I need a triple espresso more than you would believe.'

Bruce insisted he'd get the drinks, he said he was a regular and they gave him discount. He normally stopped there once a day for a break and to write up his notes while on his visits around the area to the elderly and infirm. He wouldn't take no for an answer so Kate took a seat and got her notebook ready. When he returned she took his details down and got straight to the point.

'Why were you sitting in your car in Clare Walk on Monday morning?'

'I was waiting for the Connells to come home. Mr Connell is a client; he's in a wheelchair. I was early and they'd gone to the doctors. I was only dropping off a new light pull for their bathroom. Mr Connell was having trouble getting a grip on the old one, the cord was too thin for him to hold. There was no point in me leaving just to have to come back again, so I sat in the car outside their house reading some case files. I'd turned the car around so I was facing towards the entrance to the cul-de-sac.'

'Where exactly do the Connells live?'

'Twenty-five Clare Walk, it's about three doors down on the opposite side of the road to where the fire was.'

'And you said on the phone that you were there at ten thirty?'

Bruce nodded, 'Yes, my appointment was at ten forty-five. I checked the clock on my dashboard and realised I was fifteen minutes early.'

Kate sipped her coffee and thought about it. He'd had a good view of anyone coming down the road and turning into the path that led to the back of Pink's house. 'Can you take me through what you saw?'

'Two kids. First one, then the other walking into the cul-de-sac and turning up that pathway.'

'So they weren't together?' Kate interrupted.

'No. The first kid turned up the path just as I looked up. It was the hoodie that caught my attention. It was seventy-eight degrees that day and the kid was wearing this grey sweatshirt with the hood up. Makes you laugh doesn't it?'

'Can you describe anything else about them?' Kate was trying not to speculate as to who the kid was.

'I didn't get a proper look at their face. I'm sorry, but they'd already started up the path when I looked up so I only got a sideways look. I'd say they were five feet seven to five feet nine tall, slim build. I remember their legs looked skinny because the hoodie looked several sizes too big; I guess that's how they wear them, the jeans were black and I think they had trainers on, but to be honest I'm not too sure.'

Kate was thinking it wasn't a lot to go on, but she smiled encouragingly. 'Was there anything distinctive about them? A logo on the top they were wearing, anything like that?'

Bruce screwed his eyes up as he thought about it. 'No, there definitely wasn't anything on the back of the hoodie; it was just a plain light grey one. But he was carrying a backpack, a khaki or dark green one. It was in his hand, not on his back. He was holding it down like this...' Bruce stuck his right arm out and demonstrated how the boy had been carrying the back pack like a bag; holding it by the straps down by his side. 'I don't know why I thought this, but I got the impression it was heavy. Maybe it was the way he was holding it slightly away from him, trying to balance the weight?'

Kate's interest was growing by the second. 'What about the second boy?'

'Oh, he turned up at least ten minutes later. I got a much better look at him. He was dawdling along, but walking towards the path on that side of the road. I watched him because he suddenly started kicking a small stone about as though he was Wayne Rooney or something! I mean, he was really making an effort with it - and he had great control.'

Bruce gave Kate a very accurate description of Dean Towle. Kate thought that if his description of Dean was that good then his description of the first boy must be pretty accurate too. 'And you didn't see the first boy come out before the second boy followed?'

'He didn't come out.' Bruce was adamant. 'The second boy went up the path and a few minutes later the Connells turned up. We were in their kitchen when we heard the explosion. I called back at the Connells' today. They had a card, given to them by a policeman doing house-to-house enquiries. I thought I'd better call the number in case you were interested in what I'd seen.'

Kate stared at him. He was damn right they were interested. 'How difficult would it be for you to cancel whatever you've got on for the rest of today?'

Bruce looked up from his coffee, surprised. 'Well actually the Connells were my last visit. I'm supposed to go back to the office to tackle a mountain of admin.' He grinned, 'I'll happily cancel that if you think I can help.'

'Thank you.' Kate was beginning to like the guy. She didn't often talk to witnesses who were so straight-forward and sensible. 'I'm going to make arrangements for you to give a formal statement to one of our CID officers at the station and then work with a photo fit technician to get a picture of the first person you saw - while it's still fresh in your mind.'

'A sketch artist? Is that what you mean? I don't know if I can give enough detail to be any real help, like I said I only got a sideways look.' Bruce looked a bit anxious.

'It's all done on a computer these days. Don't worry, the

people who make up the images are amazing, they'll take you through it and you might be surprised how much detail they can capture.' Kate reassured him. She didn't tell him she thought it was a long shot, but they had to give it a go because it was all they had. She called the incident room. DCI Stacey was still out at Clare Walk so she spoke to the Office Manager and set everything up. Kate didn't want to let the witness out of her sight until she'd got him safely back to the station and handed him over. Luckily, he was quite happy to leave his car and travel back with her in the CID car.

She double parked at the front of the building and quickly handed him over to Ginger, who was waiting for them. She went back to move the car around to the car park and was just pulling away from the kerb when she heard the call going out over the radio. The Control Centre was giving information about a missing four-year-old boy. She turned up the volume.

'Darren Martin is small for his age, slim build, has collar length dark blond hair and was last seen wearing a pair of red shorts and brown flip flops. He was bare-chested. He has extensive bruising to his upper torso and is profoundly deaf. He's reported missing from his home...'

The CID car rocked violently as Kate heaved on the steering wheel and did a u-turn in the middle of the road.

***

CHAPTER THIRTY ONE

'What are those idiot police up to? Aren't they ashamed of themselves? They can't manage to find one man when he's only five minutes away from his own front door and now they've lost a kid.'

There were several shouts of ridicule from the onlookers as Kate got out of her car. She thought they had a point. Several small children grabbed her hands but she disentangled herself outside the entrance to the Martin's apartment block. The stench in the hallway was worse than usual and someone was playing Elvis music very loudly from a flat upstairs. A young uniformed policeman came along the passageway towards her before she got to the Martin's door. Kate recognised him, but couldn't remember his name. He obviously hadn't made a big impression on her.

'Tell me.' She stopped him.

'Todd Martin was sleeping rough at The Castle, Ma'am. Someone called the tip line. Do you know where The Castle is?'

Kate stared at him. A sick feeling was climbing up her throat. *Darren had told her.* He'd told her he'd seen his dad at The Castle and they'd all brushed him aside. No one listened to him. Patricia had said he was making it up and she'd let it go at that. *Of course he wasn't making it up.* Darren trusted her, maybe more than anyone else in his little life and she'd ignored him. *What the hell had happened to him?*

'It's a small concrete shed thing, disused, has been for years, Ma'am. It's at the back of that patch of wasteland behind The Crown pub. The kids play war over there. It's called The Castle because whichever gang of kids controls it has a fortress.' The uniform explained it to her.

'What about Todd Martin?' She demanded, her voice harsh.

'Gone. We searched the place a couple of hours ago. Some of the kids, including Darren, turned up while we were there. When we got back here everyone thought the kid was with everyone else. Patricia Martin doesn't seem too fussed; she thinks he'll turn up, and she's probably right, apparently he takes off sometimes. Greg Thomas came out here with me. He called it in, he's concerned in case there's a chance Darren is with Todd – or has gone off to find him.'

Kate was having difficulty staying calm, 'Is DI Barnes here?'

'Haven't seen her, and I feel as though I've smoked forty fags since I got here. The air in there is thick with smoke. There's not even a decent cup of tea.' He started to make his way outside but the look on Kate's face stopped him.

'So, Todd Martin - a nasty piece of low life and top of our 'wanted' list - was within a mile of his own home and he's managed to avoid arrest *again*? Well done, you really are Marville's finest aren't you?' Kate gave him the benefit of her biting sarcasm.

The officer looked put out. 'Well, he'd gone by the time we got here,' he said, defensively.

Kate wasn't going to let him off the hook. 'When was Todd last seen?'

The officer looked blank. 'I'm not sure. I only heard that someone knew he was out there.'

'Oh, *someone* saw him. *Someone* called us to let us know where he was.' Kate was getting angry. 'I wonder if we can find Darren by ourselves before he comes to any harm.' Kate never shouted, but when she spoke in whispers it was far worse. 'He's four years old. He's deaf, and his father, who *you* can't find, beat him black and blue last week.' Kate's eyes stayed focused on the man's face for a couple of seconds longer than was necessary, and then she turned and walked back outside.

'Is Todd going to hurt Darren again?' Abraham tugged at Kate's arm, staring up at her with interest. 'Me mum says he could kill him next time. Is Todd going to kill Darren, Kate? He'll be dead then. Will his mum be sad?'

Kate managed to drag her eyes down towards the small boy. 'No,' she reassured him, 'Todd is not going to hurt Darren again, because this policeman and lots more policemen are going to find him.'

'Well, a patrol car is on the way but I don't think there's going to be a lot of spare manpower from the...' the hapless officer didn't get any further.

Kate shot him a look that cut him off mid-sentence. She marched over to the growing crowd of onlookers, dragging a happy Abraham behind her. Squinting against the glare of the sun in her eyes, she put a hand up to get their attention.

'Please, I need some help,' she shouted. All heads turned towards her. Slowly a hush fell. 'Does anyone know where Darren is?'

There was a general murmur and shrugging of shoulders.

'He was at The Castle when the coppers got there Kate, but that were earlier. He wouldn't have stayed out there on his own, like.' A woman called out.

'Did he come back with anyone?' Kate asked.

There was silence. In the excitement of having the police searching for Todd Martin on his own doorstep no one had noticed what had happened to the small boy.

'Little sod. He ain't gone far, we'll find him.' The Toad stepped casually forward from the group and to Kate's enormous surprise, took control. He told the kids to run back and search all the places they knew Darren liked to play and sent the adults and the older kids off to cover the immediate surrounding area.

Abraham let go of Kate's hand and ran off excitedly. This was better fun than The Castle. Now they had a real mission. Every one of the kids wanted to be the first to find Darren. Kate knew they'd turn the place upside down looking for him. It struck her as bizarre that they were all yelling the boy's name, although they all knew he wouldn't be able to hear them.

The Toad shouted after them as the adults started to spread out. 'Meet back here, but find him first.' He looked across at Kate, pulled his mobile phone out of his pocket and starting to text furiously as he grinned at her. 'Half an hour... maybe less, he's here somewhere.'

Kate grinned back and nodded, 'Thanks Toad.' She handed him her card with her mobile number on it. 'I think that's twice this week you've come to the rescue. If you carry on like this we'll have to give you a Good Citizen Award.'

The Toad slid the card into the back pocket of his jeans and shrugged, 'No biggie.'

One skinny juvenile delinquent with a mobile phone, which was probably nicked, Kate thought, but he'd managed to organise a manhunt in seconds.

The uniformed officer Kate had met in the hall was leaning against his car sipping from a mug of tea someone had given him.

If he thought he had nothing better to do for a minute - he was wrong. 'Get rid of that and follow me.' Kate strode past him and marched back towards Patricia's apartment. 'Get on the radio. I want a dog unit up here in the next five minutes. I saw Sgt Barry's name on the duty board. His Lulu is a genius at finding lost kids. Tell them it's on my request. Then start knocking the doors in this block. I want to know the names of everyone that is either living here or stopping here. Do you understand?' She turned her head quickly to look at him.

He nodded sullenly; his radio already in his hand ready to make the call.

'Report back to me as soon as you're done.' She left him.

The door of Patricia's apartment was open. Kate walked straight in and through to the living room. Greg Thomas was sitting at the dining room table filling out a missing person form. He looked worried. Josie was sitting opposite him. She was trying to help him with the details but she looked nervous and scared. She was talking around her thumb, which was stuck in her mouth as she worried away at the skin around the nail with her teeth.

Kate went over to the girl, crouched down and put her arm around her shoulders. 'How are you getting on?' She looked pointedly at Greg.

'Ok Ma'am, we're getting there.' He returned her look and Kate knew instantly that everything wasn't ok.

'He's got blond hair and brown eyes, but I don't know how tall he is. I don't even know how tall I am.' Josie was distraught.

Kate squeezed her shoulder. 'That's ok, it doesn't matter a bit, don't worry.'

'But you need to *find* him.' Josie started to cry.

Kate squatted down until she was at eye level with the girl. 'Look at me Josie. *Look at me.*' She pulled Josie's hand away from her face and squeezed her fingers. '*Every* police officer in this division knows Darren. They know *exactly* what he looks like. I know you're being a really big help to Greg here,' she looked across at Greg who nodded, enthusiastically.

'She's been amazingly helpful.'

'But what you *can* do; just to help them even more, is see if you have a photo of Darren somewhere, something recent maybe? Can you do that?'

Josie sniffed loudly and nodded. 'He had his picture taken at nursery. Me mum wouldn't buy it cos it were five quid, but Nana Penny paid for it. I'll find it.'

'Good girl, that's *exactly* what we need.'

Josie disappeared around the kitchen partition.

'Where's Patricia?' Kate asked Greg.

'She said she needed to lie down. I let her go because she was being a bit... difficult.'

Kate raised her eyebrows.

'She's a bit pissed, Ma'am. She's had a couple of cans of strong lager.'

'Leave her there. As soon as we find Darren he'll be taken into protective custody.' Kate kept her voice low. 'Todd was sleeping rough nearby, which Patricia probably knew about. Darren is going to a place of safety as soon as we find him. That little boy is going to sleep in a proper bed for once. As far as I'm concerned Patricia can't protect him. She can hear about it when she sobers up.' Kate suddenly had another thought. 'Where's Josh?'

Greg shrugged. 'No idea sorry, we haven't seen him.'

Kate shook her head, 'This just keeps getting better and better.'

It was Lulu and Abraham together who found Darren. Lulu picked up a scent from the t-shirt that Darren had worn that morning and took off at a run, dragging Sgt Barry behind her. Although everyone was told to stay back out of their way and let them get on with it, Abraham decided the instruction didn't apply to him. He galloped behind them, his chubby little legs running flat out as he tried to keep up.

Following a zigzag pattern around the apartment blocks, Lulu lost the scent momentarily and circled, nose to ground until she got it again and headed straight for an apartment block at the end of the row. Kate ran after them, catching up with Abraham on the doorstep and holding him back as Lulu and her handler tore up the stairs.

'Stay with me Abraham, stay with me. I don't want you to get hurt.' She gripped his hand tightly as he pulled against her.

'They're going in my house. I want to find Darren!'

There was a shout from upstairs. 'Gov! Can you come up here?'

Kate had no choice - she had to take Abraham with her. As she entered the apartment, identical in layout to the Martin's and just as grotty, her mind was churning with one thought over and over, *please let him be ok, please let him be ok.*

'In here.' Sgt Barry called from the first open doorway on the left. Kate looked in and saw Lulu sitting quietly beside an old fashioned double bed on a wooden frame.

'Under there - I can't reach him and he doesn't know me. Poor little bugger's terrified.' Sgt Barry pointed.

Before Kate could do anything Abraham dropped to the floor, squirmed under the dog's nose and stuck his head under the bed.

'I got him! I found him!' He shouted excitedly, 'I got him!'

Kate had to lie flat on the floor to fit her upper body under the bed frame. Darren was curled in a ball, his back against the wall at the far side of the bed. Tears streamed down his grimy little face as he shook with silent sobs.

Kate reached out her arms as far as she could towards him. 'Come here baby. It's ok, come to me.' She squirmed as far under the bed frame as she could get and stretched out her hands. 'Come to me baby.'

For a second Darren just looked at her, tears spilling over his eyelashes, and then he scrambled towards her. Kate grabbed him, lifted him gently out and pulled him up into her arms. She hugged him to her, stroking his hair as he wrapped his arms around her neck and clung to her. 'Ok baby, everything's ok. You're safe, everything's ok.'

She wished he could hear her. She wished she could talk to him. She knew he'd understood the police searching The Castle. He'd seen his dad there and no one had believed him. Did he think Todd was going to hurt him again? Was there something he couldn't say that he wanted to tell her? She swung him round gently, rocking him, comforting him.

'I found him, I did!' Abraham grinned up at her.

'Yes you did.' Kate agreed.

Lulu went into a dance of ecstasy as Sgt Barry threw her ball.

***

CHAPTER THIRTY TWO

As Kate struggled to open the sunroof on the car she couldn't get the look on Darren's face out of her mind, the look he'd given her as he cowered under the bed in Abraham's apartment. He was such a frightened, *sad* little soul. His deafness made it a hundred times worse. She had no idea what he was thinking; what he wanted to tell her and she felt so sorry for him. She needed to get her act together and actually take the British Sign Language course as soon as possible – she'd been meaning to do it for ages. Even if she had to use some vacation time, she needed to be able to talk to Darren.

There would be an emergency case conference called within a couple of days, and no doubt a plan would be put together to get him back home as soon as possible. But for now she was relieved not to have to worry about him. She wouldn't agree to Darren going home until Todd was back in custody.

Her mobile buzzed, but she couldn't get a free hand to it before it rung off. She grabbed it and looked at the ID in the message screen. *Stacey*. She plugged in her hands free and pressed re-call.

'Have you crashed?' Stacey didn't bother with pre-amble. 'Are you in a ditch? Is an ambulance required or the service helicopter?'

'No to all of the above.' Kate was perplexed by his impatience. If he was trying to be funny, it wasn't coming off.

'You were expected back here.' He snapped.

'Darren Martin was missing and our officers needed some guidance.' Kate felt her stomach rumble. 'And I'm hungry.'

'Right.' Stacey let out an audible sigh. 'Speaking of which, according to the FLO who is with Pink's wife, Josh Martin turned up with his little brother in tow and told Anne Pink her husband owed him money, something about work he'd done in the garden. She gave them fifty quid. She said the little brother looked sad and just made funny noises at her. She felt sorry for them.'

'What?' For a moment Kate was incredulous. Josh had gone looking for money from Pink's wife knowing Pink had just been burnt to death? She didn't believe for a second Pink owed him money. She believed Josh had found a way to exhort cash from a vulnerable old lady, and had used Darren to bunk up the odds. He was Todd Martin's son through and through.

'I'm waiting for a report from you on the arrest you made this morning - and whatever else it is you and Astman have been doing. Then I find out you went off on your own to pick up a witness, dumped him at the station and disappeared. Where's Astman now? Look, never mind, just get back here. There's been a development from the search team - I'm calling everyone back for a briefing at six.' Stacey changed subjects but was still in a foul mood.

'I'll be there shortly.' She hung up. *What the hell was eating him?*

Instead of rushing back, Kate decided to stop at a coffee shop where she paid a ridiculous amount of money for a croissant and a large double shot latte. She sat outside at a bistro table, taking her time while she drank her coffee and thought about her report. She hadn't really got anywhere. Steve had confirmed Andy Frazier's alibi for Monday morning - which meant that following up on the can of petrol found in his shed was probably a waste of time. Andy's association with Pink was still unclear, other than the seedy fact that the boy had used Pink for his own benefit. Bisby, on the other hand, was only involved in the attack on Dean. He wasn't linked to Pink because he wasn't Pink's type. He was from Sri Lanka - black, with a square, muscular body. Kate thought about that some more. Maybe that was more useful to her than she'd realised. She pulled her mobile out and called Steve.

It took him several rings to answer. 'Are you still with Bisby Alouni?' She asked.

'Been here about ten minutes, Gov. Hang on, I'm just moving to the hall – see if I can get a better signal.' Steve's voice was muffled, 'Ok, that's better. What do you need?'

'You said Bisby was posting stuff on Facebook when he was in hospital. Try and get him to show it to you on the computer.

Pretend you don't know how it works, get him to talk about it, see what he's got on there. I was hoping Gina Godden was on it, but Ginger can't find her. Ask Bisby if he knows Gina, try and find out what the story is with her and Andy Frazier.' Kate paused, 'Is Bisby's mother there?'

'Yes,' Steve lowered his voice, 'and she's prayed for me already.'

Kate laughed. Mrs Alouni was a Pentecostal Christian who despaired of the trouble her youngest son got into. 'Bless her. She's obviously recognised you for the dreadful sinner that you are. I don't care if you get converted, just keep as friendly with Bisby as possible, I think he might be useful.' Kate was about to hang up when she thought of something else. 'Did you hear anything about a development from the search team before you left the nick?'

'Yes. I can't really talk now, but it's something to do with an escape route from Pink's garden.'

'Well at least they're still working out there. There's a briefing at six, so I'll meet you at the office.' She hung up.

Before she had a chance to put her phone back in her bag it rang again. She didn't recognise the number that was on the screen, so she answered formally, 'Kate Landers.'

'Kate, I'm so glad I managed to catch you. I need to talk to you. I've gone through some stuff here, old records and photos and I've got a boy; a boy that I think Pink might have had a thing for. I think Pink was threatened because of it.'

Kate recognised Rick's voice, the coach from the MCSC, but she was caught off guard and it took her a moment to realise what he was saying. 'A boy from the football club you mean? Do you know his name?'

'Michael Bowden. Look, I can't explain it over the phone, but I'd like to talk to you, I feel really bad about this.'

Kate looked at her watch. 'Where are you?'

'Still at my office.'

Stacey would have to wait for his report. 'I'll be there in ten minutes. Get the coffee on.' Kate fumbled in her bag for her car keys. *Michael Bowden: MB. The initials on the mouth organ found in Pink's shed were MBB.*

***

CHAPTER THIRTY THREE

Colin would have run a book on the boy Kate was studying in a glossy photograph being one of George Pink's targets. She wouldn't have bet against it. The boy ticked every box; he was young, dark haired and beautiful. Michael Bowden was twelve years old, he had a tidy 'Prince William' hair cut; the fringe brushing his eye lashes but the sides cut short framing a smooth heart shaped face. He looked like a character from a nursery rhyme.

'Lummy, he's a nice looking kid.' Kate held her coffee cup out for a re-fill. 'Are there any other photos of him?'

'I haven't seen any.' Rick told her. 'After what you said about Pink and what he was doing, and the stuff about his trousers, well, I couldn't stop thinking about it. I just feel so damn stupid! Why the hell didn't I realise? I should have seen what was going on. If I'd paid attention instead of just trying to stay out of Pink's way because he wound me up so much, maybe Dean...?'

'Ok that's enough, stop.' Kate looked at him sternly. 'In every single case of child abuse that I investigate there's always someone saying exactly those same words; blaming themselves and thinking about what they could have done differently. Paedophiles are devious, intelligent and skilled at making sure their secrets don't get out. Pink acted whatever part suited his needs in getting access to boys and avoiding suspicion. Whether it was being an annoying busybody or a dedicated volunteer, Pink was manipulative. He approached the boys when you weren't around; when he knew he was safe.'

'You don't understand.' Rick looked wretched. He leant his elbows on the desk between them and rested his head on the fingers of his left hand, 'I always thought I got on well with these kids. I thought I'd built up a bit of a relationship with some of the more difficult ones. Why didn't any of them tell me?'

Kate had seen this reaction so many times in her career on the CPU, the wrong people blaming themselves. 'Philip and Joan have a great relationship with Dean. He never said a word to them about Pink. Josh Martin, Andy Frazier, however many others there have been - *none of them told*.' She walked over to the corner of the desk and perched right on the edge, close to his shoulder, her knees almost touching him. It had the desired effect - he sat up straight and looked at her.

'Right,' Kate met his eyes and gave him a small smile. 'Now buck up and tell me about Michael Bowden.'

Rick blew a breath out through pursed lip and told the story.

He'd been thinking about the photograph he'd let Kate borrow, the one where Pink had his hand on Tommy Bowden's shoulder. It made him feel ill; knowing what Pink was doing. Then he'd started thinking about Tommy's brothers. Tommy Bowden was the middle one of three boys. Michael Bowden was the youngest - he was twelve. Michael was a delicate looking boy, whereas Tommy had similar colouring but was much stockier.

Tommy had a slightly 'off centre' look about him; it was his face, the boy had a large kink in his nose where it had been badly broken, and at thirteen he suffered from terrible acne around his jaw and neck.

The older brother was something completely different. At sixteen Brin Bowden was a fighter, a boxer and a street fighter. Brin's face told the story of his career; scars over both eyes, another on his chin and the same kink to his nose as Tommy. Brin was a scraper in every sense of the word.

'The first time I met Brin was the time he walked in with Michael and threatened Pink.' Rick leant back in his seat and laced his hands behind his head.

Kate had been listening quietly, not wanting to interrupt, but there was something she didn't understand. 'Was it only Michael and Tommy who came here, not Brin?' She asked.

'Yes, but they only came for a couple of months. Tommy was mad keen on the football, always the first here and the last to leave. Michael would join the training sessions occasionally, but mostly he just sat and watched. I got the impression they were supposed to stay together. Tommy couldn't come unless Michael came. Neither of them had any kit - I got boots and stuff out of the lost property cupboard for them. Tommy got a bit excited a couple of times; he would just walk up to another player and thump them. I'd sit him out on the sideline to cool off and when he was allowed back on he'd bound up to whoever he'd smacked and make up.'

Kate was engrossed listening to Rick talk. She was beginning to feel a real sense of admiration for him; for his work at the centre, but she had more questions, there was something she still didn't understand. Why hadn't the older boy protected his younger brother?

'But if Pink was trying something on with Michael, why didn't Tommy look out for him. I know he's only a year older, but he's bigger and he seems a lot more of a hard case.'

Rick shook his head, 'Tommy was a bit slow. Football was the only thing he was any good at. He could barely read or write. For some reason the other boys accepted him, maybe because he was just a big dopey puppy. Some of them even sort of 'adopted' him, took him with them down the shops, that sort of thing. I think Michael had to come with him because he was supposed to look out for Tommy, rather than the other way around.'

Kate was losing the thread. 'Ok, so Tommy couldn't look out for Michael, for what ever reason, and we're going to assume that Pink tried something on with Michael. But Pink didn't know about the older brother, Brin?'

'No-one did. I told you, the first time I met him was when he threatened Pink. I was here, in my office when I heard raised voices coming from the corridor outside the gym. By the time I got there it was all over - well almost. Pink was backed up against the wall, looking as though he was going to have a heart attack, with Brin right up in his face. I heard Brin say something like, 'So you understand me do you?' And Pink just stared at him. He was too frightened to move!'

'Had Brin hurt Pink?' Kate leant forward and looked at him intently, her mind churning.

'Let me finish!' Rick grinned at her in mock rebuke.

Kate grimaced; mouthed 'sorry' and leant back to listen. In spite of the topic they were discussing she found herself enjoying his company. He wasn't boastful about his sporting accomplishments and although he was a professional trainer, with a number of lucrative contracts, he was giving something back by coaching football at the centre. She shut up.

'I shouted something and Brin turned his head to look at me - but he had Pink up against the wall and he didn't let him go. I couldn't see it at first, but down by his side he had Pink's left thumb bent back in a pressure hold. Brin looked at me then back at Pink and I thought he was going to head butt him, but he just glared at him and let him down with a jerk. Pink nearly collapsed, he was practically crying, nursing his hand, bent over in a heap. Brin started to walk away and of course I went to help Pink. I shouted, 'Hang on, I need to talk to you,' but Brin didn't even look back. He just said, 'We take care of our own' and he was gone, taking Michael with him. I mopped Pink up, but he wasn't really hurt. He seemed more scared than anything.'

'So Michael saw all this?' Kate interrupted before she could stop herself.

'Yes, he was standing behind Brin.' Rick held her eyes.

'Did you ask Pink about it?'

'Yes. He didn't want to talk about it. He said something like, 'load of nonsense, a misunderstanding.' He absolutely refused to take the matter any further and I didn't ask Michael because I figured if there was something he wanted me to know he'd tell me. I only saw Brin once after that.'

'When was that?'

'About four weeks ago. Brin turned up with Michael and said he wanted to thank me for all I'd done for his brothers. He shook my hand. The boys were leaving.'

'Why were they leaving? Do you know where they went?' Kate got her notebook out of her bag and found a blank page. She started to make some notes.

'Sorry, I should have said at the beginning; the Bowdens are part of a big family of travellers. They moved on.'

Kate closed her notebook and stared at him.

***

CHAPTER THIRTY FOUR

'W' as there something you wanted?'
Raymond Greggs looked up, startled. There was no one else in the reception area; she was talking to him. He stumbled as he stood up.

'Are you waiting for someone?' The woman peered through her protective glass window at him impatiently.

'The detective lady... '

'What?'

'Yes, I'm waiting; I mean I have been, for the detective lady.' Raymond couldn't get the name out. He felt stupid and was embarrassed for himself. He tried again, 'Sorry, yes, I've been here since this morning. I'm waiting for the detective.'

'What detective? Who wants to see you?'

'No one *wants* to see me. I need to speak to Detective Inspector Kate Landers. I was told to wait.' There, he'd got the name out.

'Who told you to wait?' The woman sounded as though she doubted anyone had told him any such thing.

'I spoke to the gentleman on this desk this morning, about eight o'clock. He said Detective Inspector Landers was busy, but I could wait.' Raymond tried to get some confidence in his voice.

'What? And no one's spoken to you yet?' She was appalled, either because she thought this was nonsense, or because he'd waited so long. He wasn't sure which.

'I'll find out.' She disappeared into the office area behind the counter. Raymond had absolutely no idea what she'd gone to find out. He wondered if she was coming back. Should he sit back down?

She was back.

'DI Landers is still away from the station and she may not be back for some time. Is there someone else you could speak to?' She looked at him questioningly.

'Thank you, thank you very much, but no, I need to speak to DI Landers. I don't mind waiting some more.'

The woman looked steadily at him; she seemed to soften slightly. 'Look, you could be here for hours and there's no guarantee that DI Landers will be able to speak with you this evening. What about tomorrow morning - if I let her know you're coming in again?'

Raymond's palms were sweating and he could feel moisture on his top lip. He got his clean hanky from his front pocket and wiped his face. 'Thank you, yes. I'll come back tomorrow. Is eight o'clock ok?'

He made it to his car before he started to cry.

Kate took the front entrance to the station and buzzed herself though the security door, but Mary, the receptionist stopped her before she reached the stairs.

'Raymond Greggs left about ten minutes ago. He'd been waiting since eight o'clock this morning. He won't talk to anyone else. He says it's about the murder investigation and he's coming back at eight o'clock tomorrow morning. I know its Saturday, but I assumed you'd be in.' She said, briskly.

Raymond who? Hadn't she got a message about this person first thing this morning? Why had he waited so long and why would he only talk to her? Kate was perplexed. 'Someone from the Incident Room was supposed to talk to him. Did he leave a contact number?'

'No. He wants to see *you*, he refused to speak to anyone else and he wouldn't leave his details. But I know he'll be back.' Mary was adamant.

Kate nodded, she was racking her brains and coming up empty. She had no idea who Raymond Greggs was. She got to the foot of the stairs just as Ginger jumped down the last five steps swinging on the handrail like a big kid. His eyes lit up with pleasure on seeing her.

'Hello, Ma'am, the DCI has been looking for you. Great stuff about that witness, Bruce Jeffries - he's been here all afternoon. At least we've got something to go on now.' He landed in front of her, grinning.

'Yes, thank you Ginger.' Kate continued up the stairs with slow dignity. Before she arrived at the third floor, a sergeant and two detectives had cheerfully warned her that the bosses were looking for her. Kate just smiled and kept climbing. Checking her text messages she saw she'd missed one from Steve.

GEE GEE NOT GINA.

Now what the hell was that about? Kate tried to call him but the call went straight to voice mail. She stuck her phone back in her handbag and managed to duck into her office without bumping into Stacey or Knowling. Andrea was bent over a desk, one hand holding her head as she focused on a report she was writing. Glancing up, she grinned as Kate pulled the door to behind her and turned the lock.

'Hi Gov, has the DCI or the Super spoken to you yet?'

'No, but I understand they would like to.' Kate threw her handbag down and headed for the bathroom.

'*Understatement.* You might want to wear your stab proof vest when you go out there.' Andrea grinned again and turned back to her work.

When Kate emerged she had a clean t-shirt on, her hair was brushed and she was wearing lipstick. If you look shabby you feel shabby. It was something else her father had taught her - always dress up if you think someone's going to give you a dressing down.

'Any news about Colin, is he going to be ok?' Andrea was concerned.

Kate immediately felt guilty - she'd put it to the back of her mind. 'I honestly don't know. No one's called me and I don't want to hassle Sarah. I'm sure she'll let us know when there's something to tell.'

Andrea nodded, 'Pretty shitty though. I really feel for him. The press haven't got hold of it yet, but after what happened with Bev and baby Crystal they'll have a field day when they find out about Callum. The Commander was closeted with Knowling for about an hour earlier, no doubt making sure that we've got our arses covered.'

'Our first involvement with that family was when Colin picked Callum up and took him to the hospital. If social services had concerns about them before that, well they didn't share them. I've talked to Knowling about charging the parents with manslaughter. I want Colin to know they're going to prison for a long time.' Kate's tone was grim.

Andrea nodded. 'There'll be a public outcry if they don't. Barmy was sounding off about them earlier. All I can say is it's a bloody good job she's not the custody officer – they'd never survive.'

Kate found herself nodding, but then all of a sudden, without conscious thought on her behalf to indulge or encourage it, the weight of frustration and exasperation fell on her as though from a great height. She understood how Barmy, and probably most of her colleagues, were in full outcry against Callum's parents, and even wished serious harm to befall them. But how was that different to how they felt about Pink? About how he got what he deserved for being a kiddie fiddler? About *maybe* not looking too closely for whoever was responsible? There was no difference. She couldn't lecture them on the meaning of their oath if she didn't demonstrate her belief that '*With fairness, integrity, diligence and impartiality, upholding fundamental human rights and according equal respect to all people,*' actually meant *all people*, not just the ones that weren't child abusers.

'Anyway, at least there's a bit of good news.' Andrea was still chatting on, 'There's been deep joy and celebration over the finding and locking up of one Todd Martin, especially after the fiasco at the Barracks. It's been a bit of a carnival around here since he arrived at the custody suite. Even Knowling was reported to have been seen grinning in the canteen.' Andrea lifted her head, throwing her thick mane of hair over her left shoulder and out of her eyes. 'Although he soon stopped when you went AWOL.'

'What?' Kate didn't know Todd Martin had been picked up. 'How did that happen?'

'Sorry, thought you'd heard. He was at Accident and Emergency, and by all accounts looked like one. Still managed to give the uniforms a hard time when they got there though, little shit that he is. Barmy's taking the credit for some reason; not sure what she had to do with it. She's dealing with Todd at the moment. Someone went to tell Patricia about it and she asked if that meant she could have Darren back.'

'No, she can't, not until there's been a case conference.' Kate was adamant, 'How did they know where to find Todd and how did he get hurt?'

'The hospital rang it in. I don't know how he got hurt. Barmy said someone had given him a hiding. Someone at the hospital said he'd been pushed out of a car outside the A and E entrance. He was kicking off, swearing and threatening everyone. Barmy went out with a couple of uniforms to get him. Word has it she gave him a '*serious talking to*' on the way back.' Andrea rolled her eyes.

'Shit! Don't tell me about it, I don't want to know.' Kate was appalled.

It was the same 'less rights than others' thing. It was well known that Barmy had been moved from the CPU because she'd physically laid into a retired Headmaster. He'd sneered at her when she arrested him for abusing his housekeeper's son and she'd thumped him. She couldn't deal with child abusers without wanting to punch their faces in, and on that occasion she'd lost control. Kate knew it was only due to Knowling's intervention that the man hadn't pressed charges. Barmy could have been arrested for assault.

An enormous thud against the door made them both jump. Before either of them could move another thud shook the doorframe. Someone was trying to barge the way in. There were several grunts that sounded suspiciously like very bad swear words from the corridor outside.

Kate and Andrea looked at each other. *Steve.*

'Hang on!' Kate quickly turned the lock back and pulled the door open before he used his famous kicking talents against it. She had to step sharply back out of his way as Steve charged through the doorway.

'Why's the door locked, Gov? Guess what I found out?' He obviously hadn't meant her to answer the first question, and he didn't even acknowledge Andrea. Kate just stared at him, waiting.

Steve pulled his tie off and flung it over the back of a chair. Undoing his cuffs and the top four buttons of his shirt he leant across Andrea to open the bottom drawer of Colin's desk. He took out a freshly laundered cotton shirt; turned, pushed open the door leading to the bathroom with his foot and pulled the shirt he was wearing over his head as he went. Kate stared at the muscles on his back and then swivelled in her chair to look at Andrea. *What the hell?* But Andrea hadn't even looked up.

'I tried to call you but your phone was switched off.' Steve called out, 'Did you get my message?'

'What? Yes, but it didn't make any sense.' Kate shouted back. There was no reply. All she could hear was the sound of water running. A few moments later he emerged, buttoning up his clean shirt and smelling faintly of aftershave. Kate was getting impatient. 'What did you get?'

Steve picked up the coffee pot, topped her cup up and poured himself one. He didn't offer Andrea one. 'Bisby Alouni is a switched on kid. If he wasn't mixed up with the likes of Andy Frazier I think he'd have a chance of making something of himself, and he's bloody funny.'

Kate sighed, 'I get it that you and Bisby have become bosom buddies but is there any chance you might get to the point?'

'Gina Godden is on Facebook, but she's called Gee Gee; it's her nickname. I told Bisby he'd have to keep up with all his mates online because he can't bloody walk and I pretended I didn't know how Facebook worked, like you said. He couldn't wait to show off and explain it. I acted thick and kept asking questions so that I could have a good look at stuff he was connected to. Gina Godden has some interesting posts and there's a video clip she's posted of herself dancing... its jailbait stuff, very provocative. Bisby said all the boys in his year have seen it. They think she's hot but she's trouble. She used Andy and then broke up with him. Bisby doesn't believe she ever actually slept over at Andy's place, but Andy's so gutted about the break-up he tried to bribe her to come back. He gave her two hundred pounds.'

Kate stared at him. *Bloody hell!* If Andy Frazier had two hundred pounds she had a pretty good idea where he'd got it. 'Did Pink give him the money?'

'Yes. According to Bisby a few of the kids who play football at the centre knew Pink was a 'Shirt lifter who liked 'em young', *his words*. Andy turned up at the centre a couple of times and Pink made a beeline for him. They all thought it was a joke, but Andy was leading Pink on. Pink took photos of the boys playing football and always had a camera with him. A couple of weeks ago Andy called him into the changing room, dropped his kegs, mooned at Pink and told him to take a photo of his bum. Bisby thought it was hilarious. He said Pink nearly creamed himself. Bisby described

Pink as 'infatuated with Andy', always waiting for him to turn up, always following him about, trying to talk to him. Andy gave him enough encouragement and then he hit him with the sting.'

Kate was astonished. Andy was a little yob, but he was obviously a much more devious little yob than she'd given him credit for. 'So he asked Pink for the money?'

'Yes,' Steve nodded. 'He told him that he needed two hundred pounds to get his girlfriend back and he told Pink all the dirty things she would do, making out she'd let him have sex with her; stuff like that. Then when he'd got Pink all hot and bothered he told him that if he helped him out with the money he'd help him out. All of this took place at the centre. Andy never actually went to Pink's house.'

'I like that.' Andrea had been listening intently, 'The user got used; makes me feel warm and fuzzy inside.'

Kate wasn't quite so happy, 'Help Pink out with what? What happened?'

'It went sour. Andy got nervous after Pink got him the trainers. I think Pink must have realised he'd been had, and he got nasty; threatened Andy.'

'Threatened him how?'

'Something about the photos, it was something about showing them to someone else. He said some things that really frightened Andy. Bisby said he tried to laugh it off, but he was worried. Again, according to Bisby Andy was trying to keep a low profile for a while but then he heard that we were interested in him after Pink got killed and he thought Dean had dobbed him in.'

'So basically, Andy used Pink for money because Gina was using Andy for money. Interesting, but unless you're going to tell me that someone killed Pink to protect Andy?'

'No need - Andy stole the camera.' Steve grinned.

'What?' Kate sat back on her desk, astonished. 'Has he still got it?'

'No.' Steve shook his head. 'He got rid of it.'

'Shit!' Kate swore. There might have been other stuff on the camera that they could recover, maybe even photos of other boys.

'But I know where it is.' Steve's face split into a wide grin, 'Gina Godden's got it.'

Kate nearly slapped him for being so bloody theatrical but she wanted to know something, 'Why was Bisby so happy to tell you all of this? Aren't he and Andy mates?'

'Not anymore.' Steve sipped his coffee, 'Andy told him he was only going to give Dean a slap, and to film it for him. Bisby had a go at Andy for going too far when he kicked Dean on the ground and Andy told him to fuck off. So, Bisby downloaded Gina's dance video and showed it to everyone on his phone. There was loads of piss taking about Andy going out with a slapper and Andy tried to punch Bisby in the head. They hate each other.'

Kate thought about this for a second. She was about to say something but stopped and looked at her watch. She jumped off the desk. 'Briefing, come on.' She was out of the door before he'd put his cup down.

***

CHAPTER THIRTY FIVE

Kate found an empty spot near the front of the incident room. She leant against the windowsill and someone moved over so that Steve could fit in beside her. It struck her that she and Steve were now being treated as a team. Colin had only been gone five minutes, and the whole station seemed to have slotted Steve into his place, it annoyed her.

Stacey walked in briskly and went straight to the board. 'We've got a statement from a witness who was in Clare Walk on Monday morning.' His voice cut through the chatter as he put the likeness up on the board of the person Bruce Jeffries had seen in Clare Walk just before Dean Towle turned up. 'White, five feet seven to five ten, slim build, wearing black jeans and a grey sweatshirt with the hood pulled up around his face...'

'The uniform of the delinquent.' Edwards drawled, as a groan went up from the room. 'I could take a walk around town tonight and bring in a dozen kids that match that description.'

'A delinquent carrying a backpack - which could have concealed a can of petrol and a knife.' Stacey snapped, 'And, at least we now know there was another youth, one that's yet to be identified, in the vicinity. There are no teenage boys living in any of the houses adjacent to Pink's and no mention of any one matching that description visiting on Monday. So what was he doing and where did he go? We're putting together a press package; putting it on the front page of a couple of local papers.'

Stacey turned his attention back to Kate. 'I'm waiting for the boys who have been involved with Pink to be interviewed and eliminated, or otherwise.' His stare was a challenge but Kate wasn't in the mood to play. She moved across to the board.

'Andy Frazier was brought in this morning in connection with the assault on Dean Towle. He has an alibi for Monday, which checks out. He's admitted the assault on Dean and has been charged. Since then we've discovered that Andy was using Pink, not just to get new trainers, but to get cash; at least two hundred pounds, which he gave to Gina Godden in an effort to make her go out with him.'

'That's very romantic.' Edwards interrupted again, playing the clown. 'If he was looking for a date he could have got a Tom in Brook Street to give him a really good time for fifty quid.'

'And is there a point?' Stacey said, sarcastically.

Kate's eyes met his and held the look before turning and addressing the room with authority. 'Andy Frazier and Dean Towle have been eliminated as possible suspects. Josh Martin took money from Pink and threatened him by saying he'd tell the police about Pink coming on to him. *But he didn't do anything about it.* He's since conned Mrs Pink into giving him more money. A clever ploy now that his source of income has gone. Bisby Alouni wasn't a target for Pink and doesn't fit this description.' Kate pointed at the picture of the youth in jeans and hoodie. 'The Toad doesn't match Pink's target group either...'

'He apparently knew about Pink's activities, he's capable of playing the vigilante.' Stacey stopped her.

The look on Kate's face told everyone that she disagreed. She couldn't prove The Toad wasn't involved, but she didn't believe for a second that he was. She changed tack. 'There's new information about another boy Pink may have targeted, a Michael Bowden. His older brother, Brin Bowden, threatened Pink.'

'Are you talking about the travellers?' Ginger asked. 'They've gone; left a couple of weeks back.'

'You're right.' Kate added the information to the incident board, and then stood back and faced the DCI, 'But we should be able to trace them. The County has a service for gypsies and travellers which includes education for their children; they may be able to help.' She paused, her eyes thoughtful, 'What's the story on Todd Martin?'

'He's being interviewed by DI Barnes.' Stacey said, dismissively. He was concentrating on the new information she'd put up. It all fitted with what he'd said from the start; one of the boys or possibly someone close to them was responsible for Pink's death. And they had some new physical evidence. He turned back to the room, effectively blanking Kate.

'The search team have found what could be the route the attacker took in leaving the scene.' He pointed at the large scale drawing of Clare Walk. 'This house is the last in the row that backs onto the footpath behind Pink's. The couple that live here are out at work all day so weren't at home on Monday morning. The fence and gate at the back are six feet high and the gate is kept locked. The wooden panels either side of the gate have small wooden spikes, about four inches in height, but one's been snapped off. The occupant is sure it was still there on Sunday night, and the damage looks new.' Stacey paused, playing for effect, but he had their full attention.

'The whole panel has been removed and is with Forensics. If the spike was snapped off when someone grabbed it to haul themselves over the fence, we may get prints or fibres.'

'How would they get out of the back garden?' Steve spoke up. 'Could they just walk out the front, onto Clare Walk?'

Stacey was annoyed by the interruption, but several other members of the team started asking the same question. He raised his hand for silence, 'They could get out onto Clare Walk by climbing over a wrought iron gate at the front, it's set slightly back from the house and it's an easy climb.'

Ginger spoke up again, 'There were people out on the street very quickly after the explosion, Sir. Wouldn't someone have seen them?'

'All the attention was on Pink's house.' Kate said, quietly, 'No one was looking that way. Someone may have seen them - but not taken any notice, and there's another way out of Clare Walk at that end of the cul-de-sac.' She glanced back at Stacey, realised she was stealing his thunder and took a step back.

He nodded, curtly. 'It's not obvious, but there is a cut through, just here.' He pointed to the map and all eyes followed. 'There's a gap between these two houses; it doesn't go anywhere, but there's a hole in the fence at the end big enough for someone to squeeze through. It leads to the car park at the back of the industrial estate. Again, we're looking at this section of fencing for any physical evidence that may help us, but we need to identify a suspect.' He stopped and looked around the room, waiting until all eyes were on him. 'It has come to my attention that some of you may think whoever killed George Pink did society a favour. It's very likely he was a paedophile with a fixation on young boys and that he was grooming vulnerable kids. *However*, if there is anyone on this team who feels that we shouldn't be doing everything in our power to catch his killer, I invite you to leave the team now.'

There was a stunned, embarrassed silence.

Kate was astonished. She hadn't expected Stacey to come out with a speech like that. It was a pity Barmy wasn't in the room to hear it. She looked across at Edwards. He caught her look and one side of his mouth turned up in an amused grin. If he thought all child abusers should forego their protection under the law and be castrated – he was keeping it to himself.

Stacey nodded. 'Right then, I want a renewed effort over the next twenty four hours; make sure we get something solid.'

Conversations broke out around the room as the team digested the new information. The board was criss-crossed with data, but they all knew that without a suspect, without someone to hunt - to tie the data to, it didn't get them anywhere.

Stacey had to raise his voice to get their attention. He gave instructions for house-to-house enquiries to be followed up again in Clare Walk.

'We nearly missed a vital witness; let's see if we've missed anything else. I want the industrial estate covered. Did anyone see this boy in the car park on Monday? And let's get a trace on this Bowden family - find out where they are now. Has this Brin Bowden been back on our patch recently?'

As the briefing broke up Stacey drew Kate to one side. 'When I tell you to come back and report I don't mean anytime that suits you!'

Kate bristled, 'It was important to get the information from the coach, and not just because Brin Bowden threatened Pink. Michael Bowden may have been a victim; he may need professional help...'

'This is not just a child protection enquiry!' Stacey exploded, 'We're investigating a homicide. I brought you in only because there are kids involved in this case and I expect you to use your expertise to get evidence that will...'

'Excuse me, Sir,' Ginger stepped up behind Kate and

interrupted, 'Superintendent Knowling needs you in his office right away. He's got the Commander with him and he wants to know where the Press Officer is.' Ginger scurried off. Stacey glared at Kate, 'Speak to me tomorrow.' He turned and walked away.

Kate was seething. She needed to get out of there. She scanned the room until she spotted Steve. 'Get a car and meet me at the front in ten minutes.' Her voice was louder than she'd intended.

Steve looked up, surprised, and glanced at his watch. He'd been about to head down the pub with some of the CID boys and get a couple of cold beers down his neck. 'Where are we going?' He asked.

'To get the camera.' Kate walked out.

'Christ Almighty!' Steve complained to Edwards, 'Doesn't she ever stop? There goes my Friday night!'

Edwards grinned happily at him. 'Where's your staying power for fuck sake? You've only been with her for four days. The lovely DI Landers doesn't stop - not ever. You need to buck your ideas up if you want to survive. There's a book running on who'll get the collar on Pink's killer, and Kate's the favourite by far. I don't think you're allowed a bet though, not now you're partnering up with her.' The grin turned to a smirk.

Steve had a sudden desire to punch Edwards in the mouth; instead he took his wallet out, extracted a ten-pound note and slapped it on the desk next to him. 'I'm putting a tenner on myself.' Walking away he thought he'd probably just thrown his money away, but it was worth it to wipe the smirk off Edward's face.

***

CHAPTER THIRTY SIX

I t was late. The original meeting time had been changed. The delay panicked Bishop at first but now he was in a state of excitement again, waiting for the boy to arrive. He heard the door push open but as he spun around the lights went out and he froze. With no windows to let in natural light he was in pitch-blackness. He could hear the boy moving towards him and his dick started to stir. *Games, huh? Sex games in the dark?* He was definitely up for that. He touched himself through the front of his trousers.

'I've got something for you.' He called out, smirking. He could just make out the shape of the figure crossing the room to his right. 'Do you want to feel for it?'

The first hint of unease came when he caught the smell. It was faint, and in the fleeting moment that it passed his nostrils he thought he recognised it, but then it was gone. He blinked several times into the darkness. He'd left his glasses in the car. They slid off his face when he got sweaty, and he planned on getting sweaty.

The figure slowly moved around to his right, but there was something wrong, and for the love of him, Bishop couldn't quite decide what it was. Goosebumps broke out on his arms as a prickling sense of alarm spread over him. 'Stop pissing about and come here.' He said, loudly. *What the hell was the kid playing at?*

He took a step backwards, and bumped into a metal rail; part of the animal holding pens that filled one side of the building. He smacked his hip on it so hard that he stumbled. He flung his right hand out feeling for the rail to steady him; afraid he was going to fall. He'd just got his fist around it and was lifting his head when a violent slap caught him on the side of his face and knocked him back. He was completely off balance, the shock and pain made his head reel as he lost his grip and his spine jarred painfully against the railing behind him.

'What the Fuck?' Something ripped into his right thigh. The excruciating pain that followed took the breath from him and he went down, howling. He was half lying, half sitting on the hard concrete floor. Blood seeped warmly through his fingers as he pressed his hand against his leg trying to stem the flow. His mind tried to make some sense of what was happening to him. It was telling him to get up, to fight, fight for his life, but he stayed where he was, panting and crying through clenched teeth as his blood poured onto the filthy concrete beneath him.

Then his head snapped back again and his skull crashed into the railing behind him as another slap, harder than the first, connected with his face sending a knife blade of agony up into his skull. There it was again, the smell, now it was right in his face. He was dizzy and his lips were wet and trembling. Why were his lips wet? Was his nose bleeding? He couldn't tell; there was pain everywhere, excruciating pain.

'If you think your leg hurts, wait until I stab you in the balls.'

He dragged his eyes around and tried hard to focus on the face looming over him. Nothing made any sense. A gloved hand reached out and touched his forehead, pushing his hair out of his eyes. The touch was as gentle as a mother's but he recoiled from it.

'Hold still.' He was scolded, and then he felt it, felt the blade pricking through the crotch of his trousers and pressing against the skin on his groin. He didn't move. He was going to wet himself, but he didn't move. He bit down on his lip to stop himself screaming.

'Mum! The taxi's here!'

The Godden's front door was flung open, but Gina wasn't paying attention to who was behind it. She'd started to turn away before she realised it wasn't a taxi driver. A look of panic flashed across her face before she recovered and stared at them moodily.

'Can we come in?' Kate was already over the doorstep with

Steve close behind her leaving Gina no choice but to move back and get out of their way. Kate had had enough of pussyfooting about; she wanted the girl to know she meant business.

Gina's mum appeared at the top of the stairs. She was done up like a dog's dinner for a big night out. Glossy curls bounced around her bare shoulders, a pink halter neck mini-dress leaving little to the imagination as she teetered down the steps in silver stilettos. She was throwing a black wrap around her shoulders when she realised there were two detectives in the hall and no taxi driver. She stopped and looked at them in confusion.

It took Kate two minutes to make her change her mind about going out.

As she went back upstairs to get out of her glad rags and into her jeans the taxi driver arrived and Steve sent him away.

'We'll get the kettle on!' Kate shouted up the stairs. She deliberately ignored Gina; not giving any indication of why they were there, she let the girl stew with anxiety as she set about cheerfully making coffee. Steve followed her lead and didn't even look at the girl. When her mother eventually reappeared, Kate explained, very bluntly, why they were there.

'Gina lied to us yesterday. She's been involved with Andy Frazier far more than she let on.' Turning to look at the sullen girl Kate kept her voice low, keeping things calm. 'You need to tell us the truth, *right now*, Gina. We know about the money and the camera - they came from a man who was *murdered*. I want you to hand over the camera and tell me exactly what happened. There's absolutely no reason to make this difficult.'

Mrs Godden chewed at her bottom lip fretfully, leaving red lipstick on her teeth. 'Look, I've got no idea what you're talking about. What camera? Why do you think Gina has it?'

'Andy Frazier thinks Gina is his girlfriend. He gave her the camera because he'd stolen it from George Pink - a man who had given him two hundred pounds to give to Gina, a man who was murdered shortly after this happened. I don't care about the money, Gina, but I need the camera - *now*. Its material evidence in a murder enquiry, do you understand how serious this is?'

Gina pulled at her fringe, her eyes on the floor, refusing to look at Kate. She gave a rude shrug and turned her back on them. Mrs Godden suddenly sprung across the kitchen, gripped her daughter's shoulder and shoved her roughly towards the door.

'Go in the other room - go on! Go and sit down and don't move until I tell you to, I want to talk to the police.'

Gina started to protest, but her mother didn't want to hear it. 'Do it! Just go in the next room and do as you're bloody well told for once.'

Kate wanted something from Gina before she left, 'Give me your mobile phone please.' She held out her hand expectantly. She didn't want Gina texting or ringing anyone while she was alone in the next room.

Gina wasn't giving it up easily, she hesitated for a second, her eyes full of loathing, but Kate wasn't about to let a thirteen year old test her. She took a step forward, the look on her face giving the girl no option. Gina reluctantly handed over her phone and Kate passed it to Mrs Godden.

'Thanks. It will be ok, just let me talk to your mum for a minute and then we'll get this sorted out, alright?' She held the girl's eyes.

Gina shrugged one shoulder, 'Whatever.' She slouched off into the lounge, closing the door behind her.

'I don't know what to say? Why would she do that? Why would she make that boy give her so much money?' Mrs Godden left her coffee untouched. She poured herself a large glass of wine and gulped at it quickly as she stared at them, bewildered and angry.

'Because she could.' Steve said quietly.

'Shit!' Mrs Godden closed her eyes, 'As if I didn't have enough problems. Go ahead, talk to her, see what she has to say for herself.'

Gina was curled up in a corner armchair, nervously biting her nails, her pale blue eyes sullen as her mother led Kate and Steve into the lounge. Kate suddenly understood what Joan had said about Gina; about her having a cruel streak behind a pretty face. There was something in her eyes that was calculating, as though she was working out the next move; judging the odds.

Kate sat down and gave her a pretty clear description of how Pink had died. Then she explained the huge police investigation that was going on, emphasising the seriousness of the situation Gina was in. 'What's your dream, Gina?' Kate locked her eyes on the girl's, completely focused on her.

Gina was thrown by the change of topic. 'I'm going to be a model.' She said bluntly.

Kate put on a look of surprise. 'I thought you'd want to be a dancer.'

'Well maybe, but I want to be a model first.' Gina bit into her nail again. 'Why did you think I want to be a dancer?' She was happy to keep the topic away from money and cameras.

Kate's forehead crinkled as though she didn't understand something. 'Steve saw a film you posted on Facebook, the one where you're dancing? I haven't seen it, but you obviously *want* people to see it, so I thought you must be pretty good.' She watched as Gina mentally struggled for something to say; something that wasn't going to get her into more trouble.

'It was only a *joke*. I was just messing about, having a laugh.' She glanced at her mother nervously and shrugged. 'All the girls at school do it.'

'Were you just messing about when you told Andy you'd go out with him? Were you having a laugh when he got two hundred pounds from Mr Pink and gave it to you? Because that's what happened isn't it?'

'I hate him! I hate Andy Frazier, he's stupid and he's a bully. He picks on small kids; thinks he's big, like, but he's pathetic, there's no chance in the world I'd be with him.' Gina was spitting the words out.

'So, you never intended to be his girlfriend but you got him to give you the money anyway?' Kate thought she could see where this was going. At the grand age of thirteen Gina Godden had discovered the power that a beautiful face and body can have over a man. 'Gina, Mr Pink is dead. You have money and a camera that belonged to him.'

'I never took it! Andy took it.' Gina shouted, she was getting rattled.

'*For you*, he took the money and the camera for you. Isn't that right?'

'That man had lots of money! Andy showed me the trainers he'd paid for. He was laughing about him being an old tosser, like, called him 'Pink the perv,' with more money than sense. He said something about if I was a boy I'd have got money off Pink too. I thought that was bloody stupid, so I asked Andy to get me the cash just to see if he would, then he turned up with it and I had to take it. He didn't steal it - the man gave it to him! I never went out with Andy. Whoever said that's a liar.' Her eyes flashed defiantly.

Mrs Godden was looking at her daughter as though she'd never seen her before. 'Where's the money now?' She asked, 'What did you do with it?'

'I bought that new handbag.' Gina muttered around the side of her fist.

'You paid two hundred pounds for a handbag?' Mrs Godden was incredulous, 'What the hell were you thinking?'

'Do you have any of the money left?' Kate wasn't interested in a handbag.

Gina shook her head. 'The bag was a hundred and sixty quid like, and I spent the rest on make-up. If you don't believe me I'll show you the receipt for the bag. I haven't done anything wrong! It's not my fault Andy Frazier's a tosser.'

Kate thought how unattractive Gina was when she pouted. 'Andy Frazier also gave you a camera. It could be very important in helping us investigate Mr Pink's death. Where is it?'

Gina didn't answer.

'You can search her room if you like, I'll help you.' Mrs Godden said.

'I don't have it, honest! I never wanted the sodding camera, I don't have it.' Gina's eyes flashed. She tucked her knees up under her chin and scrunched back into the chair like a small child.

Kate looked at her steadily and waited.

'I don't, I'm telling the truth!' Gina looked at her mother pleadingly, but by the look on Mrs Godden's face Kate wasn't sure if she'd ever trust her daughter again.

'Tell me *exactly* what you did with the camera after Andy gave it to you.' Kate wasn't buying the act. She let the silence hang, knowing the girl was getting more uncomfortable by the second. Gina crossed her arms over her knees and buried her head. Kate leant towards her and spoke quietly.

'Gina, Steve and your mum are about to go upstairs and search your room, then, if we don't find the camera I'm going to go through the contacts on your phone and your friends on Facebook and question each and every one of them about it. As we stand at the moment I'm prepared to believe that you didn't know the camera was stolen and that you accepted it from Andy as a gift, but you *have* to hand it over. It's up to you. Shall I send Steve upstairs to start the search?'

Gina mumbled something without lifting her head. Kate didn't catch what she said. 'Say that again.'

'I said I gave it to Dean Towle.'

'Why?' It was the last thing Kate had been expecting her to say.

Gina lifted her head enough to give Kate a stroppy look. 'Because I felt sorry for him.'

Steve glanced at his watch as they climbed back in to the car.

'Are you supposed to be somewhere?' Kate cocked one eyebrow at him, 'Have you left some poor girl in the lurch?'

'No.' Steve shook his head, sorry that he'd checked the time. He didn't want her to think his mind wasn't on the job. But she didn't sound annoyed, more like she was teasing him. 'Can I ask you something?' He looked across at her.

Kate nodded, settling back in her seat and pushing her hair away from her face. 'As long as you can ask and drive, I don't want Gina to think we're sitting here talking about her, she's looking out of an upstairs window.'

Steve didn't glance up. He put the car in gear and pulled smoothly away from the kerb. 'Why did you tell Gina I was going to search her room with her mum? Shouldn't you have searched it?'

Kate tilted her face towards him and grinned. Her face was animated and, considering the bloody long day they'd had, she seemed full of energy. It was just beginning to get dark outside. Steve was disturbed to find himself looking at her mouth, thinking how small and white her teeth looked against her lip gloss.

'You've never been a thirteen year old girl have you?' Kate was playing with him.

He decided to focus on the road. 'Not recently, Gov, although I did make a very striking Marilyn Monroe at a Rugby Club fancy dress bash a few years back. Several people commented on my legs.'

'But not in a *good way*, I'm guessing.' Kate said, solemnly. 'As I *have* been a thirteen year old girl, I can assure you nothing would bring greater horror than the thought of not just my mum, but a *man* searching through my things. Thirteen-year-old girls like drama and secrets; they don't even want their mums in their bedrooms. Think about how she would feel with you looking through her underwear, finding her tampax, looking at her diary and God knows what else. Gina would rather die. I thought the suggestion might encourage her to talk.'

'Makes sense. I don't think she told us the whole truth though.' Steve voiced his thoughts.

'Which bit don't you believe?' Kate turned in her seat and looked at him with interest.

'I don't believe she felt sorry for Dean. Gina Godden has been using her female charms to run circles around Andy Frazier - who's a little shit - but he's a street wise little shit and she's got him around her little finger. She obviously lies to her mum, although looking at Mrs Godden when we first turned up you can see where Gina gets some of her ideas. Her mum lets her run around looking like a tart - those shorts she was wearing tonight barely covered her arse, and she made a point of bending over and giving me a look at her thong. She's trouble, and I don't believe a girl like that would feel sorry for a kid like Dean Towle. I think she gave him the camera for another reason.' Steve glanced across at her as he changed gear.

Kate was surprised; it was quite a speech. 'Which is exactly why we're going to ask Dean about it.' She pulled her mobile out of her bag. 'You're right, there's more to this story than she's letting on. I wouldn't be surprised if she suddenly turns up wanting to talk to us again. Right now we need to get the camera back before it ends up somewhere else. I'll give Joan a ring and let her know we're on our way, hopefully it's not too late.'

It was Philip who answered the phone. He said Dean was watching telly and he'd get the kettle on for them. As Kate put her mobile back in her bag she heard a low rumbling and realised it was coming from Steve's stomach. He put his hand on his belly as if to cover the noise and grimaced, 'Sorry, Gov, I've missed a meal somewhere.'

Kate suddenly had a flash back to Colin telling her she had to feed him. 'Listen, when we get there I want you to take the lead with Dean. You've built up a relationship with him, so you play it as you see fit. Take it gently, but we have to have the camera. I'll help Joan make you a sandwich.'

There was an easy silence between them as Steve drove and Kate wondered what would happen to her department with Colin gone. Who would replace him? It was a difficult role to fill - the CPU group were a tight knit bunch in a demanding job. She needed someone that would fit in smoothly, someone who would add strength to the team; she didn't need any more drama or complications. There were plenty of qualified detectives, but you could be a bloody brilliant copper and never be able to work child protection - Barmy's premature departure a case in point. Kate had lost count of the number of occasions when she'd brought a suspected child abuser in for interview and one of her colleagues had asked for 'five minutes alone in the cell' with the suspect. She understood where they were coming from, but she would never condone it – plus, putting your fist down someone's throat was unlikely to elicit a confession from them.

They had pulled up at some traffic lights and she realised Steve was looking at her. She turned her face towards him questioningly, 'What?'

'What do you think is on the camera, Gov?'

Kate shrugged, 'There might be absolutely nothing on it. But did Andy steal it because there's a picture of his bum on it, or because there's something else on it he's interested in? Gina doesn't need a camera; Andy didn't gain any credit by giving it to her, so I think he was using her to get rid of it. Why not just chuck it? He gave it to Gina after he'd beaten up Dean and he knew we were looking for him. He didn't want us to find it, but he didn't know his dad had told us about Gina, so I think he wanted to leave it somewhere where he could get hold of it again. Why? What else is on it that Andy knows about? Pink may have taken pictures of other victims. Try and think like Andy Frazier for a second. Could he use the photos to blackmail someone, or embarrass someone? It's *exactly* the sort of thing he would do.'

'It would have to be something he thought he could gain from.' Steve started to speak, but Kate hadn't finished.

'Andy stole the camera just before Pink was killed, what if the killer also wanted the camera?' Kate hadn't really thought this idea through properly, but it was taking shape in her head. What was on the camera that made Andy hold onto it? And why did Gina give it to Dean?

Steve's head suddenly jerked around towards her so fast he startled her, 'Do you think there's a photo of Pink's killer on the camera?'

'Wouldn't that be nice?' Kate thought it was too much to hope for, 'And we'll recognise him straight away because he'll be wearing a grey hooded top with black jeans, and carrying a rucksack.' She was being sarcastic, but you never knew, she'd been in the job long enough to know that stranger things happened.

Steve wasn't put off, 'Worth a thought though, Gov, there's got to be something on it we're not supposed to see.'

***

CHAPTER THIRTY SEVEN

'They're here!' Dean yelled as he yanked open the front door, 'They're here already!' He went scooting back down the hall into the kitchen cum dining room, leaving the door open for them to let themselves in. Kate gave Steve a sideways look - *What the hell was Dean so excited about?* But Steve just shrugged. He was as bemused as she was.

'Hey, what's up?' Kate looked at Joan and Philip questioningly as she joined them at the kitchen table.

Joan got up and went to the kettle, 'Dean wants to tell you.' She said, but she was smiling.

Dean looked like he'd just scored a winning goal. He was so excited his words came out in one big rush. 'The phone rang and Joan answered it and it was for me and I didn't know who it was 'cos I don't ever get phone calls, and I don't know who would know my number.' He ran out of breath and had to take a big gulp of air.

Steve looked at him in astonishment and Kate burst out laughing. She bent down and put her hand on his shoulders. 'Whoa! Hang on mate, I can't keep up.' Her eyes narrowed as she looked at the scars on his face. Pink bits of new skin were beginning to break through and the bruising was going yellow around the edges. She smiled reassuringly, 'Start again... *slowly*.'

Dean looked up at Steve and there was a look of pure desperation in his eyes. He wanted something, and he wanted it really badly - so badly he could hardly get the words out.

'You got Andy for kicking my face, Joan told me you did. You had him at the police station and he told you he'd done it and he has to stay away from me now, don't he?'

228

Steve nodded, 'Well, he's been charged with assault, which means he's going to go to court and the judge will decide what to do about it. And yes, he's been warned to stay away from you. You don't have to worry, Dean.'

'I aint, I needs you not to charger, I mean *charge* Bisby and make it so's the judge don't have to talk to him.' Dean was still rushing his words. 'Can you fix it? Joan said if I told you and it was alright maybe you could fix it so's he don't have to be in trouble, *please.*'

Joan stepped in to help. 'Dean, Steve doesn't know what the phone call was - you have to tell him properly. The poor bloke's got no idea what you're blabbing on about!'

'I am telling it!' Dean was getting frustrated. Steve tried to help him, he squatted down to look Dean in the face, 'Yes, you are. I'm listening, now, who was on the phone?'

'*Bisby.* Bisby rang. He said he were sorry, he said he never wanted me to get hurt and he felt fuck... I mean really bad, AND...' he took another deep breath, 'He wants me to go to his house! He says I can come and play on the computer and he's got Internet and everything and we can hang out.' Dean stopped and his face grew serious. 'He means it, he aint just saying it. He even said sorry to Joan! You can fix it about him and the Judge can't you?'

Steve looked across at Kate and winked. 'Well, Kate's my boss; it's up to her to decide.'

Kate put her most serious face on and looked at Dean as though she was thinking very hard about something. 'Can you keep a secret?' She asked him.

Dean nodded his head solemnly, his eyes huge.

Steve wondered what the hell she was up to - *what secret?*

Kate lowered her voice almost to a whisper, 'Steve's father is a *very* important Barrister, and Barrister's are people who work very closely with judges – they're really the only people who are important enough to talk to Judges, so Steve can do things that other people can't do.'

Dean looked up at Steve as though he'd just discovered his new friend was really Batman.

'So, as you've helped him so much and this is a special case... what do you think, Steve?' She gave Steve a look as though she was asking for his help.

Steve played along, although he had no idea how she knew about his father, 'I'll work it out.' He promised.

Dean looked so relieved Kate wanted to laugh and she had to distract herself. 'Joan, Steve might die of starvation any minute - as apparently I made him miss lunch. Could we make him a Sandwich or something while he messes about with Dean?'

'Cheese and pickle or cheese and ham?' Joan was already looking in the fridge.

'Can I have ham, cheese and pickle please?' Steve said politely, and then turned to Dean, 'Quick, let's go in the other room, mate, before she throws something at me.'

After Joan had taken Steve a stack of thick cut sandwiches Kate asked her about the meeting between Gina and Dean in the park. Joan explained he'd only been gone about half an hour before he came back. He hadn't said anything about it and she hadn't asked him. When Kate told her about the camera Joan frowned with worry and Philip looked up from his newspaper.

'I don't know anything about it,' Joan said, 'I didn't see him come in with anything. God, is this ever going to end? I just think he might be turning a corner and something else happens. I told you Gina was trouble; why the hell would he take a camera from her?'

'Gina is very good at getting boys to do exactly what she wants.' Kate took a seat at the table, 'I'm more interested in *why* she gave it to him than why he took it.'

'You can't blame Dean. If that girl asked him to hide a loaded gun for her he'd do it.' Philip said.

'And shoot his bloody foot off!' Joan pulled out a chair and sat down, exasperated.

There was the sound of someone running up the stairs, a door banging and footsteps running down again. They waited. Five minutes later Steve stuck his head around the door, 'Ready to go, Gov?' He asked.

Kate gave him a questioning look and he nodded. 'It's ok - I've got it, but Dean doesn't want to talk about it anymore this evening and I've told him that's ok – he can talk to us when he feels ready.'

'Well, thanks for the coffee, and for feeding my colleague.' Kate got up and nodded to Joan, 'I'll call you tomorrow.'

Joan nodded, relieved.

It was a subdued Dean who showed them out. 'Did you find Brian?' He looked up at Kate, hopefully.

'We're looking. We haven't found him yet, but we'll keep looking.' Kate promised.

As they pulled away Kate saw something in Steve's face that she hadn't seen before; anger? No, that wasn't what it was, although it was something close to it. He was thinking about something, something upsetting.

He took one hand away from the wheel and wiped it across his forehead.

'Gina told him to hide the camera. She told him it was his 'insurance', and that it would keep him out of trouble - but he doesn't know what's on it. She told him to keep it until the fuss died down.'

'What did she mean 'keep him out of trouble' what trouble?' Kate didn't get it.

'About Andy, *that trouble*, that's all he could say. I don't think he really understood either; but he thought if he was in trouble because he was in Pink's garden, or if Andy came after him again, having the camera was some sort of get out of jail free card. Gina just told him to hide it where no one would find it and not to tell anyone. He thinks Gina was trying to help him – and he's crazy about her; in that bloody awkward thirteen year old boy way.' Steve glanced sideways at her, a small grin playing across his face.

'Are there photos of Dean on it? Did he look?' Kate still wasn't sure why Gina wanted Dean to have it. Had she told the truth? Did she feel sorry for him?

Steve's jaw tightened. 'When I asked him, he was almost crying; said he'd tried to but he didn't know how to make it work and he was afraid he'd break it. I told him we'd been to Gina's house and he wouldn't have to explain to her why he didn't have it anymore. Poor little bugger was relieved to hand it over - Christ, no wonder he needs a friend.'

Kate was sympathetic but she was worried, 'let's hope he *didn't* break anything. Check it in with the evidence officer and get the techies to download it tomorrow - it's too late to do anything about it tonight.' She suddenly remembered she didn't have her car at the station. Steve had picked her up from her house so many hours ago she'd forgotten about it. So much had happened - the investigation was moving forward; but they still hadn't identified a suspect and she still needed to find Brian.

'I'll wait and give you a lift home if you like, Gov.' Steve hadn't forgotten she was without a ride, 'It seems a nice place you have - very countrified.'

Kate nodded, 'It's quite small, it's a stable conversion, but there's only me there most of the time. My daughter's away at college, so it's peaceful.' She slid down into the seat, tiredness pressing down on her suddenly.

'So you're divorced.' Steve said, making an assumption.

'Widowed. Look, you don't need to wait for me, I'll get a traffic car to drop me off.'

'Ok.' Steve didn't know what to say after that.

***

CHAPTER THIRTY EIGHT

He knew he wasn't going to bleed to death but knew he was still going to die. He didn't want to die.

Tape bit into his injured thigh, stopping the flow of blood from the knife wound but cutting off the circulation to his lower leg. Bishop tried to balance on his good leg, but he felt sick with the pain and he was afraid of falling. He was blind, the same heavy tape wrapped around his head, covering his eyes. His blindness was terrifying. His hands were wired behind him to a metal rail separating the animal pens. He'd struggled and tried to keep his hands out and free, but the point of the knife pricked the skin on his groin and the fight went out of him. Now he was focused on staying upright, and fighting the panic, trying to stay calm. He needed to think, he had to find a way out of this, but every ounce of his being told him there wasn't one.

With no sight, his other senses tried frantically to compensate. He smelt the baked concrete under his feet and the ancient smell of thousands of animals that'd passed through these pens on their way to their own deaths. The shed was isolated; he knew for a fact the loudest screams wouldn't' be heard – he'd tested it.

He licked at the blood on his upper lip, trying desperately to think, to gain some control over his mind, to calm the terror that was overwhelming him; draining his energy quicker than the pain. Suddenly his knee collapsed sideways and he went down heavily on his injured leg. His good leg shot out from under him. As he scrambled to keep his balance the wires cut into the soft flesh of his hands; his full weight was suspended on his wrists behind his back. He screamed out, but his cry was cut short as a gloved hand gripped the front of his throat and squeezed, forcing his head back so hard he thought his neck would break. He was going to pass out. He wanted to pass out - anything to get away from the bastard agony.

'Stand up.' The words were whispered into his ear and he was yanked upwards by the hold on his throat.

Instinctively the foot of his injured leg tried to find leverage, to help push him up until a fireball of pain exploded through his calf, up into his knee and thigh and he went down again, his head hanging.

'I can't, I... please.' He was sobbing now, blood mixed with tears dripped into his mouth.

'Stand up.' The voice was pleasant, encouraging, cheering him on. 'Come on, you can do it.'

He put what strength he had left into the effort and slowly dragged his body up until he was almost standing. 'Why?' He could only whisper. He swallowed the blood in his mouth and tried to turn his head towards where he thought his attacker was standing. 'Why? Turn me in; have me disgraced - I'll go to prison. You don't have to do this.' He was still crying but his voice was coming back.

Silence. He turned his head again, his imagination feeding his terror. Then he heard the knife. He heard it slice through the air, and then nothing in the world would have kept him upright. It pierced the fabric of his trousers and dug into the soft flesh of his testicles.

He screamed

Kate didn't invite the traffic boys in for a cuppa. She knew they'd jump at the chance, but she'd managed to keep up with their cheerful chitchat in the car and now all she wanted was to get inside the sanctuary of her home and collapse. Getting a wine glass from the kitchen dresser she was surprised to find she was out of Merlot. How had that happened? She found a decent bottle of white in the rack on the inside of the fridge door and decided that would have to do. She kicked her shoes off, tucked her legs under her and curled up on the old leather sofa. There was a hollow in the cushions that had moulded to her shape over the years. Was she drinking too much? It was only a fleeting thought, easily dismissed. There was no way she'd be able to sleep - not yet; a glass of Chardonnay would help.

Now that she was alone in the privacy of her home and sanctuary she could acknowledge the feeling in the pit of her stomach as a great big dollop of guilt. She'd snapped at Steve when he'd assumed she was divorced. He wasn't the first person to jump to that conclusion, to assume that as a single mum bringing a daughter up on her own she must have failed at the marriage thing.

I didn't fail at marriage; I had a great marriage, I was good at marriage. My husband didn't leave me - he died. I was going to spend the rest of my life with him - but the rest of my life was only a few short years.

That's what she really wanted to say, but 'widowed' was simpler and less likely to make him feel like a shit. But she'd made him feel like a shit anyway. As soon as the word was out of her mouth she'd felt the way it cut into him, embarrassing him, scorching whatever it was he was going to say next into silence.

Kate sipped her drink, called herself a bitch and wondered if she had the energy to make it up stairs. It wouldn't be the first time she'd slept on the sofa. Her father had turned up in the drive one afternoon with it sticking out of the back of his Volvo estate. She'd spent an hour on the phone to him the night before; never once mentioning how lonely she felt, how vulnerable and so *bloody sad* she was, wondering if she'd ever wake up and not hurt because there was a huge empty space in the bed and a much bigger one in her life.

Angel had been her salvation. She was nearly three when it happened, and three-years-olds, *thank God,* are busy little people hell bent on rushing towards the big new world they're discovering; rushing towards it with scrapped knees and a million questions and the need for tickles and cuddles and *life to move forward*. So Kate got up and got on with it, grateful that her daughter had her daddy's eyes, so she only had to look at her face to remember him.

But Kate's own father knew her too well. Dragging the sofa into the house he'd sat her down, pulled her into his shoulder, covered her with a blanket and held her while she cried it all out.

It was fifteen years since Duncan had been killed, and she still hated the word 'widow', it was such an ugly word. The sofa had got better with age. *Which is more than I have.* Kate shook her head and, smiling, forced herself to her feet. She needed to buck up; she was only feeling melancholy because she was tired. She put the wine bottle away - she needed a shower more than she needed another drink. Stripping off her clothes in the bathroom she stood and looked at herself naked in the mirror. *Long legs, no boobs.* It wasn't going to get any better. At least she still had a flat stomach. *Probably because you forget to eat.* She stood in the shower for a long time with her head tilted back, letting the hot water wash over her, but the tension remained.

She set her alarm for five thirty so she could get in a run before leaving for work. She'd only have time for three of four miles, but at least it would wake her up and clear her head. She wondered what it would be like to have Rick as a personal trainer. She decided that if she ever had the money and the time she'd hire him.

Kate crawled into bed naked; her hair still damp, but she felt better. Her last thought before falling asleep was; *Angel's coming home tomorrow, she'll soon fill the house up with noise. And what the hell is on that camera?*

***

CHAPTER THIRTY NINE

Kate watched as Steve pulled into the station car park just ahead of her. He was early; it was only seven thirty. She was surprised and assumed he'd be heading towards the canteen and a bacon butty before the briefing, but then she remembered he was going to interview Adam Dyer in prison. She would be on her own today.

'Morning, Gov.' Steve didn't smile as he held the door open. Her hair smelt clean as she passed him.

'You still on for the prison visit?' She asked as they climbed the stairs to her office.

'I'm leaving straight after the briefing; I need to do my write ups before I get going.'

The embarrassment of last night's referral to her marital status wedged itself between them. It made Kate feel tired, tired of being a widow, tired of the awkwardness of explaining and the problems of *not* explaining. She wanted to say something, something to break the tension, but nothing of any use came into her head so she quickened her pace and walked briskly ahead of him, relieved they weren't spending the day together.

The briefing was packed, it was standing room only, but it was clear there were more setbacks than successes and Kate recognised an atmosphere of 'disengagement'. They were going through the motions but the energy was missing. There was none of the usual vigour or *intensity* that drove a murder investigation.

They'd failed to identify a single witness who'd seen anyone emerge from the front garden of the house with the broken fence post, or in the industrial area behind the cul-de-sac. There were still people to talk to but it wasn't looking promising. Local papers had agreed to run a picture of the kid Bruce Jeffries had described, but they also wanted to run the story about Pink being a suspected paedophile, so the Press Officer was currently locked in battle with them.

Kate looked around the room as Stacey droned on. He was

trying hard to make nothing sound like something and the team were getting restless.

Eventually, Stacey wound down and Edwards stood up to give his report. He was holding a mug of coffee in one hand and trying to read from his notes in the other. Kate saw his hands tremble; he was either hung over or needed a drink – maybe both. He spoke slowly, but with just enough edge in his voice to make people pay attention.

'A number of former associates of Pink's have been spoken to – mainly in Hockley. Without exception they fall into one of two camps; they either think he was a saint, or a complete pain in the arse.'

A couple of sniggers went around the room, which Edwards acknowledge with a nod before continuing. 'Pink was employed as a Facilities Manager with the County Council before taking early retirement and moving to Hockley. He was responsible for supervising contract work being carried out in schools around the district.'

Kate's eyes met Steve's and she nodded – they were both thinking the same thing: *A suspected paedophile working in schools – perfect!*

'We tracked down his former boss at the council, he described Pink as...' Edwards checked his notes, 'an utter bloody nuisance. We were relieved when he asked for early retirement because it saved us the trouble of firing him. He was an obnoxious old git.' Edwards looked up – he had their full attention, 'And this was *after* I'd told him Pink had been murdered. To say his colleagues didn't like him would be putting it mildly. None of them had a good word to say about him, but we didn't find anyone that was suspicious of his behaviour with children, or that might have held a grudge serious enough to kill him.

'In Hockley he worked on a casual basis maintaining the grounds around buildings used for Sea Cadet training, and volunteered as a minibus driver with a Methodist Church and a youth group called 'Key Kids Klub'. Not surprisingly, it was the church and the club people who thought he was a saint. We're still waiting to talk to someone from the Sea Cadets.'

'So our victim, *who had a thing about young boys,* worked and volunteered in areas that gave him plenty of access to kids. Doesn't that tick all the boxes for your profile?' Stacey gave Kate a questioning look. 'And that's all very entertaining, but it doesn't exactly get us anywhere.' He turned back to Edwards.

'One other thing,' Edwards ignored the sarcasm, 'He was employed on a casual basis at the MCSC and was never subject to a CRB check. But, he was clever enough to walk away, *unblemished* after messing about with those boys in Hockley, so it wouldn't have made any difference. He'd kept his name off the Sex Offenders Register, so no-one was any the wiser.' Edwards threw his plastic coffee cup in the general direction of the bin in the corner and sat down.

'What about his finances?' Stacey changed the subject.

Natasha stood up. She looked nervous but spoke clearly. 'No money worries, Sir. Pink has fifteen thousand pounds in a savings account and another six thousand tucked away in a couple of ISAs. He inherited sixty thousand pounds from a relative, an uncle, the year he retired... '

That got everyone's attention. There was a decent amount of money floating about, certainly enough for a motive.

'There's one main bank account, in his name only. Anne Pink has an account with a building society. She has a state pension and a hundred pounds a week paid into her account from Pink's bank on a direct debit. George Pink has a pension from the council and there's a monthly payment of one thousand pounds paid into his account from a rental agency in Hockley. Pink owns a house, which he rents out. I've checked with the agency, they handled all the arrangements; the tenants are a young married couple. The man at the agency said he didn't think they'd ever met Pink. The bungalow in Clare Walk is rented through the local office of the same agency - Hicks and Hughes. There's no mortgage payment, the Hockley house is owned outright. There's a life insurance policy on George Pink with Anne Pink as the sole beneficiary.'

'How much?' Stacey interrupted,

Natasha looked for the entry in her notes. Kate was impressed that the young woman was staying calm; not letting Stacey ruffle her. 'Fifty thousand, Sir.' Natasha read it out, 'There is a will, but we don't know the details. As you know, Mrs Pink is having a difficult time at the moment so we're not using her for information. She's not been very well and she's gone a bit...

confused. Pink regularly withdrew two hundred pounds a week in cash, although utility bills were paid by direct debit. No credit card debt and no big purchases in the last two years.' Natasha turned over a page in her notebook, 'There are no regular payments to any agencies or clubs, but we did find some regular card payments to a magazine distributor which Pink paid over the phone.'

'I don't suppose he was ordering Gardeners Monthly?' Edwards quipped.

'He ordered 'Bad Puppies', a gay porn magazine featuring young men.' Natasha gave Edwards a direct look, but her face had turned slightly pink.

'Get a warrant issued for the will.' Stacey snapped, 'That's a lot of money in one way or another. Who benefits from his death?' He turned and gave Kate a hard look, 'Camera?'

She stepped forward and turned to face the room, waiting for quiet. 'Pink took photographs of the boys at the MCSC. He was particularly interested in Andy Frazier. Andy let Pink take a photograph of him mooning, but the two of them fell out when Pink realised Andy was leading him on to get money out of him. There was an argument where Pink threatened to show the photographs to someone else. We don't know who that other person was, but we think Andy was frightened enough to steal the camera. The camera was passed from Andy Frazier to Gina Godden and then to Dean Towle.' Kate was speaking quietly, but all eyes were on her. She pointed out that the camera had been stolen a day or two before Pink's death.

'Talk to the Frazier kid again, find out what that's all about.' Stacey said, impatiently.

Ginger stuck his hand up, 'Do you think this other kid is on it, the one in the grey Hoodie?'

'I have no idea, hopefully the technical guys will let us know later, but what are the chances of us getting that lucky?' Kate grinned.

There was a general buzz of conversation around the room as several uniformed and CID boys started offering bets, but the noise stopped when Barmy walked in. She let the door bang shut behind her, effectively getting everyone's attention. 'Todd Martin was in The King's Head from eleven on Monday morning until he and his brother got thrown out by the landlord at three. Rule him out - he's a waste of time. *But* he is on his way back to prison.'

There was a smattering of applause and a few frank comments around the room. Stacey rapped his knuckles on the desk to bring them back in line, 'Ok, let's get back on track. We're still working on the theory that this person,' he tapped the photo-fit on the board, 'used the route through the neighbour's garden to get away. I want the focus kept up locally - someone, somewhere must have seen this person or knows who he is.'

The briefing went on for another fifteen minutes before jobs were allocated and Stacey released them. Kate decided to walk out with Steve as he left for Bristol. She was giving him a couple of pointers on conducting the interview with Adam Dyer when she caught the look on his face and decided to shut up and let him get on with it. She gave him her sideways grin; trying to make a joke out of it, let him know that she wasn't pissed at him, but all she got back was a blank stare which made her feel stupid. *Oh well, he could have it his own way.* Kate pulled three packets of Benson and Hedges out of her bag. 'Give these to Adam.'

'How do you know he smokes?' Steve shoved the fags into his pocket.

'I don't. But even if he doesn't, cigarettes are a currency inside. It might help him warm to you.'

As she stepped back into the hallway Mary stuck her head out of the reception room, 'Mr Raymond Greggs has been here since eight o'clock waiting for you.'

Who? It took Kate a moment to recall who Greggs was. Hadn't he waited all day yesterday for her? She looked into the dreary reception room. A pleasant looking man was sitting very still with his back against the wall. He nearly jumped out of his skin when he saw her, but he managed to get a grip on himself and looked up at her expectantly.

There was such a desperate look of hope on his face that Kate felt immediately guilty.

'Mr Greggs? I'm Kate Landers,' she held out her hand as he jumped up, 'I'm so sorry you've had such a long wait, would you like to come in?'

The look of utter relief on his face made the hairs stands up on the back of Kate's neck.

***

CHAPTER FORTY

Raymond Greggs was struggling to string a sentence together. As she settled him in the interview room Kate's interest in him grew. He was like a frightened rabbit. What on earth was he so afraid of? She leant towards him and smiled reassuringly. 'Tea or coffee? I'll drink coffee so strong you could stand a spoon up in it, but I'm sure I can find a decent cup of tea?'

Raymond's face crumpled and the massive effort he'd been making to hold it together ended as enormous sobs racked his body. His head dropped onto his chest but his hands didn't move, not even to wipe the tears from his face, they rolled down his cheeks as he wept.

Kate wasn't embarrassed when men cried. It had happened to her so many times she really didn't think too much about it. She sat and waited, knowing the storm would pass and he would start to talk, and when he did it was likely that the floodgates would open and he wouldn't be able to stop.

Raymond eventually leant back, pushed his hand into the front pocket of his trousers and pulled out a hanky to mop his face. 'I'm sorry, *I'm so sorry.*' He could only whisper.

Kate quietly crossed the room and picked up the telephone receiver on the wall phone. She punched four numbers and waited for someone to pick up.

'DI Landers here, I need a nice strong cup of tea with plenty of sugar and a strong black coffee in interview room four please, as quick as you like. Thank you. Oh, and find some biscuits.' Then she sat back down and waited for Raymond to talk.

It was painful, agonisingly painful and slow. Raymond started, then stopped, started at a different place and then stopped again. His story started the day after his tenth birthday, the day his father placed him in the care of the local authority. As Kate listened to his slow precise speech, she knew that this story had never been told before; he had never said it out loud, not to anyone.

'Why did your father give you up and put you in care,

Raymond?' she asked quietly.

Raymond was sipping his tea so that he could think before answering, 'My father didn't like me.' There was no emotion in his voice; it was as it was, he wasn't looking for sympathy.

'What happened to your mother?'

'Died. I don't know when, my father never told me. I was very young. I just grew up knowing my mum was dead. My father resented the fact that he'd been left to raise me, it wasn't easy for him, so I went into care.' Raymond wiped his face again.

Kate nodded, encouraging him to go on.

'I had an uncle. He was married but they didn't have any children. He and his wife took me out for the day every Sunday. What I mean is, they took me to church; their church, they were religious you see?' Raymond paused, breathed in deeply and closed his eyes. 'That's how I met him, at church. *Uncle George,* I had to call him Uncle George. He drove the van sometimes for the youth outings.'

Silence again. Kate could see he was struggling to find the right words.

'I... I,' another false start, 'I loved him. At first I loved him. I wanted him to be my dad; I wanted to live with him. I dreamt about being with him all the time. He was the dad I should have had. I thought God had sent him to take care of me. Then I just wanted him dead. Then all I could think about was how I was going to kill him.'

Kate's facial expression never changed; there wasn't a flicker of movement from her. George Pink, *Uncle George,* was dead, but Kate doubted Raymond had killed him. Everything her experiences had taught her about human behaviour told her she wasn't talking to a murderer. So why was he here? She knew the answer before she asked the question, but she asked it anyway, 'What changed?'

'Uncle George didn't love me, not the way I needed him to. What I thought was love wasn't it at all. He was besotted, even *in love* with me maybe, but only for a little while.'

As she looked into the eyes of the man opposite her Kate saw a ten-year-old boy who was bewildered and sad, but above all was dreadfully *lonely.* Kate could only wonder at how much he'd been hurt.

'He said he loved me, he told me it all the time. Every time he put his arm around my waist, every time he put his lips on my face he told me he loved me. He never stopped saying it. He told me I was special; very, very special, and that meant something. But I was eleven by then and I realised he wasn't right. There was something wrong with him; he wasn't right in the head. He was just this pathetic, very unhappy person who wanted to be with me all the time. He would break down and cry, just like a baby, and he... well, he *needed* me, but I just wanted him to love me and me alone. I didn't have anyone else; no one cared about me. I wanted him to love me more than he loved Brian, but he couldn't, Brian was the *special* one.'

Kate tried to stop the flare of surprise that flashed in her eyes, but it was too late. He'd said the name and she'd flinched. She leant forward onto her elbow, her eyes fixed intensely on Raymond's face.

He paused again in confusion. 'You know about Brian?'

'Do *you* know him?' Kate answered with a question, but Raymond looked bewildered, as though his story had taken a wrong turn. 'No, no, I mean I couldn't. Pink had been with Brian before, before I met him, a couple of years before. But he still loved Brian, much more than he loved me; he talked about him all the time - that's what made him so unhappy. I think I reminded him of him; he told me I did - I was just a substitute.'

His eyes held the hurt that was still alive and the bitterness of his failing to be the special one. 'I couldn't take his place, and I wanted to, I really wanted to.'

Kate had no doubt he'd tried. A young boy confused at his abandonment, to all intents and purposes an orphan, then getting the attention that he craved; however it was offered, only to discover that he was a stand-in. But why was he a substitute? Had Brian moved away? Had Pink's relationship with the other boy been cut short? *Was Raymond Greggs the link to finding Brian?*

'How did Pink know Brian, was Brian in care too?'

'I don't know. I didn't know who Brian was, I just knew that I reminded him of this special boy; *his Best boy*, the one he really loved.' Raymond's voice cracked.

Kate's forehead creased into a frown and she pulled on her upper lip with her teeth, perplexed. 'Why wasn't Pink with him anymore? Where had Brian gone?'

Raymond sat back in his chair, a look of profound sadness on his face. 'Brian was dead.'

Brian had died as a child.

Kate's mind couldn't get past this fact. Had she been looking for a ghost child?

Raymond obviously thought that if Kate knew about Brian then she should have known he'd died.

'How do you know that?' Kate was astonished. 'Did Pink tell you Brian was dead?'

'Yes, he was still crying for a dead boy years after it happened – after he'd gone.' Raymond's ability to talk confidently was growing as he spoke. His stuttering and stumbling were behind him as he told his story. It was what he'd come here to do, and as it unfolded his relief at the telling was evident.

'Do you know anything else about Brian? How old was he? How did it happen?' Kate asked softly.

'Twelve, Brian was twelve, just...' Raymond stopped. Something was tripping him up, making it difficult for him to get the words out.

Kate asked the question again. 'How did he die?'

Raymond answered so quietly that Kate almost thought she'd misheard him.

'George Pink killed him. I don't know how, I just know that it was his fault. That's why the man was possessed... or obsessed, I'm not sure which, but it was guilt you see? He was responsible for Brian's death - the boy he loved more than anything else in the world.'

She sat back, stunned. She was doing the sums in her head and thinking how badly this didn't add up. Brian had died more than fifteen years ago.

'Raymond, do you know anything about a mouth organ? It was in a tin in Pink's shed. Was it something to do with Brian?'

Raymond's mouth twitched at the corners, almost a smile, 'He kept it did he? I'm not surprised. MBB, is that right, the initials on it?'

Kate nodded.

Raymond ran his hands over his neatly combed hair, and then cupped them behind his head, leant back and stared at her intently.

'One Sunday, I was with him in his shed, it was like a kids den - coloured lights strung around the ceiling, pictures of footballers on the walls; magazines, all sorts of stuff. He'd been to the pub and had a drink and his breath stunk, I couldn't bear it. He was trying to cuddle me but the smell was making me feel ill. He was a bit pissed and I pushed him away and he fell over. At first I thought he was angry, but then he started babbling, going on about my face; how he wanted to touch my sweet face.'

Raymond's voice cracked and he had to clear his throat before he could go on. 'I called him a smelly old goat. I told him 'If your precious Brian was here he'd tell you that you stink, he wouldn't want you, no-one wants you! Next thing I knew he was crying like a baby. He took this old green tin down off the shelf, took the mouth organ out and started stroking it against his cheek. He was crying so hard, sobbing 'My Best Boy, my poor, poor Brian.' It was something he'd given to Brian and he'd kept it after he died. MBB: *My Best Boy.* I think that mouth organ was probably his most treasured possession.' Raymond lowered his hands and rubbed his eyes, 'I hated him by then.'

'Why are you here?' Kate asked quietly, 'What made you come here today to talk to me?'

'I'm going to Canada.' Raymond said it as though it was as simple as going out for a coffee.

'Sorry?' Kate didn't understand.

'Cheryl, that's my wife, did I tell you about her? No, well we have a plan; we're going to Canada. I have a job that I can do there and we won't have any trouble getting in. I need, no *we* need, a new start. I just want to be better than I am. I want to be something for me, for Cheryl, for *us.*'

'But why wait for me, why couldn't you tell this to one of my colleagues?' Kate had no idea why he had singled her out.

Raymond looked up, a shadow of sadness masking his face, 'Because you're the child abuse detective.' He stated it as a fact; undisputed, 'Pink was responsible for the death of a boy, a twelve-year-old boy he said he loved, a boy who looked like me. I wasn't special to him. Oh, maybe I was for five minutes, but not for long. What I need to know is - was Pink a child abuser? Is that why this happened to him? I heard he got arrested for it once, but nothing happened. Someone wanted to kill Pink and they actually did it. I loved him once, and he was besotted with me, but I didn't know about any of that – not then, not the abuse stuff. I just thought he was a bit soft in the head; daft or not right or something.' Raymond stopped and shook his head, 'Sorry, I'm not making much sense, I'm confused. I want to know – I *need* to know. If Pink was a child abuser why wasn't he stopped? Why didn't you stop him?'

Kate heard the question and it hit her that she didn't actually know the answer. *Was Pink a child abuser?*

'Did Pink ever make any sexual advances towards you? Was there anything sexual in his relationship with you, use of pornography, or photographs... anything like that?' Kate suddenly had a vision of a band wagon hurtling along, everyone jumping on for the ride, with Stacey sitting up front.

'Nothing,' Raymond Greggs suddenly looked exhausted, 'that's why I need to know. Like I said, I don't think he was right in the head – a grown man crying and wanting to cuddle me like that all the time. Just a sad old git really, I thought he was like that because of what had happened to Brian. I was devastated when I realised I couldn't take Brian's place, but then I thought I'd maybe had a lucky escape. Whatever had happened to Brian might have happened to me.'

Kate stared at him. For once her life she was speechless. She didn't know what to say.

Two cups of tea and two ignored messages from Stacey later Kate showed Raymond Greggs out. As she watched him walk away his head was up and he was in control of himself again. She mentally crossed her fingers for him, for Cheryl and for their new life in another Country, hoping the past wouldn't follow him.

Kate wanted to get back to her office, make a strong pot of coffee and start a search for a sudden death report of a boy called Brian in Warwick many years ago. If someone was seeking vengeance for Brian's death why would they wait so long? It seemed unlikely, and yet she couldn't let it go, not completely, not until she knew what had happened to him.

***

CHAPTER FORTY ONE

There was blood, not a huge amount, barely more than a trickle but it told Steve a lot. He looked at the side of Adam Dyer's neck. A thin red line dribbled down from a narrow slash wound and stained the collar of the boy's prison issue shirt. Someone had had a go. Either that or the boy had made a pathetic attempt to slice his own throat, and he didn't seem suicidal, just wary.

There was the usual show of sullenness and tough guy shit, but Steve knew it was a sham - it always was. Once they were locked up these young lads craved any distraction, anything to trick their minds away from the fear, the violence, and the fight just to get through the day. Adam Dyer was glad to see anyone - even if it was a copper. He'd been locked up for three months. No family to visit him, no friends, just the occasional 'officialdom', and they were paid to do prison visits. So Adam might be doing the 'don't give a shit' stunt, but he was scared, he was lonely and he was pathetically grateful to see anyone.

'What happened to your face?' Steve leant over the table and tried to get the boy to look at him.

Adam shrugged, 'What happened to yours?'

Steve grinned. 'Rugby, but I doubt you're playing that in here. Bit of bother?'

'No, ice skating.'

Steve ignored the sarcasm, 'Fine. Next time run your blade over the other guy's face instead of your own.' Steve knew how to play this game - a pissing contest with a seventeen year old wasn't really a contest at all. Adam was fighting his nerves. He was pretending he didn't give a toss about why Steve was here, or anything else for that matter.

'Look, you can tell me to fuck off if you like or you can help me.' Steve's tone was casual, but Adam looked up, his eyes questioning. Steve kept talking. 'George Pink was burnt to death in his shed. He was assaulted and set on fire, the door locked so he couldn't escape.' Steve paused and waited for a reaction.

There wasn't one. Adam sat perfectly still, watching him, expressionless. Steve ploughed on. 'Look, I know that Tony Contelli hung himself because of something that happened with Pink. Tony was your mate and it seems like you both had a shit deal over what happened.'

'Yeh, right...' Adam snorted in his throat, the blank look on his face turned to one of contempt.

Steve was confused, 'Ok, maybe worse than a shit deal - you were let down, badly. Pink had tried it on with you and he'd slapped Tony about when Tony stood up to him. And you were two little troublemakers, kids in care, just a big fat nuisance to everyone. You told your story, but it seemed like no one believed you and Pink walked away scot-free. I understand how screwed up Tony must have been, how messed up things got afterwards.' Steve wanted Adam to understand he was telling the truth, he really was sympathetic, but the expression on the boy's face didn't change.

'You don't understand shit,' Adam slouched down low in his seat and stretched one long thin leg out in front of him. He looked up and met Steve's eyes with a look of intense scorn. 'Tony and I set it up. We set that idiot up, like, for money, only we never got any.'

Steve hesitated. *What the hell was this about?*

Adam's eyes held Steve's and he visibly made his mind up.

Steve recognised the exact moment when it happened - when Adam decided to talk to him.

'Tony topping himself weren't nothing to do with Pink the perv.' Andy said it as though they were discussing last night's football match. 'It's a good name though, don't you think? Tony thought it up, he always had names for people, it made us laugh and it stuck - Jeez, everyone started using it. One time we saw him cleaning out the minibus. Tony got this big bit of cardboard and wrote 'Pink the Perv Pimped my Ride' on it and stuck it on the windscreen. Fucking hilarious. It did Pink's head in though, nasty bugger.'

Steve was still stuck on the bit about them setting Pink up. If it was nothing to do with Pink and they'd made up the stuff about him being a pervert, then what the hell had happened to Tony?

'Why did Tony hang himself?' He asked the question.

'Because he was better off dead.' Adam threw the words at Steve as though daring him to challenge them.

Steve didn't react. He sat motionless, waiting for Adam to tell him why, to explain what the hell had happened.

'The sicko stuff, that's what did his head in.' Red patches appeared under Adam's eyes as he spoke, 'That's what he couldn't live with. We thought we were so fucking clever; it took us ages to come up with the idea. And Tony... he acted like he was a hard case, but he couldn't handle it. He got so scared sometimes he'd throw up; puke all over himself. We thought it would stop; we thought we were totally brilliant, like, that we could stop it and make some money at the same time.' Adam spoke so quietly Steve had to lean in to hear him properly.

The boy shook his head and a thin dribble of blood started to slide down his neck towards his collar. 'I don't give a fuck what happened to Pink the Perv, but it had nothing to do with me or Tony.' He lifted his eyes to meet Steve's, 'And you don't know shit.'

Steve had no idea what the boy was talking about.

Kate liked the Technical Support officer who was working on Pink's camera, but she only knew him by his nickname, 'Bunny'. She didn't know why he was called Bunny and she knew better than to ask, knowing it would be something unsavoury. He was a civilian member of staff and was bloody good at his job, so much so that the fact that he didn't give a shit about anyone's authority, had a slightly bizarre personality, and could often be heard singing to himself whilst he worked, was largely overlooked by senior officers. He was also a flirt and was at least fifteen years younger than Kate.

He burst into song as she took a seat next to him. '*Isn't she lovely, isn't she wonderful*' he crooned. He was wearing designer jeans with a crumpled Abercrombie and Fitch shirt and white plimsolls.

Kate looked him up and down and wondered what they were paying techies these days as she thumped her fist against his thigh and gave him the benefit of her disapproving look. 'Show me photos.' She demanded.

Bunny stopped singing and pulled his chair forward so that he could crouch over his keyboard. He opened a file and a sheet of thumbnail size pictures filled the screen. 'Long or short version?'

Kate rolled her eyes, 'What do you think?'

He grinned, 'Short version it is. It's a 10.2-megapixel camera with an 8gig memory card added. I've got about two hundred photos recovered and down loaded so far for you to look at.'

'Two hundred! Bloody hell, how many are there?' Kate was appalled.

'Maybe fifteen or sixteen hundred,' Bunny said, cheerfully, 'and I'm guessing you want all of them.'

Kate nodded slowly, 'Show me.'

'Right, it's not very exciting; there's no blood, or gore or dead babies or anything.'

'Fine by me.' Kate stared at the screen.

'Don't frown, there's still enough stuff to have fun with.' Bunny grinned.

Kate gave him a sharp look but he ignored her. He opened the thumbnails one at a time. The first dozen or so pictures were of tall purple flowers with lots of trees in the background. *'If you go down to the woods today...'* Bunny sang softly, until Kate punched him in the leg again. Then he opened up several photos of, what Kate assumed, was the back of Pink's house.

'See, told you - *dead* boring.' Bunny was trying to be funny.

Kate was perturbed. Paedophiles often put seemingly mundane pictures in front of photos they didn't want discovered as a way of hiding them. It was the same as hiding a pornographic movie in a case with a children's film title on it. She leant forward to study it more closely. She was looking at a photo of Pink's shed, but it was more like a timber and brick room built in the garden. More pictures of Pink's garden followed and then suddenly the scene changed and she was looking at a landscape of a green field lined with trees on one side and a country lane on the other. In the distance she could see some sort of structure built on a square concreted apron surrounded by metal railings. The next photo showed the same low building taken from a different angle showing fields on three sides. Kate thought she recognised it but couldn't remember where it was.

Then the photos changed to pictures of boys playing football. She made Bunny go through each photo slowly while she tried to identify individuals. One team was playing bare-chested and she spotted Dean in several shots. Some of the photos weren't very well focused, or were in shadow, but it didn't look like Pink was targeting one particular boy – that was until Andy Frazier appeared in a shot.

The first photo of Andy had been taken from a distance. He was walking across the back of the MCSC with Bisby a step behind him. Several more photographs of Andy followed and Kate began to feel like she was seeing him through the eyes of a stalker. Pink was *following* Andy; from a distance, but in some of the photos he'd used the zoom to get a close up. One of the photos showed Andy giving the finger straight to camera.

'Blimey,' Kate put her hand out as the next photo flashed up, making Bunny hold it on the screen,

'I'm sure that was what Pink wanted.' She tilted her head at the monitor.

Andy Frazier was leaning against a brick wall, one leg bent at the knee with his foot on the wall behind him. He was leaning back, nonchalantly, his t-shirt worn around his neck like a scarf; his bare chest and flat stomach wet with sweat. His thumbs were hooked in the pockets of his baggy jeans; so low on his hips they barely covered his crotch. His head was turned sideways, eyes looking somewhere off in the distance. He looked like a young David Beckham.

'Actually I think this is what he wanted.' Bunny opened the next photo. It was a close up of a smooth bare backside; so close up in fact that it filled the screen and it was impossible to see whose backside it was. Kate thought it must be the picture of Andy mooning that Bisby had told Steve about.

Bunny clicked on the next picture and the scene changed dramatically. Standing inside, what had to be the changing rooms at the MCSC, Andy had his back to the camera. He was facing the white tiled wall, his lean body starkly accentuated by the cold, bland background. His hands were thrown upwards on either side of his head, as though he was caught up in the rapt worship of something wondrous, but unseen. He was stark naked.

Kate sat back in her seat, crossed her arms and looked straight at Bunny. 'That's a bit more than 'mooning', wouldn't you say?'

Bunny nodded. 'The next one is taken by the cameraman *of himself* - a self-portrait you might say. It's just his hand holding his dick.'

'Are you serious?' Kate raised her eyebrows.

'Sorry, 'fraid so.' Bunny wasn't making jokes about it. He pressed a key and the picture opened up.

'That's George Pink entertaining himself,' Kate said adamantly, 'you can see his right foot - he was wearing those shoes when he died.'

'But even that's not as interesting as this next one.' He smiled as though he was just about to thrash her at poker. 'The *big* question is why did he take this photo?'

Kate stared at the image that filled the screen and sat back in shock. She was looking at a photograph of herself.

***

CHAPTER FORTY TWO

Pink had taken a photograph of her walking down the front steps of the station. She was alone and, by the way her hair flew straight out behind her, it looked as though she was in a hurry. Kate stared at the image, trying to figure out when it had been taken. It couldn't have been that long ago. She leant in towards the monitor studying it closely. In the background a uniformed officer was standing on the station steps, holding the door open for Stacey, who was wearing a civilian jacket, probably going off duty.

'Can you zoom in?' She turned and faced Bunny, 'Can you see who that uniform is?'

'Traffic officer David Bench, known as 'Park'.' Bunny grinned at her. 'Way ahead of you.'

Kate rolled her eyes and turned back to the screen. The photo had been taken in bright sunshine and she was wearing jeans and her short sleeved white blouse, which she'd only bought at the start of the summer - so it had to be in the last couple of months.

Why would Pink take a photograph of her? She'd never heard of him before last Monday. She was certain their paths hadn't crossed, but he'd obviously had some sort of interest in her. Kate's internal alarm started to shrill loudly.

'Who else has seen these, who knows about them?' She asked, quietly.

'Just you, Gov.' Bunny was being serious for a change.

'Leave it like that will you? Just leave this with me for now.' Kate needed time to think this through.

Bunny shrugged. He didn't have a problem with that. He didn't have too much interest in her authority, but Kate was the Detective

Inspector on the Child Protection Unit and that cut her a whole bunch of slack that Bunny wouldn't be inclined to give to anyone else.

'No worries.'

Kate left Bunny, and, with no better idea of where to start, wandered over to the incident board. Everything they knew, all the keys points of the case, was on the board and it told her nothing. Nothing that was any help in figuring out what the photos were about or what Pink was doing.

She went back over her interview with Raymond Greggs. He'd been very close to Pink for a couple of years but he was as confused about the man as she was - there were more questions there than answers. She started to type up her report on the information from Greggs, hoping some inspiration would come to her.

As she wrote she realised she'd have to tell Dean about Brian, but what could she tell him? How could she explain that Brian had died? She felt sorry for Dean; he'd been through so much in the last week and all because he wasn't good at telling time. If he'd got the details right and turned up at Pink's when he was supposed to... Kate sat bolt upright, suddenly struck by the dreadful realisation that she'd missed something. *What was it Dean had said when she asked him if he was supposed to go to Pink's house with someone?* She put down the report and pulled up the transcript of Dean's interview at Hope House. With a growing sense of urgency she scanned the transcript until she found what she was looking for. She read it through twice, and then grabbed her bag and ran down the stairs.

When she walked into Joan's kitchen ten minutes later Dean was making milkshakes and making a mess. His face was full of disappointment when he realised Steve wasn't with her.

'I need to talk to you, Dean,' Kate spoke quietly, getting his attention, 'I've made a mistake and I need your help.'

Joan raised her eyes questioningly – did Kate want her to leave? The slightest shake of Kate's head told her she needed to stay, so Joan sat down at the table and buried her head in a gardening catalogue.

Dean looked up, curious.

'I asked you about something and I didn't pay enough attention to the answer, I've made a mistake.' Kate was still speaking softly, making him listen to her. Dean shrugged, like it was no big deal.

'I asked you if you went to Mr Pink's house with anyone, the day of the fire. You said you were supposed to go with the dog, but you couldn't find him. What dog, Dean? You don't have a dog, so whose dog were you supposed to take with you?' Kate leant forward, searching the boy's face.

In the background Joan stopped reading the seed packet adverts and watched her young fostered child. Kate got the impression Joan knew about the dog, but she needed to hear it from Dean.

'It ain't *a dog*,' Dean looked baffled, as though he had no idea why Kate had got this so wrong, 'It's *The Dog*; a *him* - he's a person.' The way he said it suggested everyone knew this, and Joan was nodding her head - but Kate still didn't get it.

'I said *The Dog*. I know I ain't got *a real dog*, I ain't allowed one 'cos I'm in care.' Dean was playing it for all it was worth, making sure she understood how poor and hard done by he was. Kate realised what he was saying; what he'd meant in his first interview and she felt her stomach clench. There was *another* kid, someone else who was supposed to be at Pink's house that day with Dean, but she'd missed it. Who on earth was *The Dog?*

Without a word Joan got up and left the room. Kate stared at Dean, waiting for him to tell her. What else had she missed? Had she been so upset about the row with Stacey and being tasked with the murder investigation that she'd ignored important information? Had everyone else who'd been there understood what Dean meant? Philip must have - he hadn't commented on it, or questioned it. Maybe Mivvie did too, she was there, she didn't ask about it either. Mivvie would know Joan and Philip didn't have a dog.

Kate was devastated. She'd missed a crucial part of the interview because she was upset with Stacey for taking her away from the CPU, was cross with Knowling for not supporting her and pissed off with Steve for flirting with her social worker partner. Great Detective Inspector stuff this was. Any more of this and she'd be a legend due to her own stupidity.

Dean started sucking his drink noisily, waiting for her to ask the obvious, so she played along. 'Help me Dean,' she looked at him pleadingly, 'I don't know who The Dog is - you need to tell me.'

Before he could answer, Joan reappeared in the doorway. She was holding what looked like a large scrapbook with several bits of paper hanging out of the pages. The book was bulging with stuff and Joan was trying to hold it together as she walked in. Placing the book on the kitchen table she pulled her spectacles down off the top of her head, perched them on her nose, and opened the front cover. 'There's a photo of The Dog in here somewhere.' She said.

Kate ran up the stairs to the incident suite and passed Ginger in the hallway, 'Where's the DCI?' She demanded.

'In a meeting with the Commander, Ma'am, he'll be back for the briefing.'

Kate caught the cautious tone in his voice and her eyes narrowed, 'What's happening?'

'Don't know Ma'am.'

'But?' Kate gave him a look that told him she wanted to hear whatever he had to say.

'But the Commander didn't look over the moon when he turned up and there were... 'words' earlier.'

Kate was confused. Bloody Ginger was talking in riddles, 'What do you mean 'words', between who? Say what you mean.'

Ginger took a step closer to her; lowering his voice as though he was afraid he'd be overheard. 'DCI Stacey wanted to pick up the guy from the MCSC, the coach, Rick Hart. He and Knowling had 'words' over it and the DCI *decided* to leave it for now.'

Kate stared at him, appalled. What the hell was Stacey thinking? There was no evidence that Rick was involved... or had any knowledge for that matter, of Pink's activities. What was Stacey trying to achieve? Was he under so much pressure to get an arrest that he was going off on wild goose chases? She didn't believe for a second that Rick even knew about the photos of Andy Frazier.

Ginger was watching her reaction with concern, 'Anyway, the idea is off the table... for now.'

Kate would have to tackle Knowling at some point. Bringing Rick in for questioning would be a colossal mistake. 'Ok, Come with me.' She nodded.

Ginger followed her into the offices, 'Gov?' He was looking at her expectantly; he knew full well that something was up.

'*The dog*,' Kate's voice gave away the sense of agitation she felt at her own incompetence, 'Dean Towle was supposed to go to Pink's with *the dog*, but he couldn't find him. He didn't mean a *dog* - it's a boy's nickname.'

'Sorry?' It was Ginger's turn to be confused.

'Eddie Lead is the dog, as in *dog lead*. Dean thought we knew that. Eddie told Dean he'd meet him on Monday but the arrangements were a bit vague. Dean was expecting to meet Eddie outside the MCSC. Eddie knew Pink had invited Dean to his house and he said something like, 'Going to Pink's? Ok, I'll meet you,' which made Dean think they were both going. Eddie didn't turn up, probably because Dean was an hour early, so Dean went by himself and ended up face down in the garden with flames licking the back of his neck.'

'So this Eddie guy, is he a friend of Dean's?' Ginger realised the implications of what she was saying.

'No - that's just it, Eddie's older than Dean. Dean's exact words were: *he's an awesome mega skateboarder, but he ain't got no mates, 'cos he don't want none.*'

'So why did he say he'd go to Pink's with him?'

'Dean doesn't know, but he felt happier about going because he thought there'd be two of them. When he thought he'd missed Eddie he still went, hoping Eddie might already be there. Here, Joan had a photograph of Eddie.' Kate took the print from her bag and handed it over, 'It was taken a month ago, so at least we know exactly what he looks like. Put his name into the system - see what comes back.'

Ginger studied the picture without comment and then handed it back.

Kate stared at it for the umpteenth time since Joan had dug it out of the book. The photo was of Dean having a go on Eddie's skateboard; wobbling unsteadily, arms outstretched like a trapeze artist for balance. Eddie was watching from the grass verge. He was slim with an athletic build, but his shoulders were hunched; his hands thrust deep into the front pockets of his baggy jeans. There was something about him; *vulnerability* was that the word she was looking for? Kate wasn't sure, but she couldn't take her eyes off his face, there was something mesmerising about him.

Eddie's head was down and he was looking up from under a dark fringe plastered to his face with sweat. There was a peculiar stillness about him; separating him from everything around him. Something dreadfully *sad* about his young eyes, something that pulled at her, making her heart ache for him – and she didn't have the foggiest idea why. She'd seen it on Joan's face too. When she'd lifted the photo from the album Joan had gazed at it for a moment, holding it in both hands, as though she was reluctant to hand it over. The look on her face as she'd held out the picture and pointed to the image of Eddie was something close to wistfulness, or maybe broodiness, Kate wasn't sure which, but Eddie Lead was a heartbreaker.

'Gov?' Ginger was walking back with a piece of paper in his hand. Kate gave herself a mental shake and looked up.

Ginger started reading from the sheet in his hand. 'Edward Norman Lead, fifteen years of age - he's on record.'

'Why?' Kate was thrown, caught off guard.

'We're getting the full details now, but I've got his home address, he's in care with the local Social Services. Eddie Lead is in foster care.'

Kate leant back against her desk and folded her arms, her mind racing off in several different directions at once, '*Shit, that makes four.* Four boys we know about who are in some way connected to Pink and are, or have been in foster care with the local Social Services.' She stared at Ginger as she reeled off the details, 'Dean Towle is in foster care. Andy Frazier and Josh Martin have both spent time in care recently, but are back with their parents. Eddie Lead was *supposed* to go there with Dean and he's still in local care.'

Kate held out her hand and Ginger handed her the piece of paper with the details on. She didn't recognise the address but the name rang a bell, Mr and Mrs Murphy were fostering Eddie Lead. Wasn't that the people Andy Frazier had stayed with? She could get more information from Social Services - but it was Saturday and they were closed.

'Is Eddie a CPU case?' Ginger asked.

Kate shook her head, 'No, this is the first I've ever heard of him.'

Natasha walked up with a computer print out, 'Your boy was arrested for razzing in June, Ma'am. He was brought here, questioned and released to the care of Social Services.'

'Who was the arresting officer?' Kate barely gave her a chance to finish the sentence.

Natasha scanned the sheet, 'PC Thomas, Greg Thomas. I've just seen him, he's in the canteen.'

'Get him... please.' Kate wanted to hear this story. She wanted to know everything there was to know about Eddie Lead.

'Wrong place, wrong time,' Greg Thomas remembered the case well, 'The boy got scooped up in the clean sweep operation and brought in, but it was pretty clear early on that he wasn't with the Razzers.'

'Tell me.' Kate was perched on the side of the desk and Ginger was leaning against the wall, leaving Greg the chair. He was happy to help, anything to avoid going back out on patrol.

'You remember the problems we had last June, Gov? Those idiots razzing through the town centre a couple of times? They caused mayhem, knocking little kids down and barging into old people. Bags and purses got stolen, a couple of people got hurt?'

Kate nodded. The craze had started in London on certain underground networks and had spread to shopping centres. Large groups of teenage boys, with nothing constructive to do, stampeded through the shoppers, whooping and hollering and putting the fear of God into people. They wore the obligatory hoodies with scarves tied around their faces like bandits so it was difficult to identify them on CCTV. There had been such an outcry in the local papers that the Chief Constable had been put under severe pressure.

'Well, Clean Sweep was us razzing the razzers.' Greg gave her a cheeky grin, 'We'd got some intelligence about when the next event was taking place and basically we outnumbered them. Twelve boys were brought in. I remember Eddie because there was something different about him. I knew almost immediately he wasn't part of it - he never once spoke to any of the others. He had a skateboard with him, which he carried like it was an extension of himself, and there was something... well, he was just so *quiet*. The others we'd brought in were all yelling the odds; swearing, making a nuisance of themselves and what have you until the custody officer got them sorted out. Eddie was a world apart from that. He struck me as being a bit of a lost soul.' Greg looked a bit sheepish, as though he'd said something unmanly.

Kate thought she knew exactly what he meant and she'd only seen a photograph of Eddie.

'Anyway, we had good film footage; it was easy enough to eliminate him, although it took a bit of time to get it sorted, and off he went.'

'Who was his appropriate adult when he was interviewed?' Kate asked.

'That was a bit odd,' Greg paused; thinking back, 'I spoke to his foster mum on the phone. I'd just about managed to tell her what had happened when she started having a major drama; crying, saying something about 'my poor baby,' it was completely over the top if you ask me. I got the impression she was a sandwich short of a picnic. Eddie's fifteen, hardly a baby. But then she couldn't, or wouldn't come to get him. We had to get the duty social worker in - the poor kid was here much longer than he should have been. I guess he's just one of those sorts.'

'What sort?' Kate didn't understand what he meant.

'One of life's victims.' Greg shrugged.

'Ma'am, phone,' Natasha held out a receiver, 'It's DC Astman.'

Kate had to lean across the desk to reach it. For a moment all she could hear was a roaring noise, then Steve's voice cut over the din. He was on his car phone and he sounded excited.

'Your mobile's off, boss. I've been trying to reach you to make sure you'd be there when I get back. I've got some unbelievable information for you. Stay there, Gov, I'm ten minutes away - I'll meet you in the office.'

There was a click followed by a dial tone. He'd hung up.

***

CHAPTER FORTY THREE

'Adam Dyer didn't tell me to fuck off, in fact he was quite happy to chat.' Steve shouted from the bathroom. Kate sat back on her desk, her frustration growing.

Andrea walked in and gave her a questioning look. Kate shrugged, 'Steve's got some info from Adam Dyer, but I'm losing the will to live while he gets around to telling me what it is. Do you know a kid called Eddie Lead?'

Andrea took her cardigan off and slung it over the back of her chair. She looked hot and bothered. 'Got mistakenly pulled in for razzing when the uniforms did that operation in town last June - that Eddie Lead?' She asked.

'How come you knew about that and I didn't?' Kate was wide eyed with surprise. She wondered if she was starting to lose the plot.

Andrea's large square jaw dimpled as she grinned, 'I happen to be a totally brilliant detective.'

Kate looked at her suspiciously,

'And I met Greg Thomas on the fag corner – he's a bit of a gossip.'

Kate rolled her eyes, and then turned towards the door connecting to the washroom. 'Astman! If you're not out here in two seconds I'm sending Lulu in.' She yelled.

'Is Lulu cute?' Steve yelled back.

'She's a ruddy great Alsatian - trained to kill people who wind me up, so stop doing your bloody hair and get out here!'

Steve was rolling his cuffs back on his shirtsleeves when he appeared in the doorway, 'They set it up, Gov, Adam and Tony, the accusations against Pink - they set it up.'

'What?' It was the last thing she'd expected him to say, 'Why?'

'Because they were desperate, and Pink was a fool who suited their purpose.' Steve was enjoying his moment of revelation. 'They planned it between them. They knew there were boys who went to Pink's and got money for helping him in his garden. There'd been all sorts of rumours about it; and Tony invented the name 'Pink the Perv.' They didn't like him because he was a 'miserable old fart' but he hadn't actually done anything to them - nothing criminal.'

He'd lost Kate - she had absolutely no idea what he was talking about. 'So it wasn't true? Tony and Adam were setting him up? But why, what was it they were so desperate about? What are you on about?' She demanded.

Steve crossed to the coffee pot and poured himself a mug full, his face serious, 'Tony Contelli was being regularly and brutally assaulted by his social worker in Hockley. It started almost as soon as he got placed in foster care, and the bloke was violent, so the boy got hurt - he didn't have anywhere to turn. But what really pushed him over the edge was when he found out he'd been filmed. He was blindfolded and tortured and some bastard filmed it.' Steve paused, watching Kate's reaction, making sure she followed.

'The people whose job it was to protect him were responsible for the abuse. Adam and Tony were too scared to do anything about the social worker, because he had total control over what happened to them and was a sadistic bastard. But they thought if they set Pink up and got him in trouble with the police – and at that time half the bloody neighbourhood were already calling him a pervert thanks to them - they could blackmail him by saying they'd drop the charges if he paid them. More importantly they believed the social worker would run scared and leave Tony alone, or better still, the boys would get moved to a new area and out of harm's way.'

A growing sense of dread was descending on Kate like a bad migraine. This was a major nightmare scenario - and it could only get worse. 'But it got dropped anyway, and nothing changed,' she said quietly. She thought she knew where the story was going, 'Pink was let go, so they couldn't blackmail him, and worse still - both boys stayed where they were, which I'm guessing means the abuse didn't stop.'

'Worse. Even when Tony got banged up he was still only fifteen and the social worker visited him inside. Tony couldn't escape from him. No wonder the kid topped himself. What he couldn't live with was thinking that other people might be watching the films, watching what he was going through and enjoying it. Tony couldn't live with that.' Steve was still watching her face.

'So we've got a social worker in Hockley who's a sadistic child abuser *and* filmed the abuse?'

'*Exactly*. That's why I was trying to call you. I'm sure Boz and Maggie would like to hear about it. This bastard needs to be picked up.'

'What's his name?' Kate glanced at her watch; the briefing would be starting any minute.

'John Bishop.'

Kate stared at him in horror. The sense of dread exploded in her chest.

'*Shit!*' Andrea swore loudly and swung around in her chair so fast she banged her knee painfully on the side of her desk, 'Fuck!' She swore again.

Steve glanced sideways at Andrea, then back to Kate, a small look of puzzlement just beginning to cross his face, 'You know him?'

'John Bishop is a social services team leader responsible for foster care placements,' Kate's voice was calm, 'but he's not in Hockley anymore - he's here, he works for our social services department. *Shit.*'

The look on Steve's face was a mixture of both shock and anger, 'And Pink and Bishop knew the same boys.'

Kate pinched her forehead with two fingers and tried to think what this meant. George Pink had lived in Hockley before he moved to Marville. Bishop was a social worker in Hockley and had moved to Marville as a team leader. How long ago? She couldn't remember, was it two years since Bishop had arrived on the scene at social services? The link between George Pink and John Bishop were the locations and the same vulnerable boys.

'There's something else.' Kate quickly brought him up to speed with the information about Eddie Lead. 'So that's four kids on the list who were in foster care plus Adam and Tony in Hockley. Bishop would have worked with all of them. But why did Bishop only target Tony and not Adam?' It struck Kate that Adam Dyer was projecting; telling about something that had happened to him, but making out it had only happened to Tony.

'Definitely not Adam, Bishop didn't want him,' Steve was adamant, 'Adam Dyer is HIV positive, which Bishop would have known because it's on the kid's records. Even a sicko like Bishop wouldn't go there, especially as there were lots of other boys to play with.'

'Then we don't have a victim.' Kate looked at Andrea who met her eyes, shrugged her shoulders and nodded, agreeing with her.

Steve looked at Kate in disbelief as he realised what that meant, 'But you just said he's *here*; he's responsible for placing kids in foster care homes. He's the *leader* of that team. The bastard is on *our patch*.'

Kate glanced quickly at her watch again and made a decision, 'Briefing. I'll give a selective update on the photos from Pink's camera and take responsibility for the delay in finding out about Eddie Lead. Don't say anything about Bishop; it's too sensitive, we need to get that information in front of Knowling first, understand?'

Steve nodded, and held the door open for her. 'You're the boss.'

'You haven't got a victim.' Knowling told her what she already knew, 'And without a victim, you don't have a complaint - and you certainly don't have any evidence, nothing that's going to let us arrest Bishop.' He leant back in his chair, tapping the end of his pen against his bottom lip. He was talking the problem through, dissecting the information, but it kept hitting the same brick wall.

Kate had insisted Stacey meet with them in Knowling's office after the briefing. She was trying to work the problem out calmly, but she was rattled,

'Adam Dyer has no reason to lie, there's nothing for him to gain, so why would he even bother mentioning it?' She was struggling to keep the frustration from her voice. She'd ignored the fact that both Stacey and Knowling were disgruntled with her and had plunged straight into Steve's bombshell. Now they were into the problem of what to do about Bishop.

'He's a foster placement *team leader*,' Kate ran one hand through her hair and blew her fringe out of her eyes, 'Talk about sending a wolf to guard the lambs! He was in Hockley working with boys in care and then moved here and got promoted giving him even more control over these kids!' She looked at Stacey, 'If we're talking about ticking boxes for a profile, Bishop ticks them all.'

'Do you have any evidence that Bishop and Pink knew each other?' Knowling looked questioningly at her.

'No. But even *if* there's a connection between Bishop and Pink – other than the fact that they both moved from Hockley to Marville round about the same time, there's no evidence that Pink was sexually abusing *anyone.*' She saw Stacey roll his eyes, but she ploughed on. 'Not one of these kids has said they were physically assaulted by him. And Raymond Greggs, who was as close to him as anyone, said that Pink cuddled him and kissed his face because he was broken hearted about a boy who'd died. *That's it,* nothing more sexual than that! On the other hand Bishop was apparently torturing Tony Contelli and filming it!'

'You've only got Adam Dyer's word to support that. And he's admitted lying about Pink when he and Contelli made up the allegations about him.' Stacey retorted angrily, 'He just might have seen an opportunity to pull our chain and entertained himself by making up some bullshit about his social worker. Why not? He's probably back in the prison canteen right now laughing with his mates about how he wound us up. Pink was stabbed in the genitals and burnt to death. What motive have you got for that if he wasn't a sex offender?'

'Everyone believes Pink was a sexual predator. Tony and Adam were the ones who gave him the name 'Pink the Perv' in the first place, but we don't have a scrap of evidence to say he was anything other than a 'cuddler', a pathetic character who was used by some of our local toe rags when they found out they could get money out of him.' Kate looked to Knowling for support, but none was forthcoming. He stood passively behind his desk, arms folded, watching her.

'Tony Contelli killed himself - nobody made that up.' she said, trying to keep control over her voice.

Stacey was dismissive, 'It's not the first time some kid hung himself in a Young Offender's Institution. It happens. They find themselves banged up for the first time; can't cope with the isolation, the bullying, there could be any number of reasons why he did it.'

'This is all guesswork at the moment,' Knowling decided to join the discussion. 'Bishop and Pink may or may not have known each other. All of these boys were, or are in foster care where Bishop had access to them, but most of them were visitors to the MCSC, where Pink also had access to them. It may be a coincidence – but were Pink and Bishop attracted to the same boys? And this stuff about Eddie Lead – you don't have enough information about him. We're investigating a murder and we don't know anything about a boy who obviously knew the victim and should have been at his house the day he died.' Knowling raised his eyebrows as he spoke. He was playing devil's advocate.

Kate wanted to strangle him.

'What about Bishop?' She didn't bother trying to hide her exasperation, 'Dean Towle, Andy Frazier, Josh Martin and now Eddie Lead - Bishop has been involved with all their cases... and dozens more. We need to cut off his access while we find enough evidence to build a case.'

'You don't have enough to arrest Bishop.' Knowling spoke softly, but he was adamant.

Kate felt like screaming, 'Bishop could well be out and about this weekend continuing to abuse boys that are in the care of social services. Are you going to risk that? We'll talk to the kids, but it needs proper planning and a couple of good interviewers... ' Kate had another thought, 'and we can't risk Bishop getting to the kids before we do. We might find someone's who's willing to talk; we'll need to move quickly, but you have to work with the social services management and get Bishop out of the way.'

'Adam Dyer wasn't lying,' Steve, standing quietly in the corner watching the conflict, suddenly spoke up, 'I believe him. His best friend killed himself because he was too scared to tell anyone what Bishop was doing to him. He knew no one would believe it. Are we going to prove him right, just accept that Adam couldn't possibly be telling the truth - when other kids could be suffering the same fate as we speak?'

'Of course not,' Knowling snapped. He wasn't going to be accused of standing on the sidelines by a DC who'd only been in the department for five minutes, 'There are two separate issues here – and you don't know if they're linked. The boys who were involved with Pink have all been less than eager to tell the truth. Some of the same boys may be able to tell us about the activities of John Bishop, but they're not the most credible witnesses. Without physical evidence we'll be fighting the CPS to take it on. At the same time it's a highly sensitive situation that could blow up at any minute. The Social Services are already reeling in the wake of the baby Chrystal and Baby Callum stories; this needs to be handled carefully, with the proper people involved.'

'Eddie Lead can be interviewed tomorrow.' Stacey tried to make a decision, but Kate cut him off.

'You *can't* talk to Eddie, or any of the others about Bishop until Bishop is taken off the scene. Eddie is in care; you'll have to talk to him with his social worker present. You can't do that until Bishop is dealt with.' She was getting more and more annoyed.

'We can talk to him about *Pink*. We have a witness who saw a teenage boy turning into the path behind Pink's house shortly before he was burnt to death, and, as you reported, Eddie Lead was planning to visit Pink on Monday.' Stacey glared at her.

Kate wasn't about to cave in, 'You've got a description of a slim person wearing a hoodie - it could have been my grandmother based on that.' Her frustration was making her reckless.

'That's enough!' Knowling put his hand up to stop the argument, 'We have something to work towards. I'll speak to the head of social services and share our concerns. I'll ask that Bishop be suspended from the Children and Families Division while an investigation is conducted. You need to establish whether or not Pink and Bishop knew each other, and you need a victim or witness that's prepared to make a statement and, if necessary, go to court.' He nodded at her, emphasising the point, then he opened the door, 'Thank you Kate. Get your reports made up before you leave.'

Kate realised she was being dismissed from the meeting. She wanted to say something about Rick Hart; ask if Stacey was still intending to bring him in, but the look on Knowling's face was a warning. For once she took the sensible option and did what he wanted her to do - she left, taking Steve with her.

There were vending machines at the back of the incident room that dispensed a variety of drinks for those that couldn't be bothered to go to the canteen or make their own.

'Give me money.' Kate held her hand out, palm up, towards Steve. He stuck his hand in his pocket and handed over a variety of coins. Kate selected a bottle of sparkling water. 'What do you want?' She stepped towards the hot drinks machine.

'A cold beer,' Steve put his right hand out and leant against the wall, effectively barricading her in, 'And then I want another cold beer - but I'd like to know what you're planning to do, Gov. I thought this was all about Pink being a child abuser? Now I feel as though we're groping about in a fog, trying to avoid a shit storm.'

'So, welcome to child protection work. You're getting NATO coffee.' Kate fed money into the machine without looking up.

'NATO?' Steve didn't get it.

'White with sugar, you're going to need the energy.' Kate carefully lifted the brimming cup out and handed it to him with his change. 'We only know about John Bishop because of what's happened to Pink. If Pink hadn't been murdered we'd be none the wiser - we wouldn't even be looking at Bishop. You went to talk to Adam about Pink and this stuff about Bishop just came out of nowhere – which is why I believe it's true. *Plus*, You're not that crap a detective that you wouldn't spot a kid like Adam Dyer spinning your wheels, whatever Stacey wants to think.' Kate put her bottle down on the counter and held her hand out again, 'Let me have a sip of your coffee.' Steve handed it over.

Kate's eyes locked on his face as she took a sip and winced before handing it back. 'That's vile.' She took a deep breath in and leant her head back, stretching her neck to ease the tension, forcing her shoulders down as she breathed out. 'Gerry Crane is head of the Families and Children Division. He's already in trouble over their handling of Chrystal's case and Callum's death; this will just about finish him off. Knowling won't have any trouble getting Bishop taken out of action while we investigate - but we'll have to work fast and find someone who'll talk to us.'

Kate realised the enormity of what they were facing. Bishop's whole case file, here and in Hockley would have to be looked at.

'Or we could find the film with Tony on it.' Steve didn't sound very hopeful. 'I'll start with the CEOP in case it's been posted on-line.'

Kate nodded, but she was thinking about something else. 'Go and see if Bunny is still around. Get the photo we've got of Eddie over to him and see if he can match it with any of the photos from Pink's camera. I'll call Rick and find out what he knows about Eddie; if he ever saw him with Pink, or if Bishop was ever seen at the Centre. That's about all we can do until we know what the plan is.'

'We're going to follow a plan? You mean from the Super and DCI Stacey?' Steve voice was sarcastic as he threw his empty plastic cup in the waste bin.

For the first time all evening Kate smiled and Steve looked at her in surprise, he wasn't sure what he'd said to entertain her.

'I didn't say anything about *following* the plan.' Kate frowned with disapproval, 'I just said we'd know what it *was*. My plan is to get to every contact, every source of information that we can possibly dredge up and keep at it until we have the evidence we need to make an arrest.' Kate realised that the tension of earlier had collapsed. There was too much going on - they didn't have time for any awkwardness.

'Great! Oh, but I'll have to drive so that you can play your 'let's go and arrest someone music.' Steve cocked one eyebrow at her, suppressing a smile.

'Don't mock. It will come, trust me.' Kate was determined, 'Gina Godden and Andy Frazier are lying to us about something and Andy was fostered by the same people that are fostering Eddie. There's a bigger story here; we're not seeing half of it yet - and didn't I just ask you to do something?'

Steve gave her a half grin, turned and made his way over to the board to retrieve Eddie's photo. Kate flung herself into a desk chair, grabbed a phone and dialled Rick's number.

The Incident Room team members who'd been close enough to hear snippets of the exchange passed looks to each other that spoke volumes. The atmosphere in the room started to fizz as anticipation grew. There was something big unfolding - they could feel it.

Rick's phone went to voicemail and Kate was surprised at how disappointed she felt; she'd been looking forward to talking to him. She didn't feel it was something she could leave a message about, so she asked him to call her when he had a minute and clicked her phone off.

Kate was still working on her reports twenty minutes later when Knowling and Stacey entered the room and all heads turned to face them. Knowling walked smartly over to where Kate was sitting, put one hand on top of her desk monitor and leant towards her. 'I need to see you in my office.'

Kate gave the mouse a final click, closed her report and rose daintily to follow him out. Stacey waited for them to leave, his face unreadable, before he spoke. 'Anyone who had Sunday off will be disappointed. See the duty officer for shift changes.' He looked around the room, silently warning anyone who felt like complaining, but there wasn't a single comment. Satisfied, he nodded and walked out.

'Right,' Ginger leapt up and rubbed his hands together, 'who's coming down the pub then?'

***

CHAPTER FORTY FOUR

'There's been a phone call from Sarah.' Knowling indicated Kate should take a seat but she remained standing, suddenly anxious. *Why would Sarah call him and not her?*

'Colin's been admitted to hospital.' Knowling raised his hand and cut her off as she was about to interrupt, 'She didn't call you because you're too close. She's not blaming you, but you're the *Queen of child protection*, her words not mine, and she's upset.'

'Why is Colin in hospital?' Kate felt her stomach twist in a knot. Of course Sarah should blame her, why wouldn't she?

'He's suffered a break down and he needs professional care for the moment. Sarah's upset because Colin broke down, crying in front of the boys and she blames the service, us, for what's happened.'

'Well she's right.' Kate was devastated. 'You allowed Stacey and Barmy to commandeer me away from the unit when we were understaffed and Colin was under enormous pressure. I saw how stressed he was and I ignored it. I got wrapped up – allowed myself to be dragged into this enquiry; didn't give him the support he needed. We did this, you *know* we did.'

'*We* didn't do this, there are always...'

'Well we *let* it happen!' Kate didn't let him finish, 'He won't come back. *If* he's ever able to return to duty he won't come back to the unit. We've just lost a bloody good child protection officer.'

'*Sit down Kate.*' Knowling pointed at a chair.

'Have you got worse news for me?' Kate stayed on her feet.

'I've told you what I know; we'll support Colin and his family in every way that we can. Now *sit down.*'

Kate hesitated for a second longer before lowering herself into

272

the chair. She was tired of fighting with everyone.

'Now listen,' Knowling's voice was firm, 'I'm bringing in help from Hockley. Boz and Maggie will be here on Monday. You're going to need them and Steve to help identify any victims linked to Bishop. I'm meeting with the head of the Families and Children's Department in half an hour. I've dragged him away from a dinner party, so he fully appreciates the seriousness of my call. Bishop will be suspended and supervised.'

Kate tried to speak but he cut her off.

'You can't do it all on your own, so don't bother arguing. In Colin's absence I'm making Andrea up as Acting DS and Steve's secondment will be extended - indefinitely.'

Kate wasn't sure what she thought about that, but he didn't ask her opinion. 'I'm calling a conference for Monday morning to plan the way forward. Now bugger off.' He waved his pencil towards the door.

'But, what about...'

'For Christ's sake! Will you do as you're told for once? Try and remember this is a team effort?' Knowling exploded, 'You're a bloody good detective - the best when it comes to understanding the warped mind of a child abuser, but we have to separate the child protection issues out of the mix of this murder enquiry. If you took a breath for a second you'd realise I'm trying to help you; although you seem hell bent on sticking your own neck in the noose half the bloody time!' Knowling saw the mix of defiance and anxiety on Kate's face and his voice softened, 'I don't want to see you before eleven o'clock tomorrow. Take a couple of hours off; have a lie in, run up a hill, whatever it is you need to do to get some perspective.' He pressed his lips together supressing a smile. Kate was passionate and tough and there was no doubt that she was a fighter, but she was vulnerable because she cared, probably more than she should. Knowling took a deep breath and pointed at the door again. He needed her to leave - before he did something unprofessional.

Steve was leaning against the wall in the hallway, waiting for her. 'Are you coming to the pub, Gov?'

'Can't, I'm busy.' Kate barely looked at him; her mind elsewhere as she jogged down the stairs with Steve in step beside her, 'We're re-grouping first thing Monday to work on Bishop with Boz and Maggie.'

They stepped out into the sunshine. A group of officers and support staff were gathered between the door and smoker's corner loudly discussing which pub should be graced with their custom. As Kate and Steve paused on the station steps a pale yellow mini turned into the yard. It was an eye-catching, limited edition with white stripes painted down each side of the bonnet. Kate was busy checking the message screen on her mobile as Steve left her to join the group waiting on the corner. The mini came to a halt in the middle of the yard and the driver's door was flung open. A pair of long, smooth brown legs appeared, ending in a pair of dainty pink plimsolls. Steve's interest peaked as he got a brief glimpse of a firm, slender body and a swish of white blond hair as the girl turned sideways to grab something off the back seat before she started to climb out.

'*Bloody hell!*' His eyes followed the girl, 'I'm usually a tit man but she can wrap those legs around me any time she likes.'

There was a horrified silence. Kate turned her head and gave him a look of such intense hostility he felt his stomach drop, and then she ran across the car park and into the girl's outspread arms.

'*Prick!*' Ginger spoke under his breath, 'You've just lusted after Kate's teenage daughter. Kate's going to kill you.'

Steve went pale. He stared at Ginger in horror, his heart beating wildly somewhere just below his throat, 'Oh, fuck!' He turned back, but Kate and the girl had already got into the mini.

'Prick,' Dave 'Park' Bench repeated the insult, 'you're seriously fucked. She's still at school.'

DC Edwards thumped Steve on the arm and grinned unsympathetically, 'At least I only fancy her on the quiet. Come and have a drink - it might be your last chance.' He threw his fag end towards the metal bin but it missed, landing on the concrete path.

The mini swung out of the car park and without hesitating pulled straight out onto the road. 'Bless her little heart - she drives just like her mum.' Ginger shook his head as the mini disappeared.

Steve felt sick. He couldn't believe how badly he'd fucked up – and he'd done it twice. 'What happened to Angel's dad?' He asked, 'I put my bloody great foot in it asking Kate if she was divorced.

She told me she was widowed, what happened?'

There was a general shrugging of shoulders; glances passed between the men, but no one spoke.

'Look, I've humiliated myself enough already; my career in the CPU is in the fucking toilet, so would someone please tell me before I shoot myself?' Steve was pleading with them - he'd had enough of being the new boy.

In the end it was Edwards who took pity on him, 'Duncan Landers was in the job, traffic officer, frigging brilliant driver. He was on a training exercise when a couple of losers botched a robbery and his car got caught up in a high-speed pursuit. Trouble was; there was intelligence that Duncan didn't know about and a twat straight out of Bramshill, with no fucking idea what he was doing, was supervising our response to the incident. Cut a long story short, we lost two men. Duncan was one of them.' Edwards paused, pulled a packet of cigarettes from his front shirt pocket and fumbled trying to get his lighter to work.

'Major fuck up that should never have happened. Of course everyone was very *sorry*.' Edwards shrugged. 'A few people went out of their way to have *words* with the twat who'd fucked up and he had the decency to have a nervous breakdown; took medical retirement, moved away, good riddance.'

There were general nods of agreement all round, but Steve needed more answers. 'How did they die? Duncan and the other bloke, what happened?'

Edwards took a long drag of his fag. 'Their vehicle was on a collision course with our would-be robbers - a couple of drugged up crazies who had made a pact to take some coppers out before they got caught. Duncan and his mate, Tetley, didn't have a clue, just thought they were helping out; trying to tail a suspected vehicle. Duncan wasn't even driving. He was in the passenger seat. The crazies rammed them and pushed them off the bridge at Cowle End - it's a thirty-foot drop there - vehicle was crushed. Duncan was still alive when they reached him, but he died before the fire service could cut them out. A fireman managed to get in close enough for Duncan to speak to him, but he couldn't help him and whatever Duncan's last words were, well... that's something only the fireman and Kate will ever know.'

Steve felt totally and utterly wretched, sick to his stomach.

Edwards raised his eyes, giving him a cold look. 'Kate got the insurance money and a pension, and her family aren't short of a bob or two. She could have married again; moved away, started over, you know? But as soon as Angel started full time school she joined up. Some people think she gets breaks because of what happened - that she got help making DI, that sort of thing.'

'Total bollocks.' Ginger swore.

Edwards shrugged, 'He's right. If anything it's harder for her. She's the real deal; works her bloody socks off and wears her heart on her sleeve. It's only people like Barmy who don't fucking see it.'

'Barmy is so screwed up with jealousy and so frigging unbalanced all the time we're waiting for her to self destruct.' Park Bench told him.

'But as you've already self destructed, you can be the first to get a round of drinks in.' Edwards gave him a rueful grin, 'And Kate doesn't talk about Duncan; so if you ever, *ever* fucking mention that we've told you, you'll find yourself on dog shit patrol in the park - got it?'

Steve nodded, thinking it would serve him right if Kate made a formal complaint. She could report him and his career would be blighted, if not over. As he trudged after them he had no idea how he would ever be able to face his boss again.

Angel took Kate straight to Starbucks where she ordered something that came with an extra shot and cream and Kate ordered a double espresso. It was a ritual; something they did every time Angel came home. She was bubbling with news about school and sport and her plans for the holiday, full of energy and sheer bloody enthusiasm, sweeping Kate along with her. After popping back to the station to collect her car, Kate followed her back to the cottage where Angel dumped her entire bag of clothes into the laundry basket and trailed belongings around the house as she unpacked.

It was nearly midnight before Angel crashed out, fast asleep in her room, but Kate's brain wouldn't wind down. She padded out to the kitchen in bare feet to put the kettle on. As she waited for it to boil she realised she'd forgotten all about the photos of her on Pink's camera. She hadn't mentioned it to Stacey, or Knowling. She'd wait until she knew what else he'd taken photographs of - maybe something would make sense then. She checked her phone but Rick hadn't returned her call. She wondered how he spent his Saturday nights. *He's probably out with his girlfriend, enjoying himself like normal people, not worrying about how to keep paedophiles off the street.* Kate let the thought go. Whatever happened, come Monday there was going to be enough work to keep them all busy.

She was going to need a bigger team.

Steve Astman climbed out of a taxi, fished about in his wallet for a tenner to pay the fare and decided this might just be the stupidest idea he'd ever had. As the taxi pulled away from the kerb he turned and walked up the front path to a familiar door. He knocked before he completely lost his bravado and did a runner.

He quickly looked around as he waited to see if she would answer. He really didn't want anyone to see him, not here, not at this time of night. He wasn't entirely sober, but if he'd been sober he wouldn't be doing this. There was the sound of footsteps behind the door and a face appeared in the glass half window above the letterbox.

'*Oh shit,*' he suddenly realised he didn't know if she lived with someone; if there was a boyfriend. The chain slid back and the door opened throwing light from the hall across him. He raised his right hand and waved, slightly unsteadily, 'It's me.' He realised he'd just stated the bloody obvious; she could *see* it was him.

Aunty Sharon leant against the doorframe, crossed her arms over her chest and grinned at him. Her eyebrows rose in an unspoken question. He was starting to regret the impulse to turn up at her door. She was laughing at him and any minute now that door would shut in his face and he'd have to walk back to town. He tried again.

'I've been a prick.' He looked down at his shoes. 'I've messed everything up.' He felt so bad about what had happened with Kate's daughter. He wanted to tell Aunty Sharon about it, but now he'd said the first words he felt sick to his stomach again. He thought he'd better leave.

'I'm sorry,' he mumbled and turned to go, but a hand caught hold of his right elbow. He was yanked inside the hall and the door was kicked shut behind him.

'Well?' She was standing very close to him.

'I made a comment, a *very stupid* comment about Kate's

daughter, 'cos I didn't know... no one told me and I was a prick. Kate hates me. The girl is still at school for Christ sakes, but I didn't know.' He was babbling and he knew it, so he shut up and looked back at her. God, she looked adorable, all sun tanned and shiny and fresh, and she smelt of flowers. Steve looked down - and for a moment he stopped breathing. Aunty Sharon was wearing a tiny yellow vest top with matching cotton shorts. Her boobs pushed up over the front of the vest, round, fat and delicious, her nipples pressing lovely little cheeky points out towards him. He wanted to bury his face in them. She was sex on a stick. He gulped as he remembered to breath and she threw her head back and laughed, throwing him into confusion again.

'I've been a prick,' it was all that seemed to come into his head, 'I'm sorry, can I have a coffee?' He looked at her hopefully. Maybe she wasn't going to throw him out.

'Come here.' She reached up with her left hand and cupped it behind his head. She pulled his face towards her and, without taking her eyes from his, poked her tongue out and ran it over his bottom lip. Steve had to steady himself with one hand behind him on the wall; otherwise he'd have fallen into her. She was licking his lip and watching him. It was too much; he felt himself pressing against the front of her shorts.

Aunty Sharon lifted his arms up and slowly pulled his shirt up and over his head, taking it off and flinging it behind her. She pressed both her hands flat against his bare chest; just holding him back from her, searching for something in his face, her eyes locked on his. Then she smiled, and to his utter astonishment took his hand and led him upstairs.

***

CHAPTER FORTY FIVE

Kate had 'run up a hill' as Knowling had called it. She had also finished Angel's laundry, cleaned the kitchen and had a shower, but Angel still hadn't made an appearance. She wondered if her daughter was ever going to get up. She glanced up at the kitchen wall clock. It was five minutes past nine - still early in the land of teenagers. She took her coffee and her mobile outside to the garden, sat back on a wicker sun lounger and rang the station to find out what was happening. She justified it by telling herself at least she'd have a heads up before she went in. She was surprised when Andrea answered the phone.

'I was just going to call you, Gov, there's a shit storm going off all over the place here.' Andrea's voice was calm, but there was an undercurrent in her tone that made Kate frown.

'What's happened? When I left last night there was a plan to deal with Bishop, they haven't changed it have they?'

'Oh no, the plan's good, it's just that they can't bloody find him - he hasn't been seen since Friday. There's a high-powered meeting in half an hour between the bosses and some big wigs from Social Services. I'd stand by if I were you, Gov. I'd put money on this all going tits up. In fact someone's started a book on Bishop being responsible for Pink's murder, and the odds are shortening.'

Kate swung her legs over the side of her chair and sat up, phone clamped to her ear. 'Did anyone report Bishop missing, or is it just that we don't know where he is?' She wondered if he'd done a runner. It didn't seem likely, Steve had only come back with the information about him yesterday, and he hadn't been seen since the day before. *So why the hell couldn't they find him?*

'Apparently, there was a meeting in the evening he was

279

supposed to attend, but he blew out and left suddenly, telling people his mother had fallen down some stairs, which wasn't true – someone's checked. He never made it home and she hasn't heard from him – has no idea where he's got to...'

Kate heard the insinuation in Andrea's tone, 'Tell me, what's up with the mother?'

'Um, other than the fact that she's, apparently, a cantankerous witch with selective hearing?' Andrea asked.

'Says who?' Kate was getting a very bad feeling.

'A very reliable source.' Andrea wasn't prepared to elaborate.

Kate changed the subject. 'Where's Steve?' She asked.

'He's here somewhere.' Andrea's voice was unusually brittle and dismissive. It wasn't the first time Kate had picked up on bad vibes between her two colleagues. 'What's he done now?' The last thing she needed was conflict on her team.

'Nothing, he's just...' Andrea hesitated, 'I'll tell you another time – it doesn't matter right now.'

Kate let it go. 'Where's Stacey and Barmy?'

'The DCI is with Knowling. Everyone's hoping he'll stay there for a while; he's been crashing about yelling at everyone all morning. Haven't seen Barmy, but something came in about some evidence in Pink's case, I think she's on that.'

'I'm on my way in. I'll be there in an hour.' Kate took Angel in a cup of coffee before she left. 'I have to go to work,' she leant over and kissed the back of her daughter's head, 'I'll get back as soon as I can.'

Angel rolled over and opened her eyes, pushing long strands of hair away from her face as she forced herself awake. 'I'm going shopping with Bridget and then we're coming back here for a girly evening. We're getting pizza so you don't have to worry about me. Go catch bad guys.'

Kate smiled and leant down to give her a quick squeeze, 'I'll try. What sort of pizza?'

'Hawaiian double crust, extra pineapple.' Angel grinned, but it turned into a yawn. She snuggled back down under the duvet.

'Save me some.'

Kate was still eight miles from the station when her mobile rang. She checked the screen: *Knowling*. 'Morning, boss,' she said cheerfully, 'I'm on my way in.'

'Where are you *exactly?*'

'I'm still my side of Berton Bridge.' Kate heard the tension in his voice and her scalp prickled. She automatically took her foot off the accelerator, slowing down.

'Then don't come here, go to the old farmers market, where the animal auctions used to be, it's off Chancer Lane.'

'Sorry, why?'

'Listen, will you? The fire service has found another burnt body in the old auction shed.'

Kate's foot hit the brake and her eyes flew to her rear view mirror, but there was nothing behind her. 'How long has it been there?'

'Don't know. Get over there, Stacey's at the scene and the team are on their way.'

Kate only had one thought. 'Who is it?'

'That's why I need you at the scene - it could be Bishop, but there's no positive ID yet. You know him, go and have a look. We don't have anyone there who knows what the man looks like.'

Kate's stomach was clenched so hard it was stuck to her spine.

'He's your case,' Knowling reminded her, 'so the line between child protection and homicide just got crossed again. I've got Gerry Crane here, Bishop's boss; I need to know what to tell him.'

There was a pause, and Kate could see her boss in her mind, sitting at his desk, fiddling with a pencil. He was struggling to say something else.

'I need you... on this. Talk to me as soon as you can.' He hung up.

Then she felt it; felt the tingle of anticipation. It was the feeling of being 'on point' of being right in the middle of this *stuff*, it was exhilarating. There was absolutely no doubt in her mind that it was Bishop in that shed. She took her foot off the brake and stamped on the accelerator.

'He's not having a good hair day.' Greg Thomas remarked casually as he wrote her name on the log. Kate knew he meant the victim, but she ignored the black humour and grabbed a white suit, mask and gloves from a box.

A fire engine had parked up on the concrete apron a hundred

yards from the shed. It was as close as they could get, there were too many metal railings around the building; remnants of the old animal penning system, but it was a convenient hard surface, ideal for setting up a vehicle park and RVP. A designated entry point had been made through the police cordon. A uniformed policeman, who looked about twelve years old, was happily directing the arriving police vehicles, chatting to each driver through their open windows as he waved them through, pointing to where they should pull in. He looked like a car park attendant at a car boot fair.

The firemen were draped nonchalantly around the fire engine, happily watching the growing circus and waiting for some revelation. Kate recognised most of them - they'd been to the same crime scenes before.

'Hey, Kate! You know we're here for you, dear,' One of them called across to her, 'but this is the second time this week.' One dead body wasn't nearly enough to stop a bit of piss taking.

'Morning, Kate, nice day for it.' Another fireman she knew only as 'Dollop' commented dryly.

'It always is.' Kate smiled as she climbed into her suit. She liked firemen, sometimes a whole lot more than she liked policemen.

Police 'do not cross' tape was wrapped around trees and posts keeping back the inevitable onlookers, including a bunch of kids on bikes. Kate thought back to when she'd pulled up outside Pink's house in Clare Walk; there were *always* kids on bikes. It was as though an unseen secret signal went out, drawing them in. Within moments of a police incident kicking off some kids on bikes would turn up, like ants at a picnic. Kate frowned as she thought about it, they were too far away for her to see if she recognised anyone. A couple of uniforms were patrolling the cordon, if they had their wits about them they'd be keeping a close eye on who turned out to watch.

Watch the watchers.

But kids were generally ignored – maybe that was a mistake. She'd once told Colin the reason the police threw such a large cordon around a crime scene was not just to protect evidence, but also to protect sensitive members of the public from overhearing the banter that went on between the emergency services.

A sudden loud bang made her jump and she felt her heart rate rocket; she spun around, her eyes scanning the area for the source of the noise.

'Oh hell! Sorry!' A SOCO had dropped a large metal lamp stand. A fireman went over to give him a hand picking it up. As Kate turned back towards the shed she had a sudden recollection of looking at the exact scene in front of her before, but it took her a second to realise why she recognised it. George Pink had taken a photograph of this site, exactly as she was looking at it now. She'd looked at it with Bunny.

Stacey suddenly appeared at her shoulder. 'Have you been inside?'

Kate looked up sharply, something in his voice making her wary. 'I thought I should wait for you.' It wasn't true, but Stacey liked the lie. 'You think its Bishop?' She watched his face.

'Right, possibly, but I've never met him and it's a bit grim in there.' The DCI was visibly shaken. Kate held his eyes for a moment then braced her shoulders and ducked inside the old wooden framed doorway.

The firemen watched with interest as she disappeared. 'I've got a tenner that says she'll throw up.' Dollop said, pleasantly.

'Well, if she does I've got a ruddy big hose here ready to wash her down.' His mate chipped in and there were immediate snorts of derision and ridicule throughout the group.

'In your dreams.'

'We'd have to get a bigger fire tender before you get to hold a big hose.'

It was harmless banter to keep the demons at bay. They knew exactly what Kate was walking into - they'd not only seen it, they'd *felt* it. It had touched them.

Kate took one step inside the shed and almost recoiled in horror. She stood absolutely still, her heart pounding through her chest, her stomach clenched painfully as bile filled the back of her throat. She was breathing in evil. It was in the shed and it was reaching out to her, trying to engulf her. It was something only a very few people knew about, simply because most people never see a crime scene where the gates of Hell have cracked open and the demons have run riot. You don't only smell evil - you can *see* it. It swirls in small wisps of blackness so dense that you can feel it's velvet touch brushing provocatively against you. It sounded like paranoid nonsense, but it was horribly real.

Kate forced a long breath of stale air out through her lips and got a grip on herself. She wasn't going to be sick - she'd smelt evil before. As her eyes adjusted to the darkness she felt as though she was looking at a set from a horror movie. One metal industrial lamp hung from the centre of the ceiling but most of the scene was cast in shadow.

Bare concrete block walls, studded in places with ancient metal rings enclosed an area divided into two halves. One side was a holding area separated by metal railings, the other side, where Kate was standing, was a roughly concreted open area with a dug out drain running directly down the centre. Two windows on her left had been boarded up with metal sheets. There was no natural light and no air. Sweat ran down her back and chest; making rivulets through the middle of her cleavage until her bra was damp and her t-shirt stuck to her.

'Well?' Stacey was behind her, holding his mask to his face, his eyes were watering in the toxic atmosphere.

Kate took three steps closer. The corpse was slumped forward; hands tied behind his back to a railing in the centre of the room, legs twisted under him, most of his weight suspended on his arms. The back of the body was badly burnt; only small, straggly strips of cloth were left sticking to the black crust. His head hung sideways and ugly blisters, fat and swollen with fluid, stood out on his neck. The face was tilted upward, mouth open, his scorched lips pulled back over brown teeth.

'It's John Bishop.' Kate turned on her heel, pushed past Stacey and out into the air. She ripped the mask and paper suit off, struggling as she yanked it over her feet, and chucked it in the bin as she strode over to the group of firemen. 'I know you've got a flask of tea somewhere - hand it over.' She ordered. She needed a coffee, but firemen didn't carry coffee, only hot sweet NATO tea.

'Take it it's him, then?' Dollop asked, as she sipped at the flask cup, which had miraculously appeared from a duffle bag. Kate nodded slowly, stretching her eyes wide in thanks for the tea, or in answer to the question, it didn't matter which - they got it.

When Stacey walked over to join them the flask disappeared.

'The Commander is on his way with the fire investigator, they'll be here in about five minutes.' Dollop told him.

Stacey nodded, 'Good, we'll hold off until they get here. Kate, I need you to come with me.' He walked away along the row of parked vehicles. Kate had to jog to catch up with him. 'Superintendent Knowling is going to brief Bishop's boss as soon as the next of kin have been informed; ironically, he's already at the station. I don't think we'll have any problems getting full co-operation. Astman will meet you at the Social Services building in an hour. Get a list of teenage boys that Bishop was responsible for and take a look at his office.'

'Get Steve to find Bishop's secretary, Michelle... somebody, and bring her in, she'll be useful,' Kate interrupted, 'Oh, and there's a couple of photos of this location and that shed on Pink's camera.'

'What?' Stacey stopped and turned to stare at her, 'Well, there's no longer any doubt that Pink and Bishop are connected.'

'And yet we only heard about Bishop yesterday and today we're looking at his body.' Kate said, 'That's a bloody great coincidence, Sir.' She didn't want to voice the thought that had wormed its way to the front of her mind - didn't want to think about the possibility that they had a vigilante on the team.

'Except he was dead before Astman got back with the information.' Stacey used both hands to wipe the sweat from his face, 'We won't have a time of death until the PM, but it could be more than twenty four hours.'

Kate was astonished. 'Who found him?'

'Not *who;* what.' Stacey pointed at a man in his fifties who was leaning on a walking stick chatting to a uniform. A black and white Springer Spaniel sat obediently at his feet. 'It was a bloody dog.'

***

CHAPTER FORTY SIX

'You didn't like him very much.' Kate was struggling to be polite to Michelle. Bishop's secretary had arrived at her office looking like a tart on a night out - big hair, tight t-shirt, too much lipstick, but stupidly excited at being involved in a drama. When Kate told her Bishop was dead, she clutched her hands to her chest, rolling little girl eyes at Steve and asking for a drink of water. It was a sham put on for their benefit and Kate knew it.

Michelle looked up and pulled a face. 'It wasn't just me; all the women detest him. He was always sneaking up and touching you, rubbing himself on you, his hands, his knee, whatever he thought he could 'caringly' get away with.'

'Caringly?' Kate didn't understand.

'This month's new buzz word. He thought if he put 'caringly' into anything he could get away with murder and he thought it made him funny.' Michelle snorted, the noise exploding from her nose.

Kate *really* started to dislike her. She changed tack. 'What happened on Friday?'

'His mother fell. She lives with him, or he lives with her, not sure which.'

'What time was that?' She already knew this wasn't true.

'He was supposed to be taking a conference but then he said he had to go, so it was just before the conference.' Michelle's answer wasn't very helpful. Kate wasn't sure if she was being vague on purpose or she really was as thick as shit.

'What time was the conference?' Kate tried again.

'I'll have to look.' Michelle took a key from her bag, unlocked Bishop's office door and leant over his desk to switch his computer on.

Steve looked at Kate and shrugged, 'She might have said she had the bloody key.'

Kate sighed, 'Let's hope she's got the password and access to his diary.'

Michelle looked up from the monitor. 'What do you want? There's a work calendar on his computer, he's got a desk dairy in this drawer...' She used another key from the bunch in her hand to open the top right hand desk drawer, pulling out a large grey desk planner. 'And he's got a digital thingy.' She looked around quickly. Her eyes fell on a jacket hanging on the back of a chair in front of the desk, 'He must have forgotten it again. Try the inside breast pocket.' She nodded at Steve.

He picked up the lightweight coat and fished out a sleek Dell PDA. Michelle grinned at him, and to Kate's complete horror, she started wriggling about, doing a victory dance. 'Told you! He got that free off some rep, pretending he was trialling it for the department. He was always blagging stuff.'

Steve wasn't smiling, 'Don't suppose you know the password for this one?'

'HOT TRIGGER, two words, both in capitals. Strange though - I mean it's strange that he left it behind if he was going home. Although I suppose he wouldn't really need it. It looks like he just took his own mobile.'

Kate stopped, wanting to slap her. Steve fed the password into the palm pilot and the theme tune to 'Mission Impossible' blared out.

'He thought he was James Bond, or something special,' Michelle said, sarcastically. 'I wish he'd known we all called him 'Hideous Homer', he wouldn't have been so bloody pleased with himself.'

Kate gave Steve a look. Nothing had been said about his comments last night about Angel. By the time she'd dashed home, stripped out of her stinking clothes from the fire scene and into fresh ones, Steve had already arrived at the Social Services office with a very pale looking Gerry Crane who was now shut in his office making phone calls. Kate knew the boys had made a night of it last night. She'd seen a couple of them at the scene earlier; bloodshot eyes hidden behind dark glasses, chewing gum and trying to get the taste of dead camel out of their mouths. But Steve looked fine, *almost too chirpy*.

'Five o'clock.' Michelle called out. 'The conference was here at five o'clock.

'Gov?' Steve held out the palm pilot, making sure Kate could see the monitor but shielding it from Michelle. The digital diary was divided into lines, each line representing an hour of the day. There was only one entry on the page for Friday. In big bold letters right across the line that started with the time 6.00pm was one word: DOG.

Kate's eyes met his and she nodded, 'Tell Crane we need the CCTV footage from the front of this building for Friday. Call the office and get a uniform here for the rest of the day. I want to keep a check on everything that goes in and out.' She turned to Michelle. 'I need a print out of that calendar for the last month, and the access codes to that computer.'

Michelle looked wistfully after Steve as he left the room, but she did what she was told.

Kate walked back into the open plan office. She needed access to files. Gerry Crane didn't look as though he was up to making any helpful decisions about anything; she needed someone practical to work with. Her mobile rang. She looked at the screen and frowned: *Journalist.*

'Hi Kate, I owe you, so this is a courtesy call. We're running it as the main story on the local TV channels today before the big boys get hold of it. John Bishop is dead - a social worker, dealt with foster kids. He's the body at the old auction shed, burnt to death just like George Pink, who was accused of molesting young boys. What's your take on the connection?'

Kate tried to stall him, 'I'm aware there's an incident at the old auction site. However, no formal identification has been made, and won't be until after immediate family are informed.' *Where the hell was he getting his information?*

'It's Bishop. You'd better tell the family before they see it on the telly; it'll be on at three, live from the scene.'

Kate sighed, 'I always took you for a professional, but if you want to report on unsubstantiated rumour... '

'Kate, see sense, I'm just warning you, that's all.'

She hung up and called Stacey. 'You've got a blabbermouth at the scene. Local news people know its Bishop, and they know the MO is similar to Pink's - it's on TV at three.'

Stacey exploded. 'What are they going to say? Bishop's mother has only just been told, but she's not been given any details. She's a cantankerous old biddy according to the family liaison girl and I *do not* want to have to go over there to start talking about torture and burning.'

'Call a press conference for three o'clock,' Kate suggested, 'They won't want to miss an official briefing, but they can't be at that and film from the scene at the same time.'

Stacey thought about it for a second, but he knew she was right. 'I'll speak to the Press Office and get DI Barnes to set it up. Where the hell are these people getting their information?'

'DI Barnes is pretty good at routing out a gossip, Sir. There can't be that many possibilities.'

'There are plenty of possibilities! The crime scene has been crawling with uniforms all morning.' He hung up.

Kate called Mivvie Levin. She was the most practical social worker she could think of.

'Hey Kate, I'm not duty social worker this weekend so I'm thinking this is not good news.'

'Sorry, no. John Bishop was found dead this morning, similar MO to George Pink. I'm at your offices with a lady called Michelle, who's been incredibly helpful,' Kate smiled at Michelle as she looked up, 'but I really need your help. How soon can you get over here?'

The pause at the other end of the line stretched out until Kate thought she'd lost the connection.

'Look, I'll be there in half an hour, *fuck*! This is insane.' Mivvie swore.

'Oh, it's going to get much worse than that.' Kate assured her.

***

CHAPTER FORTY SEVEN

Eddie lay very still and listened carefully to everything she said. He didn't believe a single word of it. He twisted across the bed and threw his legs out over the side, letting the cool air get to them. As he rolled away from her she stretched her hand out towards him, rubbing the back of his shoulder, caressing him.

'I love you. You know that don't you? It's ok.' She whispered, 'It's ok.'

But it wasn't.

He didn't believe he was safe, didn't believe it was over; there was no safety, not for him. It wasn't true. He wanted it to be true, more than anything he'd ever wished for in his whole life he wanted it to be true, but it wasn't. Nothing he'd wished for had ever come true.

Happy? What did that mean? How could he ever be happy? His life up until this moment couldn't suddenly be wiped out as though it had never happened. He couldn't suddenly forget the last twelve years as though they didn't exist, he was still the boy who had lived that life. Whatever she promised him, whatever she said she was doing for him, *had* done for him; nothing would make the past go away. The past would never go away. It was like the air that he breathed - it was always there.

Eddie tried to think of a time when he had been happy, a time before his life in foster care, a time when it was just him and his mum and she had taken care of him. He shut his eyes and tried to recreate the feeling, the *happy* feeling - the safe feeling. Funny how it was so easy to bring the scared feelings to the surface, but he had to really try before he could remember a happy time.

He had one memory; one he could drag back if he lay still and thought about it hard enough... it was his fifth birthday and he had a blue balloon.

Eddie threw his right arm over his face and stretched back across the bed. He knew she was watching him but he ignored her; faded her out in the way he had faded so many people in his life out. He took himself out of the room, out of himself and hunkered down, breathing deep, dragging it back.

He'd been so excited at having a balloon. He'd loved its bright colour and the noise it made when he batted it. He'd loved the way it floated away from him, across the kitchen of their little flat. He'd run after it, batting it up in the air with his fist and squealing loudly as it bounced up and away from him.

By keeping perfectly still and concentrating with all his might he could bring the feeling back, the feeling of that excitement, of being that happy, the joy of having a blue birthday balloon.

He could picture his mum as she was in that moment, standing with her back to the counter, laughing at him. Eddie tried as hard as he could but he couldn't picture her face. He couldn't remember the last time he'd been able to recall how she really looked. He didn't have a photograph or anything to remind him, and even though he knew he must have remembered when he was little, her face had faded from his memory, leaving just an impression of her outline and the *presence* of her.

She'd been holding a cup of tea. In his mind she was always holding a cup of tea, it seemed to be what she did. 'It will burst,' she'd said. 'It will burst and you won't have it anymore.'

But he'd jumped and batted it with his fist and, as though she'd jinxed it, his blue balloon floated onto the counter and touched the hot kettle.

And he didn't have it anymore. Happiness didn't last.

Eddie rolled over and looked at the face of the woman lying beside him and knew that she was a liar and that being afraid was what lasted.

'I was five.' He spoke so quietly he wasn't sure that she'd heard him, but her eyes focused on his with such intensity he knew she was listening. 'I couldn't get her to wake up. I kept trying and trying. She had her eyes closed and her head rolled when I shook her shoulders, but I couldn't get her to wake up.' Eddie paused and sucked air into his body, forcing it down, forcing himself to breath. Just saying the words made his chest burn with pain.

'I was so hungry. I thought she'd wake up any minute and get my tea. I started crying because my mum had wet herself. The bed was wet and I could smell it and I knew she'd never do that – she'd never wet herself. Maybe that's when I knew she was dead, she was really dead.'

Eddie had to stop and take another deep breath. The woman reached out her hand and ran the very tips of her fingers gently over his cheek, her eyes brimming with tears.

'I was...' Eddie choked on the words, breathed in so deeply he made himself cough, and started again. 'I was locked in; I was locked in the house. I tried to get help, but I was locked in. There was a packet of cornflakes in the kitchen – the only thing I could reach, so I ate them out of the packet and then I stayed with her; slept next to her, talked to her, holding her hand all the time until someone came.'

'How long?' The woman asked, the tears now streaming unchecked across her face, 'How long was it before someone came?'

'Three days.' Eddie's voice was hoarse with the emotion of it. 'Someone told me later it was three days. I just remember the hunger and knowing that I was alone. I didn't know if anyone was ever going to come.'

The woman closed her eyes. It was as though she couldn't bear to see his pain, could not bring herself to witness it. It was too raw and too close to the agony she'd lived with for so long. She couldn't bear it.

Eddie reached up and took her hand, 'Tell me about the boy who died. Tell me about Brian.' He whispered. But then her face turned towards him and her eyes found his and he couldn't keep it in any longer. He started to sob, and once he'd started he couldn't stop.

There was something unsavoury about Bishop's secretary. Kate labelled her manipulative and devious and disliked her intensely. She winced when Michelle snorted through her nose for the umpteenth time.

'You can't get the CCTV, it's Sunday and Frank don't work on

Sunday. Gerry can't help you, he's called 'Choccy' around here; as in 'chocolate teapot', bloody useless.' Michelle thought this was hilarious.

'Gerry can call Frank and ask him to come in.' Kate said evenly.

Michelle smiled at Kate in a way that suggested Kate was simple, 'Not on a Sunday. Frank won't want to get a bus here on a Sunday, and he doesn't drive.'

Kate's patience ran out and she stopped being civil. 'If that's the case I'll send a bloody police car to his house to pick him up!' she snapped.

As if on cue, the door leading to the corridor pushed open and Steve appeared. 'Gerry doesn't have access to the CCTV stuff. He's trying to get hold of someone called Frank.'

Michelle gave Kate a smug look.

'Find out where he lives and send a car to pick him up. I want him here in the next twenty minutes.' Kate wasn't messing about. If she needed to put a bomb under these people to get action, well, so be it.

'Will do,' Steve nodded towards Kate's jacket, which she'd dropped on the back of a chair. 'Check your phone, Gov. Michelle, can I borrow you for a minute?' Michelle nearly fell over her own feet in her hurry to go with him.

Kate waited until they were out of the room. Whatever she needed her phone for, Steve obviously didn't want Michelle to witness it. He wasn't very subtle, but she had to grudgingly admire his tactics. She'd missed a call from Stacey. She pressed the hash key to return the call, and waited exactly three seconds before he answered.

'What have you got?' Stacey didn't bother with niceties.

'Bishop was in the office until five on Friday. He's left his Palm Pilot in his jacket here, sir, which means he left in a hurry. There's an entry for Friday at six o'clock.' Kate hesitated, she was about to establish Eddie Lead as a suspect and she was reluctant to do it.

'So, what was he doing?' Stacey was agitated, barking at her.

'It doesn't say. The entry says 'Dog' which could be Eddie Lead, but it doesn't say where, and it may not be about Eddie.' She knew that sounded lame.

'Did Bishop work with Eddie Lead?'

'Yes. He was team leader for foster placements and Eddie is in foster care.' Kate admitted.

'Did Bishop own a dog?' Stacey asked the obvious.

Kate had to admit she didn't know, but she doubted it.

'Right, we'll pick Eddie Lead up and bring him in. The duty social worker can act as appropriate adult. What else have you got on Bishop?'

'We're waiting for someone to gain access to the CCTV from the front of the building and the car park. If we've got him on film leaving here, we'll know which way Bishop went. If he went into town he'll be picked up on other cameras. Do you know what car to look for?' Kate's mind was racing ahead, figuring out how to track Bishop's movements when he left his office.

'Oh, we've already got the car, it's been towed in. It was parked about a quarter of a mile away from where he was found, tucked away down a lane. It's a bloody great Jag – hard to miss it. What about the case files?'

'I've got someone on their way to help me get access to them.' Kate rubbed her forehead, she badly needed some coffee. 'I'll get a list of names and have a quick look to see if anything jumps out, but we'll go through them in more detail tomorrow after the planning meeting when we've got more manpower.' She had no idea how many cases they were talking about. There could be dozens.

'Right, don't spend too much time fiddling about now, just seal Bishop's office – make sure no-one gets access to it, do you understand? And bring the CCTV tape and list of names back with you. Briefing's at six.' Stacey hung up.

'Grandmother and eggs,' Kate said into the dead phone. Stacey was letting the pressure get to him. She stuffed the mobile into the back pocket of her jeans, and started poking about in Bishops desk drawers. Paper clip holder, stapler, it was all office stuff. She flicked through his desk diary. All he ever did was go to meetings. She felt let down, but she wasn't sure what she'd hoped to find. The door pushed open and Mivvie walked in.

'What the hell is going on Kate? I've just bumped into Gerry and he's barely coherent. He mumbled something about 'unfortunate incident.' *Really?* Is he joking? His foster placement team leader being burnt to death is slightly more than an *unfortunate incident* wouldn't you say?'

'Thank God you're here - can you get me some files?' Kate wasn't the slightest bit interested in what Gerry Crane was doing.

Mivvie registered Kate's no nonsense attitude and her eyes narrowed, 'Whose?

'Any boy Bishop was responsible for placing in foster care. Look for a target age group of ten to fifteen.'

Mivvie's face clouded with confusion for a moment but then realisation dawned and she understood, 'Shit! Are you saying what I think you're saying?'

'I'm not *saying* anything.' Kate drew her words out slowly, making it clear that nothing was official yet.

Mivvie was stunned. She sat down sideways onto a desktop and stared at Kate. The look on her face turned from shock to one of cold hard anger, 'There's something... something you need to know before this really gets going. John Bishop was a total and utter bastard.'

Kate nodded, she understood, 'I need the files, any boy between the age of ten and fifteen... please.'

'You know what the politics are like around here, are you clearing it with Gerry?' Mivvie was almost whispering.

Kate didn't want to hear it, 'Just get the files. Sod the politics, we can work it out later.'

'Fine by me.' Mivvie hopped off the desk and started towards the door, but Kate wasn't finished. 'Eddie Lead is a priority; I need anything and everything you've got on him.' Kate found herself on the receiving end of a long hard look before Mivvie turned away and walked out of the room.

***

CHAPTER FORTY EIGHT

They were gathered in Gerry Crane's office, leaning on various desktops and cabinets. No one wanted to take a seat.

Gerry Crane looked ill. 'How many?' he asked.

'All of the case files have sections missing.' Mivvie told him, 'The jacket covers are there, but some of the files have been removed and replaced with recycling paper, so unless you comb through the file you'd never know. I've looked through eleven cases; boys who were given foster placements by Bishop and are in the right age group - they've all had stuff removed.'

'Who has access to these files?' Steve asked.

Gerry Crane leant forward and ran both his hands through his hair in despair. His career had just turned into a train wreck. 'The Foster Care Team, other social workers who are involved with the child or its family, admin personnel...' his voice trailed off.

'So, *only* people who work in this building.' Steve wanted him to be specific.

Mivvie laughed out loud. 'Plus anyone who came in and out and was unsupervised. So foster carers, cleaners, school teachers who popped up for a chat, medical people... just about anyone who might be involved in a case conference. Oh, and add police officers to that.'

Crane looked pleadingly at Kate; a drowning man seeking rescue. Kate almost felt sorry for him, but he was Head of Department and the buck stopped with him.

'It's not a secure system,' she told Steve, 'you need the key code for the door to access this floor, but once you're inside you can get into any of the rooms, you'd just need to know where to look.' She turned back to Crane, 'What about soft copies?'

'Yes of course. But we're still trying to transfer data over; a lot of the archive stuff isn't copied. We had that problem with the formatting and the case file masks didn't work the way they were supposed to...'

'Is there specific information that's missing from all the cases?' Kate cut him off and looked to Mivvie.

'Personal information; background details, photographs, medical histories, that sort of thing, but it's a bit difficult to know what's missing unless you know what was in there to start with.'

'I don't understand, why would Bishop do that?' Crane was staring at the ceiling as though some revelation would suddenly come to him and everything would be ok. Mivvie just shrugged - she had no idea.

'It may not have been Bishop.' Steve said, 'If Bishop's killer had access to the files there may be another...'

'Who's Eddie Lead's social worker?' Kate cut him off, changing the subject.

'Bishop. He was Eddie's caseworker in Hockley. Eddie moved here about the same time as Bishop, so it was in his best interests to keep the same caseworker. When Bishop was made team leader *technically* he didn't have to keep the case, but he seemed keen to maintain the relationship.' Crane's eyes darted from Kate to Steve and back, a look of abject horror on his face. 'Oh my God.'

Kate kept her face expressionless, but an incredible sadness washed over her. No wonder everything about Eddie screamed 'victim'. The poor kid was under the care of an abuser in Hockley, and then got sent to a new home in a new town only to find the bastard waiting for him. Another more sinister thought hit her. 'Who fostered Eddie in Hockley?'

Crane took an age to answer; the enormity of the crisis was sinking in. 'It would be in his file.'

Kate looked to Mivvie.

'Which we don't have.' Mivvie confirmed.

'Are there records in Hockley?' Kate was determined the information must be available *somewhere*. There was something she needed to know. 'Was Eddie ever in the care of the Pink's? Did they foster children in Hockley?'

Crane thought for a moment, 'Hockley division would know if

the Pink's were foster carers, but I think Eddie's records were all here, with us. We can ask Hockley... but its Sunday.'

Kate wanted to scream. 'Get your opposite number at Hockley's phone number and give it to Steve - he'll ask them.' She looked across at Steve, 'I need a list of the social workers responsible for these cases.' Kate's tone left no room for argument, 'And if Bishop received telephone messages on Friday how would they be transferred to him?'

'Reception would have transferred the call, or taken a message.' Mivvie answered.

'I'll need to speak to the receptionist.'

There was a look that passed between Crane and Mivvie. Kate waited for the bad news.

'Our receptionist left suddenly last Monday - we've had a temp. I don't have a contact number, I'd have to ask the agency... and it's Sunday.'

Kate took a deep breath. 'This would be a good time to call your senior team, Divisional Directors and so forth. There's a briefing at the police station at six o'clock. The post mortem is tomorrow.'

The colour drained from Crane's face.

She beckoned for Steve to join her in the larger office and closed Crane's door behind them. 'Call the incident room. Whoever's searching Bishop's house needs to look for those files.' Before she could say anymore Mivvie came out and joined them.

'Just when I thought we'd had enough bloody drama for one day. Mrs Murphy, Eddie's foster mum, just called. The stupid woman is completely hysterical. Apparently there are fifty policemen at her house looking for Eddie.'

And then Kate knew; she knew exactly why Mivvie looked as though she wanted to punch someone, but she asked the question anyway. 'Where is he - where's Eddie?'

'They don't know. He's been missing since Monday.'

***

CHAPTER FORTY NINE

Stacey looked strained and Kate understood why. Not only was he now overseeing the investigation into two murders, it now looked increasingly like there was a child abuse scandal on their patch involving a senior member of the Social Services Children's Department. It was a nightmare scenario and Stacey was in unfamiliar territory. Knowling was keeping a close eye on things and she had no doubt that the Commander was also taking a special interest. There would also be intense interest from the media, so Stacey was in the spotlight and he needed results.

'DI Barnes is interviewing Eddie's foster carers now, but according to her they're as thick as shit and about as helpful.' Stacey didn't mince his words, 'Mrs Murphy told Bishop on Thursday or Friday that Eddie hadn't been home for a couple of nights - but they've admitted they haven't seen the boy since Monday morning.'

Kate was astonished, 'Why did they leave it so long before making a report, why weren't we told?'

'They will be asked those questions. Apparently Eddie took a bag with some spare clothes and his skateboard, so it looks like he planned to leave.'

'Has he got any money?' Kate barely waited for him to finish speaking.

'As I said, we'll know more when DI Barnes gets back.' Stacey snapped. 'The only photo we have of Eddie is the one you brought in – the Murphy's don't have any.'

He looked across the room to where Ginger was updating the incident board and Kate followed his eyes. The board had been extended to make room for the information on Bishop. Arrows linked his name to Eddie Lead, Andy Frazier, Josh Martin and Dean Towle, while other arrows linked the same boys to George Pink. There was another list of names linked to Bishop - the seven other boys that Bishop had been responsible for, who were in foster care, and in the target age group, the ones whose files had been tampered with. There was only one additional name on Pink's side: Brin Bowden, the boy from the travelling family who still hadn't been located.

There were two additional links between Eddie and the two men. One showed all three had been residents of Hockley up until two years ago when they'd all moved to Marville within months of each other. The second showed that they were surmising that Eddie had planned to meet with each man on the day they'd died and that he'd been missing since the day Pink was murdered. Kate knew a high level discussion had taken place where it had been agreed that the two deaths were linked and that they were, in all probability, looking for one perpetrator and that Eddie Lead was top of the list.

'Eddie's foster carers don't know who any of his friends are or who he could be staying with.' Stacey turned back to Kate.

'Well, Dean Towle told me Eddie doesn't have any friends and doesn't want any, but Eddie's older than Dean and I don't think they know each other that well.' Kate stopped as she saw Natasha coming through the double swing doors backwards, pushing them open with her bum. As she turned around Kate saw she was carrying a coffee pot on a tray with three cups. She'd brought coffee from Kate's office and was diplomatic enough to bring Stacey one. Kate decided the girl was definitely CPU material.

Stacey took a cup and started heaping sugar into it. 'What about at school - anyone he might hang out with? You've got more contacts with kids out there than anyone else in this division - *find someone*. The local television channels have identified Bishop and, having ignored all the advice we gave them, are treating it like the next thrilling episode of a bloody soap drama! So far we've been able to keep a lid on any speculation about paedophiles, but that's not going to last. There'll be plenty of shit hitting the fan soon; I want to make damn sure none of it sticks here. The briefing's been put back until seven, maybe later, see what you can do before then.' Stacey walked out taking his coffee with him.

Kate scowled after him. *Bloody fast track coppers - always go into melt down when the pressure gets turned up.* She put her hands on the top of her head, leant back, and thought about Eddie. Had he gone missing before? They wouldn't know until Barmy came back from the foster carers, but were they reliable? Had they left it a couple of days to report him missing because it wasn't unusual for him to be out for a couple of nights? If that was true - then either they knew where he went, and weren't worried, or they didn't know and weren't bothered. Kate had a feeling it was the later.

'What are the chances he's sleeping rough?' She looked at Steve. 'If he's outdoors he could be anywhere - we couldn't find Todd Martin and the entire bloody division was looking for him.'

Steve rubbed his crooked nose with a knuckle while he considered it. 'He's young and fit and it's been hot enough. But he's on foot and I can't see that he's got too much cash on him. What's he been living on since Monday? He's got to eat.'

Kate nodded, but she was worried. Why had Eddie run away? It didn't look good, but maybe that was the point, maybe Eddie realised he'd be a suspect, maybe that's why he was running. But where would he go? She had an idea. 'What about his old foster home in Hockley?'

'The woman I spoke to at Hockley social services is going to call when she finds the details.' Steve shrugged, it wasn't ideal but they'd just have to wait.

Kate was trying to think how many kids she knew who were the same age as Eddie. Colin had a much better network with teenage boys in the area than she did. He'd have already been rounding up the usual suspects; gleaning information from a dozen different sources in his laid back, unflappable way.

Natasha distracted her. 'Ma'am, there's a call for you; front desk transferred it, a Rick Hart, says he's returning your call.'

Kate leant over the top of Natasha's desk to take the receiver from her. 'Kate Landers,' she said formally.

'Kate, I'm sorry.' Rick sounded flustered, 'I've been away all weekend at a bloody awards thing. I forgot the frigging charger for my mobile and I've only just picked up your message. I didn't want to call your mobile in case you weren't working today.'

'Did you win something?' Kate smiled, faintly surprised at how pleased she was to hear from him.

'What? No, I was presenting something.'

Kate knew she'd thrown him, 'Well thanks for calling back. Do you know a boy called Eddie Lead?' She felt Steve watching her and she turned to face him. He was leaning against the desk, his arms folded across his enormous chest, a stupid smirk on his face.

'Sorry? Yes, he's called The Dog - he's a skater kid. I wouldn't say I know him very well - I'm not sure anyone could say they know him well, but I've met him a few times. Umm, why?' Rick was having trouble keeping up with the conversation.

'Are you free now? We need to talk to you.' Kate raised her eyebrows at Steve, giving him a hard look.

'Well, I'm in town, at The Applewood - it's a sort of posh cafe place on Deal Road. Do you want to come here?'

'We'll be there in ten minutes.' Kate hung up.

Steve didn't know where they were going but he already had the car keys in his fist, waiting for instructions.

'The Applewood - we're meeting Rick at the Applewood, and what was that look for?' She demanded.

'Sorry?' Steve's face was blank.

'You were smirking. When I was on the phone... you were smirking.'

Steve held the door open for her, 'No idea what you're on about, Gov.'

<hr />

Fifteen minutes after Steve had driven Kate away from the station, two teenage girls dressed identically in denim miniskirts, white t-shirts and pink sparkly pumps arrived at the front entrance. There was a brief argument on the steps as the shorter girl persuaded the other to go inside, eventually grabbing her hand and pulling her through the door. They crowded together in front of the glass reception window as though they were conjoined twins.

'Can I help you?' Mary's voice was stern.

'We need to speak to Kate, the detective lady.'

'What are your names?'

The girls looked at each other, uncertain. After a nudge from her mate the taller one spoke up, 'We don't want to say - but Kate knows me.' She started to chew her thumb.

Mary sighed, 'I'm sure she does, but she's not here at the moment and I can't give her a message unless you tell me your names.'

More silent looks passed between the girls. The shorter one gave a slight shake of her head - they'd made their minds up. 'It doesn't matter then.'

Mary wrote down the time and their description.

The Applewood was almost deserted. The weather was too nice for people to waste it being indoors. They found a corner table by the window that had enough space for two big men to spread themselves out. Steve ordered a burger and Kate agreed to share a plate of chilli nachos with Rick although she didn't really want any. When the food arrived Kate talked instead of eating. She gave Rick the bare details about Bishop - not because she didn't trust him, but because there was no reason to describe the horror of Bishop's death.

'I know who he is, he was at the centre once.' Rick said, surprising her. 'He was looking for Andy Frazier. It was when Andy was in foster care; apparently he'd gone missing for a couple of days, the bloke seemed very agitated about it. I only spoke to him for a minute, I hadn't seen Andy so couldn't help him.'

'By the look on your face I take it you didn't like him.' Kate said, bluntly.

Rick shrugged, 'A wet handshake.' He looked at Steve, who nodded his understanding, but Kate didn't get it.

'Bishop had a soft, clammy handshake.' he explained. 'And he kept licking his lips while he was talking – very off-putting. No, I didn't like him. He was fat, blunt and obnoxious. Andy called him his jailer.'

'Seems fair enough,' Kate nodded, amused at how vehemently honest Rick was about his feelings. 'What can you tell us about Eddie Lead?'

'Does your interest in Eddie mean he's a suspect?' Rick made an intelligent guess, but his face was full of concern.

'At the moment Eddie is missing from his foster home and hasn't been seen since Monday. We need to find him, anything you can tell us about him will help.' Kate didn't answer the question.

Rick's eyes met hers and he nodded, understanding. He wiped his fingers on a napkin and sat back in his chair. 'Have you met him?'

Kate and Steve both shook their heads.

'So you won't have seen him on his skateboard.' Rick's eyes looked off somewhere over Kate's shoulder, 'He's unbelievable, I mean *really* amazing, to get that good he must spend hours practicing. I've seen some stuff on the X-games and the likes, and he's easily in the same class.'

'Do you know who he skates with, where he practices? Are there other skaters he hangs out with?' Kate started firing questions.

'Is she always like this?' Rick looked at Steve, a mocking smile on his face, 'Or does she listen sometimes?'

Steve knew better than to answer.

Kate hid how foolish she felt by giving him a sarcastic look, but he was right; she wasn't giving him a chance to speak.

Rick started again, 'I met him after a home football game at the MCSC. We'd won and the boys were full of themselves, getting a bit rowdy, hanging around outside. I heard shouting and saw a crowd gathered in the car park. I assumed it was a fight - went running over ready to break it up, but what I saw stopped me in my tracks. Eddie was on his skateboard doing tricks, using the metal rails, some planks, even jumping off the wall. He was all over the place and it was effortless. I've never seen anything like it. I was mesmerized, but then one of the kids yelled, *Show Lion the one on the pipe!* And that was the end of it. Eddie looked up, saw me, picked up his skateboard and walked away.' Rick paused as the waitress put down two glasses of coke and a black coffee.

'I jogged after him. I'm always interested in kids with any sort of athletic ability. I introduced myself and started chatting; asking questions about his skating, but he wouldn't talk to me. He wasn't rude or anything, he just stood there, eyes on the floor, not saying a word until I asked if he wanted to come back to the Centre for a cold drink, then he said 'No, thank you,' very politely and left.'

'But he came back?' Kate asked a question before she could stop herself and Rick smiled at her.

'Andy Frazier told me who he was. I told him to let Eddie know I would cordon off a piece of the smooth concrete area around the centre and find equipment for him to use if he wanted to come back. A couple of weeks later he turned up and we built a makeshift course. He skated, we watched and he left. He came three or four times over the next couple of months. One day I gave him a Tony Hawk DVD. He thanked me and took it with him. Andy told me later that Eddie was in the same foster home as he and he wasn't allowed to use the DVD player. He'd only kept it because no-one ever gave him stuff.' Rick's eyes held Kate's and she saw the sympathy he felt for the boy.

'This is what I know about Eddie Lead: he's intelligent, polite and the most painfully shy kid I've ever encountered. His skating is a world he's created for himself. I've never heard him say more than a handful of words to anyone. It's as if he can't connect with people. I think Eddie has been hurt, or let down so badly by people that he doesn't trust anyone - not a soul. I've never met a kid that was so... alone.'

Kate and Steve exchanged looks. *Was Bishop or Pink to blame for that hurt?* Kate thought back to Greg Thomas' description of Eddie, *He's just one of life's victims.* What the hell had happened to this kid that everyone who'd met him felt the same way? 'Did you ever see him with George Pink?' she asked.

Rick thought about it, 'Pink was usually around when the boys were outside. I only saw him talk to Eddie once. I think he was offering to get him some more stuff to use for his skating.'

'Do you remember when that was?' Steve asked.

'Yes, it was the last time I saw Eddie, the week before last.'

'Can you remember anything that was said?' Kate pressed him.

Rick screwed his eyes up, thinking, 'Pink was offering to help him; said he could get him stuff. I thought he meant stuff for him to skate on, but I was making an assumption. Eddie shook his head and walked away.'

'Do you have any idea where Eddie might be?'

'Not really, but Andy Frazier was at the same foster home with Eddie for a couple of weeks, have you asked Andy?'

Steve pushed his plate aside, 'I can't run - I'm too full.'

Rick looked confused.

'Andy likes to make us chase him.' Kate explained.

'That sounds about right,' Rick grinned, 'when you find Eddie, will you do me a favour? Will you tell him he can come to the MCSC or my place and watch the DVD?'

Kate's mouth formed a thin line as she nodded. It was obvious Rick thought Eddie was just a lonely kid who needed help.

As they got back in the car Kate had to ask Steve who Tony Hawk was.

'You're kidding, right?' He looked sideways at her as he started the engine.

She raised an eyebrow at him. 'My daughter plays volleyball, she's never skateboarded - I don't know anyone who does.'

'Right,' Steve wondered if his Governor also lived in a bubble. 'Tony Hawk is a legend; most famous skateboarder in the world, a total genius, the first guy to land a nine hundred.'

Kate looked at him blankly, 'Lovely.' she said, sarcastically.

'Two and a half full revolutions in the air.' Steve could see he'd lost her. 'Where to, Gov? Do you want to pick up Andy Frazier?'

'Andy Frazier is a liar,' Kate pulled the sun visor down and checked her reflection in the mirror, 'I want more information before we speak to him again. Let's go and visit Aunty Sharon.'

She missed the look on Steve's face.

***

CHAPTER FIFTY

A loud yapping started up behind the door before Kate had a chance to ring the doorbell. She gave Steve a questioning look, *when did Aunty Sharon get a dog?* But he was studying his complexion in the glass door panel.

'Let me help you – your hair's fine and your nose is still crooked.' She mocked him.

Steve looked embarrassed, his eyes falling to his feet. He was saved from more ridicule when Aunty Sharon threw the door open and beckoned them in. In her arms was the silliest looking puppy Kate had ever seen. It was a cross between a rough coated terrier, a Corgi and a small fat cushion.

'What on earth is that?' Kate was laughing as they trooped into the house.

Aunty Sharon looked hurt. She clutched the puppy to her chest protectively, planting a fat kiss on the top of its head before dumping it unceremoniously onto Steve as he squeezed passed her. 'Here, take Skip into the conservatory - he likes you. I'll get the coffee on. I thought you might be popping over.'

Steve wrapped one huge shovel of a hand around the plump ball of fluff and did as he was told. Kate already had her feet tucked under her on the wicker couch when he joined her. He wasn't sure whether he should put the puppy down, or keep hold of it.

Kate held her arms out, 'Give it here.' She was laughing at him. 'You look more uncomfortable than you did when baby Mickey was dumped on you. Not a dog person then?' The puppy squirmed and nuzzled into Kate's neck as she lifted it against her shoulder.

'That's not a dog.' Steve brushed dog hair off the front of

his shirt.

By the time Aunty Sharon reappeared with a jug of espresso the puppy was asleep. 'He's called Skip, as in 'found in one'. She explained, 'What moron throws a puppy in a skip for Pete's sake!'

'I take it Skip has a new home?' Kate grinned.

'Nooo, I'm just fostering him until he can be found the right family.' Aunty Sharon frowned.

'Right.' Kate didn't believe it for a second.

'Take it you've been busy?' Aunty Sharon changed the subject, 'Bishop... John Bishop, same scenario as Pink, I heard. What the hell is going on, Kate? Bishop was responsible for foster placements... but word has it he might have had a bit of a sideline going, a little hobby?'

Kate was incredulous. The whole bloody neighbourhood knew what was going on. Local intelligence was better than police intelligence.

'I guess you already know you've got a gossip at the nick? Someone's got a big mouth. Details of how Bishop was found were all over town within a couple of hours. Horrible, gruesome stuff, so bad you'd want it to be made up. The story is Bishop was tied like a hog to a rail, tortured, stabbed in the balls and set alight.' Aunty Sharon's voice cracked, and she cleared her throat.

'Barmy's on it.' Kate was visibly disturbed by how much detail her friend already knew. Barmy had been tasked with uncovering the source of the ruddy great leak that was spewing information out onto the street. 'What did you mean by *Bishop had a little hobby*?'

'Films. The rumour is that you were after Bishop for taking pornographic films of some kids who were in foster care - but someone got to him before you did.'

Steve nearly choked on his mouthful of coffee. He banged his coffee cup down so hard Kate was amazed it didn't shatter. 'We might as well be running this investigation on frigging Facebook! In fact we might be doing better if we were. I don't pity whoever the culprit is when Barmy catches them.'

'Have you heard anything about Andy Frazier and a girl called Gina Godden?' Kate abruptly changed the subject.

'Pretty little Gina... his pretend girlfriend? What about them?'

'Pretend?'

Aunty Sharon gave her a quizzical look, 'I thought you knew?'

'Knew what?' Kate started to get the prickle of anticipation behind her ears.

'You probably don't want to hear this,' Aunty Sharon was happy to enlighten her, 'but that whole thing is a smoke screen. Andy Frazier is a bloody great nuisance, a trouble maker of the first order, but he's just trying to cover up the truth, keep his little secret.'

Kate was astonished. This was exactly why visits to Aunty Sharon were so worthwhile; her intelligence was golden – better than any police data system. She was about to ask the question; ask what the secret was that Andy was so desperate to keep, but all of a sudden she realised that there was something going on. Call it woman's intuition, call it anything you like, but suddenly she knew. Aunty Sharon was watching Steve. Kate saw the look on her face and she *knew*. For a moment she was completely derailed, she almost said something but stopped herself. It wasn't any of her business... except it was, and she didn't like it. Whatever was going on between her friend and Steve, she didn't like it one little bit.

'What secret?' Steve asked the question.

Aunty Sharon let a dramatic pause hang for a moment, building the suspense, and then she turned sideways to meet Kate's eyes, 'Andy Frazier is gay.'

'I thought so!' Steve exploded, 'He's got 'closet camp' stamped all over him.'

Kate was struggling to drag her mind back to the conversation. 'What? How do you know?'

'Gaydar, I've never been wrong yet.' Steve was much too pleased with himself for Kate's liking. 'It occurred to me that morning when we chased him, something about the way he was playing with us, and all that messing about when he was at the nick – pure camp. Boys don't keep gay porn under their beds unless they like looking at it. We didn't find any girly magazines, did we?'

Kate was stunned.

'Come on Kate,' Aunty Sharon said, 'He looks like one of those Abercrombie and Fitch adverts. You really didn't know?'

Kate shook her head, annoyed, but not sure what or who she was annoyed with. 'Not a clue.' She admitted.

'So he's only pretending to be interested in Gina? She's his cover story?'

'Well, Lilly-Bee, she's Gina's best friend,' Aunty Sharon started to explain, 'she told me Gina knows about Andy. Whatever is going on between those two is purely a business deal.'

'Lilly-bee?' Steve snorted.

'Lillian Beatrice, it's shortened.' Kate snapped at him. 'So this is about money? Gina's helping Andy keep a secret in return for money.'

'I think there might be more to it, but you'd have to ask her.' Aunty Sharon topped up Kate's coffee cup and took the sleeping puppy from her. 'You could try asking Andy of course, but he'd only lie to you.'

Kate didn't answer, she was thinking about whether Andy was really a homosexual, or he believed he was because he'd been sexually abused. It was certainly possible that he'd been conditioned and sexualised by his experiences with men. The picture of him leaning against the wall, shirtless, looking off into the distance, suddenly entered her head. Aunty Sharon was right about the way he looked, and he was doing it *deliberately*. He knew Pink was watching him and he was being deliberately provocative. He'd even posed naked for him! Andy Frazier knew exactly what he was doing. There was an increasingly blurred line separating victims and villains in this case and she needed to make some serious progress - fast, but more than anything she needed to find Eddie.

'Do you know Eddie Lead? He's called The Dog. He was in foster care but he's gone missing and I need to find him.' She looked at her friend hopefully.

'No. No idea, but I'll ask around if you like.' Aunty Sharon looked from Kate across to Steve, her eyes resting on his face.

'Right, thanks.' Kate jumped up, startling Steve with her eagerness to leave. She wanted to talk to Aunty Sharon about what was going on between her and Steve, but she wasn't going to question her in front of the man. The woman obviously had the bloody great hots for him. She wondered how far it had gone.

Back in the car Steve waited for her to tell him where they were going.

'Back to the nick.' Kate pulled her sunglasses on, 'Do you fancy Aunty Sharon?' As soon as the words were out of her mouth Kate could have bitten her tongue. *So much for not saying anything!*

Steve's head spun around so fast he nearly gave himself whiplash. 'Sorry Gov?' He stalled.

'Nothing, forget it.' Kate decided she didn't want to pursue it. She didn't want to hear the truth from him, and she didn't want him to lie to her.

'I want to know exactly where Andy Frazier was over the weekend.' She changed the subject. 'At the moment he's our best link to finding Eddie Lead. I'll send Boz to pick him up and question him again. Someone new on his case might make a difference.' Kate settled back in her seat trying to concentrate on the case; trying to figure out the complex lines of the investigation, but all she could think was that Steve's secondment had been extended and she wasn't sure she wanted to work with him anymore.

She knew something had changed as soon as she walked into the briefing. Kate realised, that for her cynical 'let's hear it for the vigilantes' colleagues, the case had suddenly become sexy. She looked around, taking in the banter and murmurings of speculation that were spreading. They loved anything scandalous and sordid, and this case suddenly had it in spades. Stacey pointedly ignored Kate as he got them to quieten down and started with the time line, focussing their attention on the board behind him.

'John Bishop drove away from his office at five and turned right towards town. At five twenty he's at the HSBC Bank on the High Street getting cash out of the machine. Then we lose him, but his mother, Mrs Bishop remembered him taking her to a beer garden recently, a pub near The Green where he seemed to know the barman. We got a positive identification at the Queen's Head where the Barman said Bishop had arrived alone, drank two pints of lager and left just before six.' Stacey had their full attention. The discovery of Bishop's burnt remains had racked up the energy level; they were soaking up every ounce of information.

'CCTV picked him up again - heading out of town and that's the last we see of him until this morning. We still need to establish exactly what time he ended up at the shed.' Stacey turned back to the board.

'Where does he live?' Natasha called out.

'Not in that direction.' Stacey pointed to the map again,

showing the location of Bishop's house. 'At around eight fifteen this morning a Mr Geoffrey Haines made a triple nine call from his mobile. He was out walking his dog along their normal route around this wasteland area. His dog was off the leash and was going berserk at the shed door. Haines was alarmed when the animal refused to come back when called. He went to investigate and smelt burning.' Stacey was in full flow, all eyes following his marker to a photo of the shed. 'Same MO as George Pink, apart from the level of violence used.' He put a couple of photos on the board and the room fell silent.

'What was he doing there?' Edwards was looking at the photos of the location, 'It's in the middle of nowhere.'

Stacey looked across at Kate; his face marked by deep black circles under his eyes, he looked tired and irritable. He stepped back, in effect handing the briefing over to her.

Kate felt no sympathy for him. She moved in front of the board as every head in the room turned towards her. 'He may have been meeting Eddie Lead.' She told them, 'Bishop was Eddie's social worker in Hockley and kept his case when they both moved here two years ago. Bishop knew Eddie was missing from his foster home but, for whatever reason, he kept it to himself.' Her eyes moved from face to face as she spoke, pulling her audience in, holding their attention.

'The location where he was killed also appears in photos taken on Pink's camera, but we haven't established a solid link between the two victims. It may have been a location that Bishop used for meeting boys; just outside town but remote enough for privacy.'

'So were they working together, Bishop and Pink? Messing about with these kids, using the shed?' Edwards asked.

'We don't know that, or why Pink photographed the location.' Kate said pointedly.

'Are any of those other boys missing?' Natasha was looking at the list of names.

'No,' Kate shook her head, 'we've made contact with parents or foster carers and they're all accounted for.'

Everyone was studying the list of names and the information on the board. A search of Bishop's home had recovered a large amount of pornography, some of it sadistic, together with a number of sexual aids. They'd also recovered a cheap photograph album from a drawer in his bedroom. In it were photos of a much younger Eddie Lead, Tony Contelli and Andy Frazier, together with three other boys as yet unidentified. Next to each photo someone had drawn big red lips with a felt tipped pen and the words 'HOT!' and 'SEXY BOY!' scribbled across the page. Kate was relieved there were no pictures of Dean Towle. So far they hadn't found any films.

'Everything we know at the moment about Bishop indicates that he was a sadistic sexual predator, a career paedophile.' Kate told them, 'We need to throw a circle around this, put Pink and Bishop in the middle and move outwards until we find the crucial link. I want the Sex Offenders Register trawled for anyone that has connections in Hockley or Marville and could have links with either victim.' She looked at Natasha and decided to give the young PC some encouragement. 'Work on that with Ginger.' The girl's face lit up but she nodded seriously and started scribbling in her notebook.

'Both victim's lives will be examined... what connects them? Other than the fact that they had connections with these boys.' Kate pointed to the board, 'is there some other way in which their lives were linked? Who knew, or had dealings with both men? There's a lot of background that still needs to be covered.' Kate squared her shoulders and waited until there was silence and all eyes were on her. She let the silence hang for a moment longer before she spoke.

'Every time I step outside this building a member of the public tells me exactly what's going on in this investigation. The whole bloody town knows what we're doing. DCI Stacey and I have spoken about this.' She looked from face to face. 'And anyone who wants to impress their girlfriend or their mates with some juicy stories had better think very carefully about their career options. Let me be very clear about this, there will be no more leaks.' She was furious that details of the case had got out.

There was an awkward silence and looks passed around the room. The source of the leak had been a hot topic of conversation all day, with everyone having a favourite theory. At the moment the money was on a new probationer - the one who'd been directing the vehicles at the site of Bishop's murder.

She handed back to Stacey, but he only wanted to talk about

Eddie Lead and how everything had to be done to locate him - he was still their main suspect. Kate was dismayed. As the briefing broke up she abandoned Steve and went looking for Knowling. He was in his office, two fingers typing and trying to read his own dreadful handwriting from a legal pad on his desk.

'Do you want to dictate and I'll type?' She offered.

His eyes lifted from the screen, 'You're not my bloody PA,' He snapped, 'and there's nothing wrong with my typing - I'm concerned with accuracy.'

'Probably just as well... you couldn't afford me.' She tilted her head, trying to read his notes upside down.

Knowling stopped typing and leant back in his chair, 'What do you want?'

Kate's face grew serious, 'I want to put off working with Social Services on identifying other victims. We were rushing ahead with it because we needed to build a case against Bishop, but his murder changes everything. And I'm concerned that we're focused on Eddie Lead as a suspect and not looking at the other possibilities, which is dangerous.' She paused and took a breath, 'The DCI is fixated on him.'

Knowling watched her, waiting.

'What if someone inside the child protection services is responsible? Someone who'd discovered what Bishop was up to? They could have taken information from the boy's files to slow us up.' She voiced the thought that had been rattling around in her brain for too long.

'Have you got someone in mind?' The intensity of his look made Kate uncomfortable.

'No, but we could be jeopardising the investigation by getting into the mix with Social Services on the child protection issue. We need to identify any other victims so that they can get the proper help, but we don't need to rush about, there's no child in imminent danger, not anymore. Give me a couple of days to keep going on what we've got. Social services are up to their necks with the fallout – enough to keep them tied up for the moment, and I want to find Eddie.'

Knowling looked at her thoughtfully, 'I thought you'd made up your mind Pink wasn't sexually abusing these boys? So what links Pink to Bishop?'

'I don't know. But the way these men were killed is cruel and dramatic; someone's making a statement. All that stuff that was found at Bishop's place fits exactly with what Adam Dyer told us about him - so it makes sense he was also telling the truth about Pink. He and Tony set him up, and it started a chain of events, cast a shadow over Pink that he never shook off. Half the bloody town were talking about him being a pervert and yet there hasn't been a whisper about Bishop. Unlike Pink, Bishop had legitimate access to these boys and enough control over their lives to hold them in terror.' Kate pushed her hair back with both hands. 'He was obviously a clever bastard. Adam Dyer said there was a film made of Tony Contelli being assaulted by Bishop. We've given the details to the CEOP but so far it's not ringing any bells – so, remarkably, it may not have found its way onto the Internet. Maybe we're going back to retro.'

Knowling raised his eyebrows at her questioningly.

'Back to the old way. Colin called it retro vintage abuse... before the wonders of the World Wide Web. I think this might be a perfect example of that – making a film of the abuse and *not* sharing, or only distributing it to a trusted, select few. If the film is as horrible as I believe then restricting its distribution makes it a lot more valuable.'

'Like a limited edition?' Knowling said.

'Exactly. And what if there's more than one film? When Tony killed himself Bishop wouldn't have stopped – people like him don't stop, they find someone else, maybe that someone else was Eddie.' Kate hated the idea, but the more she thought about it the more it made sense.

Knowling shook his head and looked at her thoughtfully, making her wait. 'The Social Services Director has asked for some time to deal with their internal situation. I can give them what they want - in the spirit of co-operation and such crap.'

'Can I still get some help from Hockley?' Kate knew she was pushing her luck but she had nothing to lose. 'Maggie and Boz have already been seconded and I need their help. You don't need to cancel the arrangement.' She held his look. She knew he was going to agree; he was going to let her keep the manpower, but he wanted to make sure she knew who was actually in charge.

Knowling pointed his pencil at her. 'Don't take the piss. You can keep Maggie and Boz and I'll give you a couple of days - but that's all, so you'd better get a result.' He paused, 'You don't want it to be Eddie Lead... you don't want him to be responsible, do you?'

Kate stared at him, unable to answer.

'Well then, you need to find him, and fast.' Knowling's eyes bore into hers, his voice soft but adamant. Kate swallowed, for some absurd reason she felt a bit choked.

'I'll find him.'

She closed the door behind her as she left and wondered why she hadn't mentioned the photos of her and Stacey on Pink's camera. She fished her phone out of her pocket and called Angel to tell her she'd be another hour or so, then went back to her office and changed into dark blue jeans and pumps before going looking for Steve. She found him still in the incident room sitting next to Ginger and looking at something on a computer. He looked up in surprise as she threw her car keys at him. 'Where are we going?'

'To buy some chocolate buttons.'

***

CHAPTER FIFTY ONE

Kate made her way to the counter at the front of the Deli-come-coffee shop that Steve would never have found if he'd been on his own. It was tucked between a florist and an off-licence down a little side street off the centre of town. They'd already made a fast pit stop at a late night news agents where, to Steve's confusion, Kate had hopped out and bought two bags of Cadbury's chocolate buttons, before hopping back in and giving him directions to the Deli. She hadn't offered an explanation, so he didn't ask.

She hadn't said more than two words in the car on the short journey over and he was waiting to find out what the hell was going on. He was pretty certain she hadn't dragged him out to be sociable. He was worried she was going to start up about him and Aunty Sharon again - not that he was going to tell her anything.

Kate had her purse out and was leaning across the dark mahogany counter. She didn't have to wait long. She was soon picked up on the server's 'hot' radar and he scooted over with a smile that was a little too welcoming. 'You alright love? What can I get you?'

'Hi,' Kate beamed back; she could play this game. 'I need the biggest glass of very cold chardonnay you can find, a large cappuccino, and...?' She turned to Steve - she didn't know what to order for him.

Steve was confused, for a moment he'd thought the cappuccino was for him, but now he realised she was ordering *three* drinks. 'I'll have a pint of Fosters, mate.' He nodded at the man, who was already pouring Kate's wine into a large glass and staring at her cleavage at the same time.

Steve looked around while he waited for his drink. Bleached wooden floor, lots of modern beige and cream furnishings – a typical boutique type place. It seemed like exactly the sort of place Kate would choose to drink in. 'Are we meeting someone, Gov?'

Kate gave the server another smile and took a sip of her wine before she turned to face him. 'Charlie Winsome, otherwise known as The Jockey', she nodded.

Steve raised his eyebrows and stared at her.

'I want to talk to him about the film Adam told you about. He might be able to help us.'

Steve was confused. 'Sorry?'

'Charlie served eight years for sexual offences with children; got released years ago, but it was before I was on the CPU and he doesn't hold a grudge. For some reason he seems to like me.'

Steve was still staring at her. *Was she serious?* He took a long sip of his beer. 'And he's coming here to meet us?'

'No. This is his favourite place to sit and have a quiet coffee and I thought we could just drop in and have a chat. He won't mind, like I said, he likes me.' Kate picked up the cappuccino and started across the room. 'He'll be in a booth at the back.' She turned the corner at the end of the counter. Although the place was fairly busy with what were obviously locals, most of them were out in the garden gathered around ashtrays on wooden tables. Kate made her way to a snug booth built into the back corner. Sitting with his back to the wall on one of the benches was a small man, neatly dressed in a navy blazer with a white shirt and narrow maroon tie. He was studying the crossword in a newspaper, peering over narrow black-framed glasses and holding the paper under the pool of light from the small brass lantern on the sidewall.

Steve gave him the once over. He took in the scraggy loose skin on the back of the hand holding the paper and rheumy eyes straining to read. The way he was dressed, Steve thought he had to be in his sixties... maybe seventies, even.

'Why's he called The Jockey?' he asked as they made their way towards the booth, 'Or am I asking the bleeding obvious and he actually rode horses?'

Kate glanced back at him over her shoulder. 'I'll let you read his file, it'll soon become clear.'

Steve's face said *I don't believe this,* but she'd turned back away

318

from him and didn't see it.

'Evening, dear.' Charlie Winsome looked up from his paper and gave Kate an amused half smile as she set his cup down and placed the two bags of chocolate buttons next to them. 'Bless you.' He gave Steve a hard look as they slid into the booth opposite him.

'Steve's new on my team.' Kate said, by way of introduction.

Charlie tilted his chin, but his eyes never left Steve's face. He nodded almost imperceptibly to himself and then turned his eyes back to Kate and pressed himself comfortably into the back of the booth. There was no effort to shake hands.

'Bishop.' He spoke with the quiet rasp of a man who has smoked since the age of ten. He knew why Kate had come looking for him, and why he was enjoying a free coffee and some chocolate.

Kate nodded.

'This isn't computer stuff. If it was you wouldn't be talking to me. Pictures, film? What is it?' He folded his paper and put it down on the seat next to him.

'Did you know Bishop?' Kate's voice was quiet, although there wasn't anyone close enough to overhear. Next to her Steve shifted in his seat; she could feel the belligerence emanating from him, the scorn. She regretted bringing him. He didn't understand and she didn't have the inclination to explain it to him. She just needed him to behave and keep his feelings to himself.

Charlie was shaking his head. He coughed into his hand, 'Never met the man.'

'But you know *about* him.' Kate stated it as a fact.

Charlie's thin lips parted to reveal a row of small stained teeth. 'Me and everyone else, darling, but you already know the gossip. What you want is something more, something you can get your hands around.' He turned his face to Steve; the corners of his mouth turned up as he looked at him indulgently. 'Maybe you could explain to me what it was that Bishop enjoyed with these children? Give me something to work on?'

Steve's whole body stiffened and his shoulders seem to swell to twice their width as he leant forward across the table. 'Why would you want to know that? Does it do something for you - hearing about torture, about the violence that these kids were subjected to?'

Kate closed her eyes and pressed her thumbs into the side of her nose. Charlie was deliberately provoking Steve and Steve was biting. He was giving Charlie exactly what Charlie wanted.

'Shut up Steve.' she said quietly, without looking at him.

Charlie's eyebrows bobbed as he lifted his coffee and took a small sip. 'Torture, eh? So you *are* looking for something special. Don't think I can help you.' He smoothed his tie and smiled again, but his eyes were dark. 'And if you want to talk to me you'd better find your manners young man.'

Before Kate could intervene Steve exploded. 'You've got to be joking! I don't need...'

'That's enough, both of you!' Kate snapped. 'Go and have a look outside.' She gave Steve a hard look.

Steve turned to look at her in confusion, his face set with anger.

'Please, go and have a look – see who's outside.' Kate tilted her head towards the door leading to the garden. 'I'll only be a couple of minutes.'

He stared at her for a moment longer, then grabbed his glass from the table and left.

'Why do you have to do that? Why do you have to be such a pain in the neck?' she asked Charlie as soon as Steve was out of sight. She was cross – she didn't have time for this nonsense.

Charlie shrugged. 'He had it coming. Your friend might be big, but his intelligence doesn't match his size. That was too easy. If you want to hold hands with the likes of him that's your business, but like I said, I don't think I can help you.'

'Yes, you can.' Kate smiled and nodded at him, playing to his ego, 'You might be the only person who can. And you're right. I'm looking for something special, something that's got a limited, maybe a *very limited,* circulation.'

Charlie coughed again. 'Give me a clue. I'm not saying I can help, I'm just saying give me an idea of what I'm looking for – Bishop, right?'

'Probably.' Kate nodded, 'We think there's a film of him and at least one young boy, a teenager but looks younger, nasty stuff.'

'How old; not the boy, I mean the film.'

'Not that old.' She opened her bag and pulled out two small copies of photographs. One was a head and shoulders shot of Tony Contelli, taken when he was arrested, the other was the photo of Eddie Lead – the one where he'd been watching Dean on his skateboard, but Dean and the rest of the background had been cut out making the image of Eddie even more striking.

Charlie studied them silently until Kate held her hand out and he reluctantly gave them back. As she tucked them back into her bag the photo of Eddie caught her attention again. With the background erased and nothing to indicate what he'd been looking it struck her how isolated and *haunted* he looked. Charlie didn't miss a thing. 'Beautiful, that boy is beautiful.' he said, a note of wistfulness in his voice.

Kate looked up sharply. 'Don't. You can't mess with me Charlie; you know that. Are you going to help me?'

Charlie drained his cup. 'I've got your number.'

Kate stood up, 'Thank you.' She stepped away from the booth and spotted Steve standing just outside the door. He'd been watching her the whole time. He didn't look happy. Kate sighed as he came back inside and strode straight past her. She waited until they were in the car and he was pulling out of the car park.

'When Charlie was in prison he was sectioned; placed in seclusion away from other prisoners for his own protection. Six weeks after he went down he was attacked. His skull was broken; his jaw smashed, most of his ribs kicked in, even his kidneys were damaged. His face was given such a going over he was unrecognisable.'

Steve's eyes never left the road, but he nodded, almost in satisfaction. *So what? It happened all the time. Someone turned a blind eye and paedophiles who'd preyed on innocent young children got a hiding. Steve wasn't about to feel sorry for the bloke. What about the kids he'd messed with? While he'd been cooling his heels in the garden he'd thought about Charlie Winsome and how he'd got the name 'The Jockey', it made him feel sick.*

'And they broke his back.' Kate carried on, her voice soft in the dark interior of the car. 'He was paralysed; he won't ever walk again. You were so busy getting on your high horse that I bet you didn't see the wheelchair propped against the wall besides him, did you?' She turned in her seat, studying his face, but she saw no reaction; no softening, his jaw was still rigid with anger. 'They nearly killed him, he was lucky to survive. That's only one step away from what happened to Pink and Bishop, so if you think Charlie got what he deserved and doesn't need to be treated any better - even though he's served his time and can't go after kids anymore because he can't even put his own socks on without help – you might want to re-think your position on my team.' Kate spoke every word slowly and precisely, 'Look, when you want information about drug dealers you go to someone who has knowledge about the drug scene. Get over yourself, Steve – Charlie is a contact in exactly the same way as any scrawny little druggy you've had on the payroll, only he doesn't get anything from us, apart from the odd bag of chocolate buttons that is. I think they're pretty much his main pleasure now. And if you want to embarrass yourself I'd appreciate it if you'd wait until you're back on the *really important* fraud squad, or wherever you're off to next. I'm not sure you're really cut out for this.'

In the five minutes it took for Steve to drive back to the Station he didn't say any of the twenty things he wanted to say in reply. He didn't say anything.

Kate got home to find Angel and Bridget dipping veggie chips in salsa as they waited for the pizza to cook. There was an enormous bouquet of flowers sitting in a saucepan on the kitchen table.

'They came this morning but I couldn't find a vase.' Angel was totally blasé in the way only a teenager could be. 'There's a card for both of us, it says *I'm an idiot, please forgive me.* But there's no name.' She shrugged, 'Who do you know that's an idiot, Mum?'

Kate poured herself a large glass of Merlot, 'Pass me a pen, I'll start writing a list.'

The girls laughed.

'Well, do we forgive them or not?' Angel wanted to know.

Kate took a sip of her wine, 'Not in this lifetime.'

She didn't say it, but Steve Astman would have to pull off a small miracle to get back in her good books. *And* just what the bloody hell was going on between him and Aunty Sharon? Something had happened; they'd been like cats on a hot tin roof around each other. If he messed Aunty Sharon about, even in the slightest, whether or not he still had a job on the CPU would be the last of his worries.

***

CHAPTER FIFTY TWO

There was a gaping hole in the investigation, a hole Eddie Lead had fallen into. Boz and Maggie had arrived early and they were jamming up on the case details. Steve was more subdued than normal, but no one was paying much attention to him.

'Is there someone Eddie could go to for help, somewhere he could get money?' Maggie pursed her lips thoughtfully as she studied the board.

'He hasn't got any friends.' Boz commented, 'So where would he go?'

'How the hell does a kid end up without a single friend? It's not just odd, it's very *sad*.' Kate was frustrated by their inability to find Eddie and she was growing increasingly concerned for his safety.

'I'm still waiting for the information on Eddie's foster placement in Hockley.' Steve flicked through his notebook, 'The bloke in charge of the Children's Services only took the job last summer - he hasn't heard of the Pinks, but he's getting someone who worked with Bishop to ring me.'

'Are their records any better than Marville's?' Kate looked at Boz and Maggie.

Maggie pulled a cigarette from her purse and waved it about. She was gagging for a fag. 'They're probably worse.'

Kate didn't want to hear it. The lack of information was starting to seriously wind her up.

'We don't have any evidence of a connection between Eddie and George Pink - other than the fact that Pink spoke to him at the

MCSC when he was showing off on his skateboard. There's no indication that they *knew* each other...'

His Skateboard.

Kate raised her hand, indicating that they should all stay where they were, but Maggie waved her unlit cigarette in the air again, 'Ok, fag break,' She relented, 'but be back in ten minutes.'

Maggie nearly trod on Kate's heels in her hurry to get outside.

Kate retrieved a small DVD and plugged it into the player. Steve looked at her questioningly, but she was tight lipped and thoughtful. She didn't say a word until Maggie walked back in, then she pressed 'play' and the screen flicked into life. The film opened with a shot of the front of Pink's yellow brick bungalow. The camera operator was walking along the pavement at the front of the house. He was filming the entrance to the cul-de-sac and the narrow lane that led to the footpath between the houses; walking the route that Dean had taken, but it was the next bit that Kate was interested in. 'Watch carefully.' she told them. They all crowded in a bit closer to the screen.

The camera operator walked back to the street and did a sweep of the scene outside the bungalow.

'There!' Kate jumped towards the screen and pointed.

'Shit!' Boz swore, clasped his hands round the back of his head and rocked back on his heels.

'What? What? I missed it.' Maggie didn't know what he'd seen.

Kate rewound the tape for a few seconds and then paused it. Leaning forward she pointed at a figure in the far corner of the screen. He'd only just been captured on film; if he'd been a couple of feet further up the road the camera would have missed him.

'That's Eddie Lead. He was there when I arrived at the house and he skated past my car as I was driving away with Dean.' Kate was annoyed, *why the bloody hell hadn't she realised this before?*

'So he *was* there, but not until after Dean had turned up.' Steve said.

'Well, he was in the street shortly after Pink was killed.' Kate looked closely at the screen. Bruce Jeffries had described someone wearing dark jeans and a hoodie. Eddie was definitely wearing dark jeans but he was in a short-sleeved t-shirt and Kate couldn't see a rucksack anywhere near him.

'Maybe he was waiting to meet Dean.' Kate was thinking of

different possibilities, 'Maybe he'd turned up early, but all the drama kicked off so he stayed to watch - and the kid Bruce Jeffries saw wasn't carrying a skateboard, just a rucksack.'

'Possible.' Maggie wasn't so sure. 'But it's also possible that he'd put the skateboard down somewhere to be picked up later - and he'd just set light to Pink in his garden shed.'

'What about the rucksack and the hoodie?' Kate was still peering at the screen.

'Maybe he threw them in the fire before he legged it.' Steve suggested, 'We would have found them by now if he'd dumped them.'

Kate had to admit it was possible, but what had the petrol been carried in? There was no jerry can found in the remains of the shed. Had it been carried in something else, something that would burn?

'Or he could have just hidden them behind that garden wall and retrieved them when no one was looking. There was only one uniform on the door at Pink's house when I left, and a couple of firemen outside. A kid – even a kid with a rucksack, skating off down the road wouldn't have caught anyone's attention. I didn't remember seeing him until now.' Kate was furious with herself.

Maggie jumped as the telephone next to her started ringing, 'I need another fag,' she said as Steve reached for the receiver. But Kate's attention had turned to Steve.

'Don't apologise,' he said into the receiver, 'we're getting a pretty good impression of Bishop. What? Can you say that again?' His eyes narrowed. He put the phone on conference call mode so that they could all hear the woman's voice.

'You were told that George and Anne Pink didn't foster children when they lived in Hockley. Well, they weren't on the regular register, but four years ago they were used as an emergency stop over for a couple of cases - Eddie Lead was one of them. He was with them for about three weeks.'

Everyone looked at everyone else and Kate's heart sank. *Pink fostered Eddie in Hockley!* So there was a link between Eddie Lead and George Pink and Eddie had been in the vicinity of Pink's house moments after the man burnt to death. She wondered if her feelings about him were terribly wrong. Maggie leant over the desk, opened the window and lit her cigarette.

'That's interesting.' Steve said, evenly.

'Well, look, I don't know if this is relevant but Bishop was responsible for Eddie being placed with the Pinks – Bishop knew Pink, he recommended him.' The woman said.

Steve looked up to see Kate frantically gesturing at him, 'I want to talk to her.' she hissed.

Steve got the caller to agree to meet them before he hung up. 'That was Pauline Huxley; she's a social worker in Hockley.' he said.

'What did she say before you put it on speaker?' Kate said brusquely.

'She asked if we knew Bishop's history at Hockley. Apparently, there was a bit of a cloud over his head when he left. I got the distinct impression she disliked Bishop intensely.'

Kate looked at Boz and Maggie, but they shook their heads. 'No idea, Gov.' Maggie blew smoke out of the window, 'I'd heard of Bishop, but we never had any dealings with him when he was at Hockley. He wasn't on the child protection panel - he didn't do interviews with kids or anything like that, he just did foster placements.'

'Is it possible,' Steve leant forward, 'that Bishop was moved to Marville because there was something going on? Like those Catholic Priests and whatnot, you know, every time there was suspicion about them they got moved to a new area?'

Kate chewed her lip as she thought about it, 'Maggie, do you remember who headed up the Children's Services Department over at Hockley when Bishop was there?'

'Rogers, Keith Rogers, bit of a waste of space – out of his depth.'

Kate raised her eyebrows, 'Track him down. Find out what he's got to say about Bishop - especially his transfer to Marville. And put that bloody fag out before Stacey walks in. Boz, go and get Andy Frazier, find out what he was up to over the weekend and if he knows where Eddie is. Show him the pictures we found of him on Pink's camera. I want to know exactly what George Pink was paying him for and how long it had been going on.'

'Right, what about the photos John Bishop had of him, the ones found in the album at his house?' Boz asked.

'Keep that for now – I just want you to talk to him about Pink.'

Maggie took a long drag on her fag then casually stubbed it out on the windowsill. 'Eddie was placed in foster care with the Pink's on Bishop's recommendation, he was in the vicinity of Pink's house immediately after the fire started and the chances are he was supposed to meet our second victim, Bishop, last Friday - now he's missing. That's a shed load of coincidences... pardon the pun.' She said.

Kate was afraid she had a point. Knowling had been right when he'd said she didn't want it to be Eddie; the bloody man could see right through her. 'I need to speak to Anne Pink's FLO. There's nothing in her statement about fostering kids.'

Ginger suddenly stood up behind his monitor and called across, 'The Bowden's have been located - the travelling family? They're on a site on the outskirts of Warwick.'

'Where did you get that?' Kate held her hand out for the notes he was holding.

'Warwickshire Constabulary, Brin Bowden is in Warwick hospital. He got in a street fight and suffered a head injury.'

Kate was reading the notes she'd taken from him. Social Services in Warwick were involved with the family and had been put in contact with the social worker in Marville who had worked with the Bowdens. She was surprised to see Mivvie had been associated with the family, she didn't remember her being involved with travellers.

'It doesn't say how long he's been in the hospital. Give them a ring and find out.' Kate handed the notes back, 'Maggie, find someone helpful at Warwick CPU, see if they'll speak to Michael Bowden. I want to know what happened with Pink, what happened that made Brin nearly break his arm? Use your charm, but if there's any problem we'll go up there and talk to him ourselves.' Kate looked at her watch; it was only eight thirty. She was setting them all up for a long day, but she could feel the adrenaline starting to pump. They had a lot more information than they'd started the day with and there were plenty of actions to get on with; something was going to break soon, she was sure of it.

Maggie nodded and took the papers from Kate, but Ginger wasn't finished, 'There are a couple of girls downstairs - won't give their names. They want to talk to you, Ma'am.'

Kate's eyes narrowed, 'What do they look like?'

'Desk bloke said they look like thirteen year old hookers.'

Kate turned to Boz. 'Get Andy in and give him some breakfast. Get his father to come with him – but don't talk to him until I call you.'

'Got it.' Boz nodded.

'Steve, get a car and meet me out the front.' She was gone before he could ask why.

Kate looked at the two teenagers huddled together in the corner of reception and decided 'thirteen year old hookers' was a good description. Gina Godden and Lilly-Bee were a paedophile's wet dream. They had more lip-gloss on than clothes.

'Come on you two.' Kate walked straight past them, giving them no option but to follow her. She skipped down the front steps and out into the sunshine, waiting at the kerb as the girls caught up with her. There was the roar of a powerful engine as Steve exited the car park, spun the car ninety degrees and came to a sudden stop right in front of them with a squeal of tyres. Kate didn't react but both girls jumped and grabbed hold of each other, squealing. *Bloody Steve and his Miami vice tactics.* Kate casually pulled the rear passenger door open and tilted her head. 'Get in.'

Lilly-Bee took Gina's hand and pulled her into the back of the car. Kate slammed the door, put her sunglasses on and climbed into the front passenger seat. Steve was staring out of the front windscreen, behaving like a getaway driver and paying no attention to the two girls in the back.

Kate swivelled in her seat to look at them. They were almost sitting on each other's laps. Gina was chewing the skin from the corner of her thumb as Lilly-Bee clasped her other hand.

If they want drama I'll give them drama. Kate smiled. 'I take it your mums are both at work?'

Both girls nodded, they were wide eyed watching her, wondering what she was going to do with them.

'Ok, I'm not supposed to talk to you unless we have an appropriate adult present. But, as you called in yesterday to see me and Lilly-Bee has spoken to Aunty Sharon, I'm guessing there's something you couldn't tell me before?' Kate rolled her eyes at Gina. 'So, here's what we're going to do. Steve is going to drive us to Aunty Sharon's house – by the scenic route, and if you just want to have a little chat in the car while we're on the way, well that's ok.

Then I'll get Aunty Sharon to call Gina's mum and tell her where you are, deal?'

Gina looked at Lilly-Bee, who nodded. Steve was already pulling out into the traffic.

'Good. Who's going to go first?'

Again, the girls looked at each other and Kate wanted to sigh, but instead she smiled encouragingly. 'You came to tell me *something*, and I'm guessing it's something really important. I'd like to hear it, so don't worry about what I'm going to think, or about *putting it right* or any other silly nonsense, this is just us having a chat – Steve's not even listening.' Kate let her glasses slide down her nose. 'So come on, what is it you want to talk about?'

'Andy Frazier's a loser! He's told everyone that Gina wanted to get back with him, but he made out she was a slag, like, said she'd slept with so many people she was passing diseases around! Gina were helping him out, like, pretending to be with him. But he's a total gay and we hate him.' Lilly-Bee blurted the words out so quickly Kate had trouble keeping up. She put her hand up to slow her down. She wanted to hear it from Gina.

'You think Andy's gay?'

'I *know* he is. Jayden told me.' Gina was feigning a sulky nonchalance, but she was as nervous as hell.

Kate raised her eyebrows questioningly.

'He's my cousin, he's fifteen and he's been out forever, like. Me mum says she knew he was gay when he was three because he was such a raving camp and he always wanted to hold hands with other little boys. Anyway, he told me.' Gina was speaking around her thumb, which she didn't seem able to remove from her mouth. 'Jayden saw Andy at some party getting off with another boy. I didn't know if it were a secret or what, like, cos I never really talked to Andy before. But I used to think he were cute, lots of girls fancy him, and it gave me an excuse. I went round his house and he said we could help each other out. He didn't want anyone to know he was gay, not until he was sixteen, like, cos his dad would kill him. But when he's sixteen he's leaving school and going to London...'

'But he thinks he's the best and he can do what he likes. He tried to feel Gina up in front of that Bisby, just to impress him, like. Gina smacked him and he got, like really nasty – that's when the thing happened.' Lilly-Bee butted in.

'What thing?' Kate asked with exaggerated excitement in her voice, playing along, acting enthralled. She glanced at Steve but he kept his eyes firmly on the road. She had no idea where he was going, she'd said 'scenic route' but he seemed to be taking a massive detour to get to Aunty Sharon's.

'I told him I weren't doing it anymore. He'd only given me fifty quid, even though he'd promised me lots of cash. So I told him I'd tell, I'd let everyone know he was a ponce. That's when he gave me the two hundred. He was getting money from that Pink the Perv. He had the hots for boys and had lots of money, like, and he was happy to pay. *Pervert.* Andy got the money for helping him.'

Kate had a dreadful feeling she knew exactly where this was going. 'How did Andy 'help' Mr Pink?'

'He found him a new friend, like, said it was someone new for him to cuddle. That's what Pink gave him the two hundred for. I didn't want any part of it – didn't want his dirty money, but he threatened me, said he'd tell people I was a bike.'

Kate knew who Pink's new friend was.

'And then he beat him up!' Lilly-Bee jumped in again, 'Andy really hurt him, trod on his face and everything. He's only a little kid; Gina knows him – his name's Dean, he's half the size of Andy. Even Bisby, who was Andy's best mate, like, hates him 'cos of it!'

Dean Towle – it came back to Dean Towle. He was the new friend Andy had introduced Pink to. Andy had set Dean up.

'What about the camera?' Kate looked at Gina, 'What was that all about?'

'I felt sorry for Dean, I were trying to help him. I'd have kept Dean away from the pervert an' all if I'd known, but I didn't know until after Andy had set him up.'

After you'd spent the money. Kate thought, but she didn't say it.

'Andy nicked the camera because he wanted to have something over Pink. He said he had lots of ways to get money out of him. I gave it to Dean for insurance, like. I was going to tell Andy that Dean had the camera. I wanted Andy to stop Pink messing with Dean, but then the bloke got killed and Andy thought Dean had dobbed him in.'

'When was the last time you saw Andy Frazier?' Kate asked.

'Outside my house on Saturday night, but I wouldn't talk to him.'

'So he's gone around telling lies about her, threatening her. That's against the law isn't it?' Lilly-Bee was a picture of indignation.

'And so's pimping young kids for an old pervert!' Gina cut in. 'Cos that's what Andy did, isn't it? I told him he could go to prison for that!'

There was no doubt in Kate's mind that Andy Frazier would end up in prison – one day, but not for introducing George Pink to Dean Towle.

'Are you going to arrest him?' Lilly-Bee wanted action.

Kate knew why they'd come to see her. They wanted to get Andy into trouble with the police as revenge for him spreading gossip about Gina. Kate had spoken to Gina twice in the last few days and she'd never volunteered the information about Pink and Dean – not until now, not until she was being labelled a slag by a local toe rag whom she'd happily taken money from. *Bloody teenage girls, they all think they're living in some television soap drama.* Kate looked at her watch; if Boz had found him then Andy Frazier would already be on his way to the station. She needed to speak to him before he interviewed the boy. *Villains and victims – it was getting more and more difficult to see where the line was between the two.*

Kate nodded to Steve, 'Let's drop the girls off.'

'Whatever happens Andy's going to get fucking killed - we've told everyone he's a gay and that he let Pink do it with him.' Lilly-Bee said sweetly.

***

CHAPTER FIFTY THREE

Kate desperately wanted to stop for a coffee, but she didn't have the time. She dropped the girls at Aunty Sharon's house with a brief explanation. Aunty Sharon was her normal breezy self, but Steve was still unnaturally quiet, awkward even. Kate knew she hadn't made it up – there was definitely something going on between him and Aunty Sharon and it irritated the life out of her, even though her rational mind told her it was none of her business.

Back at the car she gave Steve the benefit of her hard stare before she told him to set up a meeting with the social worker, Pauline Huxley, away from her office. She suggested a coffee shop.

'I worked with a DS on the Fraud Squad who was a bit of an alcoholic, arranged all his meetings in a pub.' Steve told her when he'd hung up. 'You're the equivalent – only with coffee bars.'

'Your point is?' Kate gave him a sarcastic look.

'No point – I'm just saying, that's all. This DS could understand all the complexities of a serious fraud case, but he'd get a bit belligerent after a drink and take a piss up someone's garden wall - at least you don't do that.' He turned and grinned at her. Now that he was alone with her Steve felt uncomfortable. She hadn't mentioned the flowers and he wasn't sure if he should bring the matter up; apologise in person, or just leave it alone. He was joking to cover up his unease but Kate wasn't amused.

'He wasn't that impressed with you, either.' she said pleasantly, throwing him completely. He decided to shut up and drive.

There was no sign of the social worker when they arrived at the coffee shop. Kate wondered if she'd changed her mind, got cold feet, but, as they got in line to order, she spotted her coming out of the loo. She introduced herself and Steve and then took a good look at the woman as they searched for a quiet table near the back. Pauline Huxley wasn't what Kate had expected. She had to be in her mid sixties, but she had a 'bohemian' look about her, with close-cropped white hair and an enormous bosom under a shocking pink t-shirt. Kate recognised a 'no nonsense' air about her.

'The news about Bishop's death is all over the office. There's some high level arse-covering going on as we speak. I haven't got long, so what do you need to know?' Intelligent blue eyes looked at Kate as she took a seat.

'What can you tell us about Bishop; about his involvement with Eddie Lead?' Kate followed the woman's lead and dispensed with any waffle.

'Bishop was completely unsuitable for his role with families and children. He'd transferred from somewhere near Birmingham. His mother lives in Marville and he needed to be close to her. I guess Marville didn't have a vacancy so the Hockley office got him.'

'What do you mean 'unsuitable'?'

'Kids didn't like him. The ability to build a rapport, *trust* with kids is imperative – Bishop didn't have it. Oh, he made all the right noises to the right people. He chummied up to the hierarchy in a way that would make you sick, but those of us who had to work with him knew better. At first I thought he was just inadequate, a liability, but as he got settled into the department and felt comfortable, *safe*, his true nature came to light. The man was a disgrace.'

'What makes you say that?' Kate wanted details.

'He was too 'touchy feely', in a way that made women uncomfortable. Oh, he was very clever; never really overstepping the line, always ready to defend himself if someone spoke up, but he was getting sexual gratification from his behaviour.'

'Did someone complain? You said something to Steve about Bishop leaving with a bit of a cloud over him.'

'The management were desperate to get rid of him. They were waiting for an excuse, any excuse. He should have been fired, but he managed to convince them it was all a misunderstanding, maliciousness from people who wanted to cause mischief for him. He was given the opportunity to transfer – and Marville got him.' She paused to pour more tea from the pot into her cup. Kate waited. She knew there was more, something important.

'We had a couple of college girls on work experience with us that summer. They were perky and fun and Bishop homed in on them like a dog to a bitch on heat. He used their naivety and the fact that he had a position of authority over them. I reported him, but Keith Rogers was in charge then – bloody waste of time he was, he was more embarrassed than anything. But both girls admitted they felt uncomfortable about the attention from Bishop and he got a slap on the wrist.'

Kate didn't think she had the full answer, 'Was there something else that forced his transfer?'

'Of course.' She looked at Kate as though she'd just stated the bloody obvious. 'Flirting with a couple of silly college girls wouldn't have forced the move. It was his relationship with a thirteen-year-old boy in foster care, a boy he was responsible for. The boy's background was one of those typical tragedies that we see all too often. Father had buggered off when he was a baby; mother was entertaining a variety of men for company and money – the usual thing. Anyway, his school attendance was atrocious, he was hanging around on the streets all day doing whatever he liked.' She looked at Kate to see if she was following and Kate nodded, using the pause to send Steve for more drinks.

'A school's officer got involved and things improved but it didn't last long. The mother found a new boyfriend; one who was a bit handy with his fists and the boy got the brunt of his temper a couple of times. The boyfriend was arrested, but sadly the mother picked the boyfriend over her son – hence the foster placement.' She thanked Steve as he put another pot of tea down alongside a double espresso for Kate.

'So what was wrong with Bishop's handling of the case?' Kate was confused. So far the story sounded like a hundred others she could tell about how foster kids end up in care. What had happened that had seen Bishop hustled out?

Pauline Huxley smiled as she sipped her tea. 'The boy had a talent for dancing. He was introduced to dance club at the Key Kids Club where they ...'

'Key Kids Club?' Kate cut her off, a look passed between her and Steve. *Hadn't Pink been involved with the Key Kids Club?*

'Yes, do you know it? It's a charity, but it receives a grant that allows them to have trained theatre and dance people work with the kids.'

'We've heard of it - sorry go on, you were explaining about Bishop's handling of the case.'

'Yes, dancing – the boy was born to dance. We encourage kids to take up interests, anything to give them a feeling of self worth. But Bishop became obsessed, started attending all his lessons and performances with him, filming it all on a little DVD camera. It wasn't seen as a problem until he started neglecting his other cases.' She stopped and glanced at her watch, 'I'm sorry, I need to start making a move soon.'

Kate nodded, 'Before you go I need to ask you about Eddie Lead... about Bishop's involvement with him.'

The woman hesitated, gathering her thoughts. 'We were desperate for emergency short-term foster placements. Bishop recommended the Pinks and they were snapped up, but they were only used twice and then, for some reason, they were taken off the books. After they'd had Eddie they didn't take any more kids. Eddie moved onto a more permanent home but there was some problem and he moved to Marville.'

'What had happened?' Kate leant forward, but the woman shook her head.

'I don't know – it would be in his file.'

Kate nearly groaned, most of Eddie's file was missing. The social worker had started to gather up her things, but Kate wanted to make sure she understood.

'Bishop recommended the Pinks as emergency foster carers and he placed Eddie with them, is that right?'

'Yes. Bishop was Eddie's caseworker. He also gave Pink a reference for his job at the Key Kids Club. I seem to remember that Bishop and Pink belonged to the same church group; I believe that's how they knew each other.'

'Do you know which church?' Steve opened his notebook.

'The First Methodist Church. It's only a little place – near the library.'

Steve wrote down the details.

'And Bishop took the offer of a transfer to Marville because he was in trouble for spending too much time with one boy.' Kate said.

The woman was about to stand up, but she paused, 'Oh it was more than that. Bishop attended a dance competition at the Key Kids Club that the boy won. One of the youth workers walked into the dressing rooms afterwards and found Bishop alone with the boy. He claimed the boy was sitting on Bishop's lap with Bishop kissing his head. He jumped off when they were interrupted and the youth worker said Bishop had an erection. Bishop denied it - he was furious, got really nasty about it. He said they'd been excited about the victory; that was all. The boy wouldn't say anything different so it didn't go any further, but it was enough, it was the excuse management were waiting for. It was agreed Bishop would move and sever all ties with the boy. Total bloody disgrace, the man should have been arrested, then fired, then shot.' She stood up to leave, 'I'm sorry, I need to get back.'

'Just one more thing, was Keith Rogers aware of all this?' Kate wanted to know if there'd been a cover up.

The woman looked at her stonily, 'Keith Rogers was fully aware – he arranged Bishop's transfer and was bloody pleased to have moved the problem off his patch.'

'Ring Maggie, tell her what we've learnt about Keith Rogers.' Kate told Steve as they walked back to the car, 'I'm calling Mivvie.' She wanted information from inside the social services camp at Marville and there was only one person she could trust to give her a straight answer.

'Morning Kate, I don't know about you, but I'm re-thinking my career options.' Mivvie sounded tired and pissed off. 'It's a bloody circus around here. Everyone knows about Bishop and the bloody hypocrites are trying to look shocked and appalled when, if they were honest, they think it's a bad end to bad rubbish.'

'Haven't you got a place abroad somewhere? Maybe we could go off for a couple of weeks; drink cocktails, lie in the sun, forget about chasing bad guys.' Kate wasn't tired but she was exasperated. She felt as though she was treading water; just keeping her head clear but not actually getting anywhere.

'Can I come?' Steve had left a voice message for Maggie and

was listening in.

Kate shook her head, 'No room.'

'What's happening on your side?' Mivvie asked.

'The Pinks were emergency foster carers in Hockley, but they only took two cases. Eddie was the last kid to stay with them and then they gave up. And Bishop and Pink knew each other in Hockley. Bishop got Pink a job at the Key Kids Club and then recommended him as a short term foster carer.'

'Shit!' Mivvie swore. 'It takes months to be accepted as a carer. They should have gone through all sorts of background checks, why isn't this on record?'

'There may have been some shortcuts. Apparently Hockley was desperate – and remember Bishop *knew* Pink, he was recommending a friend. There's also some question about the Department Head's abilities.'

'Buddies helping each other out.' Mivvie was furious. 'Have you found Eddie?'

Kate had to admit they hadn't. 'And we haven't turned up the missing papers from the files. They weren't at Bishop's house. Anyway, why I rang you – do you remember a travelling family; the Bowdens, they left Marville in June?'

Mivvie thought about it for a second. 'Three boys, right? Is that who you mean? I took a turn covering for the woman who normally looks after travellers' kids – she was off sick for a few weeks. Let me think, Michael and Tommy... I can't remember the older one's name.'

'Brin,' Kate helped her out, 'Brin Bowden. He's in hospital in Warwick with a head injury after a street fight.' She heard a sharp intake of breath at the other end of the line. 'Michael and Tommy hung out at the MCSC, Tommy played football with Rick's regular kids, but there was some sort of altercation between Brin and George Pink. Brin threatened Pink. Warwick CPU is setting up a joint investigation to see if Michael will tell them what it was about.'

'I don't know anything about it - but Michael's gorgeous.' Mivvie interrupted. 'He would have been exactly the sort that Pink would go for; small, beautiful looking boy... and from a vulnerable background.'

'But it seems whatever Pink was up to, Brin sorted it.' Kate said. 'On a different matter, do you know anything about Bishop's history at Hockley – anything about why he might have transferred to Marville?'

'His mother lives here. That's the official reason; the rest is speculation and gossip.' Mivvie was hedging.

'Tell me.'

'Something to do with a couple of college interns, someone complained that he was stalking them or pawing them – something like that, now the bastard's dead it's all coming out of the woodwork, people have been talking about it all day. I wasn't here when he transferred so I'm not sure, but I've heard that Hockley were less than honest when they off-loaded him on us.'

'Thanks.' Kate had her cover up. An ineffectual manager in Hockley had passed a problem member of staff on to another area without making them aware of the issues. This had allowed Bishop to move to fresh pastures, unscathed, and to use his ability to chummy up with the management to get a promotion to team leader. He must have thought he was untouchable - and then Eddie got transferred to Marville and back under Bishop's control. It made Kate feel sick. But why had Eddie been moved? Was Bishop responsible for that too?

'I take it Andy Frazier's got some more questions to answer. How come you're not doing the interview with him?' Mivvie interrupted her thoughts.

Kate was astonished. *Where had Mivvie got the information from – and so fast?* 'How did you hear that?' she said, evenly.

'The duty social worker told me. She's on her way to the nick to act as appropriate adult for someone called Box?'

'*Boz.*' Kate corrected her, 'His name's Boz, he obviously couldn't find Andy's father.'

'Mind you, I probably would have heard about it anyway. You've got a bloody great leak, the news about how Bishop died is all over town.'

Kate sighed, 'Yes, *we know.* We just don't know *who* the leak is yet. Barmy's been tasked with finding out.'

Mivvie burst out laughing. 'That's convenient.'

Kate was confused, 'What do you mean?'

'Just that I heard Barmy *was* the leak.'

'Can you back that up?'

'Not sure, I can try. It might just be gossip of course.'

'And then again it might not.' Kate didn't want to believe it, but Barmy was a liability – especially around child protection issues. *Damn!* She knew she should take the allegation back to Knowling and Stacey.

'Look, can you keep me updated – anything that's being said? I sometimes feel as though I'm working with my head in a bucket.' Kate's frustration started to show.

'Sure. If this Boz is with Andy Frazier what are you up to?'

'I'm going to find Eddie Lead. He's still at the top of the board as our main suspect.' Kate sounded far more certain than she felt.

***

CHAPTER FIFTY FOUR

Steve parked in front of a row of old-fashioned terraced houses and Kate checked off the numbers on the doors. She was looking for number thirty-one.

'It's the blue door, just there,' she pointed at a house two doors down from where they were parked, 'Let's hope they've got something helpful to say.'

Kate had called ahead and the door was opened before Steve barely had a chance to knock. Mrs Gibson was bustling - nervous but a little bit excited too.

Kate made the introductions, 'I really appreciate you seeing us, and we won't keep you too long.' She had to move a mountain of cushions to sit down on a tapestried sofa. 'I take it you were very fond of Princess Diana.' Every plate on the wall and piece of china in the glass-fronted cabinet bore the Princess's image.

'Oh, I loved her, didn't everyone?' Mrs Gibson was putting cups on a tray.

'I know I did.' Steve decided against moving an ancient cat off an armchair and took a seat next to Kate.

She looked at him suspiciously but his face was unreadable. 'Is Mr Gibson joining us? It would be helpful to talk to you both.' She turned back to Mrs Gibson.

'I'm sure he'll be in as soon as the kettle's boiled - tea?' Mrs Gibson was eager to play hostess.

'Love one. Let me give you a hand.' Kate jumped up.

Once again Kate realised she'd made an assumption about someone, and then having met them realised they were completely different from how she'd imagined. The couple were in their sixties and were retired, but Mrs Gibson looked quite trendy and fit. In spite of the kitsch surroundings and the homage to Princess Diana, the woman had a real energy about her, brisk and youthful.

Her husband came in through the back door just as she was carrying the tea tray back to the lounge. A tall, quiet man with a formal manner, he shook hands and introduced himself as Tim, 'Welcome, welcome.' he said with a soft Irish lilt, 'you've come to talk about Eddie. How can we help you?'

Kate perched on the arm of the settee, drank her tea and asked some questions to get a general idea of their background and their history with Eddie. It wasn't long before she started to get a very uneasy feeling; there was something very wrong. Meaningful looks passed between the couple as they tried to answer her questions and Kate knew there were things they were leaving unsaid. Steve caught her eye - he'd seen it too.

'Did you like Eddie?' Kate tried the direct approach.

Mrs Gibson's eyes went soft, 'I loved him.'

Tim nodded, 'Beth was soft on him, and the boy had something about him - buggered if I could tell you what it was. It sounds daft, but however hard we tried he always seemed... well, *sad.*' He looked from Kate to Steve and back, checking if they followed.

'What was he sad about?' Kate asked.

'He was like that when he came and he never changed. We had him for two years and whatever happened; good, or bad, even when he had all that bother, he was always the same.' Mr Gibson looked troubled, 'We just wanted him to be happy.'

Kate needed to backtrack. 'What bother?'

'Oh, we thought you'd have known. Wasn't it in his file? Oh well.' Mrs Gibson paused, embarrassed.

Here we go, Kate thought and she saw Steve sit up straighter.

'Eddie got badly hurt. Apparently it had been going on for a while; at least that's what the special doctor told us, but we didn't know, he'd never said anything.' Mrs Gibson bit her lip, her manner apologetic, 'If we'd known we would have helped him, but it was so difficult. Eddie was never any trouble, but he held himself back from everyone.' She was rambling slightly.

'How did he get hurt?' Kate tried to keep her on track.

'He'd been bullied really badly. How he managed to put up with it and not say anything, well I just don't know, but we thought maybe that's how he'd been injured.'

Kate still wasn't any the wiser. 'How had he been injured?'

There was a long silence. The Gibson's looked at each other while Kate waited. Mr Gibson cleared his throat, embarrassed, 'He was bleeding, if you know what I'm saying. We don't know how it happened, he wouldn't say. Whether it was experimenting or something worse, he wouldn't say a word. He'd been in some bother with boys in school, bigger boys, and we wondered if that's where it had happened, but we didn't know.'

Kate was pretty sure she knew.

'Is that why he had to move?' Steve asked.

'Well, yes. It seemed better that he went to a new school, a new area. We just wanted him to be safe, to be *happy*. We didn't want to give him up, he could have stayed with us, but we wanted what was best for him.'

Kate felt wretched. Eddie might have moved, but he wasn't safe. 'Can you help us find him? Does he have any friends in Hockley? Maybe someone he would have stayed in touch with, someone he could stay with?'

They both looked at her as though she'd said something very odd.

'While Eddie was here he had a birthday,' Mrs Gibson spoke so quietly Kate had to lean forward to hear her. 'I asked him to write down the names of four friends to take out for a bit of a party. We were going to Pizza Hut or something, you know?' She paused and took a deep breath before continuing. 'He sat at that table with a piece of paper and a pen for over an hour. I thought he was having trouble making his mind up; couldn't decide *which* friends to ask. When I looked he'd only written three names – his and ours. There wasn't a single friend, not one. We'd like to help you, but we can't. When Eddie left we took our names off the register, we don't foster anymore – we just can't do it, we felt we'd failed.'

There was a sombre silence in the car as Steve drove away from the house. 'How does that happen?' He asked Kate, 'How does a kid fall through the net like that? He was *injured* for Christ's sake, he'd been *raped*, and nothing was done about it?'

For Kate it was all too familiar. 'It's a conspiracy of silence. It's what Bishop and all the others like them rely on. All the way back to Raymond Greggs - none of them ever told.' It was a bleak picture and she hated it. She had to find Eddie but she had absolutely no idea where to look. She was about to tell Steve to drive back to the nick when her mobile rang. She checked the screen but didn't recognise the number.

'Kate Landers,' she said, formally, but it was Boz.

'I thought you should know, the M-Scan came back. The petrol used in Pink's murder and the contents of the jerry can found in the Frazier's shed are a match. They're waiting for the results on the petrol used in Bishop's death, but it's caused a bit of excitement here even though there are no usable prints from the can. Mick Frazier turned up at the nick while I was with Andy and I gave them both a lift home, I'd only just got back when I heard. There might be a planning meeting later before anyone gets pulled in. Andy and Mick Frazier both have an alibi for the time of Pink's death, so we need to see exactly what we've got, although the DCI doesn't know about it yet – he seems to be missing in action at the moment.'

Kate was stunned, 'Where was Andy on Friday?'

There was an ominous pause before Boz answered, 'He might have an alibi for the time of Bishop's death, but to be honest it's not great. I did get a bit more out of him about his relationship with Pink but he claims he has no idea where Eddie Lead is.'

'But we took that jerry can out of Frazier's house before Bishop's murder; it's been with us since Thursday. If the petrol from Bishop's case comes back a match too, then it must have been decanted from the can into another container *before* we found it - where's the petrol from?'

'That's the interesting thing, it's been matched to Texaco petrol...'

'There's a Texaco garage near the social service offices in Marville.' Kate interrupted.

'It's not from a local garage. They think they've tied it down to a garage eight miles the other side of *Hockley*. DC Edwards has been despatched to follow it up.'

'But Frazier doesn't drive. He made up some crap about a lawnmower, but I don't believe he'd seen that jerry can before we dug it out of his shed - he thought he was covering for Andy.' Kate was thinking out loud, it didn't make any sense, Andy and Mick

Frazier had both been at the doctor's when Pink was killed, hadn't they? She glanced quickly at Steve.

'Check out Andy's whereabouts on Friday evening, keep me informed, we'll be back shortly.' She hung up.

'Pull over.' Kate wasn't going anywhere until she'd got something straight with Steve. Andy Frazier and his father had an alibi for the time of Pink's murder, but now there was physical evidence linking them to the crime, and that didn't make any sense.

'Andy and Mick Frazier were at the chiropodist's during the time that Pink was being attacked. You spoke to the surgery – they were both there the whole time, right?'

Steve frowned. 'They were there when Mick Frazier told us they were; the girl at the surgery confirmed it.'

That wasn't what Kate had asked. 'They were definitely there the *whole time* – from before nine thirty until after eleven? Neither of them could have left and then gone back?'

A look close to panic crossed Steve's face. 'The receptionist confirmed they'd checked in at nine twenty and that the doctor was running late...'

'Don't tell me you didn't *ask*.' Kate shut her eyes and shook her head, appalled. They'd relied on an alibi that might have a ruddy great hole in it.

'Look, she definitely told me they'd waited until after eleven, she said Andy had sat slouched in the waiting room. I didn't specifically ask about Mick Frazier, I assumed they'd been together... fuck! I don't know if they were both in the surgery the whole time.'

'Was this girl cute or something, the receptionist?' Kate glared at him. 'For crying out loud! I told Stacey the alibi checked out!' She was furious.

Steve sat absolutely still, knowing there was nothing he could say to redeem himself.

'Drive.' Kate turned away from him and stared out of the windscreen.

Thankful that she wasn't looking at him anymore, Steve yanked the wheel and pulled out into the traffic.

'Where to?'

'The chiropodist's, if there's a hole in the alibi I'd prefer that we found out before Stacey does.' she snapped.

The receptionist wasn't pretty, in fact she wasn't anything much. She had a forgettable face and a condescending attitude that was annoying. Kate decided immediately that she didn't like her. Like so many receptionists in doctor's surgeries she was on a power kick; making sure everyone knew they had to get past her to get any attention.

'I've already spoken to you.' Her mouth twitched; but nowhere close to a smile before she turned away and started pressing computer keys, effectively blanking them.

Steve tried to redeem himself by taking the charm route. 'And you were very helpful, Emily. We just need to clarify a few points and you're the only person who can help us. We need to speak to you in private - this is very confidential.' He was play acting, flirting with her, but it worked. The girl stopped pressing keys and gave an arrogant flick of her hair. Giving a little wave of her hand she indicated they should wait, and then leant towards the open door behind her.

'I have to speak to some police detective people and it has to be in private, cover the desk.'

Another girl dressed in an identical high collared tunic emerged and stared wide-eyed at the 'Detective people,' more impressed by their presence than her colleague.

Kate and Steve followed Emily into a small consulting room. There were two armchairs and a coffee table but they remained standing. Kate went through the information Emily had given previously. The Fraziers had checked in for their appointment at nine twenty on Monday morning and had left at eleven thirty-five.

'How do you know the exact time they left?' she asked.

The girl shrugged. 'Everything's on the computer. As soon as anyone arrives they're logged in, when I send them through to the doctor it's clocked, when they leave it's clocked. Everything's clocked, even me. Mr. Zahani likes accurate records.'

Kate looked at her questioningly.

'He's the owner. He's a doctor, but he doesn't work here anymore.' Emily explained.

'Did Mr Frazier arrive with his son?' Kate kept going.

'Yes, he spoke to me when I clocked them in.' Emily said in a pained voice.

'Describe Mr Frazier.' Kate wanted to make absolutely sure they were talking about the same person.

'Scruffy. Greasy grey hair; smelt bad, seemed a bit thick. When I told him about the wait he had a grumble at me and then went off for a fag.'

Kate and Steve exchanged looks.

'The Fraziers sat in the waiting room in front of your desk, is that right?' Steve asked.

Emily looked at him as though he was stupid, 'Where else would they sit?'

'Where did Mr Frazier go for a fag?' Kate was losing patience.

'Around the side. We don't let people smoke near the door, Mr Zahani goes ape shit if there's cigarette butts out front. There's a little porch at the side with a big pot thing for the fag ends.' Emily did the hair-flicking thing again.

'So there were periods of time when Mr Frazier wasn't in the waiting room?' Kate pressed her.

'They went out together at one point, but the boy wasn't gone long. Most of the time he was slouched in the waiting room listening to something on his phone.'

Kate took a deep breath in, 'How long was Mr Frazier gone from the waiting room at any one time?'

'I'm busy. I don't time people in and out having a fag. He went out a couple of times while they were waiting.'

Emily's tone was so sarcastic Kate wondered if she could arrest her for something, anything, the girl was seriously getting on her nerves.

'In case you've misunderstood us in any way let me make something clear. This is a murder investigation – I do not have time to pamper to your receptionist ego. I need a direct answer right now - did Mr Frazier go out for longer than it would normally take to have a quick ciggie?'

Emily's mouth turned up in a nasty little sneer, but she'd got the message. 'Yes, and it was a bloody good job - I didn't want him stinking out my waiting room, the longer he was gone the better. When I told him they weren't going to be seen for at least an hour he shuffled off leaving the boy half asleep in a chair.'

'I'm not interested in your feelings about Mr Frazier's personal hygiene.' Kate's tone was so harsh Steve glanced at her in surprise.

He was standing besides her, looking increasingly pale but she had no sympathy for him and her patience had run out. 'How long was he gone?'

Emily looked miffed. 'They'd only just got here and he went straight out to have a fag. He came back just as I was checking in Lucy Skeller. Her mum's lovely, always brings us biscuits or something. I remember because he shuffled up and interrupted me while I was talking to them, wanted to know how much longer they had to wait, I told him at least half an hour.' Emily saw the look on Kate's face and got to the point, 'Ten thirty. Lucy's appointment was at ten thirty, so he'd been gone about an hour.'

'Did you notice anything different about him when he came back?' The skin was beginning to prickle on the back of Kate's neck. They'd got a bloody great hole in Frazier's alibi – *an hour, a whole bloody hour when he wasn't accounted for*. Stacey was going to go mental.

'He smelt worse. He must have smoked himself stupid while he was out – it was disgusting.'

'We should have known this on Friday; we had Andy and Mick Frazier in the bloody nick on Friday!' Kate slammed the door so hard the whole car rocked. Steve winced but she hadn't finished, she pushed her hair back from her face with both hands, exasperated. 'This is a total frigging waste of time! Andy Frazier didn't kill Pink or Bishop and neither did his father, but now everyone's going to be distracted trying to make some impossible scenario fit the crime because you couldn't check out an alibi properly. Where's the nearest bus stop?' Kate strained her neck looking behind her then turned to peer out of the windscreen. 'The next corner - pull over in the bus lane.'

Steve started to pull away from the kerb. He was wretched with embarrassment. 'Look Gov, I'm sorry...'

'Stay here and get your phone out while I check the timetable.' Kate ignored his apology and climbed out of the car. A minute later she was back. 'Closest you can get to Pink's by bus is the industrial park at the back of Clare Walk, but there's no way he could have got a bus there and back in the time. Have you got maps on your phone?'

Steve nodded silently and opened the attachment.

'Bring up our location.'

'What do you need Gov?' Steve flicked through screens.

'I need to prove that Mick Frazier couldn't have snuck away to Clare Walk, stabbed Pink, set him alight and made it back here in an hour – regardless of how bad he smelt.' Kate shuffled over in her seat, looking over his arm at the screen. 'Zoom out a bit; see if you can find Clare walk – there it is! It's a good fifteen minutes drive away if you take the most direct route. Frazier couldn't have known that Andy's appointment was delayed by over an hour, so unless he telephoned someone to pick him up, give him a lift, wait for him and then deposit him back at the surgery – and where did he get the knife and petrol from?'

'Well, if someone picked him up they could have had the petrol and the knife in the car.' Steve risked offering a suggestion.

Kate chewed on her bottom lip. 'But then we're talking about an accomplice; *a conspiracy* and it didn't happen! Bruce Jeffries was sitting in his car in Clare Walk for fifteen minutes. He would have seen a vehicle pulling up and Mick Frazier getting out - it didn't happen. Frazier wouldn't climb over his dirty laundry to escape if his flat was on fire, there's no way he could climb over a fence! You've met him – do you honestly believe he was having a quiet fag outside the surgery when he decided to call a friend and pop over to Pink's to commit murder? He probably just wandered about for an hour – didn't want to sit inside with the not so smelly people and the old copies of Woman's Weekly.'

'But what about the petrol?' Steve didn't want his mistake to have any impact on the investigation, but the petrol needed explaining.

'I don't bloody know, but Frazier isn't bright enough to have set this up, and remember, when he told us about the doctor's appointment he wasn't trying to give us an alibi for the time Pink was killed, we were interviewing Andy about the assault on Dean – Frazier was trying to explain why Andy might have been at the MCSC.' Kate leant back against her seat, staring out of the windscreen deep in thought. 'It's got nothing to do with Mick, it's something to do with Andy.'

'You think he was involved in Pink's death; knew about it and was maybe keeping the can for someone else?' Steve looked at her questioningly but she didn't turn her head.

348

'Possible. Or he knew *nothing* about it and someone's trying to set him up, someone who didn't know he'd be at the doctor's that morning.'

'The kid in the hoodie?' Steve made an obvious suggestion.

'Every kid we've spoken to about Pink has thrown Andy Frazier's name at us, maybe the killer knew that; knew he'd be a good fall guy.' Kate was thinking it through, 'But why? Andy's a little shit, but who would set him up for this?' Kate finally turned to look at Steve, 'And whose name *never* came up, not from Andy or Josh Martin or B.Zed – who is the one kid we *didn't* hear about?'

'Eddie Lead.' Steve said.

Kate nodded. 'And Andy and Eddie shared a foster home a couple of months ago.' She pinched her lip in concentration. 'Eddie has been under Bishop's control for years and Bishop was responsible for placing Andy in the same foster home.' Kate thought about that some more, aware Steve was waiting and making him wait. Andy Frazier had turned Pink's interest in him to his advantage. Did he have something over Eddie? Something about Eddie that Eddie wanted to protect or keep secret? It kept coming back to the boys. Kate looked across and met Steve's eyes.

'Let's go and visit Bisby, see how his knee's mending.'

'What's the plan, Gov?' Steve pulled away from the kerb, relieved the focus was no longer on the alibi cock up.

'The same as it was when we left the nick – to find Eddie Lead. If it changes I'll tell you.'

***

CHAPTER FIFTY FIVE

Mrs Alouni blessed them at least five times before they'd made it as far as the lounge.

'She wants to save you for Jesus.' Bisby grinned at Steve from the sofa where he was sitting playing a computer game on the television monitor; his bad leg propped up on a cushion. 'She's afraid for your soul. Thinks you'll be spending eternity in Hell.'

'Well, Steve could be on his way to the Safer Neighbourhoods Team – that's the same sort of thing.' Kate said, dryly.

'Give us that other controller; see if I can beat you.' Steve ignored the jibe, 'Has Dean been over for a game yet?'

'Yeh, he were here yesterday.' Bisby looked a bit sheepish, 'He said he'd talked to you about the Andy thing and the phone. Said your dad was going to fix it for us cos he's like a big judge or sommat.'

'Or something,' Steve kept a straight face. 'We'll work something out, but we need your help.'

'What?' Bisby didn't look up. He was focused on beating the pants off Steve in a racing car game.

Kate leant forward in her armchair. 'Has Andy been here since Steve last saw you?'

Bisby answered with a vigorous shake of his head, 'Tosser – we aint' speaking, why would he come here?'

'Have you heard anything about him in the last couple of days?' The noise from the game was starting to give Kate a headache.

'There's a load of stuff on Facebook about him being a shit poker. Gina sent me a message, but everyone's on about it, serves him right like, pretends he's a hard case, tosser probably fancied me.'

Gina and Lilly-Bee didn't waste any time. Kate wondered what would happen when Andy realised he'd been outed. 'Before the Facebook stuff started was there anyone that might have had it in for Andy?'

'Why, has someone given him a kicking? He wouldn't have a chance on his own. Has someone marked his pretty face? He's terrified of having his face marked.'

'No, but who might want to screw things up for him?' It was difficult to question Bisby while he was fixated on the television screen. Steve wasn't helping. Her colleague looked like a twelve year old, throwing a plastic steering wheel around as though he was Lewis Hamilton or someone. She was rescued when Mrs Alouni walked in with a tray of coffee and some pale looking wafers.

'Bisby! Turn that awful thing off, these people are trying to talk to you!' She shrilled, and then realised that Steve was playing with the 'awful thing' too.

'Thank you Mrs Alouni, this is lovely.' Kate took a cup, grateful that she now had the boy looking at her. 'Can you think of anyone? Anyone who would want to hurt Andy?' She heard Mrs Alouni suck air in between her teeth at the mention of Andy's name.

'Gina hates him big time and there's a bunch of little kids at school that he was always messing with, but I don't know their names. They're Dean's age, maybe he'd know.' Bisby's language was far less colourful now that his mother was in the room. 'Can't think... maybe Lilly-Bee, but she only hates him cos she's Gina's BFF.'

Steve looked as though he was going to interrupt, but Kate shook her head, she knew what BFF meant, Gina and Lilly-Bee were Paris Hilton wannabes. 'Ok, one more thing, what do you know about Eddie Lead?'

'He goes to my school.' Bisby frowned.

'But do you *know* him; do you know anything about him?'

'Skater; likes his skateboard more than he likes people. He don't talk to no-one, not even Andy and they was in the same home.' Bisby shrugged.

Kate was getting frustrated. 'We're trying to find Eddie - it's very important. Can you think of anyone who *does* know him, or anywhere he could go, maybe for help or to hide?'

Bisby's mouth twisted in a grimace, 'Maybe he's dead.'

Kate's heart did a double skip. 'What makes you say that?'

'That's what loners do aint it? They top themselves cos they think no one cares about 'em and no one cares about The Dog except to watch him skate. Either that or they gets a gun and shoots their school up. School's closed so maybe he went off somewhere like, and hung himself.'

'Oh Lord,' Mrs Alouni crossed herself and her mouth started moving in a silent prayer. Steve and Kate stared at each other over Bisby's head. Was that why they couldn't find him? Kate couldn't bear to entertain the thought for a second. She didn't want to consider for a moment that they'd lost another kid; not like Tony Contelli, but the thought took hold.

Eddie might be dead.

As they walked back to the car, Kate's mobile went off again. She pushed her hair back behind her ear.

'Kate Landers.'

'Mick Frazier turned up ten minutes ago and he's been arrested, but he wants to see you and won't talk to anyone else, Gov. Custody officer asked if there was any chance you could *pop back*? I've paraphrased that for the sake of decency.'

It was Ginger. 'And Frazier says could you bring some B & H with you?'

'Tell him I'll be there in ten minutes. She snapped her phone shut and squinted at Steve. 'You may have a small opportunity to impress me – can you get us back to the nick in ten minutes?'

Steve flicked his remote control, unlocking the car with a beep. 'Eight.'

Frazier was sweating and edgy, nervously rubbing his hands over his face, pushing his hair back with cigarette stained fingers. He smelt like a pub ashtray, the rank stench of his body odour filled the small interview room and made Kate feel queasy.

'I got the bus back soon as I realised what was happening. I never thought about it before, not until Andy told me about those blokes what got burnt, and that black geezer asking him about it. Fooking load of bollocks or what?'

Kate kept her face blank, ignoring the reference to Boz and

calmly waiting for him to elaborate. Frazier had hotfooted it back to the nick on a mission. There was something he needed to get off his chest and Kate had a pretty good idea what it was.

'That thing you had out of the shed; the petrol can, it aint mine, never seen it before you turned it up – didn't know it was there even.' He sat back in his chair, crossed his arms over his chest and nodded at her as though that was the end of the matter.

Kate let the silence hang for a moment, aware that Steve was fidgeting beside her but ignoring him. Eventually she spoke.

'Mr Frazier, when one of our officers found a jerry can in your shed you quite clearly told me that it was yours and that you used it for petrol for your lawnmower which you had loaned to a mate, but you now wish to change that story, is that correct?'

Frazier looked agitated, 'That's what I said.'

'So you lied to me.'

'Well I was caught on the hop like, panicked, had to make something up.' Frazier shifted in his seat uncomfortable under Kate's scrutiny.

'Why did you have to make something up?'

'It were Andy, you was after Andy and I was rattled, wasn't sure what he'd been up to but thought it had to be something bad for you to be searching the place like that.'

'So you lied to me to protect your son. Did you have any idea why we might be interested in the jerry can?' Kate's tone was harsh.

'No.' Frazier was lying and Kate knew it, she stood up and backed away from the table, he looked up at her, startled.

'Where did you go on Monday morning, the day you took Andy to have his feet done?' Kate demanded, 'While Andy was sitting in the surgery you went missing for an hour. Where were you? Because just about that time someone was in Clare Walk throwing petrol over George Pink in his shed and setting him on fire, petrol that matches what was in your jerry can – the one you lied to me about. At the moment the only *fooking bollocks* as you put it, is that you've lied and I don't think you understand how much trouble that puts you in.' Kate's voice was angry, 'DCI Stacey is ready to charge you with the murder of George Pink. We have physical evidence linking you to the crime – and there's no bail for murder charges, you'll stay inside while we find out what's really going on.' Kate pushed her chair roughly out of the way and leaned over the table fixing Frazier with a stare. 'Well?'

'I never seen it before, I told you! That's why I come back here as quickly as I could, as soon as the boy told me what was going on. I knew I shouldn't have said what I did, but I swear, I fooking swear to you I knew nothing about anyone burning. I don't know this bloke Pink, never met him, why the fook would I want to do sommat like that?'

'So where were you?' Steve said quietly. He looked at Frazier steadily until the man turned his head and met his eyes. 'Where were you on Monday morning when you left Andy sitting in the surgery?'

Kate sat down and dragged her chair back to the table, wondering why Frazier suddenly looked embarrassed. She raised her right index finger towards Steve, telling him to wait for Frazier to fill the silence.

'I needed a crap.' Frazier dropped his head, rubbing at his eyes with his fist. 'I didn't want to go in the bog in the waiting room; the door opens right there where people are sitting, I didn't want to let everyone know my business, especially with that fooking snooty cow on the desk.'

'So where did you go?' Kate softened her voice, encouraging him to go on.

'Me mate Pete. He lives off the back of the Newsagents a few minutes' walk up the road. I went off there, got me self a paper at the shop and stopped for a cuppa and a fag. She'd said it were going to be at least an hour before we got in to see the doctor - so there weren't no rush. Talk to him, talk to Pete, he'll tell you I was there.'

'What's the address?' Steve was writing down the details.

'Ok, let's get back to the petrol can.' Kate said pleasantly,

Frazier raised his eyes to meet hers, utterly bewildered. 'I don't fooking know, honest! I never saw it before your bloke pulled it out.'

'So how did it get in your shed?'

'Someone must have put it there, not Andy – he aint got nothing to do with it neither, I don't know.'

'Not very helpful is it?' Kate said, 'When was the last time you were in your shed? Before Monday - when we searched it?'

Frazier shrugged, 'I aint been in there for weeks. I don't hardly use it, there's no room for anything.'

'Is there a lock for the door?'

Frazier shook his head, 'Nothing to steal, why would I bother to lock it?'

Kate's mind was churning over the possibilities, 'So if neither you nor Andy had ever seen the can before Monday - why was it in your shed?'

The look on Frazier's face was almost pleading, 'I don't know! Easy enough to get round the back of my place and into the shed, someone's making mischief, that's what it is.'

'Who?' Kate asked the all-important question.

'Fook knows.' Frazier rolled his eyes to the ceiling.

'Do you know any reason why someone might want to set you up? Get you or Andy into trouble?'

'I don't know anything about it, and Andy's mates with everyone, but...' Frazier paused, looking unsure. 'That bloke at the social hated him.'

'Social services, you mean? What bloke?'

'The one who put him in care, that Bishop bloke. Bollocks it were, taking the kid off me just 'cos we were having a few problems. We sorts our own stuff out, right? There weren't no need for anyone to get involved in our personal business. It's got nothing to do with anyone else what goes on in my own home.' Frazier was starting to waffle.

'Why do you think Bishop hated your son?'

'He come to the house a couple of weeks back, looking for Andy. He were mad about something, shouting and swearing on the doorstep like, wanting to know where Andy was. I told him to fook off, shut the door in his face.'

Kate's eyes narrowed, 'What was he mad about?'

Frazier shook his head, 'I didn't give a shit. Andy weren't his responsibility no more so I didn't give a fook what he were so worked up about. He said something about the boy causing trouble, but he were in a right nasty mood so I slammed the door on him.'

'Did you speak to Andy about it?'

'Yeh, I told him. He said he didn't know what the bloke was on about, said he were a vicious bastard who thought he were bigger than he was. Andy were laughing like he didn't really care.'

'Mr Frazier, John Bishop was killed on Friday evening, attacked and burnt to death in a similar way to George Pink.' Kate's voice was low and intense.

Frazier smiled. 'Aye, I know – and I don't know who done that either, but it aint a great loss is it?'

Kate arranged to keep Frazier in custody while his story was checked out and they waited for the tests to come back from the accelerant used in Bishop's murder. She could apply for an extension to keep him in for further questioning if she needed to. It wouldn't hurt Frazier to sit and think about his predicament for a few hours, especially as he'd lied to her, so Kate handed him over and forgot about him. She needed to get back to something more important.

Find Eddie Lead.

***

CHAPTER FIFTY SIX

Maggie and Boz joined Kate and Steve in the incident room. It was pretty quiet. With two murders to investigate and Stacey threatening to go into meltdown, nearly everyone was out following unexciting leads and trying to uncover better ones. Natasha had increased her popularity by bringing over a tray of coffee from Kate's office only to be ribbed by Ginger for 'sucking up'.

'What's the story with Keith Rogers?' Kate looked at Maggie.

'Classic example of arse covering, terrified in case he's been found out – bloody waste of space. How the hell do people like that end up in charge of looking after vulnerable kids?' Maggie was disgusted, 'He's on some panel now, advising schools on kids that keep getting excluded.'

'So not very helpful.' Kate guessed.

'Oh, *massively* helpful. Smarmy git was only too happy to help the police with their enquiries – you know the sort. Was *very* upset about Bishop, only remembered him in glowing terms until I mentioned the complaints, then he started spluttering, said it was maliciousness - office politics and someone who was maybe vindictive because they'd been passed over for promotion. He insisted there was no evidence *whatsoever* to suggest Bishop was anything other than a caring professional who had *possibly* become a little too dedicated in his work with one child. Sorry, Gov, he wouldn't budge, but he's a frightened man, I don't think he's sleeping well at the moment.'

'Right.' Kate mentally put Keith Rogers to one side, 'What about Andy?'

'He kept up his wide boy act for as long as he could, but

crumbled a bit when he realised we had the photos. He let Pink take photos of him for money; reckoned Pink was taking pictures of him anyway so why shouldn't he make a bit of cash out of it?'

Kate almost grinned, she'd thought as much. 'Nothing if not enterprising.'

Boz nodded, 'He thought Pink was a soft touch; like taking candy from a baby – his words. He claimed he took the camera because Pink was threatening him, saying he'd show the pictures to Bishop and get Andy put back in foster care. The gist of it seems to be that Andy got greedy and pissed Pink off. Having taken two hundred quid off him he went back for more and discovered Pink wasn't *that much* of a soft touch. Andy stole the camera because he'd had dealings with Bishop before. He called him an evil, violent bastard. He wouldn't elaborate and I didn't push it, I figured we could go back to it another time, but there's definitely more there. When he heard you were looking for him he made Gina take the camera in case you found it. As for the jerry can - claims he knows nothing about it. To be honest Gov, he was worried, I'd say he was telling the truth.'

'So pretty much what we already knew,' Kate hadn't meant to sound harsh, but she saw Boz deflate and Maggie gave her a sharp look.

'Not his fault if there wasn't more to it.' Maggie said.

'Sorry, no.' Kate apologised, 'What about his alibi for Friday?'

'He was at a doss drinking with some kids until sometime after seven, when he left with Noel. The woman who rents the flat, a lovely tattooed lady who goes by the name of 'Busty', confirms he was there getting pissed on shots, but he and Noel took off when the vodka ran out. Andy remembers throwing up in the street and walking back to Noel's place where they sat outside on the wall smoking until they'd run out of fags, and then he walked home. I haven't had any luck finding this Noel bloke.'

'Talk to Bricky on the drugs squad; he'll know where to look for him.' Kate pulled a post it note off a pad on the desk and scribbled down a number, 'and talk to Aunty Sharon, tell her I sent you, see if she can help you find B.Zed. He and Noel are normally joined at the hip - take Maggie with you.'

'Great, at least we've got a decent tea stop.' Maggie grinned, she'd met Aunty Sharon before.

There was a sudden loud bang as DC Edwards pushed the door open so hard it smacked against the back wall. His eyes lit up when he saw Maggie.

'Welcome to real police work, I need a fag buddy, is any of that coffee going spare? And I hear we've got Mick Frazier in custody? Good enough, except Stacey now wants everything yesterday. How's that adorable daughter of yours, boss? Broken any hearts lately?'

Behind Kate's back Steve mouthed 'bastard' and gave him the finger. Edwards grinned at him happily. Unaware of the theatrics going on behind her Kate asked about the petrol.

'We're just starting to go over CCTV and receipts, it could take a while.' He shrugged.

Kate sent Maggie for a fag break with Edwards to get rid of him. For some reason, she didn't want to get too bogged down in a discussion about evidence with him. It wasn't that she didn't trust him – well, maybe it was a bit of that, but she knew that whatever he picked up would be spread around with high drama, and the theatrics surrounding this case were already getting on her nerves.

While they were gone she studied the interviews conducted with the Murphy's, Eddie's foster carers in Marville. The more she read the angrier she got. The couple were inadequate and incompetent. The statement Mrs Murphy had made was paranoid lunacy. Oh, it all *sounded* as though she was the caring martyr of foster carers, but the whole thing stank of self-preservation. Kate remembered what Greg Thomas had said about the woman's reaction being 'over the top', too dramatic to be real. That was the sense she was getting from the statement – and it did nothing to help find Eddie. She leant back with her hands clasped behind her head. Eddie knew where the Pinks lived *and* he'd stayed with them in Hockley. She looked across at Ginger.

'Where's Julie?'

'She came back looking for you a short while ago, think she might have gone for a cuppa.' Ginger was already half way to the door to go and look for her.

Kate studied the picture of the kid in dark jeans and a hoody while she waited. Did the person in the picture kill Pink and set Andy Frazier up as a suspect? But then if the same person had killed Bishop why didn't they wait until both men were dead before putting the can in the Frazier's shed – set Andy up for both killings? Maybe because they didn't know Andy's house was going to get searched so soon after Pink's death – it wouldn't have been if he hadn't beaten up Dean Towle. Or maybe killing Bishop hadn't been planned at that point.

Ginger arrived back with Julie in tow, Anne Pink's FLO. 'What did you get?' Kate dispensed with waffle.

'A belly full of cake, Ma'am,' Julie grinned. 'The woman bakes like it's going out of fashion. She gets all sulky if you don't eat, so much for my bikini diet.'

Kate wasn't interested in cake. 'What did she say?'

'Well it was a bit difficult, she's a real master at distraction; won't stick to the subject, just whittles on and on about nonsense.'

'Julie, did she remember Eddie Lead?' Kate snapped. She was losing patience.

Julie took the hint. 'Yes, Ma'am, they'd been asked to help out when social services were desperate for placements. Apparently she wasn't very keen; said it was her husband's idea – he'd been talked into it by a man he knew who worked at the social, and it didn't work out. She's never had kids and I don't think she knew what to do with them. Anyway, they only did it twice - foster I mean. The first time they got two little brothers, they only stayed two nights.'

'And then they got Eddie,' Kate interrupted, 'what did she say about him?'

'She said she hardly ever saw him. Eddie was at school and her husband spent a lot of time with him, but when I asked her what he was like, she burst into tears.'

'What? Why?' Kate looked at her sharply.

'It was difficult to understand. She kept saying he was a *precious boy*, but she was crying and I didn't want to upset her anymore, and there was something else - she said Eddie frightened her.'

'Why did he frighten her?' Kate was intrigued.

'She said she'd get up in the night to go to the toilet and find him standing in the kitchen, in the dark, just staring out of the window. He wouldn't even turn around when she called him. He'd just stood there for ages, motionless. She said it gave her the willies, she called him a ghost child.'

The skin on the back of Kate's neck prickled, but before she could say anything her mobile started blaring out the theme to 'The

Whacky Races.' She glared at the screen for a moment before holding it to her ear. 'Tell me.' She narrowed her eyes as she listened for a minute, ignoring the team gathered around her, said 'thanks,' and hung up. Sliding the phone back into her pocket she turned to see Maggie walk back in.

'Change of plan.' She told her, 'I want you to find Bunny, get an update on the photos from Pink's camera and call me. I want to know what else he's found.'

Maggie nodded

'Right.' Kate turned to Steve, 'Let's go.'

Steve glanced at his watch. He'd been expecting them to finish up and call it a day, but Kate obviously had other plans.

She was out of the door before he'd put his cup down.

The Barracks reeked; oppressed and rotting in the late afternoon heat. Previously scorched patches of grass had turned to dust, kicked up and blown about coating everything in a gritty brown film. Kate leaned over Steve's arm as he pulled onto the wasteland and pissed him off by leaning on the horn.

She was looking for The Toad. He hadn't said much in the call to her mobile - just asked if she wanted to talk about Eddie Lead. She was running short of options or places to look for Eddie so if The Toad knew something she wanted to hear it, and fast. She wasn't sure exactly where on the estate he was, but she knew it wouldn't take her long to find out. Abraham was the first to appear as if by magic, banging on Steve's door before he had a chance to climb out.

Kate gave him a half grin, 'At least you've got one fan.'

He shrugged, 'Just the one.'

As Kate got out more kids turned up and she was bombarded with questions.

'When's Darren coming back? Is he living in a big house with a huge bed all to his self, did he get presents, did he? Is Todd in prison? How long will he have to stay there? Did you arrest Andy? Is Andy going to prison? Did Andy kill someone, did he?'

Kate took a dribbling Mickey from Josie Martin and bounced the baby on her arms until it shrieked, 'Where's Toad? Anyone know where The Toad is?' She asked.

Abraham nearly burst with excitement, 'Me! I do! He's with me mum having a fag he is - I'm getting him. *Come on Steve!* He pulled at Steve's hand, dragging him away.

'How's your mum?' Kate asked Josie as they waited.

'She cries cos she misses Darren, she's worried in case he's scared, maybe asking for her, like. Can he come back soon?' She looked at Kate hopefully.

'I'll talk to your mum, don't worry, I promise you Darren's fine, he's safe and he's being really well looked after.' It was the best Kate could do but Josie gave her a look that said she knew when she was being fobbed off.

'Toad won't talk to Steve.' Josie said, changing the subject.

'I know.' Kate grinned at Josie and bounced the baby higher. She waited until she saw Steve re-appearing from the entrance to the apartment block looking rejected with Abraham hanging off his hand before she pulled out her phone. 'Hey Toad, get your arse down here, Steve's flashy motor is gathering dust and I'm getting bored.' She snapped the phone shut.

'He's got nothing to say, Gov...' Steve started to explain.

'Give me your keys.' Kate held her hand out.

Steve hesitated, 'Sorry?'

'Your car keys, sometimes you have to give to receive.' Kate stared at him until he dropped them into her palm.

'Toad's coming! Toad's coming!' Abraham was dancing around Steve's feet with excitement, 'Where's he driving? Can I watch?'

Steve gave Kate a look that said '*You've got to be kidding,*' but she ignored him as The Toad appeared, walking casually towards them, his face shaded by a black baseball cap. She pushed all the kids back until they formed a semi-circle of spectators and dropped Steve's keys into The Toad's outstretched hand as he passed her without looking up.

'Has he even got a driving licence?' Steve asked, in a tone that suggested he thought Kate had lost the plot.

Kate just smiled, 'Watch.'

Seconds after sliding behind the steering wheel The Toad was doing things with the car Steve didn't know it could do. He put on a display of stunt driving that left Steve spluttering in the cloud of dust his tyres kicked up. The Toad pulled the car smoothly into a sharp hand brake turn before rocketing backwards through a gap between the apartments so narrow Steve involuntarily breathed in.

The kid could drive - license or no license.

'Nice motor,' Toad told Steve as he threw the keys back to him, 'But your back end is kicking out.' He leant back against the driver's door and casually lit a fag, ignoring the kids jumping about. He took a deep drag and looked directly at Kate. 'The Dog don't have ties here, there aint no one he'd want to be with, not in Marville - he's not here. He's gone someplace else, he aint sleeping rough, he's left.'

Kate gave the baby back to Josie. 'Tell your mum I'm coming to talk to her later, take Abraham with you.' She wanted the kids out of the way while she talked to Toad, and Josie was big enough to know it. Kate shooed the others off behind them before leaning on the car bonnet next to Toad and squinting over her sunglasses. 'I can't find anyone who knows Eddie, or knows where he is.'

The Toad shrugged, 'Everyone knows someone – even The Dog, maybe he didn't leave.'

Kate was confused, 'You said he'd left.'

'Yeh, right, but what if he didn't leave, what if someone *took* him, what if someone came for him and took him - everyone knows someone.'

Kate stared at him. The Toad was right, they'd been concentrating on Eddie doing a runner from his foster home, but maybe someone had come to get him. If that was true then who, and why?'

'Is there a good skate park in Hockley?' The Toad looked from Kate to Steve, but neither of them knew. He shook his head, giving Kate a sarcastic look before pulling his phone out of his pocket and texting away furiously. 'I'll find out.' Less than a minute later he had an answer. 'There's a ramp park near the leisure centre. The Dog took the bus from town towards Hockley a couple of times and he never went anywhere without his board.'

'Did you ever see him meet anyone getting on the bus?' Kate asked.

'Nope, like I said, he aint from round here, but I thought you'd want to know seeing as how you're looking for him, he's got a hickey buddy somewhere.'

Kate had no idea what he was talking about.

'Hickey as in love bite or hickey as in Redneck?' Steve asked the question.

'Well I don't think it were a Redneck who bit him, but you never know, someone had a good go at his neck.' The Toad grinned.

Kate could see why Aunty Sharon found him so attractive, but then she remembered that her friend also seemed to have the hots for Steve and that was a different thing altogether so she put it out of her mind. 'When did you see love bites on his neck?'

'Last week - he took his shirt off when he was skating; wrapped it around his neck, covering them up like, but they were definitely there – a whole fucking daisy chain of them. He'd been having some fun somewhere, and as he don't talk to no one around here then maybe she's in Hockley, or wherever he's gone – there's a girl somewhere and she likes sucking on him.'

Kate ignored the innuendo. She was busy thinking about Eddie having a girlfriend somewhere. It was a possibility they hadn't even considered. So far, everyone had told them he didn't have *any* friends, and they'd been focused on the scenario of him taking off, leaving his foster home and going off on his own. But The Toad was right – Eddie knew someone, and whoever that someone was, there was some sort of relationship involved.

'Did you ever see Andy Frazier and Eddie Lead together?' She asked.

The Toad laughed out loud. 'That little shithead aint The Dog's girlfriend, that would be something wouldn't it? No, Frazier's a prick; deserves whatever's coming for him, but he's only in it for the money.'

'What do you mean by that?' Steve had got his heartbeat somewhere back near normal after the driving spectacle.

The Toad shrugged. 'Cash, trainers, he aint in it for the romance, he's making a career out of it - rent boy, porn star, whatever. He thinks he's clever but he's thick as shit. He aint going to be a pretty boy for ever.'

'Do you know anyone who might have a grudge against Andy, maybe want to stitch him up?' Kate kept her voice even. She was holding her face up to the last warmth of the sun, her eyes hidden behind her sunglasses.

The Toad turned towards her, one eyebrow raised. His thumbs were hooked into the front of his jeans pulling them down even lower onto his groin and exposing a bare strip of smooth sunburnt stomach, 'Like for a murder?'

Kate didn't turn her head. 'Tell me.'

'He and The Dog lived in the same home at one point... and now you can't find The Dog.' He shrugged but the implication was clear. 'Maybe you should ask The Dog – when you find him.'

If I find him alive. Kate thought.

After picking up some reports from the station to study later, Kate eventually retrieved her car and headed off. But when she arrived home Angel wouldn't let her do anything until they'd been out to eat, insisting they go to a favourite chinese restaurant in Marville. The owner made a fuss, fawning over Angel and giving them little complimentary taster dishes. Angel was driving so Kate ordered a second glass of Merlot. She tried to relax; forget about the case for a while, but it constantly swirled around at the back of her brain, disturbing what should have been a perfect evening. Maybe it was the wine, maybe it was her own bloody suspicious mind, but when they drove past Steve's flat and his car was missing, it riled her.

'Fancy a coffee at Aunty Sharon's?' She asked, impulsively.

'Absolutely, hang on.' Angel pulled a sharp U–turn, grinning at her mother instead of watching the road, making Kate grab her door handle and brace herself against the seat.

'Bloody hell!' Kate hung on for dear life.

She was already questioning her impulse, never mind her motive, when Angel pulled into Aunty Sharon's road. Steve's car was parked outside the house, almost in front of her gate - he wasn't even trying to be discreet. Angel was out of the car before Kate was sure what she was doing there. She'd already confirmed what she wanted to know, so now what was she going to do, embarrass everyone with a confrontation? Why the hell should she care that Steve was with her friend? She started to feel very uncomfortable but she had no choice but to follow Angel up the path to the front door. Angel knocked twice, waited and knocked again. No answer. Kate stepped back off the doorstep and looked up – the lights were all out.

Angel turned and shrugged, 'She must be out.'

'Must be, that's a shame. She'll be sorry she's missed you. I'll call her tomorrow, let's go home.' Kate had no idea why she was so angry.

'Shit! Have they gone?' Steve's back was pressed flat against the front bedroom wall.

'Shush! I'm trying to look.' Aunty Sharon giggled.

'Don't lean too far – I'll drop you!'

'No you won't.' Aunty Sharon wrapped her naked legs even more tightly around his waist.

***

CHAPTER FIFTY SEVEN

E verything was packed up ready to leave but something had gone wrong, terribly wrong; the police were hunting him. It was wrong, everything was wrong; they weren't supposed to be looking for him. He knew it had been too good to be true. Nothing in his life ever turned out right, never turned good for him. She'd promised everything would be wonderful, that she'd take care of him, no one would follow them - no one would care.

It wasn't true. And more than anything that had ever hurt him, the fact that she'd lied to him was unbearable. He'd let his guard down, trusted her. She said she loved him. She said it all the time, and he couldn't remember anyone ever telling him that before. Maybe his mum had said it to him before she'd died – but he didn't remember. And if his mum had loved him why did she leave him alone?

Eddie knew what he had to do - she'd explained it to him really carefully. They'd spent half the night lying in her bed talking about it, going over and over it, but he was so scared he'd already thrown up and his stomach was killing him.

Now she was crying with anger, '*Sodding Kate Landers!* We've got to fix it or they'll always be looking for you, they won't give up. You just have to do this and then we can go away, everything will be fine, I promise you. We can be together; *safe*, just the two of us, just like we've planned, it will be *over*.'

'But what if they know I'm lying?' Eddie felt sick again. He didn't want to talk to the police, he was afraid to talk to them - *to anyone*. He wasn't any good at talking.

'They won't! You know what to say, we've been over it and over it. I'll be with you. Just do it the way we've practiced, everything will be fine, *trust me.'*

Trust? Eddie didn't trust her, not now, not anymore. She'd lied to him and he didn't believe that everything would be fine. *Nothing was fine!* She promised he'd be safe, she'd promised to get hold of the films, promised him the past would be done with, gone, *finished.* But it wasn't true. She hadn't kept her promises – no one ever did.

The police were trained to know when you were lying. He wouldn't get away with it, he'd slip up and then he'd go to prison. Prison would be like being in care, but worse - he knew he wouldn't survive. And how could she say they could they just leave the country and disappear? No one would miss *him*, but she had a job and stuff. Could they just run, start a new life and no one come looking for them? He had a ton of questions but he didn't want to make her angry - she scared him when she was angry. He wanted her to be happy, to be happy *with* him. He bent down and kissed her, desperately looking for a distraction, anything to stop him thinking about prison, but his whole body shook as he clung to her and he couldn't make it stop.

A trail of bras, plastic bags, shoes and general *stuff* littered every surface of the house. Kate trailed after Angel, stuffing things into a sports bag and trying to get her ready to leave. There were kisses and hugs and Kate said all the things she always said.

'Drive safely, stick to the speed limit, I mean it... and ring me as soon as you get there. Kiss Nana and Gramps and I'll see you next weekend, I promise.'

Then her daughter was gone.

Kate felt as though they'd spent about five minutes together. This was her life on the child protection team. There were far too many bad cases, too many kids in places where kids didn't belong, and too few people to make things right. She'd promised Angel she'd be down the following weekend, whatever happened, even if they didn't find Eddie Lead.

It was unfathomable that they wouldn't find him.

Kate waved until the mini was out of sight and then glanced at her watch; it was only ten to seven but the clear sky already promised another scorcher. Maybe she could just run the investigation from her garden? It was one of those 'George Clooney and fat babies' thoughts. She felt plump, pasty and old.

She'd run first and then jump back into the fray.

By the time she got to Tockers Wood her fringe was plastered to her face and sweat was dripping into her eyes. She needed a haircut, but didn't have time to get one. Kate pushed forward, stretching out her stride, increasing her pace. Running cleared her head. She'd stayed up late into the night reading statements and reports; looking for the chink, something that had been overlooked. It was the Hockley connection that kept niggling away at her. Where Bishop had been involved with Adam Dyer, Tony Contelli and Eddie Lead, where the Pinks had fostered Eddie - and the Pinks still owned that house.

The Pinks still owned that house. It was in the financial report that Kate had eventually got to at about midnight - she'd completely forgotten they owned another property. *Who was there now?* Kate didn't know but she was going to pay them a visit and she was going alone. She felt ashamed of her actions last night. She was sure Aunty Sharon and Steve had seen them and deliberately not answered the door. Kate turned for home, trying to put it out of her mind and think constructively. She needed to make some phone calls.

She spoke to Maggie first, but she didn't have much to offer as far as the photos were concerned. Pink had taken hundreds of photos of the boys at the MSCS and Andy Frazier in particular, but there didn't seem to be anything more exciting than what Kate had already seen. Maggie didn't mention anything about finding photos of Kate – which relieved Kate greatly, especially as she realised she still hadn't told Stacey or Knowling about the photo Pink had taken of her outside the station. She sent Maggie over to the skate park in Hockley. It was on Maggie's patch, she'd know some of the kids in the area, she could find out if Eddie had been seen there recently. It was worth a try. Next she left a message for Steve to go over to Hockley Social Services; see if he could get more information on Eddie's previous foster homes. It was all she could think of to do to try and trace Eddie. And at least if she went to Pink's old house alone she could put off any awkwardness with Steve and stay clear of Stacey, both of which were good enough reasons.

Next she spoke to Ginger and confirmed that no films depicting sexual abuse or camera equipment had been found in

Bishop's house or in his office or car, nothing. Adam Dyer had told Steve that Bishop had filmed Tony Contelli, and if that was true, and she had no reason to doubt it – and Eddie had been sexually abused whilst under Bishop's control then the chances were he had been filmed too. So where was the stuff? The fact that Bishop didn't have it reinforced the assumption that there was someone else involved, at least one other person, someone else maybe doing the filming, or making the connections, acting as distributor, and they had kept the films. It was probably just one other person – that was how they'd kept their security and secrecy, how the films had been kept off the Internet and underground. Bishop wasn't that clever, someone had to be helping him, someone with the right connections.

Churning over Bishop's connection with Josh Martin, Andy Frazier and Eddie Lead and the films, Kate had another thought. Where did legitimate filming of these kids take place regularly? Hope House. Filming equipment was set up in the interview room, but there were hand held cameras and equipment for filming kids in other environments. Bishop would have had access to that at any time he wanted. She rang Ginger and told him to get a search warrant for Hope House.

Just as she hung up on Ginger her mobile buzzed again. Charlie Winsome hadn't hung about and Kate wondered how he'd got the information so quickly. When she heard what he had to tell her she almost wished he hadn't. She had to stop and pull over so that she could concentrate on what he was saying, hoping it wasn't true.

'You've got someone on your side who's running a nice little enterprise – making a tidy sum out of it and all. That's a turn up for the books aint it, one of your boys being a sick sadistic bastard? Mr Knowling won't like that at all.' Charlie sounded pleased with himself. He was enjoying being the bearer of bad news.

A feeling of dread settled over Kate, 'Tell me.'

'Bishop found a very discreet distributor and an insurance policy all in one - smart move for such a prick.' Charlie said. 'And, as this bloke is in the job he'll know what's going on with your lot, make sure you don't find any incriminating evidence, like. Probably pissed off that his little moneymaking enterprise just ground to a halt – nothing like the death of your business partner to screw things up. I don't think he's too worried. He's been pretty clever, making sure you can't get anything on him.'

'What do you mean? You're talking in riddles. Charlie, stop messing about and tell me what you're on about.' Kate snapped.

'You were right, when you suggested this was a limited distribution, you were right – it's a *strictly limited*, very specialised commodity for a couple of people with very deep pockets. That's the cleverness behind it. Bishop and his partner made a small number of very special films and sold them for huge amounts of money to specialist collectors. Vintage stuff with a high price – I aint seen it, and I'd like to, but they weren't catering to my pocket. Your lad, Eddie, has made them a small fortune by the sounds of it. That beautiful boy was the Golden Goose.'

Kate felt sick.

'Who is it? Whose the distributor?' She was trying to guess who Charlie meant, but at the same time she was afraid to guess, she didn't want it to be true, she didn't want to know that someone on their team was involved. A police officer involved in the distribution of child pornography depicting torture? It couldn't get any worse than that.

'Well let's play a little game. I'll describe him and you stop me when you've guessed.' Charlie was stringing her along.

'Just bloody tell me!' Kate realised she was shouting.

Charlie laughed, 'Stop me when you've guessed.' He taunted.

Kate had no option. She shut up and listened.

And then she hung up and called Knowling. She had to give him the problem. It was too big for her, much too big, she couldn't deal with it. What she'd learned made her feel physically ill. As she waited for him to pick up she realised that the photograph on Pink's camera of her outside the station wasn't about her at all. She was only in the photo because she'd got in the way.

And she still had to find Eddie. And she was afraid, she was afraid for his safety

She was expecting another neat old-fashioned bungalow, but the house was a substantial red brick detached property set back from the road behind a metal gate. Kate hadn't contacted the rental agency or made an appointment so her visit was unannounced. She had her warrant card in her hand ready to show her identification, but the rather harassed looking young woman who answered the door ushered her in without so much as a cursory glance. She seemed pleased to see anyone.

'Sorry, can you come to the kitchen? I'm trying to give the twins their breakfast, excuse me, and please take care, there's porridge on the floor.' The woman spoke with an accent that Kate judged to be Eastern European. She led Kate through to the back of the house where two chubby toddlers sat in identical highchairs, both trying to feed themselves from plastic bowls. Most of the food was on themselves and the surrounding surfaces. Kate realised why the woman had welcomed her in so readily, she was delighted to have company, any company - even the police.

'Hello! Aren't you gorgeous?' Kate went straight to the babies, 'Here, let me give you a hand.' She set the twins up with toast fingers to chew on then got to work with some baby wipes and a cloth until peace was restored and their exasperated mum was sat down with a hot cup of tea.

Kate kept the toddlers entertained while she asked questions, using the children as a means of making friends with the woman - who was called Agne and originated from Poland. She'd come to England to work as an au pair and learn English and had ended up staying. She and her husband were renting the Pink's house because they didn't have the deposit to buy a place. Agne knew George Pink was dead, but the agency had assured them their rental could continue. She had no family and few friends in the area and was pathetically grateful for someone to talk to. By the time Kate had helped feed the twins and clean them up she'd found out that although the house was rented through an agency, George Pink had visited every other Sunday.

'Why did he visit?' Kate asked.

'We have an arrangement for the rent. It's cheaper because he has access to go to his things.'

Kate looked at her, puzzled. 'George Pink kept things here after he'd moved?'

'Yes, it was agreed. We don't need all the bedrooms. He keeps the top room for his things and he can come and use the room. It didn't matter, he didn't bother us and the money was much better because of this.' Agne nodded.

Kate was getting the familiar skin prickling feeling at the back of her neck.

'Did Mr Pink ever bring anyone with him when he came to visit?'

'No. We only know, I mean, only *knew* Mr Pink. Oh, but there was one time when his nephew came.'

'Do you know what his nephew's name was?' Kate kept her voice even.

'One moment, I think... he was quiet, very shy. I asked if he wanted a drink, but no, and he didn't speak, Mr Pink spoke for him - he called him Edward.'

Kate didn't blink, 'Do you know what's in the room?'

Agne looked worried. 'We don't have use of that room.' she said, vaguely.

'Look, I'm not here to cause any trouble for you but it's vitally important, do you know what's in there?'

Agne got up and opened a drawer, 'Here, the door is locked but I found a spare key, go and look.'

The room was a loft extension at the top of the house and as soon as Kate stepped inside she knew she was in Pink's den. At first glance it appeared to be a small study or reading room. A tired tapestry Queen Anne chair dominated the small space. A small stained coffee table sat beside it with a huge velvet green footstool in front and bookshelves to one side. But Kate's trained eye was drawn to the more unusual items, the chain of plastic fairy lights draped from corner to corner around the room, the catalogues of children's sportswear and clothing, the television and dvd player, with the stack of pornographic films in a box on the floor. Kate picked up a prospectus for a preparatory school in Hampshire. Some of the pages had sections cut out of them. She hunted until she found the scrapbook at the back of the bookcase, knowing that Pink had cut out pictures of a young boy who had caught his eye and making bets with herself that the boy would look like Dean or Andy or Michael Bowden.

She wasn't wrong. The cloth-covered book was bulging with photos and clippings from magazines and newspapers. All the magazine pictures were of the same type - young, pretty boys with shiny hair and clear skin.

Kate sat in the armchair and opened the book on her lap,

careful not to let anything fall out. It wasn't long before she found the picture of a young Eddie Lead standing between Bishop and Pink. Both Bishop and Pink were smiling; each with an arm around the boy's shoulders, but Eddie's face was blank under his baseball cap. He looked as though he'd rather be anywhere else then in between those two men.

There were several more pictures of Eddie; some on his skateboard, some of him with Bishop. Kate studied them all. They seemed to have been taken a few years back; probably about the time the Pinks were fostering Eddie. She turned over another page of the book and her breath caught in her throat. Beautifully framed by stiff white card was a black and white print of Eddie, blindfolded, his hands tied in front of him with cord, his long athlete's body stark white against a dark, grimy background. Even blindfolded there was no mistaking the boy's terror. She studied the background closely. It wasn't clear but she'd put money on it being the auction shed where Bishop had died.

How did Pink get the photo? Did he take it? Were he and Bishop sharing Eddie – both abusing him?

Kate rubbed at her forehead with her fingers; the room was getting clammy and claustrophobic. She turned over more pages, steeling herself for more horrors but finding only more pictures of schoolboys in uniform until she came to the funeral card and the newspaper cuttings and she wanted to cry.

12-YEAR-OLD BOY DIES SAVING SISTER.

7-YEAR-OLD GIRL SAVED BY BROTHER'S SACRIFICE.

She'd found Brian.

She unfolded the aged newspaper clippings almost reverently and read quickly, devouring every word.

The paper called it a 'tragic accident' so terrible that the family were too distraught to comment, but they'd certainly got a lot of information from somewhere.

Brian and Melanie Straub had been staying with their Aunt and Uncle, George and Anne Pink, while their parents were on holiday in Egypt. The Straubs had gone away leaving two healthy, happy children and had returned home to find their twelve year old son in a coffin and their seven year old daughter so traumatised she'd lost the ability to speak.

The story said it was a boating accident. The children had been out with their uncle when the little girl had fallen overboard and Brian had jumped in to help her. The river was fast flowing and both children were soon in difficulties. George Pink couldn't swim and was trying to control the boat, trying to get close enough to haul them back in, but they were carried away on the current. Brian managed to catch hold of his terrified sister and had somehow kept her afloat, going with the current and pushing her towards the steep bank. He'd managed to push her up onto the muddy slope, screaming at her to dig her feet in and push herself back and out, away from the water, but his knees were torn open from the rocks and he was exhausted, unable to get a foothold. He'd tried to climb up to her, but fell back again and again until, with his little sister screaming and crying and begging him to not to let go, he'd slipped beneath the water. It was six hours before his broken body was found face up, trapped under overhanging branches.

There were numerous tributes to Brian, one of the most poignant from his class teacher, a Miss Jameson.

'Brian Straub was a unique and incredibly special young man. His capacity for caring and for helping others was humbling and it was an honour to have him in my class. In a world where young people are so quickly criticised Brian was a shining example for good. He was thoughtful, polite and unselfish in all that he did and he was devoted to his little sister. On her first day at big school Brian walked Melanie to her classroom and solemnly handed her over to her new teacher.

'This is my little sister,' he announced, 'she's new so she needs looking after.' He walked her to her classroom and collected her every day for the entire year. He took pride in his responsibility. Melanie's safety and happiness was his main concern, and Melanie in turn was devoted to him. He lost his life trying to protect her, not hesitating to jump into the water to save her. Any death of a child is a tragedy; the death of this amazing and inspiring young man is something almost too dreadful to bear. It was a privilege – a total privilege to have known him, we will miss him more than words can say. Our hearts go out to his family.'

The funeral card for Brian was almost too sad to read. Kate was choked; there was a lump in her throat. Brian had died while he was on a boating trip with George Pink. Raymond Greggs had told her that Pink was responsible for the death of the 'Special one' the boy Pink had been trying to replace ever since. There didn't seem to be any witnesses to the accident and only a scant reference to the fact that George Pink had remained in the boat because he couldn't swim. If he hadn't killed Brian he certainly hadn't done anything to save him.

Kate flicked over the next page and pulled out a large manila envelope. It had been folded in the middle but wasn't sealed. Lifting the flap she reached in and pulled out a seven by five inch black and white photo - a happy family scene taken in a garden somewhere. She recognised George Pink immediately. The photo had to be at least twenty years old, but Pink hadn't changed. Next to him was a jolly looking woman she took to be Anne Pink. George Pink had his hands on the shoulders of a young boy squatted on his haunches in front of him. The boy was staring glumly into the camera and holding up a shiny silver mouth organ in his right hand. Kate could clearly see the initials engraved on the front, MBB. Brian Straub was beautiful; long legged and tanned in t-shirt and shorts, his fringe pushed to one side out of his eyes. He was the image of a young Eddie Lead. Kate was gripped by the sadness of his fate. She was certain Pink had abused the boy while he was in his care, and then the boy had died. He'd never had the chance to reach his potential, for the world to see what he could be, what he could achieve.

The little girl standing rigidly next to him was like a little fawn; all spindly limbs and knock-kneed, shoulders like coat hangers, as Kate's father would have said. But there was something about her, something about her elfin face and slender neckline with bony collarbones jutting. Kate peered at the seven year old Melanie Straub and felt afraid.

She locked the room when she left and pocketed the key.

**

CHAPTER FIFTY EIGHT

She was ten minutes away from her destination when the call
came from Knowling.

'Eddie Lead has turned up, walked into the nick. Mivvie
Levin, your social worker friend, brought him in - she'd picked him
up at his foster home.'

Kate was gobsmacked. 'How did that happen?'

'He turned up at his foster home this morning and Mrs
Murphy called social services. Apparently he's been camping out,
didn't know anyone was looking for him.'

'Is he ok?' Kate was concerned.

'Seems to be.' Knowling sounded hesitant.

Kate's skin prickled. There was something going on, something
he was reluctant to tell her. 'We need a discussion before he's
spoken to. He's vulnerable, and with what I told you this morning,
I don't think he should be at the station at all. It's going to be a
difficult interview – he'll have to be asked about the films and what
he knows about who was involved, but we need to plan it out and
take it slowly...'

'Hang on a minute.' Knowling cut her off. 'Stacey isn't known
for his patience. You weren't here, so Lou Barnes is doing an initial
interview with Mivvie as appropriate adult and Stacey monitoring –
they're just going to cover some basics.'

'What? Why Barmy?' Kate was furious. 'Get it stopped. I want
Eddie out of there... we're responsible for his safety.'

'She jumped all over it and Stacey was keen not to hang about.
It was under way before I could do anything about it. It's not
playing by the book and she knows it, but I'll cut it short and make
sure Stacey sorts out protective custody for Eddie away from here.'

He sounded genuinely sorry.

Kate didn't trust herself to speak. There was a long pause while she tried to get her frustration under control.

'What about the information I gave you earlier?' she eventually asked, her voice harsh, 'Have you got that under control?'

'Where are you?' Knowling ignored the question and changed the subject fast. He wasn't going to discuss it on a mobile network.

Kate chewed her lip. She knew she'd made a mistake in asking him, but she was getting more and more angry. 'I'm going to visit Anne Pink and then I'll be in. George Pink kept a room at the house he rented out in Hockley – and he took Eddie there at least once. Look, I might have something else, but I'll call you back. And I want to know what Eddie says. Whatever else is going on that kid's had the life from hell, I want to know what's happening to him.'

'Of course you do.' Knowling hung up.

The car in front came to a sudden stop and Kate almost shunted it up the back. She was thinking about Eddie Lead at the mercy of DI Barmy Barnes and she hated the idea. *She wanted to talk to him.* But at least he'd been found.

At least he was alive.

She desperately wanted to meet him but she had something important to do first.

Anne Pink opened the door to Kate's knock and apologised for being in a mess.

'Come on in dear, come in. How lovely of you to visit. I'm expecting Sergeant Owen, your lovely Community policeman. He wasn't sure if he'd make it today, but I'm making scones just in case. He does like my scones with strawberry jam. I make my own you know?' She turned and made her way down the hall, slippers flapping on the thin carpet as Kate followed her in. A wonderful waft of baking dough was coming out of the kitchen.

'Shall I just finish this batch up and we'll have nice cup of tea, then you can have a taste.' Anne Pink beamed at her visitor. There were two trays of scones already cooling on the counter. Kate wondered if the woman was baking for the whole street.

'How are you?' she asked.

'Sergeant Owen has been a wonder,' Anne Pink busied herself with bowls and eggs.

It wasn't really an answer but Kate let it go.

'I'm glad.' she told her, 'Have you...'

'*Everyone* has been lovely.' The woman didn't give her the chance to speak, 'I've never had anything to do with the police before, but I can't fault them; *lovely* people.'

As Anne Pink babbled on Kate was convinced there was something wrong with the Pink family. Why was it only the police who were looking after her? Anne Pink was using the police she'd come into contact with as a result of her husband's murder as a substitute for family.

'Mrs Pink, you told Julie, your liaison officer, that your sister had died some time ago, but you didn't mention any other family.' Kate needed to get to the bottom of this. She needed information.

'Oh, dear, look at that, what a ninny I am.' She cut Kate off again, completing ignoring her questions. 'That's the last egg. Let's get the kettle on and then I'll pop to Cynthia's in a minute, I'm sure she'll have some to lend.' She wiped her hands on her apron. Kate gave up. She was going to have to drink tea, eat scones and take it slowly. What was it Julie had said about Mrs Pink being a 'poppet'?

She struggled to keep the woman on track, but bit by bit, and frustratingly slowly, she started to get some details. George Pink had been an only child who had been orphaned when he was very young.

'Brought up in care, his parents died when he was little.' Anne Pink whispered this information as though it was a shameful secret.

Kate kept her face blank but she'd already learnt more than was in the woman's statement.

'Where did your sister live?' Kate moved away from the 'secret' history of George Pink's upbringing. A shadow of sadness clouded the woman's face. It was the first time Kate had seen her react so she pushed it, she had to, she had to get the details. 'Was your sister local?'

'Oh no, they lived away, dear. We weren't close. Hadn't been for years... there was an accident, it was terrible, very sad.' She paused and fiddled with her apron. 'We blamed ourselves, you see? Poor George, he was devastated, he was terribly ill because of what had happened. It took him ages to recover. I worried myself sick about him. But my sister, well... she just stayed away.' Anne Pink looked around the room as if to find the next words hiding in a corner somewhere. Suddenly her face brightened and she beamed at Kate, 'Eggs!' she clapped her hands together, the sadness pushed aside, 'Let me just pop to Cynthia's, I won't be two ticks.'

Kate took the manila envelope with the photo from her bag and waited until she heard the door latch click. Anne Pink skipped back in followed by a tiny elderly lady, the two of them as cheerful as giggly schoolgirls.

'I've brought Cynthia.' Anne Pink announced, 'She wanted to meet you.'

Kate smiled a greeting but she almost winced, she didn't need any more distractions. 'Mrs Pink, please come and sit down, we need to talk about something important.'

'Shall I put the kettle on?' Cynthia asked, diplomatically.

'Would you?' Kate smiled at her.

Looking confused Anne Pink followed Kate into the lounge and sat next to her on the sofa. Kate pointed at the children in the photograph she'd found in Pink's den.

'Mrs Pink, I need you to tell me about these children and the accident.'

Anne Pink focused on the picture and her face crumpled with sadness. Fishing in her apron pocket she found a hanky and wiped her nose.

'Those are my nephew and niece, dear - Melanie and Brian, my sister's children. But where did you get this? I thought poor George had got rid of them all.' Her voice was full of waiting tears. 'Bless them. I do miss them, terribly. He was the apple of his uncle's eye, Brain was. George adored him.' She sniffed, 'It was just an accident, a terrible accident, one of those things you never think could happen. George took them out in that little boat of his and she fell in; she was always a little live wire. George didn't swim very well, but before he knew what was happening Brian was in the water and he saved her. The water was so fast and it dragged her away, but he caught her. He'd always looked after her; he wasn't going to let her die.'

Kate could see the awful sadness of what had happened was still with her; it had never left, she could hear it in every painful word.

'He drowned.' Mrs Pink whispered. 'She was saved. Brian pushed her onto the bank but he couldn't get out and she saw it...

she watched her brother drown.'

Kate reached across, lifted one of the woman's hands in her own and squeezed it gently.

She lost her voice, Melanie I mean, didn't speak for weeks, poor little thing. It was the shock. We were all heartbroken, but my sister never recovered. I'll never forget the way she held herself rigid, refusing to break down as that little coffin was carried through the church. But afterwards she closed in on herself; some people do, don't they? I think it haunted her until the day she died. She's been gone two years now.'

Two years, Kate thought. About the time Pink was arrested on suspicion of sexually assaulting Tony Contelli and Adam Dyer. Had Brian's mother found out and realised what had happened to her son all those years before? The daughter, Melanie, must have known all along, maybe she'd even witnessed the abuse. That's what this was about - a brother and sister, and a boy who resembled a ghost child.

'Are you still in contact with Melanie?' Kate searched the woman's face.

Mrs Pink closed her eyes and sniffed deeply.

'It was too much hurt. Poor George didn't know what to say to them, so he was glad in a way that they kept away. My sister never visited after the funeral. We didn't see any of them after that. I missed them, but we understood. It seems funny to hear her called Melanie, it was what she was christened, but she was never called by that name. I don't know if she'd even remember me now.'

And Kate knew it had come together.

'What was she called? You said Melanie was called something else... what was she called?' She held her breath.

'It was those ice lollies, you know? The red ones with ice cream in the middle, they were all the rage - Strawberry Mivvies. It was because of her name, Straub. Kids at school called her Mivvie and it stuck.

'How long ago did they leave?' Kate was striding up and down in front of Pink's house, mobile clamped to her ear.

'Several minutes - Eddie Lead was released into the care of social services pending further enquiries. He left with the social worker.' The custody officer was left holding a dead phone as Kate hung up on him.

Kate rang the Children's Services Department and got straight through to Gerry Crane.

'It's all rather awful here,' he said, 'we've been looking for Mivvie, but she hasn't been in yet. Let me get you the number for Eddie's foster carers.'

Kate scribbled the number down, her sense of dread mounting. She dialled and ran across the road to her car as she waited for an answer. 'Come on, come on.' she said under her breath.

Eventually Mrs Murphy answered. 'Nope, I aint seen him. We was told to ring the police if he showed up, but he aint been back.' She confirmed what Kate already knew. Mivvie had lied to them. She'd been in on the police investigation from the start. Right from the first interview with Dean Towle, right from the first time Brian's name came up when Josh Martin told them about Pink's shed. *And she was Pink's niece. She was Brian's sister!*

Kate thought back over everything Mivvie had been involved with since the start of the investigation. Kate had even called her in to the office when Bishop's body was found. Bloody hell! She was a good actress. She'd kept her cool throughout. Stunned, Kate realised she'd even suggested to Knowling that someone inside the social services network might be responsible. Mivvie was under their bloody noses the whole time! And she hadn't been with the department that long. Had her move to Marville been planned?

Kate spun her car in a tight circle to get out of the cul-de-sac. She tried to call Knowling but got his answer phone. In her mind she could see the image on the incident board. From the back Mivvie would look exactly like a young boy in jeans and a hoody. She punched another number into her mobile.

'Morning Gov.' Steve was in his car.

'Mivvie Levin is Pink's niece, Brian was her older brother.' Kate had no time for preamble. She quickly brought him up to speed. 'I need you to meet me at Mivvie's house.'

'Why is she with Eddie?' Steve was struggling to keep up.

'She's been hiding him. He must have been with her the whole time.'

'So Eddie *did* kill Pink?'

'No, I think she did. I think she killed him for revenge, and if that's true then it's also true for Bishop. They both abused Eddie and he looks remarkably like her dead brother. Where are you?'

'Just off the Hockley Road.'

'You're much closer than I am. You might get to Mivvie's place before them.' She gave him the address. 'The house is set well back from the road - Mivvie rents it. Drive past the cottage and turn immediately left, you'll be on a track that leads to a dead end near the back of her house, park up out of sight and wait for me. What's that noise?' She could hear a woman's voice in the background.

'SATNAV Sheila, she's telling me to turn around.'

Kate was driving hard and lost in thought when Steve called her back, the sound of her phone made her jump.

'Gov, they're here, and you're not going to believe this.' Steve sounded breathless.

'What? Where are you?'

'Where you told me to be at the back of the house - they just pulled up. They won't see me, they're too busy sitting in the car snogging.'

'*Snogging?*' Kate wasn't sure she'd heard properly.

'Some serious groping as well, she's all over him.'

'I'm nearly there - and uniform back up is on the way.' Kate put some more pressure on the accelerator and tried to make some sense of what seemed nonsense.

What the hell was going on?

'Now they're going into the house. I've just had a quick scout around the back and the place looks packed up. I think they're planning to leave – soon.'

'I'm just about there. Eddie's still a minor and I want to do this quietly. I'll go to the front, you stay where you are and make sure neither of them can get away out the back. I'll shout when I need you.'

There was a gravel turn around at the front of the house and it crunched noisily under her tyres as Kate stopped the car and yanked the hand brake on. As she jumped out Mivvie appeared at the front door looking dishevelled but smiling.

'Kate?' The woman stood with her back to the doorframe, hands behind her, almost nonchalant. There was no sign of Eddie. Kate hoped Steve was watching him.

'Melanie Levin I'm arresting you for the murders of George Pink and John Bishop...' Kate walked towards her, her eyes fixed on the woman's face.

Mivvie smiled, 'Aunty Anne was it? Silly old fool - she lived with that sadistic pervert for years and never had a clue. You don't want to arrest me, Kate. I did everyone a favour; I *stopped* them, both of them, something you failed to do. You're a joke, you and the social services, all going about like you're the fucking good samaritans. You had my uncle, the child abuser, *the murderer*, and you let him go! He killed my brother and destroyed my life, destroyed my parent's lives. And neither you, nor anyone else stopped him. And Bishop was right under your noses! He was passing boys around. He shared Eddie with Pink, and not just Eddie; there were other boys, others who were tortured and abused and you did fuck all about it! You had your chance - get back in your car, pretend you didn't find us, no one will really care.' Mivvie tossed her head pointedly towards Kate's car. 'Your husband was in traffic wasn't he? How do you think he would have felt about his colleague distributing hard core sadistic child pornography?' She taunted.

'Are you doing Eddie a favour?' Kate ignored the reference to her husband and the involvement of a police officer in the sex ring. She knew Mivvie was trying to rile her; distract her. She didn't take her eyes off the woman's face, but she didn't like the way she was hiding her hands.

Mivvie's face darkened, 'I saved him. He was just a replacement for Brian, one of many, and none of you could help him. George Pink was an evil fucking bastard. I saw him, I watched him *touching* Brian, but Brian fought him until the bastard got so angry he threw me in the water to teach Brian a lesson. For fuck's sake Kate! He tried to drown me to make Brian do what he wanted. My mother found out Pink had been arrested for Tony Contelli and Adam Dyer and it killed her. She knew then what had happened; knew it was his fault she'd lost her son - but that's how I found him. Tony Contelli died *and still* no one stopped him. By the time I found Eddie I knew I was the only one who could protect him. That's what we do you and I, we protect children. We're the child protectors.' She nodded vigorously, persuading herself.

Kate saw the madness. George Pink had used Eddie as a substitute for her brother and she'd done the same, only worse. Her need to protect Eddie had turned into a need for *him*.

'You're a social worker and Eddie's only fifteen. You can't protect him; you can't do *anything* with him. You're going to prison. You'll never see him again.'

Those last five words were going to get Kate killed.

Mivvie lunged, the knife coming up from behind her back.

Kate was ready, but in sidestepping to get out of the way her heel caught in the gravel and she stumbled, her right ankle twisting painfully as she tried to stay on her feet. She fell heavily onto one knee, her hands out in front of her, small stones cutting into her palms. Before she could push herself up Mivvie had her by the hair, yanked her head back and pressed the knife against her throat.

Kate managed to twist sideways but the blade sliced through the soft skin above her collarbone, drawing blood. It hurt like hell but she'd got a hand to Mivvie's wrist forcing it away from her throat as she clamoured up. Then her right ankle exploded with pain, refusing to take her weight and she went down sideways again, her hand still locked on Mivvie's wrist, desperately trying to force the blade from her hold. Mivvie yanked at her elbow and pulled her backwards as Kate fought to get to her feet.

And then the boy screamed.

It was so loud and so terrible that for a brief moment Kate's heart stopped.

Eddie was standing in the doorway of the house screaming like a tortured animal.

'Stop it! Stop it! I can't stand it! You said you *loved* me but you lied, you're a liar! You don't want *me;* you don't love *me,* no one does, no one ever loved me. You just wanted to kill them – not because of me, nothing was about me - it was all about Brian. Everybody lies, everybody!' He fell forwards onto his knees, both arms flung over his head as if to protect himself from the fall out of this awful truth.

A dreadful look of anguish fell on Mivvie's face. She turned her head, her eyes pleading, giving Kate a split second to take advantage of the distraction. She pushed herself backwards, using her weight against Mivvie's hold on her. Out of the corner of her eye she saw Steve coming and it struck her that he looked like he was going for a touchdown. Mivvie realised what was happening and dragged her eyes from the pathetic figure of the boy crumpled on the doorstep. With unbelievable strength she lunged downwards, the knife aimed for Kate's neck.

The full force of Steve Astman slammed into Mivvie's left shoulder, spinning her around and tipping her over backwards. The momentum took him with her as she went down heavily, arms flailing. Steve took a deep gash to the shoulder as he pinned Mivvie to the ground, knocking the knife from her grip and the breath from her body. He grabbed her hands as she tried to kick him, oblivious to the fact that he was bleeding on her.

Kate stood over him and read the woman her rights. Mivvie stopped struggling and started to cry. Her nose was running but she couldn't wipe it because Steve had cuffed her hands behind her back.

'Brian, Eddie...' she lifted her head to look across at the boy.

'Please, *please*,' she was begging, tears streaming down her cheeks, 'I love you.'

Eddie stood up and used both his sleeves to wipe his face. He pointedly didn't look at her,

'She got me a mobile.' He told Kate, 'It's in her car - she used it to set up the meeting with Bishop. I like Dean Towle - he's a good footballer. I didn't want Pink to mess with him. I told her about it and she said she'd take care of it. And she put the petrol can in Andy's shed 'cos he'd set Dean up with Pink. It was supposed to put you off.'

Kate nodded and was about to speak but Steve swore loudly and she turned back. He was holding onto Mivvie with one hand and holding his other arm up trying to stop the blood that was flowing at an alarming rate, the red wetness soaking into his trousers.

'Bloody thing stings a bit.' he said

'The adrenalin's wearing off. It never hurts when you're fighting, only when you stop.' Kate was concerned. 'There's a first aid kit in my car.'

'What about your leg and your neck?' Steve knew she was hurt. There was a thin gash across her collarbone trickling blood onto her t-shirt.

'Forget about me. You're going to be in trouble if I don't get that bleeding to stop.' Kate hobbled towards the BMW.

Steve dragged Mivvie to the car and manhandled her onto the back seat. She sat with her head slumped on her chest, rocking backwards and forwards, moaning.

Kate was disturbed by how much blood Steve had lost. He needed a hospital. He leant against the bonnet of her car as she pressed a dressing into the wound.

'I had the situation under control, just chose the wrong shoes today.' She looked up at his face. 'You didn't need to come charging in like a steam train; you're not on the bloody rugby field – you nearly knocked me over as well.' She was trying to keep him alert.

Steve just grinned, 'You were doing ok falling over by yourself, Gov. Luckily I left my stilettos at home today... but you're welcome.'

'Sure you didn't leave them at Aunty Sharon's?' The words, sounding as bitchy as hell even to her own ears, were out before Kate could stop them. The adrenalin rush was making her reckless. She was sorry as soon as she'd said it. 'It's none of my business, forget I spoke.' She tried to concentrate on bandaging his arm.

'Can I ask you something?' Steve was watching her face. 'Aunty Sharon wouldn't tell me how you two got to be friends – she said to ask you.'

Kate swallowed hard, not looking at him, focused on wrapping gauze bandage around his wound.

'My husband was a traffic officer, he was killed in a pursuit...' She paused, surprised that tears were welling up behind her eyes. She cleared her throat, forcing them back. 'There was an accident.' Again she stopped, her throat constricted so badly it hurt. She took a deep breath, 'Aunty Sharon's husband was a traffic officer; Tetley, they called him Tetley – he was driving the car.'

There was dreadful silence.

Steve didn't know what to say. He stood staring at her, afraid of opening his mouth, knowing he'd say the wrong thing. And then the look in Kate's eyes changed as she got herself together. He knew if he didn't say something now, he probably never would. She'd apologised to him; now it was his turn.

'I'm sorry for being such a fucking idiot. I didn't know she was your daughter.' he said.

Before Kate could reply there was the sound of a lone police siren in the distance, coming fast. They both looked up. Eddie Lead was making his way down the grass verge, walking away with his head down, fringe covering his eyes, his skateboard under his arm. Kate had never seen anyone look so lonely. But as she watched him a police traffic car turned into the driveway - so fast that for a moment Kate was blinded by the dust kicked up by the tyres.

Trust bloody traffic to make an entrance!

Kate bit back the tears again. *Duncan used to drive like that – only better.*

Knowling jumped out of the car before the driver had come to a full stop, his face grim with worry. Blood was already seeping through the dressing she was struggling to wrap around Steve's shoulder, but Knowling only looked at Kate's blood stained neck and the strain on her face and he started to fire fast, precise, no time to waste instructions into his radio.

As he hooked the radio back onto his belt and came towards her, Kate saw he was only concerned for her, but there was something – something else. He was angry with himself and she knew why.

'You knew didn't you?' She raised her hand in front of her as a warning - she didn't want him to touch her. 'When I told you about Dave Bench, when I told you that your rugby star traffic officer was distributing the worst kind of child pornography, you weren't surprised. You already knew, didn't you? Didn't you?'

Knowling stayed where he was. He wanted to grab her up, to cling to her and tell her how bloody stupid she was for going off on her own and how bloody grateful he was she was ok.

But he stayed where he was.

He knew that whatever came next would have a profound effect on their relationship, and he knew he *wanted* a relationship with her, one that would let him take care of her.

'I didn't *know*, but...'

'But you got me assigned to this case because you knew I'd find out for you. That's what this was about wasn't it?' Kate's voice was barely above a whisper, but he heard her. 'You needed to weed out the scum, avoid a scandal. You used me.'

'It wasn't *just* that. The kids, Dean Towle, Josh Martin, the others, only you could do that...'

Kate heard the sirens of an ambulance approaching.

'Except maybe Colin.' She snapped. 'But look what this did to him! And why didn't you tell me? Why did I have to hear about Bench from Charlie Winsome? Bloody hell! I guess you didn't trust me!' Kate threw the first aid box into her car, turned around and walked past Knowling so fast his head spun to watch her. She yanked open the front door of the traffic car.

'Drive me.' She demanded, looking straight at the hapless officer who was taking messages on his radio and fussing around Steve. 'Now.'

'Fuck off and drive her.' Steve told him.

Knowling nodded as the officer looked to him for approval. 'Where are you going?' he asked.

Kate turned back so slowly that for a moment she seemed to be teetering on the brink of falling, but there was nothing unsteady about the look she gave him.

'I'm going to get Eddie. He doesn't have anyone now.'

***

ABOUT THE AUTHOR

From Pam Chambers.
If you enjoyed reading *The Thirteenth Torment,*
I would love to hear from you.
You can get in touch at:
Email: pam@pamchambers.co.uk
(mailto:pam@pamchambers.co.uk)
Or through my website: www.pamchambers.co.uk
I'm also on Facebook:
www.facebook.com/pages/pam-chambers
And Twitter: @pam_chambers